LIGHTING

THE CORNERS

On Art, Nature, and the
Visionary
Essays and Interviews

MICHAEL MCCLURE

An AMERICAN POETRY Book
Albuquerque, New Mexico

Cover and text design by Amy Evans
Cover photograph © by Amy Evans

Published by the University of New Mexico College of Arts
and Sciences.

LIBRARY OF CONGRESS CATALOGING-IN-PUBLICATION DATA
McClure, Michael
    Lighting the corners: on art, nature, and the
visionary: essays and interviews / Michael McClure.
        p.   cm.—(American poetry studies in 20th-
century poetry and poetics: 3)
    ISBN 0-9629172-5-7
        1. McClure, Michael—Interviews.   2. Poets.
American—20th century—Interviews.
3. Aesthetics, American.   4. Poetics.   I. Title.
II. Series: American poetry studies in twentieth century
poetry and poetics: 3.
PS3563.A262Z469   1993
814'.54—dc20   93-7610
                                                CIP

First Printing

Love,

like a scarlet

maple leaf,

is where

one finds

it

!

Contents

Preface

Lighting the Corners seems like a miracle because it is like memory itself; it may have error in it, or strange shimmies of events just as memory does. This collection is about people I know and admire, but I'd never thought of becoming an authority on them. I knew them like anyone else might. They were, or are, a pleasure to me. This is how I know them and what we did together. I didn't expect *Lighting the Corners* to be so much about people, as I am a somewhat solitary man. However, like everyone else, I love ebullience and high-spiritedness as well as quietness and the sound of art.

I thought *Lighting the Corners* would be mostly about Nature and natural history. I've always thought of myself as a poet and a naturalist. It was my imagining that this book would be about birds and animals and forests and deserts. I see that I've almost never said anything in print or interview about Kenya, and only a little about Peru, but I'm no authority on those places any more than I am an expert on the artists and friends spoken of in this book.

My life is already longer than I imagined it would be and I'm amazed at how much I remember. I am a self-taught scholar but I didn't realize that I and all the Beats who are friends are scholars. We were treated like outlaws and we were happy to be outlaws in the brutal society of the fifties and sixties and seventies. In the political system of the eighties, everyone with feelings of humanity and love for nature was an outlaw.

One of the pieces in this book is called "These Decades Are Echoes." It's an essay in honor of Robert Creeley. There are two pieces on Robert Duncan. One Duncan piece is a memorial. The other is a conversation we had together, which Robert, after reading it, told me pleased him more than any essay he'd deliberately written. The decades are echoing in these pages. There's writing and interviewing from the fifties to the nineties. These pieces are not in chronological order, but have found an intuitive order with the help of their editor, Lee Bartlett.

These essays and interviews are somewhat like Freud's idea of the unconscious where everything exists at one time and therefore the body is destiny. Kenneth Rexroth always believed that the body is the unconscious anyway. These pieces should be read in any way or order that one wishes. There is no direction to go in them. I'd like it most if the reader started with "Writing One's Body." The reason for that is that the social layer we inhabit and the universe of discourse, which is the ongoing talk of ideas coming from ideas, is at the level of abstraction and non-reality. I mean the social whirling and the social universe are much less profound than the universe of the body, the family, and the imagination.

If we have no idea what a mouse or a wolf thinks, how can we have any idea what Bob Dylan or Dennis Hopper thinks? Walt Whitman said, "A mouse is miracle enough to stagger sextillions of infidels." The body and the imagination are miracles of stars, as are the galaxies. It's a cultural prejudice that animals and living things do not think. Of course they do. It's hopeless to try to understand Jim Morrison's ebullience without knowing how you have your own courages and passions and creativities—as does a mouse or a wolf.

Though much of this is about people and artists, it is about them as bodies and consciousnesses. They didn't model themselves, any more than did Emerson or Dickinson, on the social universe of television actors presented as propaganda by the media corporations and greedblind government. There's nothing more esoteric about the section from *Specks* than there is about the words on Bob Dylan. Read everything the same way.

Lighting the Corners is by someone who believes in consciousness and body and imagination—in fact, a very mental person who would have you believe that the body and sunlight are shapes of Reason. I can imagine that it could be fun to read this book. When I was young I'd get a new book of poems and I'd skip to a short poem that I'd wanted to read. That would lead me to another one, then that one to another. Pretty soon I began to see the sensorium of the poet—what she saw, tasted, touched, smelled, and how she approached experience and what her vocabulary was.

This collection of essays and interviews is about perception. The perceptions range from the experience of a peyote high to bundles of experience-fragments in *Specks*. I first began writing "Drug Notes" because I had read parts of Henri Michaux's book on mescaline, *Miserable Miracle*, in *Evergreen Review*. *Miserable Miracle* was nothing like the way I perceived my experience. Michaux's book, which was the narrative of his perceptions, inspired me to see my drug experiences more clearly as my own perceptions. "Drug Notes" is the earliest work in this collection. It might be interesting to read "Drug Notes" as an essay on experience and then turn to the lecture titled "Cinnamon Turquoise Leather" and see if you want to do the exercise in verbal imagination described in that piece.

I am honored to know artists like Isamu Noguchi and Francesco Clemente. Both are not only artists, but thinkers and speakers and adventurers. I give my insights of the artists as I write or speak about them, but that has no value to a reader unless it allows the reader to experience the work with her own imagination and eyes and hands more clearly. Neither of these artists created within the social whirl though the work finally inhabits that area; the art comes from a very old and very new universe of fire and nervous synapses and stone and pigment.

When I speak or write about someone or something, I am always speaking about myself, my memory, my consciousness, my ears, and eyes. We are bored if anyone speaks of anything else and we notice that society and governments are involved in an endless ploy to educate and bore us into submission. William Blake was right about the Tygers of Wrath being wiser than the Horses of Instruction and he was also right when he said that "Prudence is a rich ugly old maid courted by incapacity." I've loved to see Nature and also those who I know followed their own nature as much as they might.

I'm sorry that there is no long conversation between Ray Manzarek and me in these pages. I hope everyone will lay hands on our videotape and recording, *Love Lion*, to experience an art-symbiosis of music and poetry. I regret that there is nothing here about my writing of Frank Reynold's autobiography *Freewheelin Frank Secretary of the Angels As Told to Michael McClure*, or some experiences I had with the Hell's Angels.

My profound thanks go to Lee Bartlett, the editor of this book, who brought the idea to me and who has labored brilliantly and intensively to bring the book into being.

My deep gratitude and respect go to Uma Kukathas for her unstinting work to bring *Lighting the Corners* into the fact of its being.

LIGHTING
THE
CORNERS

Writing One's Body

HARALD MESCH: In your book *Scratching the Beat Surface* you speak of the interrelatedness of poetry and environmental consciousness. Could you trace the history of your relationship as a poet to the environmental movement?

MICHAEL MCCLURE: From early childhood I wanted to be a naturalist, then came an interest in archeology and anthropology, followed by a love of painting. When I arrived in San Francisco, as a young man, in 1954, I was involved primarily in painting and poetry. Soon I met a naturalist, Sterling Bunnell, a man of my own age who began introducing me to areas in California that I had not had the opportunity to see. With him I was able to watch coyotes and foxes and weasels and deer, and walk through savannah country, hike through the foothills, go over the mountains, and to the seashore and look into tide pools. But, early in 1955 we "Beats" gave our first reading at the Six Gallery in San Francisco. At that reading Allen Ginsberg read *Howl*, which has as its basis—in my thinking—consciousness itself. At the same reading Gary Snyder read his poem, "A Berry Feast," which is a celebration of nature, especially as seen through American Indian rites. And I read my poems, almost all of which were inclined toward nature. Including "The Death of 100 Whales," which in 1955 was an early poem against biocide by governments.

MESCH: I was fascinated by your statement that the Beat movement is part of a larger and deeper environmental movement because in such a perspective the Beat movement appears in a completely new light. How did you gain that perspective?

Conducted by Harald Mesch in April 1983 (San Francisco) and April 1984 (Munich), this interview appeared in *American Studies* (Munich) in 1987.

MCCLURE: That first became clear at the United Nations Environmental Conference in Stockholm in 1972, when I looked around and saw that in fact a great many of my friends were there. Gary Snyder was there, Peter Berg, the bioregionalist, was present, Joan McIntyre was there with Project Jonah, Stewart Brand was there with *Whole Earth Catalog*, friends of mine in the biological and botanical fields, like Richard Felger, were there. Wavy Gravy and the Hog Farm were there. We were speaking for the diversity of the environment; speaking for the whales, speaking for the preservation of diversity of human culture; for the American Indians, for the Laplanders.

I looked back and saw the connection between what we had started in 1955 and where we were in 1972. In our first poetry reading in 1955 there was an interest in mind as consciousness, in nature, and in biology. That impulse has been picked up and amplified in the rock music that we influenced (in the organismic approach of the Beatles), in the return to dance by young people which is a direct expression of the bodies as opposed to abstract pattern dancing and music that preceded early rock music. Remember the Beatles called themselves the b-e-a-t, the Beat, Beatles. Earlier they called themselves the "Silver Beetles." When they became deeper, when they felt themselves alive with a kind of surge, with what was happening in the physiological sense, they became the Beatles as we know them today. At about that time books on the environment, on environmental subjects and on conservation subjects, were beginning to pour out. They were beginning to quote the poets, and there was a real sense of oneness that was occurring.

What I'm saying is overlooked because of the newspaper image that was formed of beatniks wearing berets and sandals, playing bongo drums. There was a lot of that, but those beatnik poets were a phenomenon. They were there for the newspapers to photograph, and we weren't close to most of them. Those of us who survived continued our work.

MESCH: It is within the fence posts of the Beat–environmental movement that you have been carrying on a dialogue with Lawrence Ferlinghetti. And it is here that your differentiation between "revolution" and "revolt" seems to be central. Refusing to define the movement as a revolution, you seem to deny the political relevance. You seem to be saying that it is non-political. On the other hand you are saying: "There is but one politics and that is biology."

MCCLURE: Yes, you're right. I read that poem last year, the poem "Listen Lawrence," at the University of California along with a reading by Denise Levertov. We were reading for the nuclear freeze movement. I read the lines "capitalism will not help, socialism will not help, communism will not help." A week later, I was giving a reading with a fellow poet to raise money to give to the Salvadoran guerillas for medical supplies. So, I don't believe that because one takes a deeper approach to the reality that one can avoid politics. I go on making political gestures that I believe are necessary, that are important. I don't back away from them. I do not exist in an ivory tower because I believe that biology is the only meaningful area of change. I go ahead and make changes that I can make politically, at least those that I can align myself with spiritually. And I can align myself spiritually with the guerrillas in El Salvador, and with raising money for them. But I don't believe that helping them is going to make any kind of permanent change for Central America—which is going to be in a permanent state of revolution and in a permanent state of disarray until something can be done about the overpopulation problems there as well as the problems of colonization. The only thing that's going to make anything better for them is to find a biological solution to the problems. Some solutions to their need for basic resources and agriculture and some resolution of their overpopulation. Those are both biological problems.

MESCH: So you tend to think in longer terms, because biological solutions are not short-term solutions.

MCCLURE: Short-term solutions are not solutions. Short-term solutions are necessary simply to stave off pain and criminality and disastrous chaos. But there are no simple solutions. And people are going to have to start determining what the problems are, and they are going to have to start thinking in unity, they're going to have to begin thinking together about what the possibilities of solutions may be. I don't believe that people have begun to envision what the *problems* are.

The problems are not the wars and the starvation and the chaos that's going on. The problems are what's causing the wars and the starvation and the chaos. Those are biological. I do whatever I can, as I can do it, to align myself with causes, to confront and to alleviate war, pain, starvation. But I don't believe that I'm doing anything except helping put on surgical dressing. I'm glad to put a band-aid on whatever I can. On the other hand, some believe that if we had a socialist world, we shouldn't have any problems. But we would have the same problems we would have with a capitalist world; they just might be a slightly different color. We'd have the same problems we'd have with a communist world; they just might have a slightly different odor. The problems are deep and are permanent until we look at the whole complex of them and determine to do something which is very long-range. We're talking about a generation just to determine what the problems are, and then whatever decades are necessary, to work out the determinations in a flexible manner.

MESCH: In one of your poems you say: "In turn we give flesh to the revolution / like Che, Darwin, and Francis Crick / *creating visions not solutions.*"

MCCLURE: That's right. I really don't think that there are solutions in the sense that people speak of solutions. When I speak of a long-term solution I mean a new path.

MESCH: Would you see your poetry moving toward a new path or would you see your poetry as making the problems conscious?

MCCLURE: My poetry is to make myself conscious. And my poetry is to illuminate a reader, if he or she is interested, with what I've been able to do with my consciousness, which may be of use to them on their own. Perhaps my poetry is to broaden my sensorium, and hopefully it will broaden the sensoriums of other individuals who read it. In other words, the function of poetry, as I see it, is to create a myriad-mindedness.

I see myself wholly as an artist, as a poet. I am not a utopian. I'm not a socio-biological thinker. But I do align myself with a movement or a thread or a stream or a surge of individuals who are interested in liberation of the body, in the liberation of the imagination and the liberation of consciousness. In that sense, we may be of help to those who begin to deal with the situations that need to be dealt with. I constantly ask biologists, botanists, or bio-philosophers what we may do, what we may think about, what the situation is. That's reflected in my poetry. I'm an artist.

MESCH: There's a general saying that "poetry won't help." In other words, poetry is in an ivory tower.

MCCLURE: I think most poetry won't help and most poetry is in an ivory tower, speaking of what is generally accepted as poetry. If you look in the New York Times' book review section, what they review as poetry won't help and it is in an ivory tower. If you look in the London Times Literary Supplement, what they speak of won't help and it is in an ivory tower. So, what does one say to that? I'm speaking about people such as myself, Robert Creeley, Robert Duncan, Philip Whalen, Amiri Baraka, Diane di Prima.

At Martin Luther King Junior High School in Berkeley a month or two ago, there was a reading by Gary Snyder, Robert Creeley, and a Vietnamese monk poet. More than a thousand individuals from Berkeley came to that reading and listened to the exercise of consciousness that the deconstruction of event and autobiography presents in Creeley's work. This could only give individuals a new stance toward their own lives if they listened to what Creeley was saying, and I'm sure they did listen. Those individuals present were also listening to Gary Snyder's consciousness-deepening stance toward nature as represented in his poems. A thousand people at an event like that have widespreading possibilities. For a thousand people to have an experience that intense and that meaningful makes waves and surges of consciousness with a potential to spread throughout a much larger community. I suppose bourgeois poetry is essentially aesthetic entertainment—well within the contains and bounds of the universe of discourse. But the other, like the Creeley/Snyder reading, is an event which is a revolt against the status quo, and it is a profound experience. It is like comparing a film of the Sierras with a trip to the Sierras. A film of the Sierras will only have the function of entertainment; a trip to the Sierras is liable to change somebody's world view.

MESCH: It seems to be a fundamental requirement that our understanding of language is being transformed. For unless this understanding is transformed our stance toward reality won't change. And if our stance toward reality won't change we will not be able to act adequately in the critical ecological situation in which we find ourselves.

MCCLURE: I agree with you completely. If those thousand people are given the example of the use of language in both Creeley's way and Snyder's way, both of which are revolutionary ways to use language, they're bound to absorb some of those values and will, I believe, in many instances make changes in their own use of language, which is equivalent to their own feelings and their own intellectivity. Then we can see changes. I do think Shelley was right that poets are the unacknowledged legislators of the world. I don't think that they're the only unacknowledged legislators of the world, but they are *some* of the unacknowledged legislators of the world. Again, I'm not talking about the ones who are reviewed in the *New York Times*, but certain of those who are *not*. You see the new poetry that I am speaking of is no longer new; the poetry that I'm speaking of is a poetry about experience, it's a poetry about consciousness, it's a poetry about the senses.

Language is used in a way which is in revolt against a previous language, and it is a mutational divergence from the previous common use of language. It's in this change that we open the possibilities for a new ground upon which people may think and act. That's our duty as artists. We are not eco-politicians. We are not eco-philosophers. We are not eco-metaphysicians. We're *artists*.

MESCH: Ferlinghetti, in the introduction to your *Meat Science Essays*, speaks about you as the cat that is "willfully incapable" of understanding Camus. Camus himself may be regarded as one of the staunch defenders of the humanistic tradition in the sense of an anthropocentric position. From that position you might be accused of consistent desublimation, even of regression, of anti-intellectualism. What would you say to that?

MCCLURE: There's not anything very difficult to understand about anything that Camus says. Sartre is more challenging intellectually than Camus, and I see that what both Sartre and Camus did in founding Existentialism is extremely important to my work and to the work of my friends and to the work of many whom I admire. The primary thing that Existentialism does is deny that there is a secret beneath the surface of things. Sartre makes his insistence that that which you see is that which is. He calls it the confrontation with the absurd. He does not pretend that there is a mysterious poem lurking beneath the eyelids of stones, which makes charming symbolist art, but is a cultural mystification. However, neither Sartre nor Camus when they speak of the universe of the absurd are speaking of anything *beyond* the human universe. Both men are bound within the social level; they have no experience *outside* the social level. Their work was done at the time when important discoveries were just *beginning* to be made in the biological sciences and they did not comprehend their value or meaning. But Sartre and Camus are certainly our forebears intellectually. As much as Emerson is a forebear. And we owe much to Camus.

In regard to anti-intellectualism, I would as soon be called an anti-intellectual as not. However, I am pro-intellective. I believe in the use of the intellective powers. Intellectualism means that one assumes values with insufficient questioning of the culture of which he or she is a part. Intellectualism is equivalent to one-dimensionality as far as I'm concerned. *Intellectivity*, however, means that one has a vivid and athletic intellect.

MESCH: "Intellectivity" and "intellectualism." How do you differentiate between these notions?

MCCLURE: "Intellectivity" is the willingness to use one's perceptual integrative high-level mental capacities; "intellectual" means plugging into an already established program or grammar of those activities. So one can be an intellective giant and not have been to college. I mean you have a man who is a lumberjack who is an intellective wizard, and you have somebody who is a great intellectual but is not intellective at all. In fact many intellectuals are not intellective. Their perceptions are formed by an adherence to their program.

MESCH: One-dimensionality, as you speak of it, would mean the exclusion of what you call the mystery out of the "social bubble."

McCLURE: No. One-dimensionality, according to Marcuse, who uses the term best to my way of thinking, means that the individual in contemporary society has so little interior, individuated self remaining that the introjection of the values of society hardly phase his consciousness. They *are* his consciousness. There is only one dimension. Marcuse believes that the individual in today's society has so accepted the outer values of society that they can hardly be introjected into the personality. They are already *one*. There is only one dimension. There is not an interior and exterior dimension.

MESCH: Your return to the body—I would describe your poetry as such—would implicitly mean that your poetry is moving in the direction of re-discovering the biological self?

McCLURE: It's moving in the direction of recovering the biological self. I don't know if there's a re-discovery. I think perhaps each of us has to recover our biological selves. There is always a blockade of our process of discovery of the biological self, that is of each individual's normal personal discovery of the biological self.

MESCH: Again, from the humanistic, anthropocentric position you might be accused of narcissism. That is, the return to the body as a narcissistic move. Would you reply to that?

McCLURE: "Narcissism" is used to identify a pathological state. I've known a few narcissists who probably have some degree of pathology. But I must say that not only did I not dislike them, I rather liked them. The problem with pathological, or semi-pathological, narcissists is that they're not dependable. However, they're enjoyable to be around because they honor themselves, they enjoy themselves, they treat themselves well, which is something that many people do not do. On the other hand, the use of the term "narcissism" as it was used in the sixties and seventies as a pejorative is something like the pejorative use of the term "elitist." I have a distinct feeling that narcissism is used as a pejorative by those who, in some sense, feel inferior about themselves. There is nothing narcissistic about the experience of one's self. I see a great lack of experience of one's self in present society. Probably in all cultures there's a lack of experience of one's self, except the social self. If one experiences oneself in senses other than the social self, as long as it is adherent to relatively healthful, mammalian processes, I think it's wholly to be admired. That is, provided it doesn't cause blindness to the needs of others or interfere with the normal functioning of one's friends, relatives, and associates.

MESCH: S.P.R. Charter, the ecologist, you may know him, speaks about the necessity that we recognize and accept both self and "beyond self." Would you see that move in the direction of "beyond self" as a discovery of the biological self?

MCCLURE: The more one discovers one's *bio-self* as opposed to one's *social self*, the more one is moving out, but one has to move *in* to move *out*. The more you discover your biological person and your biological functions, the more you find your biological self. And the more you discover your biological self, the more value you can be to yourself. The more value you can be to yourself, the more value you can be to those around you. People fear such acts because they believe that their biological self is a monster. That is certainly not the case. I mean, we're social primates, and we have distinct social patterns. The more we find those deeper patterns and the less we are robotized by the cultural patterns, the better we'll be. If so-called narcissism is an escape from the robotism of the culture, I'm all for it.

MESCH: Your first experience of stepping, so to speak, out of time, "changing time itself into space," was this experience helped by drugs?

MCCLURE: Some of what I feel today has for a source the use of psychedelic drugs, but in a small way. But then everything that I feel today has in part for its source the fact that my grandfather was a doctor who loved nature. Everything that I feel today has in part for its source the fact that I found Robert Creeley's poetry when I was a young man, and so forth. I don't feel that as a poet I stepped whole from Athena's brow and had no progenitors and sources.

As one becomes aware of one's self as an organism, as a body, as a body consciousness, one says, this body consciousness is not wholly mine. Yes, I think psychedelic drugs are important, but I also embrace observations and perceptions of my fellow poets, of my daughter, of my grandfather, of Jackson Pollock, of Hans Arp, of Antonin Artaud, of Lorca, and Shelley.

MESCH: Your statement in *Scratching the Beat Surface* that we must "change time itself into space through an alchemic act then we may move in it and step outside of the disaster that we have wreaked upon the environment and upon our phylogenetic selves" seems to me to be central both in the context of your poetry and of the contemporary fundamental environmental concerns.

MCCLURE: What I'm speaking of is the Taoist notion that the universe that we perceive is an "uncarved block," that all time/space occurrences of the past, present, and future are one giant sculpture of which we're a part. It's not as if something is going to exist in the future or that something has happened in the past, but that it's all going on at once. And we're in it. If we're aware of that, there's a *proportionlessness* that is a liberating state or condition. If we understand that we're not of a particular size, of a particular diminution, or of a particular "behem-othness," then we sense that we are without scale. We're without measurement in the same way that we're without time. When we have that experience, there's a peace and an understanding that can come over us. We can make better judgments and more positive actions.

As a poet I observe moments of proportionlessness. I observe moments of bio-alchemy. As I become more practiced, or sometimes when I become more liberated through the exercise of my art, I seem to be able to call on meaningful moments more and more. But they're not something to be utilized. They're something that occurs if we exercise for them, if we create our art for them, if we pursue our discipline for them, then we notice those moments happening more and more. I'm not sure that we actually bring them about. But we can partake of them more and more if we're clear, more and more if we're less and less robotized, if we're less and less one-dimensional and more myriad.

MESCH: Would you see that alchemic act of "changing time itself into space" as coming close to what Charles Olson might speak of as the stepping out of the "universe of discourse"?

McCLURE: When we step out of the universe of discourse, we are in a more primal, more phylogenetic state, a more primal, more phylogenetic condition. I would imagine that the exterior world is more coordinate with the *Umwelt* when we step out of the universe of discourse. In other words, I believe that when we step from the social world (that has lifted itself from the earth, with petroleum and fossil fuels) back into our biological selves, that we feel a proportionlessness. The descriptions of the "uncarved block" of the Taoists are much like that state. It's an inherent condition. If, on the other hand, we step out of the universe of discourse into a tribal condition which is another kind of one-dimensionality, that is, into a tribal sociology, it's of no advantage whatsoever. We must fuse our intellectivity and our emotional force and the feedback loops of our sensorium and our perceptions to step back into our bodies. When we step back into our bodies, we are more liable to find a condition of proportionlessness, or a timelessness which is rich with the meanings of our evolution, and which is rich with the meanings of our possibilities and our extensions.

I could move out of the one-dimensionality of the universe of discourse into a tribal condition which I feel is an equally limited condition. A tribal condition is possibly as limiting to the intellective and emotional capacities as the urban life of one-dimensionality, though of course it is rich in other ways.

MESCH: As far as I can see, stepping back into what you describe as tribal would be a regressive move.

McCLURE: Cultures have certain things in common. It seems to be a common teaching of all of them that we are not animals, that we are minds. That is wrong. There was a German biologist who called himself a disciple of both Goethe and Darwin, a man named Ernst Haeckel.

He described himself as a monist because he believed that the universe itself, or all of existence, is a single, great organism or a single, great "critter" with organismic characteristics. Whitehead carries that a step further, believing that any point in the universe is a novel point of "prehension," i.e., a point of the universe experiencing itself. Our sensoriums are spirit mechanisms that light up the cave around them for the experience.

MESCH: That's beautiful. That certainly connects—for me at least— with Charles Olson's essay "Proprioception."

MCCLURE: The mystic philosopher Jakob Boehme says that the world we inhabit is created by the rubbing of the universe of celestial bliss against the universe of black fire. In other words, the strata that we inhabit is the friction between the universe of celestial bliss and the universe of black fire.

In a way Olson's "Proprioception" is the rubbing of Charles's desire to experience against his internal capacities, and then the outward projection of what he might experience. It's as if Charles becomes alight with an idea, as if he's inspired by the outer universe to an idea which he then internalizes, and that internalization calls upon itself to create some kind of rampaging bull within himself that tramples around in the inner residences of his sensorium to create ideas about that which he desired to have ideas. Then he projects outward and examines the ideas. Then, he re-internalizes the ideas and the wild bull of his consciousness tramples around again in the sensorium of what he's experienced and creates another idea which is projected outward which comes to a field which is then perceived and internalized again. You see, Charles's "system" is definitely a systemless system and that's the most attractive thing about it. Charles's proprioceptive essay is inspiring not for saying anything, because I don't believe that it says much; it's inspiring because it's an energy construct that recommends to us that we proceed in our lives with the same energy. In other words, it's like a painting by Clyfford Still. It's not a direct mimesis of nature.

MESCH: It occurs to me that one might describe it, in your own words, again as "not a solution but a vision."

MCCLURE: It's a vision. It is definitely no solution. It has no answer except to return to the inside and trample around some more.

MESCH: What was your relationship to Charles Olson? In what ways did he help you in developing your own language, your own poetics?

MCCLURE: When I discovered Charles's essay "Projective Verse," I found one of the bases for my own poetics. My own poetics has several distinct substrata and one of them is traditional prosodic poetry, like that of Blake, or Keats, or Yeats, or Shelley. Another is the modernist tradition of Pound and Williams, and particularly the poetics of Olson since I come of a later generation.

The poetics of Pound and Williams was not wholly appropriate for me since their poetics preceded the important recent discoveries made in biology and physics. I had to create a poetics of the fifties and later times that I could speak with. I do not imply a superior poetics but a poetics appropriate for my field, for my wave. Olson's recognition that the mind is a construct of the heart, of the nervous system, and his interest in the energy charge that we derive from the subject, whether in mind or in the world, as the motivating force, was a help. Also his recognition that the syllable is a unit of measurement rather than the foot or the word. That gave me a clue.

MESCH: You have an argument with Olson in your manifesto "The Rose Flush, Straight Speech, Exclamation and the Drift (1958)"—the kernel of that argument being about the anagogic and pre-anagogic. Could you comment on that?

MCCLURE: I wrote this poem thinking of that:

AND COLD TIRED EMPTY TO BE SO SPREAD IN AIR
is Hell too.
The predator's world is space. Time the instant
(taken) in the strike.
But to be spread to strike at (so many) unwanted
half-desires. Is Hell too. To be so
self-flung in so many ways. To leap
at so many half-loves. To fall back

and find that part of you
still hangs (there) so many times.

HELL PAIN BEWILDERED EMPTINESS
the part left smolders.
Does not burn clear and drifts too
upon the air. Hot Hell
is freedom.

So, it's like hot Hell, the burning of our bodies, whether it's in the mitochondrian furnace or whether it's in the aspirations of our macro-physiology as the basis for our poetry, as the basis for what we feel rather than history. Charles's field began as history. As he moves into his *Maximus Poems*, you'll find that he's trying to deal with history. He does crash through the same way Creeley crashes through the same problem. By the time he writes *Pieces* Creeley is no longer making poems about traditional concerns, but is *writing his body*. By the time Charles gets to the last volume of the *Maximus Poems*, what he's talking about is coming directly out of his own sensorium. He no longer feels that he has to have the pretext of history—names and dates. He uses them, but doesn't need them as a pretext. They've become part of his experience. It's a noble thing that Charles did, because he's the only person—the only poet—I know of who internalized history. It was a struggle for him to internalize it and make it part of his physiology. So when I had a disagreement with Charles, it's at a point where the disagreement is entirely fair. I had that disagreement with Charles in 1958. By 1962 or 63, Charles was in an entirely different stance in his long poem.

MESCH: The concept of the "field" is central to Olson's poetics. In *Scratching the Beat Surface* you also speak about the "felt," the "veldt," i.e., the field. How does that lock in with Olson's "field"?

MCCLURE: I'm taking Duncan's poem "The Opening of the Field" to mean the feeled, or the felt. With Duncan it's the field of the threshers and the dance. With Olson it's a field similar to the one that Pollock has in his painting—the area that he paints upon. For me, it's the cave that I see lit up by our senses, that which is felt is that which is alighted by our senses.

MESCH: The central image in your play *The Beard* seems to be the "velvet eternity." Does that image relate in anyway with the "veldt"?

MCCLURE: It's a field of velvet; "Velvet Eternity" is the eternity that we touch with our fingertips, that we smell with our nose, that we feel with the seats of our buttocks when we sit on a chair, when we hear the sounds of someone else who's speaking. Those are the parts of the universe that are available to our prehension, those are the parts of the universe that we light up around us when we are the universe prehending itself. The universe seems to have an unending appetition for itself, an unending appetite for itself. And it certainly would be gruesome narcissism if we felt we were anything more than points in the universe experiencing itself, or if we had any more proportionlessness than any other point that was prehending itself.

MESCH: By the way, since we mentioned *The Beard*: what is the history of this title?

MCCLURE: "Beard" is Elizabethan slang, and it means to quarrel with someone; it means to pull his beard when you "beard" someone. In fact there is an old Spanish saying, and the Elizabethans could have taken it from the Spanish because the Elizabethans had much contact with them. The Spanish saying was "Pluck not the beard of the sleeping lion."

MESCH: In *Scratching the Beat Surface* you speak at one point about the invisible observer who closes his ears to the meanings of words and only listens to the vocalization as sounds. And you suggest further on that if the intelligence is open and is able to follow the sounds it will hear something. What is actually the direction in which this hearing might be moving?

MCCLURE: I'm talking about the split between what we say we're talking about and what we're speaking of. I think what I spoke of was a man and a woman arguing about laundry tickets. But if you listen to the language, if you listen to the sounds coming out of the body, you realize that what is being spoken of is not really the laundry ticket.

It's probably about their sex lives, or about their children that they're conversing, because one does not truly speak of laundry tickets with that emotional passion, or that intensity.

In other words, we use limited vocabularies to describe our true emotional states. And that is what I'm suggesting that one listen for. I was thinking about something in my poems today. One of the reasons for the shapes of my poems is to give body language to the poem itself. In other words, we do judge by body language. We judge by shifted position or cock of head or posture or eye squint or the way the body is turned with what's being spoken. There are a lot of cues that can be given in terms of body language in the shape of a poem.

By giving a sharpness, by giving a width to a passage of speech versus a narrowness to a passage of speech, one can follow the thrust of two things. One, whether it is true in speech, and not mimesis. And secondly, there can be hidden cues as to the subject that's being spoken of as well as to the intention of the musicality of what's being said.

MESCH: So what is to be heard, what should be listened to is also the sound, the rhythm?

MCCLURE: Rhythm, volume, intensity, timbre.

MESCH: In that connection I am interested in the principle of repetition in your poetry. At one point, in *Scratching the Beat Surface*, you compare a poem by Philip Whalen to a Sung Dynasty landscape painting with the proper number of strokes, not too many and not too few. How does that relate to the principle of repetition, the working of which is observable in your own poetry? Doesn't repetition imply redundancy?

MCCLURE: Well, I don't think of my poetry as having any resemblance to a Sung Dynasty landscape painting, although I would be pleased if it did. I don't work that way. That's a comparison I made to Philip's work, particularly to that poem.

The principles, the intentions, underlying the repetition are much more organic. It is our nature to repeat. As it is another part of our nature to delicately inscribe superb, small, correctly numbered strokes to represent something. It is equally natural for us to repeat. For instance music repeats, dance repeats. Much of painting repeats, particularly today's painting, or pop art. They are all natural ways of expression.

If you begin a poem with the words, "the gesture," repeated nine times, fifteen times, the first time you hear "gesture," the second time you hear "gesture," and so forth, then the meaning does crumble. As a matter of fact the meaning disappears. Then the meaning becomes ritual. Then the meaning becomes meaning again. Then the meaning becomes something else. Then the meaning becomes a metric. Then the meaning becomes a sound pattern; it no longer has justifiable significance. Then it returns to significance. In the process of repetition of words you're playing not with one or two processes—you're playing with a number of processes. You must operate intuitively. One uses everything from deconstruction to ritualization to prosodization all in a short space. This is possible because words have such powerful meanings and significance.

MESCH: How do you feel about my observation that there is a structural similarity between your novel *The Adept*, the long poem *Rare Angel*, and your play *VKTMS*: the structural similarity being the repeated return to a scene, a horrible scene, a climatic scene? How would you comment on that?

MCCLURE: I think that's true. I was troubled about something last night and I kept thinking about it and returning to thinking about it, and thinking about something else and returning to thinking about it again. I had a hard time going to sleep. I mean that's one of our ways of thinking. We have other ways of thinking that are expansive, where we go from one delightful imaging to another. But a primary process of our thinking is to move away from a scene, to come back to the scene, to move away from it in another direction, to come back to it. We create an expanding field around the scene and that gives the scene other resonances, other connections, other possibilities.

MESCH: I would describe the essence of the climatic scene in all the instances I've mentioned as the "felt" or the "veldt." Would you agree with that?

McCLURE: The field or the "felt" or the "veldt" is what's created by moving away from the scene, coming back to the scene, moving away from it in a different direction, coming back to it, moving away from it in a different direction. That's what makes the moderation that allows us to live through primal scenes of horror.

MESCH: It's a very moving scene in *The Adept* when the protagonist kills a man unwittingly. Olson's words perhaps paraphrase it very well: "We do what we know, before we know what we do." I see the killing in this sense as an event, as a "field" in which you are included and you really don't know what you are doing, you just do it. Which is horrible because you realize that your body does what you don't know that you're doing. At the same time it's beautiful because you're completely inside what's happening.

McCLURE: That's kind of a description of the "uncarved block" that you just made.

MESCH: In my understanding there is therefore a connection between the "field" and the "uncarved block." You don't see it that way?

McCLURE: In the way you said, one could, certainly.

MESCH: There are two central notions or concepts that seem to be fulcrums in your poetry. They're "flesh" and "meat." Could you comment on the difference between and also on the mutual relatedness of these terms?

McCLURE: I don't know that I've ever contrasted the idea of flesh and meat. What I propose is that we say meat when we are speaking about flesh, since flesh seems to be a euphemism for meat. In other words, the Victorians spoke about the limb of a chair rather than saying a leg of a chair because they wanted to avoid reference to the body. "Flesh," in the English language, is a way of avoiding the fact that the reference is to a chopped-up piece of an animal—which is meat. This is not such a critical distinction anymore, in part because of my writing. I found myself titling a new lecture "Being Flesh" rather than "Being Meat." At one time I felt compelled to title my first prose book *Meat Science Essays*, so that people would understand that I was really speaking about meat. I think that's clear enough now in my own writing.

MESCH: You have mentioned quite a few forces or sources which have been formative for your poetry. But you have mentioned him only in passing though he is definitely a source—Artaud. Could you comment on the fact that on the one hand you speak about Artaud as an anti-physical mystic poet, and on the other hand, he in fact seems to have led you toward a "physicality of thought."

MCCLURE: Artaud's anti-physicality and the stance that he takes against the body requires me, as a brother—and I felt like the younger brother of Artaud—requires me to take a position in regard to anti-physicality. I must either agree with Artaud or decide how I feel. So in that way he's instrumental in helping me make the decisions I make. The intensity and the beauty and the perception of his gnostic anti-physicality requires that I accept it or that I disagree with it. And if I disagree with it, then I must have some understanding of why I disagree. Therefore it gives me a field upon which to work, or shows me that I need a field upon which to work. I choose my physicality. So, Artaud has been a major source for me. In the same way, when one reads D.H. Lawrence, one must say, I feel that this man is right or I do not feel that this man is right. And if I do not feel that this man is right, why is he not right? Thus I agree with much that Lawrence speaks about. I admire Lawrence's use of the perceptions as I admire Kerouac's extraordinary sensorium. So in the case of Kerouac and Lawrence I'm given the gift of their sensorium. In the case of Artaud I'm given the gift of his nervous system.

MESCH: Speaking about the Beat movement you point out that there is a change going on, a change of the understanding of the nature of consciousness. And one may see your poetry as forcing that change in the sense of changing the traditional hierarchy of the senses, in changing the place of consciousness, in moving it closer from the locus of thinking—in the sense of Descartes's *cogito*—to the locus of the sensorium.

MCCLURE: Rimbaud wanted an arranged derangement of the senses. We have an established hierarchy of the senses in Western civilization, with the eye being the superior and I suppose the ear is second, and so forth. I've done a lot of experiments which sometimes clearly look at mind like organism, in them I arrangedly derange the traditional hierarchy of the senses. In doing so I place as much emphasis on the imagery of hearing as on the imagery of sight, as on the imagery of smell.

The effect sometimes appears to be a loosening up of an established stance towards experience. In other words, in the creation of spontaneous images, in *Rare Angel*, or in my book *Organism*, I have often deliberately, although spontaneously, written out *synesthesia*-imaging processes which cause a startling effect upon traditional modalities of perception. The intention of the work is to give myself a view that I haven't had before. Hopefully, when someone reads such an exercise, they can take a view that they haven't had before. In other words, traditional ways of seeing things are only *our* traditional ways of seeing things. They may also be our *biologically* traditional ways of seeing things, but we can deliberately arrange or derange them. And it can be constructive. It need not be frightening.

MESCH: Let me quote a few verses from *Little Odes* and *Star*: ". . . the Blackness, the Blackness. . . ." "I move in the deep pool of the black Lily / of Space. Like a worm without a head . . . mindlessly scenting the perfumes. . . ." "I Am Lost O, in the Lily / without eyes. . . ." "Life is not thought, not Intellect, / But Perfect Creation. . . ." "Light or intellect (or soul) / is no perfection. . . ." There seems to exist a relation between intellect and sight and light opposed to a positive blackness and blindness. I wonder whether that points to a shift in the spectrum of the sensorium.

MCCLURE: Let me just comment from an entirely different direction. Since the mid-fifties I have been interested in *agnosia*, in the kind of vision proposed by the progenitors of Meister Eckhart, like Dionysius the Areopagite or like Hildegard von Bingen. I've always been interested in that idea that *one sees with blackness*, one sees through poverty of knowledge. It's only through the poverty of knowledge that we acknowledge our own blackness so that perceptions can happen. When we think we know something, there is no black field upon which perceptions may happen. Hildegard von Bingen is saying that, Dionysius the Areopagite is saying that, I think Meister Eckhart is saying that, I think Jakob Boehme is saying that, and I believe that this idea is even more common but stated in another way in Eastern thought.

MESCH: I thought "agnosia" was something you got from the East.

McCLURE: No. From the Western mystic tradition. Although one can say that agnosia is what takes place in forms of Eastern meditation. I mean one is attempting to clear the reticular formation, to make it blank, so that perception passes over. One observes the naturalness and ordinariness . . .

MESCH: In *Rare Angel* there seems to be a significant interplay between the—as far as I can see—synonymous terms: "curb," "edge," and "on the precipice." Did you intend any relation among them?

McCLURE: I was unaware of it. But there probably is.

MESCH: You couldn't comment on that?

McCLURE: The whole poem is about being on the edge.

MESCH: What do you understand by "being on the edge"?

McCLURE: Being on the edge of the explosion.

MESCH: Of the ecological catastrophe?

McCLURE: It's happening right now. We all thought that the world is going to blow up, and it is; we didn't realize how slowly it was going to blow up. Resources are being turned into cinders and gases and forests are being changed into cinderlike structures of buildings, river beds are being blown up into freeways. We're looking at the explosion in slow motion. Imagine the world a hundred years ago and a hundred years in the future.

MESCH: In your poem, "Stanzas in Turmoil," you speak of the danger, of the "brink" or of the "edge" we are on. At the same time you're saying that we're in love with this danger. Since we love it, we obviously look for it, provoke it. We obviously enlarge and enhance that danger—isn't that a contradiction?

McCLURE: I don't know that it is a contradiction. I want people to be aware, though, that it *is our primate nature* to enjoy what we're doing.

MESCH: Even if we are burning up gas and polluting the biosphere, even if we are exploding the substrata of our being?

McCLURE: Yes, and if we realize how much we really enjoy it and why we enjoy it and what a great thrill it is and what enormous machinery . . .

MESCH: But it might be stupid, too.

McCLURE: Clearly. But it is too easy to say it is stupid. We can't self-righteously tell other people who are enjoying it, when we are in the process of enjoying it ourselves, that it is simply stupid, that they are fools. So, one thing that we can do is make people understand how beautiful it is and that it is our nature to do those things and that they are beautiful *and* they are stupid at the same time for us and the future and for all life.

MESCH: It's not necessarily our nature, is it? I mean the Indians don't do it.

McCLURE: The Indians were destructive in their own ways. This is why I often talk about Paul Martin's idea (in *Pleistocene Extinctions*) that it was the ancestors of the Indians, the paleo-Indians, who wiped out twenty-six genera of megafauna, the upper tier of the Pleistocene mega-fauna, in the New World when they entered it. Everything from the wild horse to the giant ground sloths. That is called the Overkill Hypothesis. They destroyed everything from the mastodons to the forest bison. If we see that, then we say: Oh, that's what we love to do, that's what we like to do, we like to do that. We love to kill big animals. Then we say: But if we like to do that, if we go any further, we are not going to have any mammal brethren left at all. But first of all, you can't righteously take a stance that this is wrong, this is evil, this is not human. This is, in fact, entirely human, this *is* our nature. Then we say: Ah, but our nature has *other* possibilities. If we acknowledge that this is our nature, what *other* possibilities does our nature have? What else could we do that is natural? That's the critical thing that I can see. Yes, I think it has to be stopped right away but I think it has to be stopped by saying: Oh, *that's* who we are. Oooooh, I get it! I see! I understand. That's me.

MESCH: You are saying: "Politics is dead—Biology is here . . ." Biology, i.e., the revolt of our bodies, or with our bodies? How would you describe that revolt as it may take place in everyday life?

MCCLURE: There is a wonderful young man in California. He was concerned about a river that was about to be dammed, a wild river which would be dammed for the sheer fucking purpose of sending water to southern California, water that they didn't need. The young man announced to the newspapers and to all the media that he was going to chain himself to a rock in the bottom of the canyon that would be filled up if they dammed the river. And he went down and chained himself to a rock where no one could find him and they didn't dam the river.

MESCH: I fully agree with such acts.

MCCLURE: That's biology.

Bob Dylan: The Poet's Poet

Memory is a beautiful thing—as I get older I learn to cherish it. It seems so beautiful or ugly that it is often more than real. Sometimes the vision is lit up with imagination; sometimes the imaginings have the shapes of real acts and gestures we call experience.

Experience is physical matter—and there is no sense in hanging onto it. It is a pleasure to let memory pour through the consciousness like nuggets of gold and moss agates and crystals of quartz clicking through the fingers at the rock shop. One never plans to keep those stones but the pleasure of feeling them is lovely.

The autoharp Bob Dylan gave me early in 1966 sat on the mantel-piece for six weeks before I picked it up and strummed it. A black and magical autoharp. Afraid of playing music, I had always felt totally unmusical—except in my appreciation. Bob had asked me what in-strument I'd like to play (I was writing song lyrics). I said autoharp out of the clear blue though I had no picture of what an autoharp looked like. There must have been people playing them on farms in my Kansas childhood.

San Francisco poets were poor in 1965 and it was an impressive present and it committed me to music. There was the interest in writing lyrics and perhaps a new way to use rhyme.

Rock had mutual attraction for all; a common tribal dancing ground whether we were poets, or printers, or sculptors, it was a form we all shared. I spent a year and a half learning how to play the autoharp in an eccentric way and wrote songs like "The Blue Lyon Laughs," "The Allen Ginsberg For President Waltz" and "Come on God, and Buy Me a Mercedes Benz."

I bought an amplifier and stood for hours whanging on the autoharp. Obsessed with John Keats's question: What weapon has the lion but

Originally published in *Rolling Stone*, 156, March 14, 1974. Reprinted with permission.

himself, I tried to make it a song and sang it so many times so loudly that I wonder what the neighbors thought in those old days when acid rock was a baby.

In December, 1965, when we had been bombing Vietnam for eight months, Dylan read "Poisoned Wheat," a long anti-war poem of mine. One day as we were eating chicken, I handed him another copy. He left huge greasy fingerprints and he did it with great aplomb. It seemed very non-materialistic and natural not to notice the blotches. It seemed right to treat works of art as part of the transformations of life. Later I gave the copy to a woman who wanted Bob's fingerprints.

The first person to play a Dylan album for me was poet David Meltzer. It was Dylan's first album, and I heard it shortly after it came out in March or April of 1962. I could not understand what David heard in the album. In high school I knew slightly older people at the University of Chicago and in New York City who were singing like that—just some hillbilly-intellectual music that I'd gotten bored with earlier. In retrospect, Dylan must have shown a direct creative thrust without the "Art" self-consciousness of other singers.

Early in 1965 a friend of my wife Joanna came to visit and brought the Dylan album with "She Belongs to Me." The album had changed her life-image from a tragic loser to a proud artist. My wife heard and understood Dylan at once and completely, I think.

In 1965 everyone had been after me to listen to Dylan carefully—to sit down and listen to the words *and* the music. I absolutely did *not* want to hear Dylan. We had a banged-up record player in the hallway at the top of the stairs. Late at night, in the pale-grey hallway-light, Joanna sat me down in front of the speaker and told me to listen to the words. I began to hear what the words were saying, not just the jangling of the guitar and the harmonica and the whining nasal voice. The next thing I knew I was crying. It was "Gates of Eden": "At dawn my lover comes to me / And tells me of her dreams / With no attempts to shovel the glimpse / Into the ditch of what each one means. . . ."

I had the idea that I was hallucinating, that it was William Blake's voice coming out of the walls and I stood up and put my hands on the walls and they were vibrating.

Then I went back to those people who had tried to get me to listen and I told them that I thought the revolution had begun. "Gates Of Eden" and those other songs seemed to open up the post-Freudian and post-Existentialist era. No longer did everyone have to use the old explanations and the mildewed rationalities. By the time I met Bob, his poetry was important to me in the way that Kerouac's writing was. It was not something to imitate or be influenced by; it was the expression of a unique individual and his feelings and perceptions.

There is no way to second-guess poetry or to predict poetry or to convince a poet that the best songs in the world are poetry if they are not. Bob Dylan is a poet; whether he has cherubs in his hair and fairy wings, or feet of clay, he is a poet. Those other people called "rock poets," "song poets," "folk poets," or whatever the rock critic is calling them this week, will be better off if they are appreciated as songwriters.

At a party after his concert in Berkeley in 1965, Dylan told me that he had not read Blake and did not know the poetry. That seemed hard to believe so I recited a few stanzas. One was the motto to "the Songs of Innocence and Experience" which begins: "The Good are attracted by Men's perceptions / And think not for themselves."

In 1965 that first Dylan concert in the Bay Area was at San Francisco's Masonic Auditorium. In those days the Masonic seemed huge and rather plush. It was the first time I had heard Bob Dylan in person. The records were beautiful but this was better—an immaculate performance with inflections or nuances different from the albums. Dylan was purest poet. Like an elf being, so perfect he was and so ferocious in his persistence for perfection. There was a verge of anger in him waiting for any obstacle to the event.

After the Masonic Auditorium concert we went to the Villa Romano Motel, where Bob and his group the Hawks were staying, and met with agent Al Grossman. He, Joan Baez, Allen Ginsberg, and I spoke for a while. Joan said that Allen and I should be Bob's conscience. It seemed a beautiful thing to say, though not clear at the time. Later Joan wrote that we should hold Bob in our consciousness.

A night or two later, after another concert, there was a party for Bob in San Francisco. Ken Kesey bounced through the door with a few of his Merry Pranksters. Ruddy with the vigor of good health, Los

Gatos sunshine, and acid, Kesey immediately hit Dylan with something like, "Hey man, you should try playing while you're high on acid." Without a pause Dylan said, "I did and it threw off my timing." There was no way to one-up Bob or to get ahead of him at any level or any time. You knew that pop stars like Dylan or Lennon drove around in black cars and they were careful and they were very fast and they were staying where they were and they were not kidding.

Nine years later, on the plane going to meet Dylan's tour in Philadelphia, I reread Robert Duncan's small book, *Seventeenth Century Suite*. Duncan had vowed not to publish any of his new poetry publicly for fifteen years, so that no pressure would direct him to write anything other than what he wishes most deeply. By canceling formal publication he was essentially vowing to please only himself. Robert made an edition of two hundred copies of the *Seventeenth Century Suite* poems and gave them to friends as Christmas gifts.

How incredibly far it is from Duncan's private edition of *Seventeenth Century Suite* to Dylan's millions of albums. Both are fine poetry and though they seem poles apart, they almost touch in their subtle images and music. One can imagine the radiance and spectrum of the poetry between.

It is a mistake to wonder which poetry will matter thirty years from now. We should wonder what is wrong if Dylan's songs do not mean something to us today. We are all moved by spiritual experiences. For some of us the spiritual experiences can be the grossest hit songs or the most kitsch style of painting. It really is a matter of whether we are ogres or elves—or something in between drawn one way or the other at one moment and another.

The Philadelphia concert made the Masonic Auditorium of San Francisco 1965 seem like a jam session in a small nightclub. The crowd was not in their late twenties and early thirties as friends had predicted—this was an audience of nice-looking, scruffy young people in their early twenties. All in all, except for the number of bodies (making one think of the pictures of a Japanese beach), one did not mind being there. There were some of the best people around, a part of the backbone of the future—the people with hope and some enthusiasm in a country run over for eight years by the War Machine.

The lights went down accompanied by a burst of enthusiasm from the 19,000 living souls.

To open the first set, houselights came down into darkness very fast. Colored spotlights flashed to the stage and banks of colored lights shone. The Band and Bob Dylan almost ran onstage and began playing without a pause while the audience was still cheering their enthusiasm.

There were two thoughts that someone had imparted to me. One was that Bob was redoing his old songs as rock for the new generation who did not know him well. The second was that Dylan was in danger of disappearing into his own creation; that as one of the founders of the giant rock scene he had spawned so many followers, so many imitators, and Dylan-influenced groups and movements that he stood in danger of blending in among his own offspring and hybrids—ending up in the public eye as another surviving folk-rocker.

Dylan a grown man . . . a young man still, but a man. The elfish lightness of foot is gone and the perfection of timing is replaced by sureness; the nasal boy's voice replaced by a man's voice.

Another poet's singing came to mind: Allen Ginsberg at the 1966 Human Be-In singing his strange "Peace in America—Peace in Vietnam," and I was there too, using the black autoharp and singing, "The god I worship is a lion."

Now Dylan is official culture—like Brecht and Weill. He played "Mr. Jones"—in 1965 a glove thrown in the public face, a statement of revolt; now it is Art.

I could not take my eyes off the lights, hypnotized by the spots of amber, lavender, blue, red that kept playing on Dylan. The banks of lights up above the bandstand stage to the right and left kept bleeding and blinking off and on in time with the drama and melody of the songs. Bright lights kept popping in the blackness—intensely bright and silvery white in their flash. Flashbulbs! It seemed crazy that anyone sitting three blocks from the bandstand in the darkness would be setting off flashbulbs. It seemed demented.

"My God, it is a long way since the Avalon Ballroom," I thought. A long way since the artist's light shows and the smallness of the dance floors and the tribal dancers of 1966. We felt so crowded together, transpersonal and magical in those days. In Philadelphia what I saw was gigantic! The incredible subtlety of the earlier light shows was surpassed by a blending of colors, the motility of the spotlights and the sheer candlepower. The devastating volume of the music made it unpleasant trying to pick Dylan's words out of the roar.

One became aware that the enormous volume of the amplified music mimicked, as it bounced off the walls, the roar of the crowd. The music became a response to itself. The effect would trigger in the audience a response to the music. Loud cheering. When it happened I wondered if that was entertainment or ethological manipulation—or if entertainment could be ethological manipulation.

I loved what I could hear of Dylan's new love songs—they seemed inspired. The melodies, lost in the amplified blare, were not impressive but I was able to hear: "May you always stay courageous / Be forever young. . . ."

In the darkness at the end of the concert, the audience lit matches and cigarette lighters, making a Milky Way of wavering lights and cheers—a universe of tiny flaming stars.

If a scholar goes seriously into an analysis of the poetry convergent with the rock movement, there will be interesting contrasts between Lennon, Kerouac, Dylan, and Morrison. The whole thing started with the poets of the fifties. It was an alchemical-biological movement, not a literary one. Bob Dylan's "Dylan" is from Dylan Thomas, the Welsh poet so popular in the fifties. Allen Ginsberg asked if I'd heard that Dylan was titling his album *Planet Waves*. I asked Allen what he thought of that. Allen said, "Charming! Delightful! Great!" I think so too. Allen's last book was *Planet News*. There's plenty of room for feedback back and forth.

At the Toronto concert, media philosopher Marshall McLuhan and his wife were in the audience. McLuhan told me that he had played Dylan albums to a poetry class that morning. McLuhan believes that rock 'n' roll comes out of the English language—using its rhythms and inflections as a basis for melody. (Exactly what I believe—and also that it comes out of the Beat mutation or it has the same root.) The future of rock, he felt, would be the same as that of the language; that it would have its ups and downs as the language does.

As a mode, the ballad and story-song seemed mined-out, I said. Anyone can write a story-song in almost any manner and it becomes uninteresting to listen to. McLuhan felt it is the background, not the mode, that gives out. The background is violence, and Dylan was singing violently. McLuhan feels that "violence is the result of a loss of identity—the more loss the greater the violence."

Sitting among 19,000 people McLuhan said, "Gravity is like acoustic space—the center is everywhere."

I told Marshall that I wanted to go out into the hallway in the last set of the concert when Dylan and the Band played "Like a Rolling Stone." The night before I had been carried away and wept so hard that I did not want to have the experience again. This was my third concert and the incredible volume of the speakers was beginning to undermine my nerves.

I first heard "Like a Rolling Stone" when my wife and I were driving in an open MG across the Arizona-California desert with our daughter curled up asleep behind us next to our wolfhound and our pet black-and-white rat sleeping in his cage on the floor of the sports car. The moon was on the horizon. A song never hit me so hard except as a child when my mother sang to me. Much of our poetic sensibility may have its origin with cradle songs—I remember my mother singing songs from Disney cartoons and movies and reciting Mother Goose and Kipling.

After the concert there was a moment to introduce McLuhan and his wife to producers Bill Graham and Barry Imhoff and Dylan before Bob and the Band went back onstage for their encore.

Pouring sweat, his face puffy, his eyes partially blanked by the concert he'd just delivered, Bob smiled as much as he could. In the auditorium almost 20,000 people were screaming and yelling for him to come back so he could reconnect them briefly with the godhead.

When Dylan and the Band ran back onstage, McLuhan said that this was his first rock concert. Bill Graham replied: "I wish I could say the same thing!" Bill had been concerned because everything on this tour was going too well. There is a theater superstition that if small things don't go wrong then something major will.

Dylan has slipped into people's dream baskets. He has been incorporated into their myths and fantasies. They worry about him: whether he is understood, what his next album will be like, if he is appreciated by the press, whether he might get a cold and how he performs his pieces.

My particular fantasy is that he is underpaid. I would not stand in front of 20,000 people and those lights and amplifiers and do what he is doing for all the dollars in the world or for a stack of gold records ten miles high.

Bob is a prisoner of his fame and fortune. When he says, "I'm anyone who lives in a vault . . . ," he means himself. He is a real poet who lives the poems that he sings. A lot of people who hold Dylan in their dream baskets think the songs are a confection—that they are cute and sweet the way Rod McKuen is. But everything I've seen convinces me that Bob is the real thing, that he is no joke, that he has no answers, that he is a poet, that he is trapped most of the time.

The several new songs that I heard in the concerts were domestic (about wife and home) and inspirational. I hope this is the direction that Dylan is going. It would be good to see lots of young Americans put back on their feet—not through renewed faith in the old values that have been shot down, but through greater awareness of themselves on an earth that was once beautiful—and that still has pockets of beauty. I'd like everyone to begin to get some sense of what, and who, they are—and a further sense that something can be done to elevate the vicious mindlessness of politics and bio-environmental destruction and the extinction of the species of living plants and animals. A lot of poets are moving in that direction—Ginsberg, Snyder, Duncan, Creeley, Waldman.

Thinking of Dylan's poetics I had brought along some books as background material: *Seventeenth Century Suite* by Robert Duncan, poems by Gary Snyder and Allen Ginsberg, *Black Music* by Imamu Amiri Baraka (LeRoi Jones), and Kafka's "Josephine The Singer."

In *Black Music*, published in 1968, Baraka says that the content of white-rock, anti-war and anti-authoritarian songs generalizes "passionate luxurious ego demonstrations"; that the artists want to prove that they are good human beings though, in fact, Baraka contends, they are really sensitive antennae of the brutalized and brutalizing white social mass. Baraka insists that is a cop-out and the music is still wealthy white kids playing around. We should remember Baraka's viewpoint: it may be narrow but light sometimes passes through a thin slit. The Beatles didn't write anti-war songs. When asked about that they replied that all their songs are against war. There may be some beams of light in that crack too.

In Toronto I read Kafka's "Josephine The Singer," from *The Penal Colony*. A mouse-narrator relates an account of a woman-mouse named Josephine who is a singer. She proclaims herself a great artist and the other mice congregate around to hear her at the risk of their lives. But nothing will satisfy her ambition. She has a coterie of worshipful followers. Many of the mice people, however, are not at all sure that what she does, as fascinating and important as it is, is singing. They think that it may be only "piping" and perhaps it is her childishness (as she reflects simple attitudes of her people back to them) that is attractive: "Here is someone making a ceremonial performance out of the usual thing." Josephine demands freedom from the labor quota of the mouse people. But no matter how much they love her or worship her, they will not free her from the work law. Josephine disappears—perhaps she has gone into hiding—to force people to accept her demands. Anyone interested in Dylan and/or poetry should look at the story.

———————

I thought of the creation of a demigod and prophet that took place in the multicolored spotlights and amplification and banks of stage-lights—better known to the modern world than Plato or Confucius or Buddha; watched by thousands with millions wishing to see him in other cities. One can become a statue of one's self, mimicking what one is in eternity. Immortality (or its substitute) can be turned off and on and directed by voice over wires and captured on disks of black plastic. There is the possibility that the background has swallowed up the object and that we are in the process of whiting-out. If so, I think we stand in need of it.

Poetry, in a general sense, may be defined to be the expression of the imagination; and poetry is connate with the origin of man. Man is an instrument over which a series of external and internal impressions are driven, like the alterations of an ever-changing wind over an Aeolian lyre, which move it by their motion to ever-changing melody. But there is a principle within the human being, and perhaps within all sentient beings, which acts otherwise than in the lyre, and produces not melody alone, but harmony, by an internal adjustment of the sounds or motions thus excited to the impressions which excite them. . . .

So said Shelley in 1821 in A Defence of Poetry.

Ninety-One Things about
Richard Brautigan

1. For a long period I was probably Richard's closest friend and he was probably mine. He was here visiting two or three nights a week. We talked and drank Gallo white port, sitting on the floor. This was when we didn't have any furniture. We were still poor. The first sip of white port hits the mid-chest and brings on sudden intense warmth. The second swallow begins warming the shoulders. After that you slip into a sweet yellow-warm glow and become great storytellers and listeners. Richard had an open face and mobile eyes behind his round glasses— the movements of his mustache emphasized his jokes and stories. As I remember, a pint of port was thirty-seven cents. We bought it at Benedetti's Liquors on Haight Street, where we bought most of our bottles back in the mid-sixties.

2. Richard was a disciple to some extent, or more aptly a *pupil,* of Jack Spicer. He must have met poet Jo Anne Kyger through Spicer, and maybe Joe Dunn that way too. (Dunn published Richard's first book in his White Rabbit Press series.) Richard was an afficionado of Gino and Carlo's Bar, Spicer's hangout. When I first met Richard, there was something skittish about his literary background—probably Gino and Carlo's and Jack Spicer. I liked Richard because of his angelic schitzy wit and warmth.

3. I arranged a poetry reading for Richard at CCAC and I made a poster for it. It was like a boxing poster of the time. I drew it by hand, Richard face-forward with his glasses, hat, and mustache. Across from that I drew his profile, then wrote DIGGER under one and POET

Written in 1985, these notes are previously unpublished.

under the other. Richard kept that poster up on the wall forever, along with other posters, and good notices. He loved it. Everything got very old on his walls. He'd hang new things but he'd never take anything away or down. The things about him comforted him and got cobwebby. It was like an old museum of himself.

4. Richard always dressed the same. It was his style and he wanted to change it as little as possible. (I was like that myself at the time. We were all trying to get the exact style of ourselves.) Richard's style was shabby—loose threads at the cuff, black pants faded to gray, an old mismatched vest, a navy pea-jacket, and later something like love beads around the neck. As he began to be successful he was even more fearful of change. When the three-book-in-one edition of *Trout Fishing In America*, *The Springhill Mine Disaster*, and *In Watermelon Sugar* was published, it faithfully reproduced the earlier avant-garde editions of his work—including cover photos, critical comments, and pagination. It was a magic formula and Richard didn't want to jiggle it.

5. The planning of each book was a huge strategy and Richard was a Confederate general scheming a campaign. He was the same way about placing a story of his. He couldn't simply do it and be done with it. He had to go over everything endlessly. He'd phone me half a dozen times each day to talk to me about a cover photograph he was thinking up. How to do it? Who should do it? He probably phoned novelist Don Carpenter that many times a day too. He became even more obsessive about contract details with his Delacorte Press publisher and with Grove Press. It was maddening and painful and dull to go over it all with him. He'd laugh about it—but it was obsessive. He'd sweat over whether to take an advance of $60,000 or whether to hold out for $65,000; he'd torture out details regarding advertising his book. It was endless, and painful for his artist friends who were supporting him emotionally but were in near terminal poverty. You wanted to help, he needed it, but he also needed to hurt with his success. It was awful for everyone.

In his book *Marble Tea* there's a poem—a prose poem reminiscent of Blake's "Memorable Fancies"—in which Richard describes cutting a worm in half on an April morning. Part of the worm crawled toward the infinite and part towards infintesimal. Richard's success—to my eyes—cut him in half. Part of him was crawling on to creation and another part was crawling towards destruction of friends and self through booze and the birth of envy. As his writing became more divine, Richard became more sexist and more alcoholic.

6. Richard convinced his agent Helen Brann to represent my short plays *Gargoyle Cartoons* and my novel *The Adept*. Richard believed in my work the way I believed in his. His poem "For Michael" is beautiful, and his dedication to me and Don Allen and Jo Anne Kyger in *In Watermelon Sugar* is lovely. Especially so since it is his most perfect book.

7. The first thing about Richard and guns that I remember is when he was beginning to get goofy with drinking and success and he gave Gary Snyder a broken, vintage Japanese machine gun for his son Kai. "So he won't lose his Japanese heritage," said Richard.

8. As Richard became a kind of monster, his public appearances became sweeter and more like his creative, imaginative, and beautiful person of before. He was a wonderful reader—his voice was smooth as honey and warm and personal, almost sweetly drunken to the ear. And his eyes sparkled with a cross between happiness and the resignation to the ineffability of everything. It was real. He felt it. It's all there in the work and in his earlier person. At a reading he literally loved everyone and they literally loved him back. They were wowed by the beauty of his poems.

9. When my wife of the time bought a Russian wolfhound puppy we named him Brautigan. He was skinny and angular, long-faced and long-nosed, and he looked like he had loose threads on his elbows.

10. Richard and I were always showing up in the newspapers, usually the *Chronicle*. My play *The Beard* was a topic of conversation and the play's censorship was still going on, I was writing Hell's Angel Freewheelin Frank's autobiography with him, I was doing a video documentary on the Haight Ashbury. Richard had stories and reviews appear-

ing everywhere, and columnist Herb Caen loved to mention us. When either of us had our name in the paper we declared ourselves to be a "Ten Day Baron of Cafe Society." We proclaimed that we were famous for ten days and we rushed off to drink at the sidewalk tables of Enrico's Cafe where we could be admired by mortals. We drank Enrico's stemmed glasses of cold white wine in the afternoon and watched record scouts digging in for the new rock 'n' roll of Frisco, or literary agents, or visiting L.A. stars come to ogle the City of Love. After a couple of glasses Richard began to get owlish and silent with bursts of slightly tipsy talk and I began to get winishly ennobled in my own ways. I contended that nobody—not even Frank Sinatra—could be famous for more than ten days in Frisco. Often Richard and I were simultaneously Ten Day Barons of Cafe Society and sometimes we'd get on a roll and manage to keep a Barony for a month at a time with overlapping newspaper references. One rule, though, was that you could not accrue Baronhoods. A Baronhood only lasted ten days after the mention or article. A second rule was that it couldn't come from your name being in an advertisement. Richard would phone me or I'd phone him. "Hey, I'm a Baron. Let's go to Enrico's."

11. One of the things I liked most about Richard was that he was the real poet of the Diggers. He was often on Haight Street passing out papers from the Digger Communications Company. I liked that activism. Richard was doing it because he believed in it. I got so I'd go down there and do it too. And I was a lot more self-conscious on the street than he was. Richard would pass out papers from the Digger Communication Company urging all the "Seeker" youngsters at the Summer of Love to go immediately to the VD Clinic at the first sign. Richard has a poem about clap in *Pill.* It might have been a Communications Company broadside. It was his example that got me involved with the Communications Company, and I wrote a poem— "War Is Decor"—and helped pass it out, then read it later on Walter Cronkite's national television report on the Haight Ashbury.

12. Richard was crazy about beautiful women, smoothly glabrous ones with long hair and big eyes. Blonde or brunette didn't matter. He'd been considered real homely all his life (I'm sure), but like a Russian wolfhound puppy he knew better. When his sex appeal bloomed with his fame he loved it. He loved all the lovely sex around him. Real sensuality—clear and lucid like you read in poetry of the *Greek Anthology*—began to come out in his poetry . . . But that worm got split about the same time and the secret sexism began to become obnoxious.

13. Rereading *Trout Fishing* I began to fear that it would be an apolitical and purely esthetic document and there would be no comment against the monster war in Vietnam. Then there it was, near the end: the Trout Fishing Peace March. It must have touched millions.

14. It was Richard buying the house that David and Tina lived in right out from under them and their two children that was the straw that broke my camel's back. I thought he should have bought it and let them live in it for nothing. Or even have given it to them.

Suddenly Richard was wealthy and not only real tight but afraid that people would find out he was wealthy. It was a shock to him and he had broad anal streak anyway. It was too much for him to handle. I felt that he was not only after me with his success but also after David because David was like Richard's anti-type. David poured creativity, and in vast spontaneous amounts. I think Richard just had to get at David. So he bought the house and left it standing empty.

Later, Richard shot and killed himself in that house.

15. When I reread *Trout Fishing, In Watermelon Sugar*, and the early poems, I had a flash of intuition. It is wrong to look at Richard as a novelist. What he is doing seems more akin to Lautreamont, to his *Chants of Maldoror*. Lautreamont was a young South American intellectual named Isidore Ducasse. Ducasse was inspired by Rimbaud and wrote a booklength prose poem. This began a chain of thought: Richard should rightfully be compared to Rimbaud, Lautreamont . . . Baudelaire. He should be compared to the dark school of French writers, to the maudites. His suicide closes his life. Compare him to Alfred Jarry who also changed personality and became gross and fat and took ether and alcohol. Richard reminds me of the mystic poet Gerard de Nerval also. Further, Richard could be compared to the German visionary Novalis. Novalis was full of aphorisms—his works were studded with them. Richard lacked that in his writing, but it is a world of the imagination and of nature melted into the imagination, as is Novalis.

16. The tigers in *In Watermelon Sugar* are surely Blake's tygers from "The Tygers of Wrath are wiser than the Horses of Instruction." They have beautiful voices and The Nameless Hero asks them for aid in his math problems. The black world of Death is the interwound topology of the primal (unformed and still forming) material, and the unconscious, and the universe of anti-matter.

Richard lived across the street and down a few yards from the big Sears Roebuck department store on Geary Street. Sears is the Forgotten Works in the novel.

In Watermelon Sugar might have been written by an American Lorca, it has the darkness of one of Lorca's late poems: "Nobody understood the perfume of the dark magnolia of your womb. . . ."

On the other hand, *In Watermelon Sugar* on the whole is simpleminded, which Richard wasn't. What the prose lacks, as does *Trout Fishing*, is conflict. In both books Richard almost abolished interpersonal conflict to create a "gentle" (the word is used over and over) world of the imagination and sensory perception and memory melted into a pool that Richard took us swimming in, a stream that he fished in. Those two books are his great struggle to cancel conflict and confrontation. There is never confrontation because each chapter is in a new place or new situation.

One cannot create a long dramatic work without conflict.

17. Richard can be seen as a phenomenon of the Haight and the sixties. Or as an American artist. I think one might say Artist rather than either poet or novelist. I think of myself as an artist, with a capital A. Artist. West Coast writers of the period tend to see themselves as Artists, not so different from the painters or musicians they admire. Artists are free from the spectre of the possibility of monetary success or national acclaim which in those days they knew they'd never get. In the fifties Gary Snyder used to tell young poets to learn a trade, meaning there was no way to support themselves through their art; learn to be a merchant seaman or a carpenter.

18. Richard can be seen as a West Coast writer—not that his success
wasn't national or that he isn't a national artist. The West Coast looks
to the mountains and the forests and the deserts and Big Sur and
Mendocino and Puget Sound around it. When strangers visited I'd
sometimes take them across the bridge to Mount Tamalpais—or into
Muir Redwood Forest. San Francisco is part of the United States but
it is also part of the Pacific Basin and as part of the Pacific Basin we
were connected to the Orient, to Japan and China. New York looked
to Paris and London. San Francisco looks there too. In 1955, Frisco
looked like Cow Town, USA. No tall buildings. There were Asian
people all around. They had a different cuisine. Buddhism was something real to them and lots of them practised it in churches.

Kenneth Rexroth was the ideologue. He showed us that we could
define our own personal anarchism, that we were free to invent our
own mysticisms or follow old ones—agnosia by way of the Areopagite,
or Kundalini Yoga via Arthur Avalon, or practice Zen Buddhism.
Everyone was free to invent or reinvent their own intellective structures
of understanding time and space, music and painting. The West Coast
was full of deep readers who were also involved in soul-building by
means of travel and mountain and forest experience. We were different.

Kenneth Rexroth did something else, too. He showed that we could
look to the Orient for poetry and cuisine but that also we could
look back in time—we could look to 1000 A.D. to Sung Dynasty
China, or back to Buddha and Confucius and Lao Tsu in Chou Dynasty
China. Most of us did Some Oriental time-travelling by way of art and
poetry.

19. Editor Donald M. Allen "discovered" Richard—he put his faith
in Richard, publishing *Trout Fishing,* then *In Watermelon Sugar* and *The
Pill.* It was Don who brought together the San Francisco Issue of
Evergreen Review in 1957, linking up Ginsberg, Kerouac, Duncan,
Spicer, Broughton, Everson, Lamantia, and me for the literary public
eye. And it was Don who edited the major and poetry-world shaker,
The New American Poetry, in 1960. Richard was not in that anthology
as he had not made any impact as yet. Don was the first business world
literary gentleman to recognize Olson, Duncan, me, and many others.

20. Regarding information on Richard and the "Orient": Shig Murao (who was the man busted for selling *Howl* at City Lights in 1957) tells me that I should contact Albert Saijo about Richard because it was Albert who got Richard the job testing meat samples that he had in the early sixties. I'm told incorrectly that a Japanese restauranteur loaned Richard his final gun. Richard had a Japanese wife. Richard had—if I understand correctly—as big a vogue in Japan as he had here.

21. On the phone I asked Shig Murao if Richard wasn't part of the Jack Spicer–Gino and Carlo's Bar crowd. Shig said that Richard came here when he was seventeen or eighteen and hung around North Beach "in the early days." Shig said Richard liked to hang out at The Place, which was mostly a painters' and poets' bar in the mid and late fifties. Shig said Richard liked to recite a poem about pissing in the men's room sink. I don't know of that poem. Jay DeFeo had a show of painting in The Place, and Allen Ginsberg had a show of his poems hung with the flower paintings of Robert LaVigne there. The Place was the corner bar for me in 1954, the Deux Magot of Frisco; it put the X into San Francisco Existentialism. The Place was where I could get high on the beauty of Jay DeFeo's gouaches hung on the walls.

22. Poems of Richard's in *The Pill* intrigue me lot. Often the word surrealism is used inaccurately. "Horse Child Breakfast" might be called a "surreal" poem by someone, though actually it is quite lucid. Some young woman looks like a horse to Richard—probably she has a long palomino mane and sleek legs. Also, she looks like a child to Richard. I imagine she looks like a horse-child to him also, a filly. She is there the whole night and they have breakfast together, which she probably fixes, as it's hard to imagine Richard fixing breakfast. She becomes Horse Child Breakfast and Richard addresses her as such. That is not surrealism. Actually, it is a love poem owing more to Richard's imagination of Sappho's poems—to their lucid sensual and sensory address of another person than to a surreal impulse.

In fact, the use of three words—Horse and Child and Breakfast— probably owes much to Oriental poetry as we understand it. Richard was aware of Fenollosa's text on the origin of the Chinese ideogram and how elements combined to make a calligraphic character, as well as the "concrete" use of three words, not normally syntactically connected to create a verbal construct.

It's quite a delicate poem. It may be naively combining the Greek and the Chinese—but it is canny and memorable. It's gorgeous!

23. A big figure on the West Coast in the fifties was philosopher Alan Watts. He was speaking visionary Buddhism and new hipness and mystical Taoism on his radio program. The poet Kenneth Rexroth also had a great and eccentric book review radio program in which he reviewed, in the most intellectual and learned terms, everything from the Kabalistic aspects of the Shekina to the geography of Han Dynasty China and texts on Byzantine Greek theology. There were carpenters and printers and news-reporters around who were members or ex-members of anarchist–pacifist discussion groups. San Francisco was a rich network of streams to "trout about" in. Richard must have loved it all as much as I did. Vibrancy of thought was in the air. Consciousness of California landscape and Oriental thought were in the air we breathed, and it was made dark and moist by the Pacific beating on the coast of Monterey. Steinbeck country was nearby, Henry Miller lived down on Partington Ridge, Robinson Jeffers was in his tower in Carmel. Kenneth Patchen was in town. William Carlos Williams came to read for the Poetry Center. Robert Duncan had a class in poetics at S.F. State. A Jack Spicer disciple group met at Joe Dunn's house to read and discuss poetry. Brother Antoninus was in a nearby monastery after his previous career of being poet William Everson. Philip Lamantia was around—he'd been acclaimed a major surrealist poet at age fourteen by André Breton. Kerouac came to town. Creeley visited and ran off with Rexroth's wife. The buckeye on the mountainsides was in flower—everything smelled like redwood and bay. One could see the first reappearance of sea otters down the coast. I met Ginsberg at a party for W.H. Auden. I can't remember when I first met Richard.

24. An intriguing passage of Richard's in *The Pill* is "Our Beautiful West Coast Thing." It begins with an epigraph by Jack Spicer: "We are a coast people. There is nothing but ocean behind us." Richard says he's dreaming long thoughts of California on a November day near

the ocean. He says he's listening to The Mamas and The Papas. Naively he says in caps, "THEY'RE GREAT." They are singing a song about breaking somebody's heart and "digging it!" He gets up and dances around the room.

San Franciscans were inhabiting their bodies by learning to dance communal dances with Billy the Kids and Mae Wests and Florence Nightingales and Beatles' Sergeant Majors in the Fillmore Auditorium and in the Avalon Ballroom. Everyone was putting their booties down to the Jefferson Airplane and Big Brother and the Holding Company. The dances were free-form—you could make any beautiful step or wave of arm that you wanted with anyone around you on the floor. Tribal stomp! But a lovely stomp, even "gentle," as Richard would say, amid the gross amplification and the strobe lights and large moving patterns of colors on the walls.

25. It is easy to read free-form from chapter to chapter in *Trout Fishing* after dancing free-form at the Fillmore or Avalon Ballroom. You danced with the partner who was behind you when you turned around. She had on a dreamy costume and had lovely bare arms. Maybe you'd had a hit of windowbox grass and she was high on acid. She was a goddess. You were some god. Goethe said, "Experience is only half of experience." The details could shift a lot but it was all holy. When Brautigan speaks about dancing in the poem he's making reference to W.C. Williams dancing solo in his home being the happy genius of his household, but the dancing that Richard saw and did in the Fillmore helps explain the chapter structure of *Trout Fishing*. It was what people were doing.

26. Richard was five years younger than me. He was from the Pacific Northwest. I grew up in Seattle. As a kid, the newspaper comic strips that I read were probably the same ones he read. I remember "Smokey Stover," where the goofy firechief with the blank eyes and big smile tooled around in his threewheeler car from panel to panel with almost no connection and a host of weird characters. There were little signs on sticks that said "Nov Shmoz Kapop" and "Notary Sojac." I also read "Toonerville Trolley," which was often just one big panel with dozens of strange countrified and shaggy, shabby, angular whiskerandos and

old ladies and terrible children clinging to the country trolley. In "Smokey Stover" there was little need for continuity—just a good old-fashioned sense of humor and appetite for the strange and amusing—and a basically good-natured view of the world and its tiny tribulations and ambitions. A chapter of *Trout Fishing* had as many things clinging to it, and riding on it, as did the "Toonerville Trolley" on a crowded outing to Blueberry America.

I wonder if Richard read my other favorite newspaper cartoon strip, "The Nutt Brothers: Ches & Wal"? It was so far out that it made "Smokey Stover" read like Ecclesiastes or the Odes of Horace. Ches and Wal Nutt changed not only costumes from panel to panel but even bodies. Each strip was based on some far-reaching pun. It was a wonder to look at—it had whales in it and bathtubs and fezzes.

Trout Fishing reiterates the American comic strip of the period Richard grew up in, the late 1930s and early 1940s. He read all those panels and they must have delighted him. So he wrote *Trout Fishing* in panels.

I'd guess he got desperate about reaching out in *Confederate*—trying to write an *On The Road*—and afterwards he went back to what he knew, loved, and could do. Part of what he did was to make far-out comic strips, but with an enormous, liberated imagination, using only words, and childhood, and everything he ever felt, or saw, or thought that fit in. Thus, *In Watermelon Sugar* was his second big comic strip. I can't think of any comic strips like it, save maybe an imaginary one: "The Adventures of Federico Garcia Lorca in Samuel Palmer Land." Samuel Palmer was a disciple of William Blake who etched dark nightscapes of sheep and kine and shepherds walking past black kirks in the Lake Country. The funny thing is that there might be a grain of truth there—Richard certainly knew Lorca and no doubt he knew some of Palmer's works.

27. Novalis wrote, "Man is a sun; and the senses are planets." Richard would have liked that.

28. I think of Bruce Conner as an Artist. He's known now as a filmmaker but he is a master sculptor in assemblage and in wax, and there is no better painter or draftsman around than Conner. Bruce wrote

terrific rock lyrics and learned to play electric piano; he is considered by some to be a fairly fine mouth harpist. Richard thought of Bruce Conner as an Artist and he would have thought of himself as an Artist. I can't imagine that Richard thought of himself as a "novelist," except, that is, for public consumption. I don't mean that he looked down on it at all—he admired novelists. But he was an Artist.

29. Richard's mutation interests me. By "mutation" I mean metamorphosis. I love to see metamorphosis in an artist. I love Mark Rothko's change, over a period of five years in the forties, from his spirit-figure paintings to his color fields. I love Rimbaud's teenage change to explorer. I even love Dali's change from Salvador Dali to the person renamed (in anagram) Avida Dollars—the money-hungry genius satirized by André Breton. Oddly, I couldn't stand the big change Richard made in front of me from Richard to Dark Richard. Only now can I begin to appreciate it.

I've spoken about the transitions from *Confederate* to *Trout* to *Watermelon*—equally intriguing like the graceful hops of the katydid are the leaps between his first books of poetry. Only a visionary literary critic would ecstasize over *Galilee Hitchhiker*. It's a small collection of whimsical, poignant, intense to some extent, momentarily witty poems with the central thread being the changing presence of Baudelaire as an occupant of the poems. Sometimes he's a monkey, sometimes he's driving a car, sometimes he's a flowerburger chef. (This again reminds me of Smokey Stover and the Nutt Brothers. Persons change their bodies and their occupations with no rational linear reason except the pleasure of fantasy and expression.) *Galilee* is mimeographed and not prepossesing, except to the *au courant* literati who recognized that it was published by a ring of intense young poets surrounding the ideologue older poet Jack Spicer. That was in 1958.

Next, in 1959, appeared an equally unprepossessing book of twenty-four small poems, titled with a quote from Emily Dickinson: "Lay the Marble Tea." But the poet's skill has expanded! The obsessive crispy Baudelaire persona has gone and the poems are inexplicable artifacts and penetrating insights into childhood. They are both soft and terse and they lack the compression of statement that a Poundian poet would have written. These are literary poems with reference to Shakespeare,

Melville, Kafka, and Dickinson. Though the references are whimsical, they are inherent to the poems and not decoration. Richard is clearly quite literary.

In the front of this book is the first sight of Richard's trademark—his teardrop-shaped trout drawing. The book is published by Carp Press. One of Richard's fish drawings is there and next to it are the words: The Carp.

The next katydid hop is to his 1960 book *The Octopus Frontier*. It has Richard's first photographic cover, looking as deliberate and planned as the cover of *Trout Fishing*. The photo is by North Beach photographer of the fifties (and daughter of folklorist Jaime de Angulo) Gui de Angulo—she used to photograph all of us. It is a bleed photo cover showing what is apparently Richard's foot on the suckered tentacle of a large octopus. It is striking and just misses being sinister. It is startling and not funny. It is a *non sequitur* . . . and a memorable one.

The poems of *Octopus Frontier* are filled with large simple images of vegetables and pumpkins floating on the tide, a poem about Ophelia, and poems about childhood. At this point there is a recognizable Brautigan style, though it would still be hard to recognize the gleam of gold in the poetry. Now there are three stepping-stone books of poems, and Richard has been lucid and readable in every one of them, but there is no indication that this work is greatly above the level of much North Beach poetry. There's not any reason for even a keen reader like Donald M. Allen to note any of this for his important anthology.

Keats said, "Life is a Vale of Soul-making." Richard was Soul-making—carefully, cautiously, tersely, but still with some sweetness and even courtingly. The three little poem book "hops," in all their sharp-edged softness, add up to a stepping stone big enough to move him into poetry of true richness. That rich poetry shows up in the *Pill*. But the *Pill* is a "selected" poems. Richard carefully seeds and manures it with selections from these three early books. He puts them all together in the *Pill* into what he finds to be a courtingly enchanting—and otherwise inexplicable—order.

Later in *Please Plant This Book* he not only passes out the free poems by way of the Diggers, but real packets of seeds along with the writings. Richard's metamorphosis is made of little mutations, skin-sheddings like those of the instar of a katydid.

30. I like the little "Dandelion Poem" that Richard dedicated to me. He also reviewed my Beast Language poems, *Ghost Tantras*, in a mimeo magazine of the day called (if memory has it right) *Wild Dog Review*. It was one of the few reviews that book ever had. I said earlier that *Watermelon* is dedicated to Don Allen, Jo Anne Kyger, and me. Richard really knocked himself out to please people he liked or loved. He wrote a lot of poems for women he loved and men friends that he was close to, and he dedicated all his books in the most generous and heartfelt way.

31. Except for Don Carpenter—who never broke off with Richard—I was the last of his old close friends to cut away. It tears me up to think how close we were and how wonderful he was in many ways. Could I have stuck by him longer? Then I realize—yes, I could have. . . What? For a month more? A year more? But to old friends he was like a cat on its back clawing the stomach out of a hand.

32. Writer Ron Loewinson first met Richard in 1957. He says that Richard's natural form was the short story. Ron and I are probably the only two around to whom Richard had expressed his admiration of Henri Michaux's prose. Michaux's *Miserable Miracle*, about mescaline, was the take-off point for me to write my essays titled "Drug Notes." I felt I could be more truthful, more American in my description of peyote.

33. *Trout* is dedicated to Ron Loewinson and Jack Spicer. Ron confirms that Richard wrote *Trout* before *Confederate*, and that Spicer was responsible for much editorial contribution. So young poet Brautigan was helped into his first novel by Jack Spicer.

34. I told Ron that the beginning of *The Abortion* reminds me of Franz Kafka. Ron pointed out that in the prologue to *Trout*, Richard notes that Kafka learned about America from reading Benjamin Franklin. Then there's that poem, "Kafka's Hat." Then there's Richard's ever-present hat.

The situation in the beginning of *The Abortion* reminds me of Kafka's novel *Amerika*. *The Abortion*'s a real book about an imaginary America.

There is a real library in a real place in San Francisco, but in the novel it is open twenty-four hours a day and the librarian lives there and cannot leave. It is as if he were involved in a "gentle" and voluntary *Trial*.

35. Today most students at California College of Arts and Crafts don't know who Richard is. One student asked me if Eleanor Dickinson was famous—she teaches at CCAC. I said, yes, for her drawings and television documentaries. The student thought he had her seen picture on a stamp. He was thinking of Emily Dickinson. Television has collapsed time and history for these students. *Trout* collapses Time and History and Memory and the topological separations of Places. *Trout* changes channels every few hundred words.

36. Poet and critic Bill Berkson says when he went up to a radicalized Yale (late sixties) to teach, he asked who the students were reading. They were only reading Richard.

37. Ron Loewinson thinks that all of Richard's later (post-*Abortion*) works are based on a two-screen principle—shift from one location to another, then back to number one, then back to the other. This would be a desperate attempt to eliminate conflict or confrontation. It is also literary, a device. It is also romantic, turning from partner to partner and never looking at one long enough to see the flaws.

38. People sometimes mixed up James Broughton and Richard Brautigan. Before Richard was famous—on his way up—film-maker and poet James Broughton was making a film called "The Bed." It featured celebrities on a bed. Broughton filmed Brautigan for the film. Richard was thrilled about it. He was genuinely excited to be recognized as an art-celebrity by a world-known film-maker like Broughton. When the film came out, Richard was not in it. For a long time Richard went around with damp eyes, lashing his tail.

39. There is a "grandmotherliness" in Richard's *Abortion*. In addition to the smarminess of the dialogue, metaphors like "Vida and I were so relaxed that we both could have been rented out as fields of daisies" begin to become underwhelming. The dialogue is almost mincing. Not only is Richard skipping the confrontation and conflict, he's also using filler, and it's hard to put filler in such a small book. There are small dialogues about nothing at all in simple-minded phrases.

40. The American painter of the 1920s and 1930s, Arthur Dove, had a naive simplicity in his work—a simplification of landscapes or mood-scapes derived from vistas in broad, sweet, looming colors. Dove also did grandmotherly sentimental and exquisite collages using materials that might have come from grandmother's trunk or her life . . . pieces of lace, a spice label, and an elegant piece of veneer, or a page from an old letter in lovely elder handwriting of a previous generation. In doing those collages, Dove was not only American-Grandmotherly— he was French. There's something French about American-Grand-motherliness. It's perfectionistic. Sweetly anal. Exquisite. Even more than the box assemblages of Joseph Cornell.

41. To go back a step, *Trout* was written before the Fillmore dances, but I think for readers it mirrored their tribal dances in the switching of partners and chapter-channels. To paraphrase Samuel Butler, life is like a violin solo that one is playing in public but one is learning the violin as one plays. That is what Richard was doing—learning to write novels in public as they were being read. That is entrancing for a reading public but perhaps dangerous for Richard. He was always on the brink. He was always risking himself like a cautious acrobat and he was firmly trying to keep his shabby, personal, angular, wire-rimmed image unaltered. But he was also trying to become a male sex image and a wealthy artist.

42. Richard's description of the airport in *The Abortion* sounds like the world as seen by a schizophrenic—the nets of travel hanging in the air and catching people is a most real idea—most real and schizophrenic. Seeing the people as generalized robots seems schizophrenic. Seeing airplanes and airports as medieval castles of speed and so forth seems not only accurate but over the edge. This is a highly perceptive and accurate book but I'm afraid it is no longer fiction—it sounds like a "gentle" case history being written. The writer seems alienated, child-

like and incapable. It seems like an accurate set of descriptions about a real fantasy about incapability.

It occurs to me that the latent madness or hysteria is being salved by constant grandmotherliness. The hysteria a nanosecond beneath the surface is being calmed by cliches, figures of speech that are reassuring, and a willingness to be satisfied with images like "blank as snow" as capable acts of writing.

Richard, like the protagonist of *The Abortion*, did not know how to drive.

43. Richard keeps referring to the coffee spot on the wing of the plane through his protagonist. When the protagonist looks out of the cab and sees there is no coffee spot out there on the wing of the cab which isn't there—then, I begin to worry about Richard. This seems to be Richard flat-out describing schizophrenia. It is the raw stuff of mental cases.

By the time Richard wrote *The Abortion* we were both clearly "controlled" alcoholics. I wonder how much he had progressed later into uncontrolled alcoholism which may have acted as a balm of drunkenness—as per the balm of grandmotherliness in the novels. Alcohol is a numbing, godly, poisonous, liberating high.

44. *The Abortion* may be as mad and daring an act as Norman Mailer's *Ancient Evenings*. Both books are lovable for their vulnerability. I mean that both Richard and Norman dare to make themselves vulnerable. Are these voluntary acts of literature or are they uncontrollable obsessions? Great literature surely must be obsessional, and surely both of these books are obsessional.

45. Because it is so self-referential and so highly literary, Richard's *oeuvre* seems almost decadent, as if it were a part of a long tradition of intra-referential, self-referring works. Richard's works seem like Wen Fus written about other Wen Fus in a tradition of Wen Fu writers (the Wen Fu being an old Chinese form of highly literary prose poem). Clearly Kafka is there, and Michaux, and Vonnegut, and Spicer as mentor, and, I suppose, Hemingway into extremis. The writing is so *au courant* that Richard's *oeuvre* whites itself out and *seems* mindless and

spontaneous and unliterary, or anti-literary. But it is just the opposite. Richard is a highly-honed esthete writing esthetic documents and works of art of great, great refinement.

Like Baudelaire, Richard is a refined Dandy. His dress was the dandyism of Beatles style as well as Haight Ashbury style. The impoverished Dandy dresses in the most carefully chosen stylish rags of no-style. He makes an elegant sculpture of himself while he works obsessively in his garret. And as he interwinds the topology of his works, picturing himself on the cover of the work, his schizophrenia becomes its subject.

46. As I finish reading *The Abortion*, it seems inept. Richard had few adventures in his life when I knew him. He'd apparently had an abortion with some woman, he'd had a number of trips to Big Sur, and he'd had a dream that became *In Watermelon Sugar*. In the fifties none of us had had many adventures—we were poor and broke and young. Some of us shipped out to Asia and some of us had sexual adventures; some had been in the forest service; a few were criminals and drug addicts, or dope dealers, or had been through the post-midnight romance of bop at Black nightclubs and in sleazy hotels. Richard must have missed most of the few opportunities there were for adventures—he just wasn't adventurous, he was cautious. And with good reason, judging from the mental state of the narrator of *The Abortion*.

47. Our biggest adventure in the fifties (and it was huge and without proportion, on the scale of our nervous systems and the Universe) was literature, and trips of the mind through literature, and the literary wars for dominance in North Beach and elsewhere in San Francisco. Our study of poetry and each other's poetry was marvelously, miraculously intense. Richard was on the edges of that in the fifties, but he must have feasted on it mentally and in the bar life, as a whale feasts on the bloom of krill in the Antarctic Sea.

48. The opening of *The Hawkline Monster* reminds me of Richard's enjoyment of movies. It is a carefully-studied movie opening for a slightly far-out cowboy movie. To open with cowboys on a pineapple plantation in Hawaii in 1902 reminds me of movies like *Chinatown:*

the subject is popular, specific, and a little off-beat, but realistically satisfying and intriguing.

I remember Richard's pleasure in retelling scenes in movies. There's Richard in my mind's eye retelling a favorite scene (from *Butch Cassidy and the Sundance Kid.*) He tells the scene over in a precise and pleasurable way—juicy in the telling (from the warmth of a glass of wine in his shabby flat across from Sears)—but it is deliciously precise also.

49. *Hawkline* has a strong opening in the third person as compared to the mentally inept and grandmotherly sweet Kafkaesque opening of *Abortion.* (Wasn't *Hawkline* the next novel after *The Abortion?* Answer: No, I remember Richard telling me about *Willard and His Bowling Trophies*, though I hadn't seen the manuscript.) There is an enormous jump between *The Abortion* and the opening of *Hawkline.* It is not just the shift of person in the narrative—*Hawkline* is deliberately macho. Cameron and Greer are right out of macho cowboy movies. Maybe they are a split person. They are Sun and Dance, or Butch and Cassidy.

50. Richard really wanted to be MACHO—he wanted to be one of the Big Boys. It was childlike, or maybe childish. After I quit speaking to Richard I wrote an angry poem about him:

NINETEEN SEVENTY-TWO

SO, AT LAST YOUR PERSONALITY
HAS BECOME A COPROLITE!
((Fossilized shit!))
HOW
painful it was
to grow up in the fifties!
WE LEARNED:
materialism
macho-competition,
greed.
BUT STILL I CAN HARDLY BELIEVE
that you sit there telling me:
about the women you fuck,
how much money you make,
and of your fame.

As if
the last twenty years
never happened.
You seem pathetically
foolish. But there is a viciousness
in
our generation.
YOU
ARE
REALLY
SET
(like a robot)
ON OVERKILL.
And you believe
in social appearances.
You want to be like
The Big Boys.
Whoever *they* are!

I put the poem in *September Blackberries* and I didn't edit it out when I edited scores of pages from the manuscript. It meant something to me—it was a point I'd reached. It was a *node*. I saw the degree of my own materialism, sexism, and macho in Richard's actions and yet I was slightly aghast at Richard.

September Blackberries was the first book I published after the break with Richard. I hoped he would never see the poem, and I believed that he would accept our break so abruptly that he wouldn't read the book.

51. Last year Richard upset producer Benn Possett and his co-organizers at the One World Poetry Festival in Amsterdam. Apparently, Richard came on stage too drunk to read and he either read a bit or not at all, and maybe delivered an insult or several. Then he drunkenly howled and yelled and demanded for a woman who would fuck him. That must have been October of last year, and Benn was still talking about it in March when I saw him in Amsterdam. A couple of other people also mentioned Richard's scene. He was outrageous enough to anger the Dutch literary bohemians. It must have been something!

52. Shelley and Byron used to practice with pistols together regularly. They were both so highstrung that there was apprehension of a duel arising in a moment of anger. Shelley was the better shot.

53. Years ago in The Summer of Love days I asked composer George Montana why so many of the rock musicians were so terrible, and why they were listened to, and why they didn't learn their instruments. George said that was the way it is supposed to be. George's idea was that anybody could learn to make sandals, and anybody might make them and be a sandal-maker. The same with music. He believed anybody could be a musician—it was just wanting to do it that was the necessity.

I wonder if many young sixties people felt that Richard was just their casual sandal-maker novelist, and that they could themselves write just such novels as Richard did if they sat down (by candlelight on acid) to do so. Probably no one realized he had been rewritten some passages sixteen times with labor and fastidious obsession.

54. A few nights ago I had a dream with Richard in it. There was a vast auditorium as big as the Fillmore Ballroom, but it was clean and shiny, with waxed floors, and the air was clean, and people were dressed in respectable suits. A band was playing (a regular band, not a rock band) and there was an enormous circle of people and gray plastic folding chairs. It was a game of musical chairs. Richard was directly in front of me in the line and the band started playing. He just stood there owlishly, holding up the whole line. He didn't know he was supposed to move.

55. *June Thirtieth* is a terrifically good book. It does things that a book— *and poetry*—should do. It is a book of travel poems, poems about place. There is a tradition for this "genre" of book. It is the tradition of *haibun*; that is, a collection of haiku gathered into a story line. I think especially of Basho's haibun *Narrow Road to the North*.

56. *June Thirtieth* reminds me, in an odd way, of what I love about Kerouac—Jack giving me his perceptions with the lucidity and athleticism of his sensorium. I love to read Kerouac for the clarity with

which he sees the same things I see. We see differently, and thus Jack gives the lucid gift of his perceptions. With Norman Mailer it is a different case—I see things almost the same way as Mailer does, as if we are twins. But Kerouac is a little odd and quite understandable to me.

In *June*, Richard is giving the gift of a rare and delicious combination of his perceptions (sensory) and his imagination (uniquely personal). His perceptions are quite unlike mine—they would not interest me except for the potent charge of his interest. Richard can be potent and spontaneous in this little book. It is quite daring. Being in Japan is a big adventure for Richard. He's safe (God, is Japan safe), so he's less cautious. He's playing: going to Japanese bars, courting and loving women of different appearance, discovering television all over again. He's seeing flies and elevators differently. This book is fabulous stuff. And it is the right length in the sense that one doesn't feel that things are being squeezed off early.

The "quality" of the poems is uneven—as Richard notes in his introduction—but so what? It is a glorious whole and Richard is letting himself go, finding new stops in his flute. There is divinity in this book.

Thank you for these poems, Richard.

57. If someone knew nothing about Absurdism or Samuel Beckett and went to see *Waiting for Godot*, that person might think Beckett was a literary Naive. There are two things typical of Absurdist theater that are usually not commented on. Each Absurdist play takes place in a different universe with its own rules—such as people turning into rhinocerouses, vaudeville bums standing in empty fields speaking existentialist thoughts, and etc. Beckett has a different universe for each play. *Endgame* is similar to *Godot*, but *only* similar. It is a different universe. Second, though Absurdist theater is quite literary, it is heavily influenced by the popular media, using films and comic strips as sources.

Each of Richard's "novels" is a different universe. Each one (except for *Trout* and *Watermelon*) reminds me strongly of Absurdist theater. (*Trout* is complex to a degree that is unsustainable in theater, and the "decor" of *Watermelon* is too lovely to be Absurdist theater.)

58. Loading Mercury With a Pitchfork reads as dry and trashy, with an occasional smart aphorism. The "poems" are flat and Richard is trying to pretend that he—and the reader—are hearing something special in the flat prosy lines. Once in a while I'm almost convinced.

59. What's interesting about *Mercury* is that it *is* Artful. It is almost all on the same level of flatness and dryness; it all inhabits the same vibration of possibilities that Richard has chosen to write in. As ever, Richard has edited it into artful bundles. The *nature morte* of "Group Portrait Without Lions" almost works—but, of course, there are no lions. There are no lions growling, nor any gazelle blood, in any of the poems. It's a strain to read it, and I can imagine some self-horror in this book.

60. The poem "Ben" in *Mercury* is about a phone call to Ben Wright in Oklahoma. Ben is not in his housetrailer to answer Richard's call. Ben is a brilliant and intense man moving from one terrible affair to another after his wealthy Oklahoman father's death. When Richard and I first met Ben he was at U.C. Berkeley working on a paper about Mark Twain. He said the Twain archives were being ransacked and everything interesting was being stolen out of them. Ben lived in San Diego, and Richard and I saw a lot of him. Ben was tormented and hyper. He always said, "I've got the whips and jingles."

61. I finished *The Hawkline Monster* easily, but Richard's novel *Dreaming of Babylon* is awful, pathetic. I am more than a third of the way through and I feel stuck. It's hard to look at the page. This little universe was hardly worth creating and barely has enough energy in it to sustain the fact of the ink upon the page.

The novel is a double removal. It is removed in time and space to 1942. Then the private eye protagonist removes himself like Walter Mitty to his imaginary Babylon. The Private eye character is barely there as a persona (another post-Beatles loser), and to have him go off into a personal removal to his fantasy world leaves only words on the page—there's barely any coherence of "story." It is a book constructed of props: private eye, peg-legged mortician, a blonde, a gun, absence of bullets, a lovely corpse, reminiscences of the Spanish Civil War. But the props don't come together to make a story.

62. Kenneth Anger titled his book *Hollywood Babylon*, a deliberate use of the pun "babble-on."

63. *The Hawkline Monster* owes less to Poe than it does to Disney movies that Richard and I grew up watching. *Hawkline* uses the same color palette as Disney's *Fantasia*, and to a certain extent the same sleek glabrous non-threatening biomorphic monster shapes and shadows of monster shapes. The monster is ultimately cute and plays his role on the steep steps to the basement, or on the surface of the gravy bowl, or mingled with the pearls on the lady's bosom as a pattern of light. Finally, the monster becomes diamonds.

64. Poe used some of the following, but Richard used them all over and over in tandem and in rotation, one on top of another, in a musical series like a tone-row composer: doubles; revenants; periods of forgetfulness; confusion of self; childlike view of self; confusion of places and proper names of persons; interruptions; ruptures of transition; pointless dialogue. These seem, when they show up in abundance, to be like symptoms, and they are the solid stuff, the structural stuff, of *Hawkline*.

65. Some chapters of *Hawkline* seem like symptoms.

66. A description of Freud's Unconscious in *Hawkline*: "But they did not know that the monster was an illusion created by the mutated light in The Chemicals, a light that had the power to work its will upon mind and matter and change the very nature of reality to fit its mischievous mind." All things are possible to the monster—as to the Unconscious of Freud—and the monster is just beginning to learn to use its powers.

67. In *Hawkline* the monster dies when whiskey is poured on The Chemicals. Richard poured a lot of alcohol on his monster.

68. Dreaming of Babylon ends with the beautiful whore corpse tucked in the protagonist's refrigerator. To my earlier list of Poe/Brautigan symptoms I will add: inability to accept the body.

69. A few years ago I looked up and saw Jack Nicholson standing by the stairs in Cafe Sport Restaurant. Jack was facing the dining venue and he had on his HUGE Jack Nicholson smile. He was standing so everyone could see him—would see him—would notice him—would have their "minds blown" that they were looking at *Jack Nicholson*. Jack loved it. I liked him for his flagrant egoism. It was heroic. Irish.

Richard got so he liked to sit at Enrico's outdoor tables to drink (it was the most visible place in North Beach), and to be seen. He wanted to be seen, to be admired, and perhaps to be envied. He seemed to like being there by himself. He managed a look that was at once wistful, self-intent, and intriguing. He looked like the great man of himself sitting there. This was not the boyish show-off macho of running to Enrico's to be Ten Day Barons of Cafe Society. This was serious.

70. Someone describes Richard at Enrico's after he separated from his Japanese wife. She was suing him for alimony, I suppose. The friend tells me about how Richard told him the whole dismal financial story, and no doubt with juicy precision mixed with intense and slightly wet-eyed anguish. Richard told how he was being ruined, how the woman wanted to strip him financially, how she was doing it, what he was doing, and so on. Painfully detailed, yet probably Richard was not telling any personal secrets and was keeping much under the table. Then Richard told the next person who came into the bar, apparently the same story with slightly different wording. Then Richard found someone else and told the story yet again. And the next . . .

71. Bruce Conner knew Richard's wife Aki and liked her. When she wanted to get a divorce from Richard she phoned Bruce and asked him how to get hold of a lawyer. She'd been, Bruce says, some kind of an executive at Sony in Japan. Here in San Francisco, when Richard went off on trips to Japan to "do his writing," she stayed at home.

In Japan the home is the province of the woman, Bruce explains. Richard got a Pacific Heights apartment for himself and his wife. I imagine it to be large with high-ceilinged rooms and a view of the Bay. Bruce describes Richard bringing home his drinking buddies, being quarrelsome (dish-throwing), and also bringing home girlfriends. Bruce is sympathetic to Aki, though he is a firm friend of Richard.

72. Bruce reports that Aki's family was hostile to Richard when he was in Japan. Bruce stayed in Tokyo for a month to write a film script with Richard, but Richard did not show Bruce around Japan and stayed in his hotel room much of the time. The script aborted because they could not agree on a working style to compose it. Bruce pictured Magritte-like and *Troutfishing*-like ideas for the film. One idea was to show Dennis Hopper disappearing into quicksand. Bruce wanted to do sixty or so takes—he imagined Dennis would do it differently each time.

73. The writing of the script bothered Bruce because Richard would only have people on screen telling what they were doing. He would not, or could not, have them actually do actions on the screen.

I commented that none of the "novels" had been made into films. Bruce said that *Hawkline* was optioned for a film. I replied that only Disney could have done it, meaning as an animated cartoon. Later, I imagined it might make one of those strange combinations of animation and film. A real lady, with real pearls, but an animated Hawkline monster slithering around on her pearls.

74. Bruce asked me if I had any idea why Richard killed himself. Then he proposed several reasons: a. To get people to read his works; b. To emulate what Richard postulated was Hemingway's reason, i.e., Hemingway intended to kill himself when his faculties dwindled; c. Serious depression. Earlier in our conversation Bruce led me to believe that in Japan Richard might have learned from the Japanese culture that suicide is an acceptable way of dealing with problems.

75. In the late sixties, Richard phoned Don Carpenter one day and told him he'd had dinner at a Japanese restaurant with Rip Torn, and he recounted some of what he had said, and what Rip had said, and so forth. This kind of ego-building and one-upping mysteriousness

was typical of Richard. Don was excited to meet Rip, who was his favorite actor. Finally, he demanded that Richard tell him where he'd met Rip. Richard said chez McClure, then Don came by and, as he puts it, just leaned on the door and smiled. Then Don and Rip became friends and Don wrote and produced the film *Payday* for himself and for Rip. How often, how endlessly, Richard would phone with some great coup of his and tell you about someone you'd like to meet, but then not let on where it happened or who his connection was. He was trying envy and its discontent on his friends. It was unpleasant and highschoolish, but it was a fundament for what he was to do to friends later.

76. Driving back from Mill Valley after having lunch with Don I had an idea: Why did Richard kill himself? Possible answer: Because he had made his point. Clearly in the process of making his point he'd used himself up, "fried his brains with alcohol" as someone unkindly put it. That would not take into account what Richard's liver and insides looked like. I'm making a subtle "take" on human spirit. Perhaps Richard killed himself because he'd made his point and used himself up like a butterfly uses itself up in the process. If Richard's point was the fulfillment of blind groping hungers of the Freudian Unconscious, he'd satisfied a lot of them that must have looked unsatisfiable during his early life: he'd become a male sex figure to some great extent; wealthy and propertied; a successful artist; admired by those he despised in the colleges; had some adventures; tasted glory. And he had triumphed over his enemies and most of his friends. It may have have taken all of the physical and spiritual substance—and the fuel of alcohol—that Richard could manage to make such a triumph.

There are ways of looking at death. One might say that Richard killed himself in an extreme depression, or that he killed himself because his faculties were going (as per Hemingway fears). Those could be the series of impressions in Richard's consciousness preceeding his death.

In a different stance I can observe Richard's whole life and say what a grand triumph—he *won* on all scores. He got the things he seemed to want so intensely. He went from threadbare recluse born too late, unwanted child, and has-been, all the way to the stars.

Richard had made an immense number of points against his friends and enemies. It took everything he had to make the points and he ended the game. This is not to infer that this was a rational process of the conscious mind. He didn't sit there with a gun and think, "O.K., I'll do it now. I made my point." Of course, he was drunk and in agony, or drunk and numb, and uncrystallizing himself.

But Richard's life doesn't look like a failure to me. It looks like a win in the overall. Even if Richard thought he was losing, his whole life says something else.

77. One mutual friend says he bedded several of Richard's women friends—they went to him after they left Richard. He says that Richard worshipped one woman who appeared on the cover of a novel, that he went down on his knees in front of her and worshipped her. Like worshipping a goddess or a Mary or a mother, I suppose, and I imagine with maddest religious-sexual and religious-fervor bound together. She must have been Richard's first real bravissima, glorious, non-bohemian, long-legged sleek beauty with perfume and clean expensive sheets. Why not!

78. An old friend's reactions to some stories about Richard being "into bondage" is that, yes, it is likely Richard was involved in leather or whatever. He treats it casually and as a minor foible—not implying that Richard would have been very deeply involved. He believes that Richard might have become involved because it is a "national past-time" in Japan. It would be ordinary enough to be a bit intrigued after a number of sexual adventures in Japan, he says.

79. Don Carpenter disagrees with me when I say that Richard was well-read. He asserts that Richard was only well-read about Hitler and the Civil War. I reply to Don that Richard could talk about Blaise Cendrars or Michaux. Don's reply is that Richard only "read the odd stuff."

This is certainly to be taken *con grana salis* to my over-assertion of Richard's literary breadth. Richard probably could not talk for long about Spenser. He had not been to college—his reading in literature may have been delvings into the "odd" plus, however, William Carlos Williams, Emily Dickinson, Melville, Hemingway, and etc. Richard's reading was quirky, thorough, broad in the directions he chose. Probably he hadn't read the usual literary traditions of Beowulf, Chaucer, Spenser. He didn't know the college English Lit canon, but none of us cared about that much anymore because we were the New Mutations.

80. The below-zero, cold, black sombrero in *Sombrero Fallout* reminds me of the ice caves in other books. The crowd going mad and running out of control reminds me of the "body"—I mean the sexually huge out-of-control body of Vida in *The Abortion*.

81. Actress Mie Hunt is on the cover of the Japanese publication of *Sombrero Fallout*. There was a simultaneous Japanese and American publication of *Sombrero*. It reminds me of Richard's other tinkerings with topology and making novels into real and unreal events. The simultaneous printings make me think of a set of intentions similar to those behind making the cover of *Trout* a real place with the real author on it—and referred to in the interior of the novel.

I like those topologizings and meltings. They are poetic in intent, as well as egoistic. They are embedding Richard in the work as the artist of the work. Richard is using the possibilities (some new ones) of the media. Many of us were doing similar things, or wanted to.

82. *Please Plant This Book*, poems printed on seed packets, is not only a coup in gaining an audience through a startling book and object, but it also creates a new image of the book and is a true poetic act. Mallarmé said the book is a spiritual instrument. Richard made one that would spread carrots, lettuce, parsley, squash.

The free book is taken in concept from Wallace Berman—it is an extension on Berman's give-away packet magazine, *Semina*. The tondo screened cover photo and the triplication of it is also sheer Berman.

83. The screens of *Sombrero Fallout*: To use Ron Loewinson's image, there are not two but three screens. The screen that contains the sombrero that has fallen to the street is the first. The screen with the

humorist writer protagonist is the second. Screen three is the screen of Yukiko, the lost lover of the protagonist. The first screen which is the continuation of the story begun on the torn scraps of paper in the wastebasket interests me almost not at all. Richard barely tried to make the expanding story of pillage, mayhem, and civil war interesting or even amusing. I imagine that it was his strategy to not even try. It gains a little interest because there is no effort to make it believable or funny. It is odd. But I tend to sight-read those sections—I turn the pages and the words on them are obvious and repetitive.

The second screen: The screen of the protagonist/author interests me more because Richard is presenting a highly and carefully doctored self-portrait. I wonder when he is presenting himself and when he is deliberately not doing so. I wonder when he is presenting himself and thinks he is not—and vice versa.

Yukiko sleeping is the third screen. It is a worshipful portrait of the beauty of a sleeping, long-haired Japanese woman. Much of it is exquisite prose poetry. Just now I thought of Pierre Louys, though it is not like that. Still, perhaps Richard shares some things with Pierre Louys.

The Yukiko screen gives birth to another screen. Her cat has a screen all to herself and is an entity splitting from Yukiko. It is one of those rare and delicious animal portraits, and its wholly anthropocentric nature contains a wonderful believable cameo of a cat expressed in human terms. It feels like a cat. The cat chewing the soft but crunchy diamonds of the catfood. The cat lapping a drink of water but forgetting the five or six bites of food and then returning for the dainty nibbles. The self-involvement of the cat, its inherent bored indifference. As in the accurate descriptions of schizophrenic observations of the airport in *Abortion*, I am moved. Of course, a cat doesn't image the cat food as soft diamonds—but what an analogy!

84. The descriptions of Yukiko's dream life are interesting perceptions of dream life, and relationships of dreams to the exterior events—like the cats purring or stirring—are most psychologically credible.

85. Pierre Louys wrote a book titled *The Daughters of Bilitis*. My mother had a copy of it on her little shelf of books where she kept *Kristin*

Lavransdatter and Kipling's *Barrack Room Ballads* and the *Book of Stag Verse*. After almost forty-five years I remember *Daughters of Bilitis* as being an erotic but not explicit book of prose poems describing, in sensual and delicate terms, acts of female romantic homosexuality.

86. Here is an aspect of *Sombrero Fallout* that intrigues me: the description of the cat purring and the relationship of the purring to dreams, the description of the cat itself; the renderings of the dreams themselves remind me of poetry. Richard's decadent poetry is written as prose. Further, this decadent poetry written as prose is basically a comedy.

I'm not using decadent perjoratively. I mean by decadent a style that is overly aware and lush. It is playing with the edges of our acceptance by means of its delicacy and accuracy regarding a human fringe of feelings. In *Sombrero* there is a lushness at times and it is achieved with sparseness. This reminds me of certain Oriental works and is certainly not part of the English/American tradition of literature. It is contrasted to the cartoonishness of the Civil War that is started by the hat in the street.

87. On the phone Dennis Hopper tells me about sitting up late at night with Richard arguing politics. They shout, presumably extremely drunk. Richard's wife Akiko comes into the room and asks them to stop shouting at each other, but Dennis tells me that he and Richard were shouting into a corner of the room and not at each other. They had made that decision. Dennis comments on how right wing Richard's politics had become.

In large part, Richard's "politics" had much to do with my ceasing to speak to him. His feelings about women, other artists, and the growing lack of sympathy for the Digger ideals he'd help build were clearly growing into right wingism. It was awful to hear, especially when he acted sweeter and more sugary and sincere on stage or in public utterances of kindness, love, and social concern.

88. Robert Duncan in conversation is negative about Richard. He remembers Richard for writing a wonderful book called *Trout Fishing in America*, and he remembers he and Spicer going to Richard's public

reading of the book. Robert declares that Richard did not write anything else of worth. Robert dislikes—maybe despises—Richard's poetry. He sees Richard as a talented stand-up entertainer, recollecting
that people would stay to the end of long multiple poetry readings
just to hear him. That's a fact.

Clearly there were a number of people who read *Trout* and were
disappointed by all the books afterwards. There were others who bought
Richard's "package" of *Trout, Pill, Watermelon* and then read no more.
I can imagine that *The Abortion* stopped many or turned them around
in their interest in Richard.

89. Like *Abortion*, Richard's last novel *So The Wind* deals with a Kafkaesque American landscape, another example of visionary schizophrenia. *So The Wind* seems at one moment exactly right in its depictions
of Northwest small town post-Depression boyhood; at another moment
I realize the "landscape" of small town America is as unlike how it
really was (I grew up in the Northwest also) as the protagonist is
dissimilar to Richard. This double intention on the part of the artist
gives me a sense of great skill.

90. *So The Wind* is ominously depressing. I feel terrible while I read
it and I still have four or five pages to read. It is depressing to read a
novella of more than a hundred pages when one knows from the very
beginning that the protagonist is trying to call back a bullet that has
killed someone. The landscape is relentlessly depressing, from children's funerals to rundown motels to hooverville huts where old sawmill
guards live out pointless, impoverished, neat lives.

91. In *So The Wind*, the protagonist's killing of his "classy" junior high
school friend makes me think of Richard's own "murderings" of his
friends in the late sixties, early seventies. Killing a special friend seems
to be a primal event in Richard's consciousness. He did it often enough
in real life and then it returns (no, it emerges) as a subject in a novel
shortly before he kills himself. Just as the protagonist is not to blame—
not responsible for the bad luck of having shot his friend—so I feel,
in a similar way, Richard is not to be blamed for killing off his friends.

Richard's alienation and attacks on the capacities of his friends seem mindless. He was not able to control the impulses he acted out and I cannot imagine that he had any insight into what he was doing. I always felt that what Richard was doing was somehow programmed. I felt that Richard was acting out directive impulses that he had no awareness of, that he had little or no conscious contact with them. We are like that much of the time. When it is in such a crucial area as friendship and when one needed friends as Richard did, then it is tragic.

The child, the twelve-year-old boy, in *So The Wind* is as mindless as Richard often seemed. The boy is a mirroring reflection of what catches his senses, and he follows the most simple animal directives— to get some bottles to sell so he can buy a hamburger or some bullets. To blow apples apart with his gun. To try to imagine what an enemy boy might have gotten with the returnable bottles that he did not get.

Bruce Conner said he saw Richard as a tragic child. And he was. And he is.

ACKNOWLEDGMENT: *Vanity Fair* asked me to write an article about Richard Brautigan and his recent suicide in 1985. These are notes written at typing speed as I reread all of Richard's writings. The article appeared in *Vanity Fair* and these notes, none of which appear in the magazine, are published for the first time.

Talking with Robert Duncan

MICHAEL MCCLURE: Robert, those familiar with your writing know your scholarship and your studies in history, Kabala, and alchemy, as well as gnostic and mystical traditions and they are aware of your involvement with linguistics and language. I see a powerful effect of concern with biology and the biological frontier in your poetry. It seems to me that your interweaving of *Structure of Rime* with *Passages* throughout your books is a biological as well as a poetic/linguistic process. *Passages* and your poem *Structure of Rime* are streams and they meet and circle around or move through other blocks of poems like the *Dante Etudes* and the *Metaphysical Suite* and your long poems. And the long poems composed in sections appear to be something like physiological organs. The new book *Ground Work* appears to be a unified work comparable to the *Cantos* but your expression is much less "structural" than Pound's work. Your poetry seems to be organismic. It's complete with living streams, like blood flows, and it surges and explores and it does not fear to be unsymmetrical in nature. It unifies itself with its living quality or sensations. And in fact the symmetry is present.

ROBERT DUNCAN: Of course it's going to resemble blood flow since right at the forefront of my own consciousness all the time are my own orders and disorders of blood pressure and especially during the period of writing *Ground Work* my debt was that I had been for a long time in hypertension. And there are many signs of a poem having its origin in and riding the crest of a hypertension seizure.

I'm sure "Up Rising" was just before my high blood pressure was diagnosed in 1964, and it seems to me a symptom. But my thought is I'm never deliberately biological in my reference in a poem unless

Originally published in *Conjunctions*, 7, 1985.

my thought of the structure of the poem as I'm working on it is very closely worked with vowels and consonants, and again it will go back to the biological because I feel measure as body weights and shifts in the lines. Now that's different from your sense of the waves. Perhaps I didn't really have to feel the waves at all, the waves are going to be there, no matter what, because of the rush of my blood. And now having gone through the kidney failure I'm more conscious of the presence, the ruling presence, of the blood pressure. But I don't know that that's turned up in a poem. The asymmetry of a poem for me does have something to do with Schroedinger's marvelous picture from *What is Life*, which influenced me, more than biological pictures of it, Mike, I think. That is, that life is present as long as it hasn't settled into a symmetry, so that life produces itself by constantly throwing itself out of symmetry, postponing the moment of its arriving at composition.

MCCLURE: In the introduction to *Bending the Bow* you wrote: "So the artist of abundancies delights in puns interlocking and separating figures, plays of things missing or things appearing 'out of order' but these remind us that all orders have their justification finally in an order of orders, only our faith as we work addresses." There's a fellow named Sydney Brenner who was originally an associate of Francis Crick and he has made an intensive decades-long investigation of the development of the nematode worm. It's about a millimeter long and it has exactly 959 cells. It's the ideal laboratory animal for certain reasons: it's tiny size, quickness of reproduction and because its number of cells is the square root of the number of cells of a drosophilia (fruit fly) which is the square root, more or less, of the number of cells of a human being. So that one can make many projections. In the process of doing an anatomy of this 959-celled creature, Brenner has determined that these organisms are not assembled by a linear or tidy process and that the assemblage of this animal, cell-wise, is not even sequential. In fact, he determines that the development appears illogical unless one would, in my words, acknowledge there's a Dionysian or Orphic principle of organization that is involved in the development of this creature from its first cell to its last cell. The processes of organization are utterly baroque. Lineages of cells may lead to a cell that then differentiates into four or five other types of cells. An organ may be the result of cells blending together from apparently unrelated lineages of cells. So now we find out that there is no program unfolding the organism from the genetic codes outwards. There is something complex that is going on, it's punning, it is creating and removing, some structures of cells are made and then disappear.

DUNCAN: Within a structure there are programs but a program is not a whole. Programs intrigue me, but not a program that would govern the whole poem. The kind of poem that has a point just disappoints me. I think the poem with a point is one in which the poet is convinced the universe has a point. Of course, some of it's so shallow they aren't even thinking that. But in a universe created by a God with an end that's named and everything has meaning and significance toward that end that is known then you get stories and poems which point toward an end and have closure. I am absolutely a creational materialist because I do not understand the universe as anything but a creation, and also think there is only one.

McCLURE: I think Brenner sees that the development of this organism, and, by extension, the development of all organisms, is metamorphic, playful and expanding. I think, as in your poems *Ground Work*, one has this sensation that everything is going on at once. It is not sequential.

DUNCAN: Yes, that is out of Philo: God does all this simultaneously. And Herakleitos would be nearest to the universe as I feel it until we come to Whitehead. They made fun of Herakleitos and accused him of blasphemy when he said the universe created itself. The opposite of that is the Aristotelian idea that there must be a creator outside the universe: that I don't understand at all.

McCLURE: I'd like to come to that in just a minute because I want to ask you something in regard to what you say about Aristotle. But in this frontier of biology, which is no longer what we had forced on us as kids, the process is seen as a cascade of complex interactions and there is a grammar of assembly but not a program. That's the relationship I see to your work.

DUNCAN: That's exactly it. That's what a self-creating and self-originating force is. But then you have to realize that the immediate force such as myself or such as an amoeba is, in itself, only an immediate instance. So although it is self-creating, the important part of that self is the fact that the whole universe is proceeding in the same way so the interactions are far beyond anything individual. In other words, we hear them as poets, or overhear them as poets, we don't control them or initiate them at all. In writing a poem I think of my job as recognizing right away what's happening in the poem so I am not redundant and continuing to keep everything alive in the poem. That determines the length of it: I can't exceed the length of my own recognition of the presence of its very first impulse. Its opening words are not first in that sense. They're conceived of as being simultaneous, that's true.

MCCLURE: Several times in conversation you've quoted Aristotle's *De Anima* saying "the soul is the body's life." I wonder what picture that makes for you.

DUNCAN: It makes a shape. Life has a shape so you are living a shape and that's the feeling of identity and non-identity. You can't inhabit the whole shape. I'm not a Reichian. But if you suppose a Reichian life picture and you could remember the first engram, as they call it, that's really the fantasy of not just inhabiting the shape of this life but being able to remember it. Poetry is the area of what you can remember. Language itself does not cover this area. The organism, in time, is a lifetime and it extends. If you could run forward and backward in time, by the time you are at the baby you would have forgotten what the old man looks like, and you'd run to the other end, and by the time you got to the old man . . .You'd have to remember, you'd have to *re*-member.

MCCLURE: Do you think the 959th cell can't remember the first cell?

DUNCAN: They do remember in the sense of resonance. That the organism is alive means to me—life itself means a resonant continuity. And that resonant continuity is never balanced.

MCCLURE: Brenner has the idea that the original cell, or the original cells, form a—there are two systems going on (this I don't think necessarily relates to poetry alone)—that there are two systems going on. The one system is creating a sort of rough worm being and the other system is refining that rough worm being into a sharper worm. But a naturalist friend of mine has a much different thought. He thinks that the original cell of this nematode projects out an image that then becomes worm and then feeds itself back to the original cells which then sharpen themselves, so there is a back-and-forth process going on.

DUNCAN: I see, a process of feedback. And the feeling of Soul would be a feedback going all the way through time. Taking that the present is the only area in which we're conscious, then memory like prophecy becomes an area of self-creation. You don't really go back to the beginning but you read every present happening. And how you read what really happens, is creationally colored because you have to recreate and precreate—you recreate the past and precreate the future. And a form like a poem has a past and a future. Now in the poems that bore me you don't have to recreate the past or precreate the future because they're actually moving from one place to another and the point at the end of the poem is more real than all the things in the beginning.

MCCLURE: The poems we like the most are the ones where everything is going on at once.

DUNCAN: Yes, but also I still arrange my poems chronologically, for instance. So sequence is extremely important to me, or the sequence of lines is important. Although, in theory I thought the lines can go anywhere, and though I rather admire that in a poem that is not my body feel or my "me" feel. So I recognize why I don't do that in a poem. There are two systems present in all my poetry. The fact that everything is simultaneous is present; but the fact that the order is the form and that any other order would be another form. You see what I mean, the simultaneity doesn't give you a form at all.

MCCLURE: Possibly one of the reasons Books Eleven and Twelve of *Paradise Lost*, in our recent discussion group, were difficult for some of us to take, is that they become so historical in the sense of being fixed on telling a story.

DUNCAN: Milton has an outline, also. He is doing what he ought to be doing at the end of the poem. Yes, that was a thorough bore in that regard. The poem is not. While there's brilliance in its passages, and there would be an example of our feeling that that brilliance came from Milton's own deeper poetic temperament, the idea of what to do with the poem, his address in the poem is very antipoetic and he had to carry it out. You don't feel this at all in Homer. The *Paradise Lost* is not a true narrative.

MCCLURE: I want to go back to an older discussion we've had and haven't been back to in a good many years, and I wonder what you think about this now. Sapir says that language precedes thought and it occurs to me that the energy of language, which is a very physical sensation, precedes both thought and speech. It also appears that it is a more complex process than Sapir presented. I'd imagine that White-head and Olson and Creeley, as he acknowledges in *Pieces*, work like Einstein (who said he worked with his body sensations).

DUNCAN: This is what I call "feel-thinking." If the thinking has its origin in feeling then it is not brain thinking, and our computers are beginning to show us how poor brain thinking is, how limited. Because when we get a machine to imitate the movements of our bodies they're all the same, they're all limited by the brain's picture. There may be certain other intuitions present in the machine. Yes, the machine also imitates things that we know from our own kinetic movements.

MCCLURE: How do you fit in with William Carlos Williams, looking for that dance step that he carried out in his body-mind sensations?

DUNCAN: Well, those body-mind sensations are stirred up when . . . The essential thing where Williams . . . In poetry it begins with Carlyle, who said that poetry is musical thinking and musical speech, so it lies at the level of what is music. Computer music shows us what music ain't.

MCCLURE: It certainly does.

DUNCAN: I think in the first place that that isn't what I'm talking about. What music ain't ain't body. We know very well that the body itself can be inhabited in different ways. The body itself can be felt in a whole series of different ways. The body is a brain regiment. Every impulse of the brain, as the newest organ of the body, comes as an order or command. As I think of it in evolution, the brain is the organ that eats up all the calories. And the brain is new, so it is much less experienced than the hands, and much less experienced than the rest of the body. And the rest of the body tends to be fairly unconscious, and I really wonder that if we got down to a nematode whether the rest of the body *is* unconscious. Our consciousness, to us, is our brain. It usurps consciousness from all other parts of the body. Its only concept of body consciousness is for it to return and direct everything which happens in meditation and so forth. You know, through Yoga forcing your intestines to do so. Let's say I experience the failure of my kidney as a condition, as a given physical condition in the universe: it's what you are actually living in. And if you start talking about it as an illness or a sickness you're not paying any attention to the actual environment because the environment is now the one you are in. You're co-inhabiting your own.

MCCLURE: Let me insert in here in regard to the last few things you said. In speaking of the consciousness of the nematode, apparently Brenner and Crick as they worked with this creature became so respectful that they began to question their right of sacrificing countless of these tiny . . .

DUNCAN: Nematodes! Nematodes!

MCCLURE: Their respect for them grew, and I think that's a respect for consciousness that is taking place.

DUNCAN: Well, Darwin called that the vanity of the human image, which makes us worship organization in the universe. Darwin doubted it, he said it was simply the narcissus effect, that wherever you see something that seems like your own organism, that answers to your own pride in organism. Of course, what Darwin was thinking was he didn't think there was an organism in evolution itself. It was more inscrutable. And the inscrutable part of it is also what I aim at in a poem. I trust in the poem as something that "comes into my mind" that is going to be the poem. Then I start working with it, because it is all material. It isn't an idea that I "have," and I don't really think in a poem. I have no impression that I think in a poem. I don't think that's what goes on. That's why if I'm teaching I teach poetics, not writing of poems or even what is in a poem. Poetics is the part you do think. But all of that is brain thinking. I'm not devaluating brain thinking; it's quite necessary for a complex organism. If you just think of our bodies, without a brain, nothing is clearing through. But I'm interested in the eyes, the total news coming in from everywhere they convert it very quickly into "think news." Going back to biology and physics, what interests me is that both these sciences are imaginations of the world. They are not really thinking of the world. When they turn to think of the world that is usually in order to support their imagination. The astounding things, breakthroughs for us, are not their thinking out and plotting it but the combination of their intuitions and absolutely free imaginations. So science, for instance, doesn't become antiquated because in our rational process we've shown that it doesn't meet the data we have got. In the poem, too, you have to *admit* into it things that are present although they seem to make impossible the form that you felt. But that's the faith you have to have. That's the governing faith of science. It can be falsely expressed. Einstein will say that "God doesn't cheat at dice," or whatever, doesn't play games. Well, that is Einstein's own nervousness. The imagination does indeed play games, the playfulness of the imagination is expected in poetry, and we are meanwhile terrifically repressed about that playfulness when it takes place in physics. You and I are not really nervously trying to check out what kind of universe we're in. The controversies are not that interesting. We are fascinated by what we'd call the play of the mind. And "mind" is not at all identical to brain. It is the mind that has a life through time. The body after all—each cell of the body— dies. Am I right that no cell really lasts the lifetime of that organism? Organism is a matter of fact, is given in the first place, as language is. I still take it that life is created, but the body is really given. And that is just what happens with language. We're surrounded by language, we take what of it we can use. There are so many analogies. You can make analogies that we digest it, that we throw some of it away, that we shit lots of it out, that other parts of it enter into systems of nutrition. I am most fascinated now—because it's what I'm involved with—in just these elements and their balances. It is not nutrition, they're not nutrition. Jess says they have to do with electrical exchanges and all the mineral elements that I have to balance or unbalance.

DUNCAN: You'd have to be sure you're going to use only one kind of logic, and logic is—logic ought to mean what words do and don't do. And what words can't do they don't do anyway. I mean, if you understand the difference between "oughtn't to do". . . I mean, lots of logic has what words ought to do or oughtn't to do: that is of no interest at all, besides what words can do and can't do. That we can think about that, that we can frame propositions about what words actually can't do.

MCCLURE: Here are some words you said, that I gave a lot of thought to, and it is a framed proposition in my mind. You said, at a discussion group, that Shakespeare has equality of souls. And then you also added that Spenser does, and you pointed out that Whitman also has it. It's this equality of souls that's part of hugeness, the huge sensation of childhood, as I see it.

DUNCAN: Oh, yes, this is also what Crick is finding with his nematodes, is equality. There is no hierarchy of life. There are kinds of life. Now, when the helix and the proposition of DNA appeared it seemed to me a real, a true revelation, that was present in Darwin but didn't have a principle, so that people could misinterpret Darwin. Because life is a series of variations, not a series of hierarchal achievements. The original proposition about complexity is that a human being must be much more complex than an amoeba, and that just doesn't work out at all. So we find out that we're really asking each time what is going on in this organism. The non-Darwinian picture of evolution was that evolution was a constant improvement of the species and individuals of species. Well, that's exactly what Darwin hit, because the slightest change in temperature or anything else would make an entirely different condition for survival. So it is the ratios we respond to and that's the change of temperature in which some species survive, and some don't.

McCLURE: It seems that in childhood, though, that we're not applying ratio to the faces and the arms of other human beings but each one is allowed to be a star in whatever their own particular universe is. They may be minor characters in the cast of our drama, but we recognize that they're important characters in other dramas.

DUNCAN: Well, the other thing in childhood is that there seems to be a childhood style that is universal whether it's a child in Africa, or an Eskimo, or a child in New York. When you think about children's drawings and so forth in contrast to the adult arts in widely different civilizations, or the stylistic periods, children's drawings seem to belong throughout to one undifferentiated language. In Africa if a child has promise as an artist he's suddenly forced to desert his childhood style and he's initiated into the highly sophisticated and differentiated tribal art of the adults. When this realization hit Europe it was a while before they even realized what they just suddenly saw, because their own stylistic sophistication had begun to approach that point where tribal art was no longer alien. Cubism took Africa as part of its language. Adult sophistication in art is had at the cost of an extreme repression of all sorts of things you can do. Tribal art is extremely repressed.

McCLURE: Probably almost as repressed as—

DUNCAN: Whereas, for instance, the Renaissance, which doesn't have repression also doesn't have style. Style fascinates us. Now, in metamorphosis—I do think going through periods of repression, like going through a dark mood, like into melancholia, which can also go along with style—it is, when you go back to your metamorphosis figure, this strikes me over and over again, that we plunge ourselves into "cocoons" in which something is at work: the creative in us has to go inert in order for the unfolding genetic design to enter another phase. You see, the second phase isn't an improvement of the first phase at all. But it really is at a level of species and rehearsal of species that the individual hardly knows the use of. But the transformation of the worm to the butterfly is one of the most fascinating things of childhood. Because it is some sort of analogy: adolescence is some sort of horrible cocoon.

MCCLURE: I was just looking at that same metamorphosis, speaking of painting, in an adult. I love Rothko's early, what I would call "energy-spirit-surrealistic" oils. But there is a period of about five years, I think it was roughly from 1940 to 1945, where he is seeking, he is actually undergoing a metamorphosis, where he is endeavoring to move himself from that spirit-surrealism of those sprawling seashore surreal canvases to his color-fields. Those five years are like five years of incubation.

DUNCAN: Yes, and that incubation was all through New York, much of it coming out of Hoffman's teaching of color-field.

MCCLURE: It's very exciting to see what change a man can make in five years and when the change is made it is rather sudden, breaking the shell of the cocoon, getting a leg out, climbing out of the cocoon and drying his wings in the sun while he pumps air into the veins of the wing. It's a complex process but it is relatively swift when it happens. That for me was a very exciting event to discover in the catalog of Rothko's works, as in the Guggenheim Retrospective.

DUNCAN: When you started talking about the child's view, I want to point out we recreate in our mind Nietzsche's statement that we're striving to become a child, if it were put back into our picture of metamorphosis, the butterfly itself would be laying eggs and worms will now proceed with a voracious appetite—and so in a sense the butterfly can be said to be striving to become a worm.

MCCLURE: In Pollock's paintings in 1951 when he was dripping paint but faces and figures began to appear in the painting, he goes back to a kind of simplicity that could suggest that he was looking for childhood art again.

DUNCAN: I think Pollock is the creation of our art market. For instance, Miro does not look like child art the way Matisse does when Matisse is drawing because Miro is calculating and being childish which Pollock isn't. Klee is. There are styles in art. Matisse is drawing from the way the hand sees. Remember that the hand is a good part of our seeing and in order to have the technique of representation what you do is to repress entirely how much you actually are feeling. The hand obeys. I would be more than aware of this being cross-eyed so that all my sense of distance is my own sense of movement through space or my sense of touch.

MCCLURE: I agree with what you are saying. What I was guessing about Pollock is that what he was doing was very complex, very developed kind of drip painting. And there is one period in 1951 when actually beatific, huge simple faces and figures began to appear in the drip paintings. I don't think it was in his control. It doesn't resemble child art the way Miro does, but there is something childish and fresh and dancing and exuberant that's come back into the work in a new way. And it is after that that he has his crisis with painting and retreats from painting. I think it scared him.

DUNCAN: But also he drank heavily as he did, like Dylan Thomas, in order not to encounter what was going on in his work. And this can be the terror. People clinging to their personality as if that were an identity. Actually, most people don't want to encounter the feel of soul and that they are a lifetime because the terms in which they present the personality wouldn't have been present throughout that lifetime and they suddenly feel it's made up, this personality is made up. Then it can't be real. This search for the realness. Or somebody's "Do you really love me?" That is already one who has mistaken the whole nature of love and of life.

MCCLURE: And, you know, in other terms if you acknowledge that you are a star in this galaxy you find you don't want to be a star where we are blowing up Asians with napalm, or electing Reagan to the presidency.

DUNCAN: And yet if we weren't in that universe—let's pick any other ones—there could be a broody elephant thinking "I must be to blame because the lions eat dear little gazelles." And you say "But you'd never be able to eat a gazelle." "But no, how can I be happy, how can I be eatin' leaves in a world in which poor little gazelles get eaten?"

MCCLURE: Shall we take a rest?

———————

DUNCAN: When you go back to the picture of Pollock, his astounding and great paintings, the big canvases, where he was inside the canvas and moving about. In all the painting of that period there are two kinds of things that are present and they aren't necessarily the same. One of them is action painting. Well, Rothko isn't action painting. Color fields are really indwellings. What happened in the big Pollock canvases is that they were action paintings—he really enacted the very act of painting, and at the same time, since he was inside it, they were also indwellings because when we see them they do not convey what one says of Kline, that it is the will making shapes. They seem like huge networks of light and presence. So one thing in poetry and painting and music that most interests me is when it becomes a presence. This goes back to our picture of the biological. In the biological there is no bio-illogical. I'd go all the way back to Schroedinger where he shows that, in fact, the biological is not illogic within a logical universe that is mathematic throughout, because he says he knows of nothing in the material world that is not biological, that doesn't have life, that doesn't move between being born and dying. We can see that the sun is dying, we can see it of the earth. Once we understand that the earth has a lifetime, that it wasn't just made by somebody, it is *indeed* self-creating. It's like here in California where people build silly real estate on the side of mudhills. Don't they look around? Where do they think these hills with their soft contours come from? Our landscape is constantly self-creating itself by collapsing on itself. And that is what is beautiful to us, on top of that. But how idiotic, then, to start building a house on the sand. But let's get back to this picture. Jess talks about indwelling in the work you are in. It even erases any sense of being inspired. Inspiration is another thing that happens. Something comes in. Yet when things come into the poem I don't think of them as inspirations, but as material. Remember that in my poetry there is a tenure of constantly reestablishing myself, but that is different from repeating what I've done. Repeating must be something that's present in the biological, for where else would it be? I think the place where I would agree entirely with your approach is I don't see anything, any other place for painting and poetry to belong other than that they're flowerings of a biological kind out of a species, and the species does not create painting as a whole; only certain individuals create these flowerings.

MCCLURE: That leads into something else I wanted to bring up. The Romantic movement in English poetry is very strong for many of us. What I see in Shelley is not just the discovery of nature just at a moment when the Industrial Revolution was beginning to eat it up, but also I see in him the internalization of the organism into poetry. That is, Shelley's poetry absorbs and breaks the forms that precede it, and it ripples like a muscular being, and it surges forward, and it invents its own rules, as in *The Triumph of Life*. What a strange poem, and what a beautiful poem. It changes constantly, and fluidly, and daringly. So that it has the qualities of sensation, movement, fluidity, organism. A long poem by Shelley seems almost like a living being to me. I realize, of course, this is also true of Chaucer, Aristophanes—

DUNCAN: Any poem that you're going to respond to. In part it mirrors your living being, and since it mirrors your living being it seems intensely to be a living being to you. If we have no hierarchy of souls, then as a matter of fact—let us take a really "jerk" poetry, like L=A=N=G=U=A=G=E poetry is to my mind—it also is organism. And the reason I can't read it is because it doesn't answer to me, to my on-going life way.

McCLURE: I wonder if Structuralism is organism. I see L=A=N= G=U=A=G=E poetry as Structuralist.

DUNCAN: Oh, no. What is your idea of Structuralism?

McCLURE: Structuralism is where you have a schema—

DUNCAN: Oh, no, no: that is Conventionalism, because Structuralism means that you approach things and ask questions of the structure. Structuralists include the psychologist Piaget, who is concerned with the organization of consciousness, that doesn't mean you have a schema. Let's use the term the right way. Because Structuralism is extremely important for me in freeing my poetry of any sense of being literary.

McCLURE: So you want to call what I was calling Structuralism in literature Conventionalism? Where you have a set of rules that you follow?

DUNCAN: Yes, and it's a form of game, because you agree. It's like playing bridge, you agree what you're doing and you make the cards go that way.

McCLURE: I don't see much possibility for organism, or for the qualities of organism, in a Conventionalistic approach to a work of art.

DUNCAN: And yet it's got to be organistic, because organism doesn't get not to exist. In other words, it's organisms that produce those conventional forms. Now, Mike, let's look back at the species. It's got an underlying map and method. And it's only when we look at thousands of individuals do we begin to realize that there are metamorphoses going on.

MCCLURE: But the very thing that Brenner finds out when he works with these nematodes is that there is no blueprint for the organism in the genetic code.

DUNCAN: Yes, but then where do you think blueprints come from? They come from organisms. This is exactly what my objection to the idea that something can be illogical. Everything is biological. And the reason we find that we respond to certain works and not to others is because there is not just one life form, there are multitudes of life forms. I find it healthy that there are just lots of different kinds of poetry. Most of the time, having heard something once I don't want to hear it twice. Yet it is so mysterious what you can be drawn to that can seem different to you. But I think of all these as being drawn again with a life sense, of what belongs to your life and what doesn't belong to your life. When "Howl" was written and suddenly everyone rightly recognized that that was the age of "Howl"—like Eliot was the age of "The Waste Land" from 1920 clear through the end of the thirties—established poets at large responded to it so that Wilbur, who is a very solid, talented, conventional poet, and his admirers, behaved as if "Howl" were some sort of offense to whatever Wilbur wrote. But admirers of Wilbur were never going to be reading "Howl"; and the admirers of "Howl"—who had never before admired any poetry—were certainly never going to be reading Wilbur. And we've got much more variety than that at present. That's the healthiest sign of human beings, not the unhealthiest sign.

MCCLURE: For me that's the same thing as saying "All souls are equal" in Shakespeare, all souls are equal in childhood.

DUNCAN: But that does not mean that all souls are familial, or familiar. And that's what we're seeing in poetry as it's more and more vivid, it's more lively. I certainly was not saying that "Kaddish" and "Howl" were not lively, although Allen has, as a matter of fact, significantly deserted poetry for Buddhism and thinks that that's the primary reality. And he's written fewer and fewer poems. He writes long rants, and so forth.

MCCLURE: What poets are you reading right now, speaking of plurality of poets?

DUNCAN: You mean right now? Troubadors.

MCCLURE: I mean in the last three years. Classical poets and new poets.

DUNCAN: We could take that up next time, because my mind is not—

MCCLURE: You've been reading Jabès, and Homer.

DUNCAN: Yes. And in the French—I heard him at Cambridge—it was Jean Daive and I carried his *Decimal blanche* with me, practically memorizing it. Baudelaire, of course. I spent two years on Baudelaire.

MCCLURE: Are you reading the *Journals*?

DUNCAN: I'm reading the *Fleurs du Mal* but I have read them, of course. Oh, yes. Oh, yes. But I'm talking about the poetry. Of course, in the poetics program at The New College of California Robert Kenny was doing his thesis on Baudelaire, and preliminary to that he translated everything in *Les Fleurs du Mal*. He had a tutorial with me, and we compared translations. The question always with a translation is not does it represent the original poem, but what is happening in the translation. Again, if we think about two lives: there is a disproportion when a Richard Howard translates Baudelaire. We recognize right away that they don't resemble each other. What I want is a differentiation upon principles, a sense of structural signs as there is a sense of significant structure underlying biological definitions. My first reaction to Don Allen's anthology was that he should have an arrangement . . . and I did not want to be in the sort of circus where the polar bear is brought in right after the monkey is brought in right after the—and that's the way all anthologies were. Actually, it would be the polar bear then the polecat, because they're alphabetical.

McCLURE: Did Don consult you about the arrangement? I understand some of it was Creeley's suggestions.

DUNCAN: I was relaying ideas through Creeley, relaying them through Robin Blaser, and I was refusing to be in the anthology unless it had an organization on historic principles. And of course in the second anthology Don no longer arranged it. But the feeling of identity was a little intense in that period. If you remember, not only was I objecting to being in the wrong categories, but I saw absolutely no meaning at all to being in something called San Francisco.

McCLURE: This is a little bit of a change in subject, but one of the things that strikes me is how much things feel like the fifties now. I feel that there's a polarization going on, I feel there's a great sense of clarity under political oppression that's going on. And I feel a strong sense of creativity and personal identity. I feel this in the eighties as much as I felt it in the fifties.

DUNCAN: Now we've had three crops of students in the Poetics program and they're all interrelated and they're all of absolutely great potentialities. We're also in the situation of having no magazines we can contribute to.

McCLURE: And that's exactly the way it was in the fifties.

DUNCAN: Exactly the way it was then. You had the *Hudson* and the *Kenyon* and so forth. And now *The Southern Review* is doing an issue on me and, after badgering me for a year and a half, will be printing a chapter of the H.D. book. Well, this is just unheard of. In the first place, *The Southern Review* is extinct. But we have emerging, however, magazines, like David Levi Strauss's *Acts*, right here where they were emerging before.

McCLURE: Yes, I find that now I go see people like I did in the fifties. My interest in painting is strengthened, my interest in serious music is strengthened.

DUNCAN: Some of that is because our past writing now feels to us very much achieved, so we have the same problem we had in the beginning. We aren't really carrying out something, we're not still carrying something through. The fifteen-year break that I wanted between *Bending the Bow* and *Ground Work* (and the title *Ground Work* itself) I wanted to be back where I was when I was writing *Letters* and making things up.

MCCLURE: Somebody asked me what you meant with your title *Before the War*. I said I think *Before the War*, as Robert's using it, has three meanings.

DUNCAN: Yes, oh listen, I've made up a million. And at the present time I wonder what does *In the Dark* mean, the following volume. The volume doesn't answer "before the war" although every one of those suckers is living as if they're before the war. If there is a universal sense in the world today, no matter who, everybody thinks there is going to be a third world war, everybody dreads the third world war, everybody promises there won't be a third world war. And that's the only thing they're living before. Like, before the mirror. I think that's one of the strongest meanings of *Before the War*. Before the sphinx, I'm standing before the sphinx, I'm standing before the war. And my idea of a war is that you don't object to a sphinx, or to a volcano, but that you're "before" it.

Robert Duncan:
A Modern Romantic

RE–

-turn. In spring-up green freshet
turn. Delight to the eye . . .

ROBERT DUNCAN, *Letters*

Robert Duncan was everything we believed him to be. The savant and soul-maker of recent years who so many of us saw in poetry readings and his lectures at the New College was the flowering of an earlier Duncan. But Duncan's flowering was continual, and as long ago as 1954 Duncan had an enormous body of energy and genius that he exerted. When the students of his first poetry workshop at San Francisco State listened to his insights and projections regarding their poems and looked in wonder at his restructuring of their work on the blackboard, they knew something big was happening. Duncan was one of the pantheon that was pre-Beat and pre-San Francisco Renaissance and one of the heroes who walked the earth with Kenneth Rexroth, William Everson, Madeleine Gleason, James Broughton, Jack Spicer, and Robin Blaser. Those were not the good old days, but the sinister cold fifties. Duncan had been part of the World War II anarchist circles; he'd edited outspoken magazines and published a booklength poem; he'd dressed in peasant blouses and workman's boots—he'd rubbed shoulders with Anaïs Nin and Henry Miller and Kenneth Patchen. He had announced his homosexuality—in defiance of the wall of silence. He'd become domestic, one of a couple, and what he called a householder, with Jess (who studied with Clyfford Still and had turned to Romantic landscape painting).

Originally published in *Poetry Flash* 180, March, 1988 and reprinted in *New Directions Annual* 52, 1988.

Duncan was a man with nerve. In an era that twitched with dismay at the thought of having influences, he called himself a derivative poet, and he found a clear early voice in a book of Gertrude Stein imitations. His sources ranged from Dante to Zukofsky to children's books. He was writing poetry that was so breathtaking in its intellectual excitement and vivacity and so technically thrilling in its shape and structure that one hardly knew how to discuss the poems. In his book *Letters*, "Light Song" begins:

> ;husbands the hand the keys a free imp-
> rovisation keeping the constant vow . . .

We were left in a state of pleasurable awe that this most trembling, in-looking world-lover—with one eye near-sighted and the other far-sighted—was opening a door for those who chose to pass through it. Robert reiterated to all who listened that there were new voices and a new sound in poetry, and he put Levertov, Creeley, and Olson out there for anyone to see and to hear. In those days, Duncan gave solo readings of his music drama, *Faust Foutu*—for which he'd composed the music and for which he invented the voices of all the characters. Today, those jovial readings would be called performance art.

This wildly capricious man had the unflinching politics of a Blake-like visionary and was opposed to any form of fascism or totalitarianism or philistinism, or command of involuntary restriction or constriction of the living child in man or woman. In Duncan's apparent scatteredness was a solid, growing core of old-fashioned character and personal soundness that is not often seen. People around Robert wondered where the wisdom came from, where the fountain of unrelenting demands for liberty had its source, and what were the subtle sources of his swift and accurate opinions and decisions.

Thirty-five years ago this very modern Romantic poet had his pen at the pulses of what was meaningful—and he was beginning to allow the flood of his art to flow into varied channels and streams and shapes— as in his ongoing "Passages" and "Structure of Rime" as well as the individual books. Duncan saw the flowing universe of language, and he let that be the shape of his songs, poems, odes, as they bubbled out separately from their secret springs and then joined in rivers and pools and channeled to waterfalls and wordfalls.

In the Bay Area in the fifties, and for a while after that, a young poet could sense that his older artist mentors had been reading Kropotkin's anarchist philosophy in *Mutual Aid*. Kenneth Rexroth might help a young poet move all his family belongings to a new flat; in fact, Rexroth might be the one to lug a huge stove up three flights of stairs. Artist Ronald Bladen might contribute his scant earnings to finance a literary magazine. Almost everyone who could, worked at some job or craft or was a merchant seaman—and probably no one expected any financial remuneration from their art. Duncan did typing of thesis manuscripts and hitchhiked across the Bay to U.C. Berkeley to pick up the manuscripts. One could often see him there at the bridge ramp, radiating his energy, with thumb out to the air. In the evening, he and Jess would be hosts to hopeful writers and filmmakers and painters. Robert gave generously of his mind and his imagination, and unlike many poets he liberated those who wanted to listen so they could be themselves, and not writers in Robert's own manner.

Robert had much pride, but it was not hurt pride or false pride; it was pride in his art and life, and the arts and lives of his friends. At one point, my family and I were so sick with flu and poverty that Robert and Jess swooped down on us, took us away, and nursed us back to health. And I often saw Robert's intuitive understanding of infants and children in his friendship with my daughter. Duncan was surrounded by a younger generation of men and women who wanted to understand the glamour and mystery of life as he saw it and lived it. Though that generation must have seemed dense-headed sometimes, Robert kept laughing, telling stories, and reading new poems, while we sat as if enchanted, and while the bookshelves in Robert's parlor sagged, heavy with more and more that he was studying, from the *Zohar* and Sapir to George MacDonald.

When I think of Robert, I see firelight in a hearth and bronze Art Deco women with long hair, and Oz books and cats and San Francisco fog and Jackson Pollock. I think of him recounting some recent discovery in the sciences, and as he tells the technical details of a rat overpopulation experiment it becomes the story of London and Peking—and then it exfoliates to be, in a visionary way, a vast set of perceptions of the physical universe. Then, for a moment, I see Robert explicating Pound's *Cantos* line by line. Then Robert is exploring Whitehead's or Plato's philosophy. Then Robert is boundlessly denouncing a poet he believes is untrue to poetry. Then Robert is telling a story about H.D. or Laura Riding.

Then I can smell the saffron that Robert adds to the first bouillabaise I ever saw anyone make—tentacles of squid and pieces of a white fish and chunks of red fish and clams. Artists were poor in those days, and a rich soup wasn't something one got at a stylish restaurant but something one scrimped for to celebrate with. Robert was even poorer than some others, in dollars, because he was always buying paintings and books by other artists and writers. It was a rich world made with little money, before the Vietnam War brought our wealth of plastic cars and plastic televisions, and suet-and-petroleum gendered fast foods.

Robert had grown up in California; he was moved by the California landscape of chaparral and oak savannah and meadow flowers. Seeing a beautiful orange California poppy, he'd pick the ripe seedcase and put it in his pocket to plant the seed in his garden. He was always working the ground and opening up the fields and the meadows and the glades inside of himself, as the titles of his books tell. Surely an old man can be a flowering of the young man, and somehow, in some Jungian sense, if he individuates himself, then he can be like the big, simple, glorious flowers of the tulip trees that were blossoming in San Francisco on the day Robert died.

San Francisco has always been a literary province in the eyes of poeple living in industrial, overpopulated centers. As artists, we did not want to be provincial; we wanted to be modernists, and more than that we did not want to be San Francisco artists, or Bay Area artists, or California artists, or West Coast artists, or American artists; we wanted to be *artists* without all those qualifiers. As brilliant and as "major" as Rexroth was, it was Duncan who seemed to be even more international. It did not matter that Duncan was unknown or that he said he'd be happy to have just five hundred readers—the scope of intention and smoldering liveliness in his poems made Duncan seem to be the most international among us. We could imagine Robert speaking with Picasso and Cocteau and Stein and D.H. Lawrence.

But also Duncan was a time-diver. He could dive back through time into the medieval history he studied, or he could learn French and commune with Baudelaire. Or Robert would take the course of extolling Shelley, as if he were with us, and rewrite Shelley's long lyric *Arethusa*.

In the days I'm describing in Robert's life, I was listening to Brahms's recordings, and the album jackets portrayed an old man with longish hair and a white beard. One day I found a photo of Brahms as a handsome, cleanshaven, almost winsome young man, and I took a bust of Brahms and attached the picture of the young Brahms to the old bearded face of the bust, and I gave it to a friend. Like the photo of the younger Brahms, Duncan was a good-looking man in the years of his early maturity; sometimes he was stocky, sometimes slender, sometimes plump. Robert would have a period of casual dressing and then move into a time of neckties and vests and charcoal suits. In his middle age he became a serious dresser—he'd sit in his front room with a stack of books about him and his pen and notebook in hand, with Scriabin or Stravinsky on the record player.

Robert could always fall into a powerful, driven, self-centered way of speaking, and as he grew into the seventies and the eighties the scope of his wordplay broadened like the deep language world he was forever exploring in his unspoken consciousness. Robert trembled as he moved onto a subject, and then the subject would change to another and then another, and as he knit them all together in his mind he shook—his hands shook—and his eyes looked in different directions. Year by year Duncan came to seem more patrician, like some groomed lord of poetry and thinking. He seemed superhuman, and at the same time the most human.

An old friend of Robert's believes that this is the end of an era; she said that Robert formed her ideas of painting. An admirer of Robert's who is a designer and printer says that Robert gave him the image of what art is because he perceived Robert moving into poetry and becoming the art. On going to visit Duncan there was the feeling that one was meeting Yeats or Joyce or Nerval or Villon—one felt that just before entering, Duncan might have been communing with the troubador Peire Vidal or Emily Dickinson. There was a luminosity about Robert, and it grew with each decade as he lived in the aura—not really seeking it—and he always lit it up with his unexpected smile and his spontaneous, merry laugh.

From *Specks*

AH
YES,

how perfect
to be within a dream

inside
a body

in a
VISION!

How
REAL!

HOW SOLID!

I
am
the
body
!

the dream
is flesh!

APPEARANCE
is my breath!

From *Specks* (Vancouver: Talon Books, 1985).

I
AM
THE
HUMMINGBIRD

OF
CHANCE
!

"Float like a butterfly
sting like a bee"
Muhammad Ali is not a dancer in the sense that one thinks of a dancer—moving about with legs working against gravity. Ali's style of movement is different. At first it is not easy to comprehend—his head floats and his body hangs suspended from his head. In turn, his legs and arms hang from the suspended body. When Ali moves, his torso falls forward and into the direction he wishes to go—his head continues to float—and his hanging legs, in subtle balance with all of his organism, step out to catch him and support him. His skeleton moves the muscles in equilibrium with gravity. Ali does not resist gravity but in part he's moved by it—backward and forward—or to the sides. It is the most powerful and refined style of movement. Man spent five million years evolving so that his head is free to float and his body able to hang from it and fall forward to make movement almost effortless. Ali and Fred Astaire, who also floats, are adored because they show what our mindbodies recognize in them as they box and dance—a high degree of perfection in movement.

Ali is almost fearless—there is no intrusion of an instinctual primate fear of falling. Ali is always falling and continuously and almost effortlessly recovering—and doing it in sync with the floating of his head. Ali's opponent Frazier is a physical genius in his own right but of a different style. Frazier does not float and he has not mastered the fear of falling. He moves more mechanically than Ali. Frazier requires enormous energy to move himself with the power to box Ali.

Although Frazier is courageous, there is a contraction—which is clearly fear—in his muscle use. His style is to utilize the fear. Alchemically, Frazier hunches—drawing into himself—using the contraction of his body—as opposed to the free-floating Ali—to make a compression of his inner visceral systems. It is a transmutation. Frazier squeezes energy out of the center of himself, from his internal systems, and he pours it into the muscles. He does not consume the power inherent in the muscles but adds to it with the strength of his guts and organs. His power is almost superhuman—he resembles Society with its inputs of fossil fuel supplementing agriculture. Ali resembles a snow leopard or a butterfly.

The demonic aspect of Agriculture.

Honey and peaches and plums.

Some days there are no festivals.

I

AM

THE
PELICAN

OF
REASON

D
I
V
I
N
G
in the surf
!

The systemless system absorbs all systems.

Keats and Whitehead speak of truth and beauty.

Absorb the beautiful systems.

Blueberries in darkness and the light of stars.

I am given a painting of mastodons and I dream of smiling rats.

How beautiful the spotted rat is with his brain, his nervous system, his tiny muscles and the fascia within them. The fascia join at the ends of muscles to become tendons that are inserted upon the bone-sheathes of connective tissue. How lovely are the nerves that report the tension of the rat's tendons to the brain. How perfect are the dark eyes, capable of performing actions, reflecting the conception of actions. They are jewels of living jet. How beautiful is the mastodon on the tundra. How perfect is my daughter. How exquisite is the nasturtium blossom, the odor of fennel, and the fog pouring over the peaks.

Invent two principles:
   1. Cause and effect are one single explosion in the rain of Chance.
   2. Reason can overlap the edges of Chance—and vice versa.

The white table.

The black table.

The rainbow table.

The last rose of summer is the first rose of autumn.

October roses.

The personality. The rose.

Myriad-mindedness.

BLASTULA. Stage of embryonic development of animals, at or near the end of the period of cleavage, and immediately preceding gastrulation movements. Usually (in those animals with complete cleavage) consists of a hollow ball of cells.
From *The Penguin Dictionary of Biology.*

Nature is lawless. Nature drifts and surges.
We are in a flaming explosion—the cinders of it are concrete buildings, freeways, and plastic toys. Their formation continues. The explosion continues.

Let the badger loose! Praise the mustang!

The position of boulders is information.

The senses are hungers.

The buckeye butterfly is as beautiful as the California condor. The art nouveau patterns of planets and auras on its wings in dazzling russet, brown, ochre, yellow, red, tan, and buff make me want to capture it. I want to possess and fondle it with my eye. But it is too beautiful to kill.
The California condor evolved to be the vulture—the scavenger— of the giant Pleistocene mammals of North America. But eleven thousand years ago the giant ground sloth, the American elephants, and the saber-tooth were made extinct.
What will the condor do?

❊

The raccoon is incredibly graceful as he picks up bread with his tiny hands in the beam of the flashlight. He slips from a sitting position on his hindquarters forward to all fours and drifts effortlessly in any direction he chooses. He steps backward, away from our stare, without turning—or he moves forward drawn to the lovely white bread. He is able to stop—perfectly in balance and floating—in the midst of any movement and reverse himself and go the opposite direction. When he reverses there is no interruption of the smoothness of his movement. There is no stop made in a change of direction or gesture—there is no cessation. He never seems to be still and yet there is no unnecessary movement. He is vibrant with the delicate wildness in all life.

The outlaw. The wild rose.

Assuming the postures of fear creates fear—just as fear creates the postures. Either can be seen as a penetration of a very real curtain of flesh.

The essential mystery is lost and recovered—lost and recovered.

The mystery of personality and the mystery of physics.

Addiction to personality.

Personality is an addiction.

I am afraid. I am not afraid. I am brave. I am not brave. I am something else. I am many things. I am a system. I am not a system. I am beautiful.

The addiction to solutions is dualism.

Addiction to facts is short-sightedness.

Myriad-mindedness. (System within system within system surrounded by dimensions of Nothingness comprised of the interpenetration of realms.)

We are almost liberated.

Liberation is physical.

Everything I touch is spread through me and reverberates.

The taste of wild ginger remains long after the hike is over. The rain is forgotten, the exhaustion in the thighs can barely be remembered, but the acrid, sweet, and perfumey taste of the wild ginger stem remains. With it there is an image of purplish-red light on the leaves.

Walking through the herd of wild zebras, in front of the hotel at the top of the crater, I am aware of the Pleistocene. Their striped haunches ripple and twitch with consciousness of me though only a few look.

The odor spreading from the tiny island is a physical aura. It is the smell of blood, of mummifying meat, of rotting flesh, of placenta lying in the sun, of the excrement of giant mammals and of their sexuality and pheromones. It is the odor of the Pleistocene—of the age of great mammals. There is also a physical aura of mammal-energy radiating from the island. I recognize it. My sub-beings know what it is.

These auras have the beauty of sudden recognition, of terror, of cousinhood, and of the special, thoughtless ogre-hood of these near-brethren.

The sea elephants—the size and weight of small trucks—raise their heads and threaten us as we walk among them.

They are very dumb and sweet and cruel. They are mindless and comic and terrible. These giant seals have the faces of feeble-minded babies grown gray and stubbly whiskered with noses changed into trunks. They are uninvolved with morality and amorality, and are caught within the processes of their evolving instincts. They are more than human.

———————

The movie stars appear to glow with wholeness. (John Wayne, Lauren Bacall.) We respond to the three-dimensionality caused by their lighting for we wish to be whole, unified persons and sure—and free.

We hope to have cruel and beautiful and true relationships—and superhuman devotions marred only by our humane weaknesses.

We dream of being without proportion—sizeless as an image on a screen—permanent but also changing for each occasion.

We are stars. We are proportionless. We are myriad-minded. We are bodyminds. We are bulks of experience. We are cuckoos shaking the orange-blossoms from the boughs. We are boughs of orange-blossoms. We are the water moving by capillary action through the dark earth around the roots.

———————

The orange reflection of embers on the polished floor.

A flock of crows in the Douglas firs. Seen from below they make a black constellation in the daylight. They caw loudly. Each crow is a star.

Beauty is everywhere. Evil is rare. Honesty is deep as snow drifts. There is little joy.

The brains of certain invertebrates are in a ring around the mouth-opening of their gullets.

———————

It is frightening to walk through a herd of zebras but I do not show the fear.

Our sensoriums pass over an event and various particles of the event stimulate our sub-beings. Our life, which is an aggregate—a sensory model—is then brought into brighter being.

Or: we move through an event—which is a purely arbitrary segment of what we can perceive. And/or: we, and the event, cybernetically bring each other into being and shape the totality of what is perceived.

Or: all of these possibilities, or none of them, or some of them, or some of them plus something else.

The nervous system makes models of the universe that are constellations produced by the information from our twenty-seven senses, and syntheses of the senses, and synesthetic restatements of the senses. These reverberate in the body-mind which is a solid piece of information derived from the success of innumerable earlier models of the universe. Perhaps these act with fields, auras, movements that we do not understand.

The senses are extrusions of the substrate manifested through us. We test the background—the substrate—the messiah—with them.

The background—the substrate—may be compromised of intercrumplings of fields and dimensions and realms. It is no doubt as complex as the microscopic surfaces of a cell from the cytoplasm on down to the molecular level.

Reticular formation.

DNA/RNA.

Mitochondria.

Cytoplasmic streamings.

Swirling dimensions taking the shape of our senses.

Or something else.

Other things.

No things.

Outlaws. Hummingbirds. A sphinx moth.

✳

It is certain that we do not understand how we move or in what
directions—or dimensions.

———————

I BELIEVED THAT EVERYTHING
IS DIVINE
and now
I
know
it.
It is all perfect.
This is really it!
—AND IT IS ALL PERFECT. THIS IS REALLY IT!
—AND IT IS ALL PERFECT. THIS IS REALLY IT!
You and I
will
find
our home
our cave

on this

substrate

among the windblown
orange poppies

among the windblown
orange poppies

on this

substrate

WHERE
WE

ARE
MAMMALS

and gods
and goddesses

and
KINGS

and
QUEENS.

———————

Spanish longhorns escaped from the southwestern missions and throve on the native American grasses. They multiplied into scores of thousands and created a new resource—meat. The snowy winters made these survivors hardier and they discovered wild cattle behavior and learned to protect themselves from wolves. The plains grass lay untouched because the large herbivores of Texas had been extinct for eleven thousand years. The longhorns created a rapport with the grassy plains— and the grasslands flourished with the cattle. There was a mammal renaissance—a mini-revival of the Pleistocene—clusters of large herbivores dotted the land as in the past.

Easterners could eat inexpensive beef regularly and often—if it could be brought to them. They could dine like lords did in earlier times. Some men became adventurous for the wealth and excitement of beef. The mounted cattle herder—the cowboy—came into being and gave birth to the myth of himself. He flourished with the herds of mammals.

SEE, THERE IS THE BOOTED MAN
IN THE SADDLE!
The dream was meat
and

he rode
tall in the stirrups—
flushed, electric, alive
with the thunder and stink
of longhorns.
The East was hungry
but tired
of the flesh
of pigs and sheep.
NOW,
MY
DEAR,
we wear
our boots

like dreams,

dreams.
—And
SEE
that
reverberation:
the motorcyclist
in
his
black
leathers.

I asked for a statue of Kwannon, the goddess of mercy, and I was shown a tiny black deer carved in jet.

The dust specks turning in the sunbeam flash like mirrors.

In the empty room I listen to the roar of the truck.

———————

BASAL METABOLISM. The rate of energy expenditure of an animal at rest, usually expressed per unit weight. In man, basal metabolic rate (BMR) is expressed as the output of calories per square metre of body surface per hour. Measured directly or indirectly by calculation from the amount of oxygen consumed or carbon dioxide given off. From *The Penguin Dictionary of Biology*.

———————

The fragmented consciousness is intense. The possessor burns brightly.

When man is alone he is on fire. When man is Love he is on fire.

When man sleeps he is a constellation.

Alert in the forest at night.

———————

A model to remind us what we are when outside of our selves.

———————

The surge of life drifts in every direction. In a teaspoon of water from the ocean or a vernal pool, or in a cubic inch of air, are many orders of plants, animals, molds, and microbes. Life in many tribes and phyla is around always. Each one is a sensorium. Each is a jewel.

———————

Billboards line the freeways and make a dimension of the flattened and brutalized faces of advertising that stare in at drivers in their cars. The figures are represented as mindless robots of pleasure. The pleasures they show are simplified ones: macho triumph, narcissism, and sensual overcompletion. The eyes and mouth express a life wherein the body is rigid and armored rather than flexible and supple. The representations are on backgrounds with little modelling of light and shadow. They show the everpresent, omnidirectional light of the supermarket. The figures are decorated with blatant sensory symbols—black velvet, pearls, peacock feathers. Plump lips are made into sculpture by lipstick, painted toenails emerge from sandals, blonde hair flows in two-dimensional sculpture. It is the poetry of morons.

No diversity of intelligence holds it together. Merchandise is the subject—and the goal is to persuade the passing driver. There is no subtlety—it is less than human and less than anthropoid. Our primate cousins—baboons, monkeys, apes—have exquisite and detailed feelings of touch and appreciations of the softness of kisses, and of the loving stroke, and of the fires of rage and brutality. Their perceptions have a million opalescent caves in them. They have starlight on their brows. Some of them—as we do—watch the sunrise with pleasure.

The subtle and tender auras and extensions of ordinary objects and beings. The baby rabbit might be a child.

Federico Garcia Lorca in "The *Duende:* Theory and Divertissement" speaks of one of the inspiring forces of music and poetry. The *duende* is a black, demonic force of "salt and marble." It is an energy that passes historically through the Greek mystery cults and comes to the modern world by way of the gypsy Flamenco artists.

Lorca says:

> The *duende* is a power and not a construct, it is a struggle and not a concept. I have heard an old guitarist, a true virtuoso, remark, 'The *duende* is not in the throat, the *duende* comes up from inside, up from the very soles of the feet.' That is to say, it is not a question of aptitude, but of a true and viable style—of blood, in other words; of what is oldest in culture: of creation made act.

Lorca speaks of "how style triumphs over inferior matter, and the unenlightened" and he tells of a gypsy lady of eighty who took the dance prize—competing with the lovliest beauties by the way she raised her arms, threw back her head and stamped her foot. She acted with *duende*.

The *duende* is not afraid of death—if the *duende* is to be present there must, in fact, be the possibility of death.

Lorca takes pride that Spain and Mexico are countries that use death—the bullfight—as a celebration.

❄

The initiate in certain mystery cults was dressed in white robes and laid out upon a ritual bier. Above in the darkness a bull was sacrificed in the rite of the *taurobolium*. The bull screamed in death and the initiate was drenched with blood. The initiate was taken from the chamber reborn and given a new name and honey mixed with milk to drink. He, or she, was purified and ready to become at one—in bliss— with the godhead after death.

❄

Emerson speaks of the transcendental Oversoul.

❄

The mystical rebirth by blood sacrifice in the mysteries is not simply purification through the death of a substitute. The bloody act—the style of it—states that at deepest root we believe that the transcendental oversoul is connected to all by veins and arteries and capillaries of blood. Oversouls and godheads may float mystically on high, or in created dimensions and aeons of bliss, but the connection to them is through a common elixir—blood. Blood is, Mephistopheles says in *Faust*, "a very special kind of juice."

The sacrifices are like the veins of the placenta attached to a fetus that is about to be born.

❄

Wine is the blood of the grape that is transmuted. Wine is the symbol of blood that may be exalted into spirit-blood in the body of the future.

The bee colony was seen as a body—a being—a single complex creature like a man or a deer. The honey was the blood of the being.

❄

When mysteries become metaphysical and abandon the sacrifice of an animal, the real drenching with blood, the wine, milk, honey, ecstatic songs and torchlight in the grottoes—then they no longer are about the bodymind. They can no longer liberate. Liberation is of the body. It is the bodymind that is spirit as well as matter.

❋

The substrate of the mysteries was the Asian Mediterranean region and Mediterranean Europe. There were no lions in Greece by the time of Pericles. In the Roman world wild living creatures were rare and they were imported from Africa for destruction in circuses. Except for the sacred groves the large forests of the Greco-Roman countryside were extirpated. The trees had been changed into warships, fuel for cooking and smelting, and objects of commerce.

❋

The mysteries were the last taste of animal blood (man's own animal blood) in a pastoralized, cultivated, and urbanized world. The mysteries renewed the physical longing found in dreams. They renewed the hopes, fears, and desires for the long-lost phylogenetic worlds of our evolution. The still-aware sub-beings, and smoldering reverberations of the body— the mind/body—needed satisfaction.

The mysteries were acts of despair, attempts to find liberation. They went directly to the body—to cut open the flesh—so that blood might pour out. So that man might see his own blood and dream of it upon a landscape other than the devastated one on which he was born.

❋

A Pueblo Indian artist speaks of Shewanna—a power that appears to be antipodal to *duende*. Shewanna is nature in an embodiment that shows both its grandeur and its consciousness. Nature allows incredible beauty to be seen in a shape that is enormous and yet has physical boundaries. Shewanna is beyond good and evil and has majesty. As a boy, the artist was wandering through steep-walled canyons on a hot afternoon. A storm started directly above him. There were crashing bolts of lightning and booming thunder and the colors and explosions and scents of a desert storm. As he ran home through the ravines with only a strip of the sky above his head, the storm followed him always staying above him no matter which way he ran—backward or forward or down a side canyon. When he darted through his door and fell over with exhaustion, wide-eyed and awestruck, his mother knew that he had witnessed Shewanna.

There is sometimes Shewanna in a herd of buffalo, in a sunset, or in a special place on the earth. One knows it on seeing it. It is very special—it is not a herd of buffalo or place or a sunset or a thunderstorm. It is Shewanna.

Shewanna is of nature, or the spirit of nature that is the interaction of vast undomesticated environmental systems. For Shewanna to appear nature must still be open-ended—the processes at both ends of a system must be vital. *Duende* appears as nature is closed-down by man. Perhaps it is a special manifestation of deep nature—a "loop" of connections with uncultivated nature and with blood. Shewanna is primal and free.

I
KNOW
IT IS TIME
for
ENORMOUS
BEAUTY
as
well

as
the
special
manifestation.
Come,
Shewanna,

come to brothers and sisters
and sons and daughters
of otter, and coyote,
tadpole
and wolf.

Let us be done with diluted mysteries that are rhetoric—that are removed from the body. They are a froth of bubbles created by the social system.

Come,

Shewanna,

come to the brothers and sisters
and sons and daughters
of otter, and coyote,
tadpole
and wolf.

———————

When some British children were asked, "What are the twelve loveliest things you know?" one boy answered:

"The cold of ice cream.
The scunch of leaves.
The feel of clean cloze.
Water running into a bath.
Cold wind on a hot day.
Climbing up a hill looking down.
Hot water bottle in bed.
Honey in your mouth.
Smell in a drugstore.
Babies smiling.
The feeling inside when you sing.
Baby kittens."

A little girl's list went:

"Our dog's eyes.
Street lights on the river.
Wet stones.
The smell of rain.
An organ playing.

Red roofs in trees.
Smoke rising.
Rain on your cheeks.
The smell of cut grass.
Red velvet.
The smell of picnic teas.
The moon in clouds."

An Empire of Signs:
Jack Spicer

MICHAEL McCLURE: I met Spicer for the first time with Robert Duncan but I don't remember the date or the place. One of my earliest memories about Jack is when I was having some of my poems typed, in 1955. I counted all the letter spaces in a line and at the end of each line there'd be a number like "72," and the next line might say "34," and the next line might say "15," because there were fifteen letter spaces. That way, it was possible for a typist to center them correctly. I remember Robert Duncan was amused, because Spicer had seen the manuscript of these poems that had the numbers at the end of the lines—and Jack thought that it was either a poetics or "magic" that I was doing. He asked Robert what it was. Robert took delight in telling me.

KEVIN KILLIAN: They must have resembled chemical equations—Uranium 238.

McCLURE: No doubt, it looked *alchemical!* And probably I thought of it that way.

KILLIAN: I guess they were magic constructions in a way. Regarding the production of Robert Duncan's play *Faust Foutu* in 1955, Spicer was in it but later on in life he had a great deal of difficulty reading his work. Did you have to memorize the play?

McCLURE: No. We read it from the script. As a matter of fact, we all sat at a table: it was a reading of the play, only partly a performance.

Conducted by Kevin Killian in 1992, this interview is previously unpublished.

At the end, Robert performed, to the extent of standing up and taking off his pants, standing there, the naked poet. A couple of people stood up while they read their lines, but mostly it was a play reading, not a performance. There were no costumes or sets. I remember Jack had a leering presence—you know how Jack would sit bent over, with his chin stuck out, his head thrown back, and look straight out into an audience, or straight into a crowd—and maybe with his head slightly tilted to one side. It was an apparatus of his self-consciousness as much as anything.

KILLIAN: So there were no problems of "stage fright"?

McCLURE: Some of us were probably so unused to being in front of an audience saying our words, or somebody else's words, that there was an intense nervousness about it. Also, we all believed in the play; and we all believed in the beauty and intelligence and the awesomeness of it as an act of language and wit. I suspect that added to our feelings. And, of course, all of us wanted *Robert* to like what we did. So it made a complex event for a simple reading of a play. For one thing, a play reading is a different thing when there are actors doing it. They read it through before they get on a stage and they know how to put themselves in the technical capacity of giving the role some particular sense. Whereas we were a mélange: we were artists.

KILLIAN: They must have been wildly different styles of reading.

McCLURE: We had all seen Robert do it, because Robert would sometimes do the entire play himself. He'd act out the roles, and hum the music, and sing all the songs, and do any dances that were in the script. He did them not on a stage, but in one's front room.

KILLIAN: I didn't realize that.

McCLURE: Oh yeah, Robert "performed" the play, it was a reading, but it was much more a performance than what we did. There was a magic quality about our event nevertheless, because of the people doing it—filmmakers, poets, painters, composers.

KILLIAN: The *Faust Foutu* presentation was in January 1955 and Spicer left San Francisco in June for the East Coast.

MCCLURE: That makes sense, because it was a few months after Jack's departure that painter Wally Hedrick asked me to put together a poetry reading for the Six Gallery. At that time, I was about to become a father, and was working full-time at the museum, so I asked Allen Ginsberg to organize the reading. And that was the beginning of the Six Gallery Reading. Spicer's friend John Ryan came that evening and gave me a letter he'd received from Spicer. It asked someone in San Francisco to help find Spicer a job and the wherewithal to come back home, because he wanted to leave Boston. I read Jack's letter from the stage and it got applause from his friends and fans.

KILLIAN: Was it your impulse, then, to include Spicer as a San Francisco poet at a representative of San Francisco writing?

MCCLURE: I hadn't thought of that. There were few poets and we were not thinking in those terms. It was a practical matter. "Could anybody help Jack?" This was a request for much needed mutual aid: *Let's get Jack out of Boston, where he's unhappy.* It was a letter of plaint: "Help! Get me out of here!" There were a lot of people there and maybe somebody could help. It was a good idea. Which brings me to a question in your letter: you say that some people thought of Jack as being the *eminence grise* behind the plastic arts scene, while others remembered him as being a smiling dilettante, or something like that.

KILLIAN: Yes. It was hard for me to determine exactly what he knew about art, and what his real interest in art was.

MCCLURE: Let me give you another take on it. It's entirely appropriate that Jack was one of the founders of the Six Gallery. I don't think Jack necessarily knew much about the work of all the artists. A number of them coming into the Six Gallery were students of Clyfford Still— people like Jess, and there was Wally Hedrick, Jay De Feo and so on. I would imagine—and this is a guess—that Jack comes most strongly into the art scene through the North Beach milieu. I would think that

Jack comes to the art scene as much through the artists bar as any other direction. I mean, Jack spent so much time at The Place in those years that the graffiti on the men's room walls was an ongoing epic, and Jack was an ongoing subject of it, and he seemed to enjoy that. He'd go in, read the new graffiti, and come out smiling to himself.

KILLIAN: He had taught all the other painters English literature at the Art Institute.

McCLURE: I didn't realize that he'd been teaching at that point.

KILLIAN: Yes, when the Humanities Department opened up Fall, 1953, Spicer was the first English teacher hired by SFAI, taught for two years, and was fired in the spring of 1955.

I always think of Spicer as . . . well, I can't think of a polite way to put it—as kind of *predatory*. Didn't you have trouble, as a young, straight, handsome man, in this kind of very gay milieu of poetry when you first came to San Francisco?

McCLURE: Not as much as some people would have had—the reason being that many people in the places that I'd lived before were queer. (Nobody ever heard the word "gay.") Many of my friends were homosexual and they understood my position on things. In fact, I thought of *my*self as "queer." That's why I emphasize the word "queer." People would yell, "Queer!" at me when I walked down the street as easily as they would yell "Queer!" at my friend Don Love when *he* walked down the street. They weren't separating out young men with long hair from somebody who was apparently homosexual. I had it yelled at me as much as anyone. You know, I don't remember Spicer ever being predatory towards anyone.

KILLIAN: Well, Spicer would fall in love, very dramatically. I don't mean "predatory" in Duncan's sense. That's what I understand about Frank O'Hara, too, that he was so persistent he could wear one down.

McCLURE: Yes, he was a charmer.

KILLIAN: When Spicer returned from New York and Boston, he felt that the whole city had changed in his absence, and that the publication of *Howl*, the whole *Howl* trial, all the publicity, had changed his city that he had loved. The whole atmosphere was different.

MCCLURE: He was right. The earlier scene preceeded the *Howl* trial. It was centered around the *Ark* magazine, with Parkinson and Rexroth and Duncan; and it included the Berkeley Renaissance, with Jack Spicer and Robert Duncan and Robin Blaser. And although the older anarchist scene was represented at the Six Gallery with Kenneth Rexroth being the Master of Ceremonies, the absence of Robert Duncan (because Robert was in Mallorca) and the absence of Spicer allowed a mostly new group to be present that evening in 1955. If Spicer had been there; and Robert Duncan had been there, they might have been in the reading also, and we would not have had an event that was "the beginning of the Beat Generation" as much as an enlargement of the San Francisco Renaissance. But then I have an idea that the Beat consciousness is like Romanticism, or Classicism, or like Surrealism—it's a large state of awareness. I mean, I'd say Classic, Romantic, Beat, Surrealist—like that. It was Leslie Fiedler who called what we were doing a New Mutation. That's the position I hold about it, that the Beat Generation is about consciousness and is about nature, primarily, and is about the body to a large extent.

KILLIAN: When Spicer returned from Boston, he kind of gave up hope for his plays—he never wrote any more plays after 1956.

MCCLURE: I've never seen a play of Spicer's.

KILLIAN: He had been writing a series of plays, that haven't seen the light yet—Robin Blaser is still keeping them—on classical themes: *Sir Orfeo*, versions of Greek drama; and he went to New York and Boston in hopes of persuading Poets Theater to put them on, and planned to make his living as a playwright, but, discouraged by the East Coast poets, he returned. He became paranoid about the East Coast writers liking his work. But I see his attempts at theater as part of a whole movement in San Francisco, at the period, of expanding poetry into performance.

MCCLURE: Only a few people are aware of the diverse and interesting theater scene that was in San Francisco in 1955, and how much the poets were involved in it. When Herb Blau started his Actors' Workshop, the result seemed to be the collapse of the smaller theaters. The varied possibilities that had been supported before had been displaced.

KILLIAN: Wasn't the Actors' Workshop started in 1959, or 1960?

MCCLURE: It was around 1959 or 1960. When they got their feet on the ground to start presenting the first West Coast performances of the absurdist playwrights—Beckett, Genet—and using Robert LaVigne to do the sets for Genet, and getting Mort Subotnik to do the music, then I began to get interested.

KILLIAN: They did *Lear* with LaVigne's designs also.

MCCLURE: As a playwright, you had to be shown in Paris, or London, before you could be done in San Francisco at the Actors' Workshop. But there were people here like Lee Breuer—Lee Breuer, who's now Mabou Mines. As a matter of fact, the first performance ever done of my first play about Billy the Kid and the Lincoln County Range War was done with Lee Breuer playing one of the parts, Kirby Doyle playing another, Ruth Breuer playing another—right in my front room. It blew my mind, it was a beautiful experience. That was going on. James Broughton was a large part of the theater scene. You could go to one theater, and see *The Crucible*, by Arthur Miller, and go to another theater and see *The Playground* by James Broughton. The Bella Union was one of the North Beach theaters and every year it did the Poets' Follies.

KILLIAN: And Helen Adam wrote her play, too.

MCCLURE: Yes, that's just a little later than we're talking about, but not much. There was an audience for these plays, too—not an off-Broadway audience but an audience.

KILLIAN: Michael Davidson's book on *The San Francisco Renaissance* has as a thesis that poetry developed a performative aspect here.

MCCLURE: That's what the Six Gallery reading was about, and the Six Gallery reading was probably given because of the performance of *Faust Foutu* earlier in the year.

KILLIAN: Regarding the "Billy the Kid" material: Did this material belong to you, Michael, and did Spicer appropriate it—or was it a question of two artists working through the same mythos? I've talked to several people who have remarked on Spicer's use of the Billy myth, and your own use of it from your play *The Blossom* onwards, and I've even heard it said that Spicer's *Billy the Kid* is his homage to your poetry and your person. (And that Spicer's use of Marilyn Monroe in his *Holy Grail* is an echo of your Harlow character.) Or is this a case of the same mythic, manifest-destiny, Romantic materials buzzing around like bees in the zeitgeist?

MCCLURE: I couldn't tell you. I don't know how people's minds work, when it's a mind other than my own. My Billy the Kid and Spicer's Billy the Kid are so entirely opposite that there's certainly plenty of room for them to co-exist. Whether I was the source for Jack's or not I couldn't tell you. Jack's Billy the Kid is a Billy the Kid of the mind; in it Jack is listening, letting the persona create himself through his listening. And it's an intense listening. It's an idea of Billy the Kid. It has no historical foundation, as far as I can tell. My Billy the Kid stepped out of the Lincoln County Range War, and then became another kind of a creature—but he stepped out of research. So there are different provenances—Jack listened for his, and I went after mine in a different way.

KILLIAN: It's curious then. I think of it in the same way as the Arthurian materials, from which so many writers worked different treatments.

MCCLURE: My relationship with Billy the Kid and Jean Harlow is one that you don't want to interview me about here, because that would take a couple of hours to discuss. It's complex, and lengthy, a deep and intimate relationship that began in 1956, and still goes on today. And the Marilyn Monroe thing—in Spicer's Arthurian pieces in Spicer's *Holy Grail*—I really don't know if it relates to my coupling of Billy the Kid and Jean Harlow in *The Beard* or not.

KILLIAN: I imagine it just entered the poem, actually, because it was in the news that day that it was being written—the death of Marilyn Monroe.

MCCLURE: Yeah—I wrote a poem about the death of Marilyn Monroe, one of my *Ghost Tantras*—I believe it's "Ghost Tantra 39." It was written the day after Marilyn's death, in fact. It begins:

> MARILYN MONROE, TODAY THOU HAST PASSED
> THE DARK BARRIER
> —diving in a swirl of golden hair.
> I hope you have entered a sacred paradise for full
> warm bodies, full lips, full hips, and laughing eyes!
> AHH GHROOOR. ROOOHR. NOH THAT OHH!
> OOOH . . .
> Farewell perfect mammal.
> Fare thee well from thy silken couch and dark day! . . .

KILLIAN: Regarding the Charles Olson seminars that were done here in San Francisco in the fifties—I understand you were in attendance.

MCCLURE: I was not only in attendance, but Olson gave a lecture at my flat.

KILLIAN: I wondered about that. Duncan said that he had spread the subscription series out to people's houses beyond his own, but I could never figure out whose they were. The relationship of Spicer and Olson was difficult, and I think that Olson's visit here to San Francisco represented yet another threat to Spicer, who was already tiring of being knocked around by the Beat poets.

MCCLURE: Since Olson was Duncan's "mensch"—I have no doubt that what you're saying is possible. Recently I began thinking about Jack Spicer and Philip Whalen. They both have an idiosyncratic practice in their work. Phil has a wonderful poem that says something like, "I'm the last wild buffalo," you know, "I'm the last wild being here on the plains." Well, Spicer might have been not the last wild one, but the last hunted one, in the way Phil speaks of himself being the "last free wild buffalo." Spicer was the last something. Spicer and Whalen both had a system that they used—in both cases, based to some extent on William Carlos Williams. When Williams read his poetry in San Francisco, Jack Spicer wore a necktie. He said, "This is the only living being that I would wear a necktie for," and he made quite a point of saying that to many of us.

KILLIAN: Now that I didn't know.

MCCLURE: Both Jack and Philip relied on friends to a large extent, as reverberators of their work, in different ways but part of the practice of their systems grew out of that.

KILLIAN: By "reverberators" do you mean that the friends in turn would write poems in reaction, and this would start off a chain reaction?

MCCLURE: That would be Jack's way of doing it. Both of them, interestingly enough, had trouble with Olson or his system. Probably two different kinds of trouble, but in addition to the resemblances and dis-resemblances I'm pointing out, they were both troubled by Charles. And yet both were grounded solidly—in their unique ways—in Williams. Comparing Spicer and Olson, you have both of them writing from outside—maybe it was Blaser who said that about Spicer and it is a good way of putting it. Jack was writing from outside. Writing from outside has a relationship with Projective Verse. The inspiration for Projective Verse is outside, see what I mean? If you know Olson's essay on Projective Verse, the inspiration is outside—it comes to your central nervous system, and the energy of its impact on your nervous system combines with the energy of your breath then the energy of your physique creates a verbal line that bounces from you—from your nervous system, from your physique and your breath, out into space onto the field of the page. But it must come from outside. In Spicer's case, it's coming from "another" outside, and he's listening to it, and it's going in through his mind and out his hand—an entirely different process than Olson's. We are troubled not with the people who are different from us: we are troubled with the people who are similiar. I see the problem that way. I also see that perhaps Philip Whalen's trouble with Olson's system is that they are both energetic writers, rooted in Williams.

KILLIAN: Robert Duncan gave Lew Ellingham a very dramatic account of one of those Olson lectures of the late fifties—I think this was at his house—in which Olson said, "Next time I'll bring in the Tarot cards, and lay them out." Spicer brought his own set of Tarot cards, and Olson took one look at those cards and said, "That set of cards is a corrupt one—begone! I don't want to see those cards," and Jack was thoroughly humiliated.

MCCLURE: We're right into magic here, aren't we. Robert Duncan believed, as you probably know, that Ezra Pound's *Cantos* were something like a seance. He believed that Pound was calling up voices from the spirit box. Obviously *The Cantos* is everything else that it is, but in addition, for Duncan, it was a seance. So these dealings with the Tarot cards were deep and powerful to all of us at the time.

As I look through Jack's *Books* I see him as a conveyor of messages; this goes back to what I was saying about his resemblance and non-resemblance with Charles. Spicer is picking up messages with his nerves but he's not a public messenger as, say, Ginsberg would be. He is a messenger, and he is a conveyor of messages, but not a public messenger. The books in the *Collected Books* are in a number of ways comparable to painter Francesco Clemente's use of the "circuit." Clemente feels a circuit open up, and he'll do perhaps thirty or forty paintings which have a resemblance and a relationship to one another, and they're interreferential to one another. They make a cohesive body of work. Sometimes the ellipse between separate circuits will be so great that they won't look like the work that preceeded. Or sometimes what opens up looks like work he's done three years earlier. Sometimes it will have no apparent relationship to anything else he's ever done.

KILLIAN: How often have I been surprised by—"Oh, who did that picture?" "Francesco Clemente!" "What?"

MCCLURE: Exactly. Many of Spicer's poem sequences are what he called a book. He begins this with *After Lorca*. There is a special coherence to *After Lorca*—the coherence of being centered around Lorca and the caprice of the idea itself, as well as the conceit of the idea, in the classical sense of the word "concetto." The collection of Spicer's books becomes *intra*referential, not just interreferential, and the books relate to one another. It's a powerful and interesting way of building a body of work.

One of the characteristics that Robert and Jack share at the early point is their disjointedness, where one line seems to, by ellipse only, by the power of the ellipse, refer to the preceding line. This may well come from Gertrude Stein. I mean that Gertrude Stein may be one of the sources for this, although her work tended to flow and one could read it in that way. Jack went on with his own disjointedness: in fact, I think the best work of Jack's is the most disjointed. It is the most like Paul Celan, which is something I'd like to come back to. Robert Duncan densifies the disjointedness and then becomes his own Romantic self, and the disjointedness becomes parts of longer tropes of rhetoric and consciousness; whereas, in fact, Jack, continued to deal with disconnectedness. This formal structure is a disjointed formal structure—creating books, or circuits, and it works very well. Systems work if you follow them. Robert went off in another system, but I see this as one of the basic diversions. This might be somewhere close to the basic differences between Duncan and Spicer. When you get into Spicer's *The Book of Gawain,* the disjointedness is working brilliantly. For me, books work better than poems. I prefer to read a book of poems, a larger piece of consciousness. So, Spicer's system works well for me. I'm pointing out that, structually, it's a disjointed system to think with, and yet it works well in art. The poems that work best are the poems that, after the fact, reminded me most of Paul Celan, where the disjointure creates both art and a psychic event.

An outstanding quality of Spicer's is that he works in a pale palette—
he works in a paler palette than Lorca, which is one of the first things
you think of when you read *After Lorca*. You read *Billy the Kid*, and
it's a pale palette of the West that he's using—this is an artistic choice
that he's making. I also think it's part of the nervous system action,
a part of Jack's difference with Olson. He's not dealing with sensorium:
he's listening. He's gone through all that agony of waiting for the
poem to manifest itself, and then he keeps demanding, "Oh, poem,
not only have you manifested yourself in me, telling me that this is
the day that Billy the Kid had died, now you must make Billy the
Kid for me." I mean, he keeps making demands. But they're demands
not of his own sensorium, they're demands on something outside of
himself. Whereas with Olson's Projective Verse, there's the demand
that the inspiration do something with his sensorium. Both are urgent,
both are intense ways of working. So this finding your poetry outside
is in great opposition to Olson. Spicer's much more opposed to Olson
than he is to Ginsberg, because Allen's listening, too. At that time,
Allen had just been through a great period of listening.

Now, take a poem like Spicer's "The Red Wheelbarrow." A different
process is going on there, one much more akin to what we call deconstruction today. It's as if William Carlos Williams's "Red Wheelbarrow" is deconstructed—I can imagine Jack wearing his necktie when
he wrote it!—it's as if Williams's "Red Wheelbarrow" is deconstructed,
and in the space of this deconstruction, Jack's poems come in. It is a
somewhat different process. Jack is not listening for poems; they are
actually forced into existence by the hole he makes. It's like Hawking
radiation coming into being around black holes.

KILLIAN: I found it fascinating in process, and he does it with many
of his masters.

MCCLURE: I'm sure it precedes any reading of Derrida. That's a different thing. I like *The Red Wheelbarrow* and *The Book of Gawain* the
most of Jack's work, and I realize what an unusual choice that is! And
then, I like *After Lorca* much. In poems like *15 False Prepositions*, I feel
it's something like *Waiting for Godot*: the wheels are spinning, and it's

an agonizing wait, and the subject of the poems is the wait and the listening.

KILLIAN: I wouldn't be surprised.

MCCLURE: Now, I don't know about the word "disjointed," but since I've already used it, there is—an unusual aesthetic effect that is created by disjointure, of there not being a substance there. And I call this "insubstantiality," and this insubstantiality itself becomes a dominant aesthetic in Jack's work. The insubstantiality of lines of rhetoric following lines of rhetoric that are disjointed from one another creates an effect that is as much an aesthetic as *wabi* is in haiku. A haiku isn't a haiku if it doesn't have *wabi*. (*Wabi* being old-fashioned gnarly countrifiedness.) This insubstantiality should have a more elegant name: I don't know what you'd give it. But it becomes an important part of the poetry. All of this is commenting on the difference between Jack and Olson. Another person that I think of—and this is a strange comparison—is that I see a resemblance and a dis-resemblance between Spicer and Norman Mailer. Norman Mailer's last two major books were *Harlot's Ghost* and *Ancient Evenings*. These two works are not literary works at all, they are inventions of alternate lives. They are Faustian, not literary; and there's something in Jack's own, different Faustian way, something going on in alternative lives in Lorca and Billy the Kid. Enough so that it reminds me of Mailer. But I also have to say that Mailer reminds me of Mallarmé—and the way that Mailer reminds me of Mallarme is that both of them think that there is no size. Both of them feel that their emotions are proportionless, that their emotions are immeasureable, and are the size of the universe, which is wonderful. I suppose I could make a troika of Mallarmé and Spicer and Mailer. I don't know what Norman would make of that!

KILLIAN: What you're saying is also true of *The Executioner's Song*.

MCCLURE: Mailer's novel *Harlot's Ghost* is unlike anything else that exists. It's pretty wonderful—and pretty boring—and pretty majestic; and concretely existential. We all wanted to create art, not literature. I don't think any of us wanted to create literature. We wanted to create poetry. Shakespeare didn't write his plays to create literature and Melville wanted to write great art like Shakespeare, and popular novels.

KILLIAN: As the difference between what's signed on the page, and what meaning can be assigned to it, opens up this vast, scary vacuum of meaning. Allied to that, I thought not of Mailer but of Burroughs as a companion to Spicer, in that strange, spooky science fiction atmosphere created often not out of the content, but from the rupturing, the—

McCLURE: The cut-up technique. That's a point, too.

KILLIAN: And I think Mailer's latest books build on Burroughs to that extent. Not in the cut-up technique, but in the invention of an alternate universe, and the science fiction.

McCLURE: Of course, regarding Norman's *Harlot's Ghost*—it's the absolute real world of the fifties. I realize—"Jesus Christ, I could have been a CIA agent. Anybody could have." I could have literally become one; if I hadn't had the breaks I've had, I could have believed all that lying propaganda. Although I'm sure I had plenty of doses of lying propaganda from other directions. You brought up something else I wanted to reply to . . . Oh! I see that Jack's legacy also has a "division" in it—you know, two potential visions in it, and one is stuff of great poetry, or visionary pain, or agony, or even of boredom. Pain, or agony, or boredom. Not grief—never any grief.

KILLIAN: I think that the manifestation of the characters on the page— your numbering system you described, 72, 15, 20, might be all that literature or poetry allows us. This is a lesson many take from Spicer, that the substance—is the words themselves. And his linguistic training and practice allowed him to see this maybe a little bit earlier than someone like Derrida.

McCLURE: Of course, with Jack's deep roots in Linguistics.

KILLIAN: When Spicer died, he had just ordered Roland Barthes's *Empire of Signs*, which had then just appeared.

McCLURE: There's also a bestiary quality in the relationship that Jack had to people on the scene in Gino and Carlo's Bar that shows up in the poems. The poems become bestiaries. Bestiary page for Nemi, bestiary page for Ebbe, bestiary page for Russ, bestiary page for Lew, you know. Not the way Robert did it in *Letters*. In both books—all the poems are dedicated to somebody they knew, which is a real gesture. There's a difference in the way Robert Duncan dealt with admirers and workshops. Robert encouraged people to let themselves be themselves, to whatever extent they were capable of doing it. Jack gave people a direction, which is something Robert would never have considered doing. Jack must have said, "Be like me," or "Do this," or "Listen for the poem"—

KILLIAN: "Negate your own personality."

McCLURE: Duncan said, "Let it come out of you like rose petals, and just let it keep happening, and do more of it so that it'll get boring and become something else again." I see that Jack did not have a positive effect on his people. I think people who might have grown more without Jack were quite entranced with Jack. I use the word "entranced" specifically. Some of his admirers probably didn't come into their own until after Jack's death.

KILLIAN: *Lament with the Makers* opens with Spicer's version of "Dover Beach," which insists "It's *not* a beach! It's *not* a beach!" It's a no-place.

McCLURE: Isn't that an amazing poem! That's an interesting act of art. I think that's one of the other high points, by the way: "Dover Beach," *The Red Wheelbarrow, The Book of Gawain, Lorca*, I like reading *Billy the Kid* because it's so different from mine. Those are the high points for me.

The Beat Journey:
An Interview

MICK MCALLISTER: You surprised me last night when you said you were influenced by Wordsworth's long autobiographical poem *The Prelude*, because my understanding of your poem "The Poet's Mind is Body" is that you were criticizing Wordsworth.

MICHAEL MCCLURE: I certainly was. Critic Warren Tallman gave me *The Prelude* when I was visiting Vancouver in the early 1960s. I was in a stressed psychic state at the time. I was impressed with the beauty of the idea of doing an autobiography in rhyme. Warren read me some of the most interesting parts of *The Prelude* and I read some of it to Warren. Then I began to compare it with Shelley; that is, I wrote a poem comparing it with Shelley. I haven't seen my poem in years, but I have a pretty clear recollection of it. I couldn't help but weigh Shelley against Wordsworth. [McClure is handed an issue of *Caterpillar* containing his "The Poet's Mind is Body" poem and an old photograph of himself, bearded, on a Harley-Davidson motorcycle.] Oh, great— I forgot that that photo with the beard and bike existed. Where's the poem?

MCALLISTER: It's right after the picture.

MCCLURE: Yes, there it is. I wrote my poem originally on the title page of *The Prelude*.

Conducted by Mick McAllister in the mid-1970s, this interview first appeared in *The Beat Journey*, ed. Arthur and Kit Knight (the unspeakable visions of the individual, vol. 8).

The Poet's Mind is Body
& his Arm is Joy.
SCIENCE
MIND
NATURE
MAN
are toys,
he hurls about like sailboats
with painted wings.
FIRE APRIL FIRE!
FIRE APRIL FIRE!
FIRE APRIL FIRE!
But deeper blacker being grows from genes
—with sullen eye & laughing yell
and generosity that hurls his senses
into Eternity & Heaven & Hell
like poor mad Shelley
like beautiful mad Shelley
& not this fool!

Well, I went on ahead and decided I needed to be my own kind of fool, and a few years later, not forgetting Wordsworth, and strongly moved by Kerouac's *Mexico City Blues*, I wrote a book that was in 250 stanzas. They are all about twenty-five lines apiece and rhymed, and were written as fast as I could on an electric typewriter. In the first ten I had not yet discovered, or was only beginning to sense, that they were going to be autobiographical—it was at about the eleventh or twelfth that they start becoming autobiographical. The poem is named *Fleas*, and it's 250 spontaneously written, rhymed electric typewriter poems about my childhood. They hop from memory to memory like a flea, while one image lights up another. So, in a sense, *Fleas* is a long autobiographical poem. In *Fleas*, I felt that I was opening some of the same territory that's occupied by the worst and merriest of Lord Byron and the best of Terrytoons. It is like a Sistine doodle. The poem is no more serious than a doodle and yet it's the size of the Sistine Chapel, and as complex as the Sistine Chapel. It proves that childhood is a vision, which is what we lose track of so often. When we let the childhood memories slip and slide away, we forget their visionary intensity. I began to recover the visionary intensity of them. And also, fortunately, I had some interesting insights, which I'm going to continue to explore, into the way memory works. You see, I didn't plan to write a stanza saying, "now I'll tell about the time I went down to the candy shop"—instead, one memory would bring another memory into being. Sometimes memories changed in the middle of a stanza, then I began to sense how one of them would light up another related memory and that memory would light up another and that one would light up another. Then a constellation of those three, having been lit, would light up another which would seemingly be disparate but was related to the constellation of the three, when they appeared together. But perhaps it was not related to any *individual* one solo. Finally, the ending of the poem is related to the combined constellation of all the 247 preceding ones. The end is a long triple stanza, all about mowing lawns in the yards of Heaven.

Here's something slightly related. When we were traveling in Ethiopia, an imaginary character named Flip Flea joined the trip. He joined us in Addis Ababa at the Grand Ghion Hotel and wrote postcards to my friends. Later, he sent postcards from Calcutta Airport describing what it was like inside of my boot, what we were doing, what he could hear us saying, what the weather was like.

The Aloe Press wanted to do a pamphlet of poems, so I gave them seven of the 250 *Fleas*. Originally, to make sure *Fleas* was completely uncensored, I had vowed never to publish it as a book, but I published ten stanzas in *Caterpillar* magazine and the pamphlet of seven that Aloe did. Now I've found that I do want people to see them or hear them. I read the last one-third of *Fleas* at a reading for the Poetry Center in San Francisco and they videotaped it.

MCALLISTER: The constellation structure of the poem wasn't something that you imposed on the poem while you were writing it?

MCCLURE: I had no choice. It was an exploration as I went. I began to see how memory was working, and how one sight would light up another, how they happened. It all seemed like a pinball machine: one part lights up another part, and then those three make the girl with the fishing rod light up on the boat on the way to Bermuda; and that means we get a free game which means that you get five more balls which light up another bunch of things. If you call that structure then that's structure, I guess. It was a wholly engaging experience writing it.

MCALLISTER: Is the way that *Fleas* came about similar to the way the rest of your poems are written? You talk about spontaneous composition somewhere, that you prepare for days to write a poem, and then you sit down and you write it, and that's the end of the writing—in some cases at least. The place that I'm thinking about is the description of writing *The Blossom*—an early play.

MCCLURE: I said that specifically in regard to the play. There are no changes in *Fleas* except some spelling errors I have corrected. I left many spelling errors and much mispunctuation because I wanted stanzas altered as little as possible and double meanings and slips left in. Videotape is a good medium for them. If it's a misspelled word and I want to read it a little differently, I can read it that way with my voice, and the punctuation doesn't matter a whit.

MCALLISTER: Then you read them with a pause in between the "Fleas," like in between the jumps, or do you just kind of go like your memory would take you?

MCCLURE: I was doing both. It was a lot to ask from an audience to follow me. The audience was sweet—they went with it. I asked afterwards how many people were able to follow brand names from my childhood, like Wing cigarettes and names of movie actresses like Carmen Miranda. They said they sensed what they were and they had correspondences of their own and they liked the whole thing. When you're reading something more than an hour long, you gauge it; sometimes you make pauses or you get a good run going, you run with it—I played with it. The reading was a benefit for Chilean refugees. I was to read with Fernando Alegria, who in the meantime had been called away to Mexico City to speak to Mrs. Allende, the widow of the assassinated President of Chile. Alegria left a film of himself reading.

MCALLISTER: Your poems are set up on the page like pictures generally. Do you have a method for setting up lines? Do you think of line as . . . what is it you said in *Rare Angel*? You say the poem tracks vertically on the page like ideograms.

MCCLURE: No. You're mixing what the two issues are for me. I have a number of reasons for breaking a line. Once I figured out seven reasons for breaking a line, all of which I do intuitively. I've done it so long that I never think of "why."

Since the poem is symmetrical—since it could be folded down the middle, and it is symmetrical on a vertical axis, it resembles a biological organism. You know, we picture flatworm, human being, mustang, whale—even a five-pointed star—as symmetrical. The stanzas (a stanza being a cluster of lines) are sub-beings of the organism, of the whole poem organism. A poem can be an overall organism, the direct extension of our biological selves in the sense that Jackson Pollock or Franz Kline imagined Abstract Expressionism to be a spiritual autobiography—an extension of their arm's energy leaving a trail of paint. I picture poems as being the same kind of extension. Projective verse, as Charles Olson conceived it, is a related form.

MCALLISTER: The mechanics of making a poem symmetrical—the printer can make any poem symmetrical simply by counting the letters.

MCCLURE: It was a style of printing in the nineteenth century. Also Dylan Thomas did it a lot, George Herbert did it a lot, and I do it usually. My centering the poems is not mechanical. That I center is not a mechanical choice on my part. When I write poems they are centered . . . they came out centered, and I seldom write any other way because I picture it as an organism as it happens. Here's a manuscript. You can see how centered it is, and it was written, you know, waking out of a sound sleep—I just woke up and wrote this out. Gregory Corso streaked us running naked across the stage when Allen Ginsberg and I read together in New York last week at St. Mark's Church. I woke up the next morning and reached for a pen and wrote this. I gave Corso a copy of it later.

FIRST POETRY STREAK

GREGORY CORSO
your naked
torso
is not a bore.
So
here you are
streaking
at St. Marx!
(You're even in good shape.)
We're larks
of prestige.
We're grapes
speeding past
at 50,000 miles per hour
with our noses
in the press.
The stars forget to dress
and they run naked
as an ape
or cherub
through all the old cathedrals.
Death to doldrums!
There goes mooning,
beamy beamy
Corso!

MCALLISTER: Did they turn out that way when you started writing? Was it a conscious choice to make them centered like that?

MCCLURE: It was a definite shift in my feeling; I remember with my body when it happened, I have the body remembrance of everything shifting over the middle.

It *may* have happened this way. I wrote a poem called "For the Death of 100 Whales" in 1954. First, I wrote it as a traditional ballad with 4-3-4-3 meter and with A-B-C-B rhymes. Then I broke it apart so it was a Cubist poem. Then, in the new shape it slid over to the middle and centered. In my first book, everything except one poem called

"Night Words: The Ravishing," which *should* stand out differently, was centered. Centering may have started with the whale poem.

MCALLISTER: Were you doing free verse then, when you wrote "For the Death of 100 Whales"?

MCCLURE: Yes. I wrote free verse in my early teens, and then in the first year of college. I practiced poetic forms and prosody and wrote Petrarchan sonnets in the style of Milton, vilanelles, and sestinas.

MCALLISTER: Was the movement back to the symmetrical form the point at which you moved back into free verse?

MCCLURE: No, it's not that simple. There were other things in be-tween, and I may have had other earlier poems centered, but I think it was with "For the Death of 100 Whales" that I felt the shift to center as being something other than a convention. I loved the beautiful way that Williams's late poems look on the page. I never liked endless poetry going down the left side of the page. I open those books, and all the lines are the same length and they go down the page with the same margin. It seems unnatural. I suppose some readers look at my poems and say, "This can't be real." But it's uncreaturely to have those rigid endless right and left margins. They fill up pages mercilessly.

MCALLISTER: Do you revise your poems?

MCCLURE: Lots of poems are spontaneous and unchanged; some are heavily revised and some are revised a shade, trying to get them to do what I feel would be the original impulse.

MCALLISTER: And there were no revisions on the ninety-nine beast language poems, *Ghost Tantras*?

MCCLURE: I don't remember any.

MCALLISTER: After you did the poems in beast language, the "Ghost Tantras," it became part of the vocabulary of your poetry—the language of those poems. When you use beast language in your poetry after the "Tantras," are you using it as a conscious addition to your language, or are you using it because of this same kind of spontaneous impulse? The description you gave in *Ghost Tantras* sounds like possession.

MCCLURE: No, it's almost as though beast language startles itself out of me after that. I didn't really care to pursue it any further, but "Ghost Tantras" are like a war—you can't completely end all of a sudden. Everybody thinks, "Now we've ended the Vietnamese War"—it's not true. It's going to take twenty years to end it. Everybody should have known that. The "Ghost Tantras" are like that, an intense and involved commitment, although I didn't know it when I was doing it. Not that it was done in frivolity, but I didn't know that it was going to be something that would fill me that much. And then afterwards, beast language did keep coming out. I started to translate Rimbaud's *A Season in Hell* into beast language, and I wrote a short story in the form of a long roar in beast language, which is many pages long. One single roar. Earlier in about 1960, I wrote my play *¡The Feast!* in beast language. I've written small things in beast language but I don't have copies. They were poems for people, valentines, things like that.

MCALLISTER: Your poems in *The Sermons of Jean Harlow and The Curses of Billy the Kid* come later than *The Beard*, don't they?

MCCLURE: Yes. I thought I was through with Billy the Kid and Jean Harlow, and then they came back in the middle of the night, and they wouldn't go away until I'd write. It was almost against my will.

MCALLISTER: The first thing about Harlow is the "Meat Science" essay, and the first thing on Billy the Kid is your early play, *The Blossom*.

MCCLURE: Yes.

MCALLISTER: Of all the possible people to pick, how did you wind up with Billy the Kid?

MCCLURE: Well, if I tell you the framework that I see him in, you'll understand. In the play *The Blossom*, the Kid is the prophet of death; he's a mystic of death. It's as if he sees over the edge of the nineteenth century into this century and sees the rapine here; it's as if he's the tiniest hint then of what's to come now. There's still some honor and some meaning in what he's doing because it's a revenge slaying, you know, for a friend's honor. But the manner of it and the brutality of it and the numbers killed, and the style, is like a preview of the twentieth century. What he's doing is still beautiful, still is auric. That makes him like a visionary for the future. I think maybe we, meaning people like Allen Ginsberg and myself and Gary Snyder, were in a visionary position in '56 and '57, seeing into the now. I'm not very surprised, you know, by anything that's happened. I guess looking at the Korean War (I grew up with World War II and Korea happening) none of this surprises me a bit. What we're going through is a natural outgrowth of Korea as much as Korea was an outgrowth of what preceded it. All of us may have had the same relation to the present that Billy the Kid had to the twentieth century. We may have felt like we were looking over the horizon with rather visionary eyes. Also, we wanted to liberate ourselves and to escape. Some of the Kid's great acts were escapes. He made one jailbreak that was incredible. He did some amazing things—he was a physical genius.

MCALLISTER: I guess the thing that makes Billy the Kid seem so strange is that you, and you've added Ginsberg and Snyder now, the bunch of you seem like such gentle people. The two times I've heard you read, I hear people muttering, "That can't be Michael McClure." They expect a wild man. And with Billy the Kid again—this gentleness and the terrible violence of the poems. It's not that you and Ginsberg and Snyder are mellow people or anything like that but that there seems to be a schism of some kind between you—I'll say ethics for the time being—your ethic of poetry, and the ethic you seem to be living by.

MCCLURE: I've changed a bit.

MCALLISTER: Well, the violence in the long poem *Rare Angel* is in the killing of a giant ground sloth . . .

MCCLURE: The killing of the giant ground sloth was something I had no control over in the poem. I felt it was developed too poorly in the poem. I said this must be more clear, this has got to come forward in some big straight and clear rosy scene where it's understood that this is a strand of the poem. I took the manuscript of *Rare Angel* to Robert Duncan. He told me, "You can't determine the laws of that poem; it's got its own laws." And I said, "You're absolutely right. I brought it over here to hear you say that."

We live in the midst of flaring violence. I feel a great desire for liberation which I once confused with violence, and I'm more liberated now. With the liberation a lot of desire for violence dissipated. As I saw the world around me go crazy, more and more violent, I saw my own liberation grow in an entirely different way. I think my life is an interesting life historically—as any of our lives are interesting historically—because of the transition that is taking place. In my case there is the disintegrated personality seeking violence as liberation, then that need for violence dissipating, while the violence around grows so abundantly. Sometimes it's practically incandescent. It doesn't look incandescent out there beyond the window in the snow, I'll admit. But the civilization we're living in is incandescent and *that's* what I'm saying in *Rare Angel*. I realized just the other day that *Rare Angel* is not just passively recounting a vision to you. *Rare Angel* goes out there and smears itself over everything to show you what the vision is in case you missed it . . . *Rare Angel* is a vision projector.

MCALLISTER: Would you like to talk about the difference between a theatrical event and a poetry reading event? You see them as different things just as poetry and theater are different things?

MCCLURE: Theater is a play. A play is a special kind of organism. A play is an organism in which the author is the DNA, the director is the RNA, the actors are the proteins, and the limits of the play form a cell membrane, and what goes on within makes the endoplasmic reticulum of the play, and the streaming of the cytoplasm within it.

A poetry reading is a man standing up repeating for an audience the organic extensions of himself, which have subtle and beautiful interplays within themselves, but do not form a single coherent organism for the same purpose as theater.

MCALLISTER: When you write poems do you see them as visual experiences?

MCCLURE: Yes, as well as audial.

MCALLISTER: Do you think you are likely to do poems simply as an oral thing rather than writing things? Have you ever experimented with that?

MCCLURE: I have. I composed poetry into a tape machine and it didn't work well for me. I think that if I wanted to spend the time involving myself in it I would have success. I have gone in directions that have more desirable payload for me. I've learned the autoharp so I could find more music and get more rhymes into my poetry, more of a song quality into what I was doing. I don't think if I composed directly by sound or tape that it would be much different from what I do with a pen or typewriter. And so there's not much challenge to explore in that direction. My style is to use all the styles I can invent, and that way I can express given muscular feelings that I call thoughts in as many ways as possible.

MCALLISTER: How did *The Blossom* come to be dedicated to singer Jim Morrison?

MCCLURE: Jim wanted to get a theater in L.A.; several times he negotiated for one. *The Blossom* is a kind of compressed Elizabethan revenge tragedy—yet also something like Nōh drama. When writing it, I was trying to formulate a play in which the sensation of Yūgen was emanated. So it was only right that I dedicated it to Jim. Jim had Yūgen; he had clear brightness.

MCALLISTER: Do you want to talk about *Rare Angel* now?

McCLURE: Yes, you asked me about "tracking vertically," as I said in the introduction to the poem.

McALLISTER: Yeah, the line in the introduction to the poem is something like . . . "the poem tracks vertically on the page." What I wanted to ask you is how do you determine the lines, and what do you mean by tracking?

McCLURE: Oh. I have to cut back a little bit before that so I can give you the answer to those. The poem started with my understanding that many biologists believe that we think with body sensations. Einstein apparently believed he thought with bodily sensations also. So I thought, "Ah, now if I write a poem directly from these sensations, if I write with the body sensations without trying to give them predestined subject matter, but only write only what my body sensations immediately become as I type, then that will be new." Then I decided to make the stanza a full $8^1/_2 \times 11$ inch page so that there wouldn't be an issue of determining the length of the stanza. I would just go from the top to the bottom of the page and write out words as my body sensations created them. Of course, the poem *does* begin to form its own tracks. Nothing's perfect—one can't just have an abstract poem; it begins to make its own laws, demands and creates stories, and they repeat and recur, and take on a being of their own from their own selves. So the poem begins to come out of the substrate of itself, forming a murder of the giant ground-sloth by palaeo-Americans at a waterhole, and shaping the Dantean imagery near the end—with the island of Okinawa floating overall. You have the substrate of the body, the substrate of the poem, creating its own materials and surfaces; but I remain true to the idea of writing from muscle and sensation. *Rare Angel* seems really Asian, not anything in subject matter or appearance, but *linguistically*.

McALLISTER: The physical act of reading?

McCLURE: Right. It's a projected vision . . . It projected what was inside of me outside on to everything around me. I don't think I've ever written anything like it and it has become a model for me.

Drug Notes

I. PEYOTE

Cleaning the buttons is a wild experience.

You twist the knife point at the center of the dried disc of cactus. Suddenly blond silky fur begins to roil from the knife tip. Curls and twists of it fall to the table top. The fur comes out yellow-brown where it is old and dirty, and then the newly uncovered silvery locks tumble out from the heart of the button. (In among the strands are tiny seeds where once there was a white-pink blossom like a daisy.) Next the gray tufts circling the center of the button are picked off. Then you eat the cactus flesh.[1]

A mystery of the organic is cast like a benign shadow on the experience to come.

After eating the buttons there usually are two hours of nausea and malaise that precede the high. Peyote smells like a dead wet dog on a cool morning. The taste is not sweet, sour, bitter or salty, but something else—the taste of the universe. The taste is disgusting, frightening, curious, acrid, intriguing, and nauseating. The taste and malaise are enough to dissuade most persons from repeated experimenting. Peyote is non-addictive. As the high comes on, the world of your senses skitters, tilts, and opens to sizeless actuality.

The experience of peyote-high is a physical adventure. It is like climbing a Himalayan mountain. There is a vastness and timeless triumph. Because the peyote high is a *stress drama*, a stress situation, it changes our sight, feeling and thinking. Time ceases to exist. In moments of great tension or stress as the mystics know it, the elaborate and artificial structure of time dissolves and they make contact. Space becomes a *hall of glory* containing casually and invisibly what was once the monumental reality Time. You stand on the snowy summit or the

These "notes" originally appeared in *Meat Science Essays* (San Francisco: City Lights, 1964).

warm steppes of a vision. You have the view of a colossus or a tiny creature of love.

There can be a bad experience of extreme fright and demon-seeing. The baleful and threatening air and Bardo demons of Tibetan mythology come to life. The sight of space and stark reality become vertigo. The feeling of spirituality becomes horror. The air fills with threats and cliffs and chasms darkly opening and closing. Trees loom into unrecognizable living technicolor towers of twisted and sparkling hatred. There is no time and so no conceivable end to the horror. There is no place to run for all is limitless—a voice becomes a tortured concerto of mysterious evil—sounds are hideous music—the sky is orange! This is accompanied by great intellectual and emotional pain—but it is without the anguish that accompanies normal pain. A bad experience is not harmful and need not be feared. It acts as a catharsis.

Usually the peyote high is great. Everyone should think, though, about repeated and extensive use of peyote—it can cause, depending on flesh and temperament, an almost unending estrangement and alienation and ceaseless visions of nearly unendurable nature. You can spend days or months afterwards walking numbly and sitting in a room watching the play of lights upon woodwork.

The high is caused by a number of alkaloids. The most understood and experimented with is mescaline. (A mescaline high is not a peyote high but a specialized high of one alkaloid. Mescaline has been used in psychotherapy but the result is not satisfactory. Rather than temporarily breaking down personality so the patient is more accessible to the therapist it reinforces the personality as peyote does. Mescaline has fewer grossly physical effects, less nausea. It is more psychic and spiritual and more dreamy than peyote.)

Peyote affects the cellular level of the body. Also it acts on a larger morphological level. It stimulates the nervous systems and jars them to a greater receptivity of impressions and more free transmission of impulses. In addition it acts directly on the sense centers of eyes, ears, touch, etc. It works on the syndromes of physical interior self-perception in throat and stomach and other areas of physical energy that are not centered in specific organs (as known by Kundalini Yogis).

In the midst of the euphoria of sensory excitement the stomach or solar plexus can become *consciousnesses* themselves. Then there is an additional euphoria of the liberated half-beings of ourselves.

Peyote acts on the most minute of nervous-biological arrangements. It temporarily straightens synaptic chains of memories and confusions and our cyclical repeatings of thoughts and feelings—the hang-ups. It creates a revolt against habitual ways of feeling and action and frees us to make direct gestures—we walk straight to our desires without the memories of past failures and denials making a negative cloud of interference. The hand reaches and takes. But there is only desire for necessities.

The smoke of our interior meanings lies on all things. It covers in hazes and wisps that we are not conscious of seeing. Peyote clears all this away and gives the joy of seeing with bright eyesight and ears. When the tendrils are blown away the sight of a graceful pitcher and blue cups on an oilcloth covered table is stark as a vision.

To really see perspective again, suddenly and without a veil, as it truly is, is an illumination. As it is normally is WRONG! Perspective drifts and flows and is more horizontal than we know. We have learned to see by a code first invented by Michelangelo and Da Vinci. And to see colors leap into ten trillion unexpected glows and fires and radiances to see the sharp edges of definition upon all material things, and all things radiating chill or warm light—is to know that you've lived denying and dimly sensing reality through a haze. All things beam inner light and color like a pearl or shell. All men are strange beast-animals with their mysterious histories upon their faces and they stare outward from the walls of their skin—their hair is fur—secretly far beneath, they are simply animals and know it. Far far underneath the actions they make, their animal actions are still being performed as they walk and smile—and each one so different! There are old wolf men and young fox kings and otter women. They have totems that they do not know. Buildings lean and shake and tremble and the movement of a cloud before the sun changes the colors of air. Dark spaces are secrets. Light is eternity. Breathing is music made in space and it looms like a physical object. Creakings and rustlings are Nōh plays. Walls are partitions of space in vast eternity. The crisp edge and light on all things is real and true. Colors are all bright and new in Timelessness.

In the high there are periods when fantasies of great mental weight may be entered into or passed by. A parade of the history of unknown Romes with emperors, and gladiators, and goddesses raising bare arms pass by over your lap with minute sweetness. There are moments of estrangement and coldness when all is strange and unpleasant. Timelessness becomes irreality and nothing exists except the stasis of your loaded senses staring at a scene of meaningless despair. But mostly there is the sureness of looking down on real solid brilliant fact.

Descriptions of the physical appearance of the high man or woman—with reddened face and thin cheeks and lips like an Indian's (this contraction and stiffening of the face is a symptom of peyote intoxication)—and the descriptions of new images of reality, the brain-movies and visions, the oddities of sight and sense as the high comes on or ends, have all been recorded by experimenters. It is all an individual experience of the last degree. With closed eyes I saw the cathedral of the Behemoths—a golden lion the size of a continent rose over the arched door. Vultures the size of seas drifted in the air. There are visions of technicolor geometry of the cosmos radiating and flaring and fluxing. There are visionary trips to real and imagined islands. There are comic visions like kaleidoscope cartoons. White hands speak to you in sign language on a screen of black velvet. Voices echo prophecies in your ears. These brain-movies are endless—all there is to do is close your eyes. Sometimes there are open-eye hallucinations of power and glory, with monster projections spiritual truths . . . meaningful ospreys and dragons.

The greatest importance of peyote is that it is a spirit experiment beyond conception. There is no objective wisdom to be drawn from peyote though biochemistry shall probably finally treat men with some of these alkaloids. The experiences are not relative but unique and individual and concerned with clarified reality and our freedom in it.

The dissolving of Time and the cosmic super-reality of Space's vast breathing is a vision beyond value for men who can be conscious of Space for only moments in normal lives of earthly seeking.

In the high it is impossible to lie to one's self and simultaneously impossible to be self-critical. All lies and hidden desires of others are apparent. There can be no falseness in such a primal state. Peyote reinforces the personality of the high man and makes positive all definite free knowledge and good aspirations. The high comes upon objective reality as a unity. The new unity is there for man to press himself against anew. It is a challenge that is a love. All is clarified into true clarity or left standing in the mystery of an essential mystery.

Each taking of peyote is a new order and is unrelated to the previous high except by sequence and the resemblance of the sharp feelings and vision. Carrying on a search for understanding from one high to the next is unlikely. But the highs build into a totality.

In an old notebook I find:

> I have just been high on peyote for the second time. It was a miserable high of beauty. An esthetic high. Things were as beautiful as bop. I had intended to meet the Dragon of Space, to visualize him. Instead I was only a lion wandering in the mouth of the Dragon. A lovely thing, but a failure. I took twice the number of buttons that I took on my first high but I was unable to cope with them. I vomited like the Indians. I got the whim-whams—no sense trying to describe them. My mouth ran saliva like a fountain. The tears flowed from my eyes. The buttons poured from me. My face was scarlet, eyes swollen shut. After that it was sickness and high. I was left with the beautiful vision of peyote but not the consciousness of space or eradication of time. Also sounds were like strange music.
>
> The Dragon of Space is the consciousness of Space. Who can explain it? To know space extends gray and without mercy in all directions forever. Without mercy does not mean cruel. . . .

Lovers are left with the need to explain and pursue the appearance of nature, time, and space. You see them as you have always secretly known them to be . . . or as you have seen them in moments of rare sharpness. Nature seen with truer eyes is never again easily taken for granted. A delving into each factuality of being occurs after peyote. (You chase the shadows of simplicity and the everyday twistings and intricacies of sense from the normal.) The accepted blacks and whites of thought and understanding are abandoned. Nothing is taken for granted. Once *high* there is a change forever. The moves of lights and colors upon objects are tested. What are they? *How* are they? The meaning of being a beast and spirit in a universe of objects is constantly at test. No casual or causal laws are accepted so easily after the high.

For some in the high there is a glimpse of a final strangeness and alienation—a complete true sane madness. It is a glimpse seen by many men many times. Physicians who believe mental illness is a disease and not a struggle of the soul and spirit in threat of dissolving are wrong. A man who has seen complete cold fiery-colored emptiness with all of the flashes of lights and radiances and solids in its splendor of shallow chill hollowness carries the sight forever. He cherishes what he can create beyond the emptiness, and he puts what he can into that emptiness to warm it. Finally, perhaps, a deep enough measure of wisdom may come over him so he can love what was always there before his discovery. Perhaps then he may love the things that preceded in existence the new works of his hand and brain.

(I mean to say: A man who has discovered a cold, bare universe may begin to warm it, as an artist does the world, and when a man has made enough warmth, or art, he may love again the warm things that preceded his discovery of iciness. But he cannot love till he creates warmth enough to feel the old loves.)

Coming upon a sharp and perfect sight of reality a grail-search to explain it must begin. The old long standing spirit laws of morals, art, and science are destroyed. New or older laws that are found to be true are reinstated. Reality is not as it seemed! The old truths found out to be falsehoods are abandoned till perhaps they are true again (if ever)! What does it mean if Time can cease to exist? What does it mean that we have bound up our senses and that man is a beast of the infinite?

The complexity and richness of peyote dissolves the preconceptions of those who take it. All gratuitous choices, such as taking peyote, are a risk for that is part of life. The risk is that of giving up warm preconceptions for a cold unknown where all must be made anew. I went farther into life and matter than I knew. But it was all truly an extension and intensification of the way I was already going. Later I found fear, horror, and self-blockading but it was of a nature I would have come against regardless—and it is without regret. PRAISE to all things that bring closeness to the Universe!

GAAHHHHHHHH!

Normally mankind sees vibrations and projections of himself on all things. He views through a smoky mist of spiritually, physically, emotionally, tortured and twisted screens.

The screens, the clouds, are actually thrown into the air and they accumulate. They exist in the nervous connections of the brain and centers of sense throughout the whole body. Peyote draws the projections back to the interior beneath our skins and they dissolve and leave the world vivid. (Once they are cleared away there can be no doubt we literally project them.) Even seated before a table—the silverware, an ashtray, a candle, are a thicket of our fears, past relations, and the suppressed and unfulfilled half-desires that they call to mind. No wonder peyote causes you to go out and to walk with freedom. If the simplicity of a domestic scene is a miniature of oppression, what must the world be? To walk a hundred yards in total freedom is to live forever in eternity—freedom for an instant is beyond measure and is immortality. Huge and free.

Actions begin to follow immediate channels untempered by internal confusions. We see and feel what is happening! A walk from room to room is a thousand-year journey of depth and breadth, not a passage in one dimension. The eye, intellect, imagination, and emotions are free to see Space, and Space is there!

Murkiness is a habit. All ideas of science and poetry may be checked against sensory truth. All men can experience truths and judge them. Anguishes holding back clarity disappear when Time dissolves. All things exist in space alone and there is not grief of mortality or consciousness of life's transcience.

Sharp divisions between inert and organic disappear. A spectrum and flow of intensities of spirit and life-meanings is visible. The life in "inert" things is seen and the "death" in organic things is visible. Falsities tremble and there is esthetic shaking and rapture. The possibilities of Love disappear and become reshaped and re-evident. This can take place in a single high or in a course of years following peyote. Engagement with the world and air and breath become possible to any man after peyote. I know that insects are truly BEASTS and individuals, and I always knew it. How fresh and real the knowledge returned. The understanding sharpened more than ever before. Always I had known of the life of plants—BUT THE ROSE!! And to see the cold space between myself and men and women—and not to lie of the sight! Oh yes it is there. . . !

AHH, I'LL GO NO FARTHER!

BUT YES, I will. . . . Combined with the religious rapture and reveries of great expansion and supersight and hyper-benevolence, there is the eradication of the *thought of the object* that rises between the sight of the object and its meaning to the man who sees and touches. The object, the spoon, is exactly what it is, no more nor less to hand and eye. It gleams! There is religiousness—no other word names the height of human feeling that includes the personal and quiet active ecstasy of being a cohesive and singular being within all. There is no barrier between you and what you sense. There is no thought of a spoon. It exists in its most primeval, barest and most vibrant spirit state. It is there to be used, seen, touched or not. There are no inversions of desires—but only the immediate: thirst and hunger and their satisfactions. Water in the mouth is an Ocean moving in the cave of the Universe. We live in a void and we carry the void with us—it is an emptiness that we fill with the traces of our gestures. We warm it and enlarge it or it darkens and closes upon us!

Previously formed hierarchies called *levels of being*, made for convenience in mortal life, pass into nothingness. They turn on their heads and flow one into another and they cease.

It is a titanic state where ideas of proportion and measurement sometimes bringing misery in company with convenience, are gone. (Can real Science be measurement? Or can measurement be real Science or Art?)

One may walk quietly without shades of self-criticism or fear of emotions like gratitude or humility. Not that gratitude or humility are necessarily false—but there is no threat of them to cast a blight on primal simplicity.

All real things are instant and available. No explanations are needed. All things and emotions are completely themselves alone. It is the view of Herakleitos the philosopher—and it is more too. It goes further than Herakleitos. He could see the melting of all things but not the *blessing* of the flow. He could only see the flow was cold and hot and wet and dry—*but we know so little of what he thought!*

It is the first and last atheist view. This state is triumph of the real coming through the senses. It is a divorce of man from the cast solidity of life and it gives him a chance again that he may marry the life of his days—but as a wedding of his choice.

Divorce

Vision

Blessing

II. HEROIN: A CHERUB'S TALE (FOR MICHAEL LEWIS)

Heroin is a mild thing. After shooting it I can barely imagine what draws a man to addiction. But many find it answers needs locked in their muscles and genes. Some junkies seem to have a family weakness or an inherited masochistic genius that leads them to love of heroin. The weakness could be a strength if there were no heroin.

The flash is a tremendous experience—a great physical cloudy blast in the body—particularly in the head, arms, and chest. It is a sensation of great warmth and swelling. Then there is a swift convulsion of the muscles, and sometimes vomiting that clears away to the pleasantness.

The flash, for me, was not good. A big experience, but not one to seek out. The moment after sent me to write a poem . . . the poem was written and the moment was gone. (Ahh, but wait. The needle came out—I thought I was suffocating and leaned on a table. My chest contracted and expanded, my stomach turned and stopped. Was I dying? Was a huge globe of air in my heart? I had seen bubbles as large as coffee tables go up the fine spike—was I dead? With fear-of-death and with hope I looked into my compadre's face. He laughed at me.) Ever after heroin there is a warmth in the chest that lights up at mention of it.

After the burst of pleasure, a feeling of liberation and bodily expansion, there comes a new state, an aftermath. That is the high.

There is no combat with circumstances or events—no boredom or intensity. Sitting on a bed or a trip are the same. There is quiescence even while moving; there is an inviolable stillness of person. You are a warm living stone. In a fast open car you are a herculean vegetable— the wind on your face is a pleasant hand. You half-nod at the passing of scenery. Eating and drinking are the same but without interest. You can feel yourself exist in a place or activity but without feeling of responsibility. There is nothing to drag you. You have *occurred*.

A new kind of self takes over—there is not so much *I*. I is an interference with near-passivity. This is a full large life—there is not much criticism, anything fills it. Rugs are as interesting as a street.

Whatever is spoken is as meaningful as any other speech. Life and colors had a distracting sharpness before. You are glad they are toned down, you make a study of yourself and nod on the passage of occurrences—everything is smooth and of the same emotional weight. New correspondences are made, unusual things link with the common ones. There is time to study a face—thoughts are traced on it that you had not seen before. Suddenly you understand an old friend. Time does not bother, painful thoughts are fluffed like a pillow. A hand seems larger while you study it—it has details! Comparing the high to normality, you ask where the daily pains are; they are curious. You sort through them wondering why they are problems. They look different and easy. You take them apart and put them together in new ways— you find a few answers. Eyes and thoughts drift to something else. You go somewhere or you sit. You notice coincidences.

Everything that was held back burst out with the flash and not much is left except a kind of easiness. Life is an unruffled flow of the disrelated. If it bothers, you don't think about it.

Sniffing heroin is different. There is meaning to the popular confusion of narcotics and sexuality.

Usually before sexual pleasure we defy the universe and the world. We are swollen and tense with the apparent necessities of life. Often we live in a pervasive anger. Sex sweeps away the defiance and, after sex, in brief but unmeasurable moments there is a universality. There is a realization of tenderness and completedness. Love has been given and garnered . . . body and senses relax into new receptivity. There is a willingness to see and listen and to be heard and touched. Our imaginations drift in the darkness—or into sleep. Or we stand up and move, feeling freedom and ease. The bed in darkness is a throne. Predisposed tensions are eased. The still coolness of the world is a quiet adventure.

The pleasure of sniffed heroin is like those moments but more elusive. (How great it must be for those who can't fuck.) It is nearly the same beauty. The high resembles a state of bliss. Both dissolve tight definitions of beauty and allow due and honor to be paid to everything. New ideas and meanings enter. Perhaps this is the *flash* in slow motion. As the pains slip out the new possibilities enter.

There are previously unseen quantities and qualities of life, new perceptions of the daily real and of the body. They are almost indefinable. A loosening of ways of thinking and the visible beauties that things have when we are relaxed. The taste and sounds of things are more gentle and full and the mind weaves trails around the senses. Meanings of the visible are slightly enlarged. In the happiness water may taste like a liqueur—for an instant there is liqueur in the glass! Then it is water again—*how good water is!* Is the matchflame a castle? How solid and still the room is. People talk to you and notice you— they smile and speak.

The common things are sometimes wild. It can do no harm to know them. We bring back awareness with us after sex and after the high. They both open us.

Awareness springs when desires are conceived of and when they are satisfied—and sometimes through the use of drugs.

Satisfaction brings rest and better functioning of the life processes. Heroin gives momentary satisfaction. Conception of desires brings a rush of energy to fill them. Heroin gives you some liberty of imagination and rest to conceive with.

Heroin brings a small physical satisfaction. Even if it is mild, it is unique and true. It brings some rest and if it is not great blissful wholeness-making rest, it is a step toward it. Heroin can light the dullness of life and show there is no drabness except the one we make internally. Outside things are as they have been always—ready to be seen with interest.

It could help bring some self-damned men back to their *senses*. (It could only *help*.) Opium was used in treatment of the insane. Like wheat or air, heroin is an existent combination of chemicals. It should have exactly that importance. Heroin should be judged by individual experience of it.

Heroin experiences can be memorable if they come in time of need and lend strength or ease. With sniffed heroin there are two states of high. The first follows the sniffing immediately and lasts from two to four hours. That is the state I've just described—like the high after injected heroin, it is subtle. It can be lost or forgotten if necessary duties impose. The high has to be guarded and held to—it does not overcome you or sweep you away to another earth. The world seems to be in a state of calm excitement. The intellect fastens on to the immediate and sees *into* happenings and makes expansions. There is an edge of clearness. Relaxation settles upon everything like a soft cotton blanket. Decisions are keen and amiable—though if the man high is bothered he may become angry. He wants to hold on to the high.

The second state can come the next day, evening, or after a long period of calmness and rest. It is an even larger relaxation, a good languor—spirit condition becomes keen and there is a restful laziness. It is a definite state. You are making some piercing of apparent reality. New nameless emotions happen and unseen sights come. Reality has a welcome weirdness and is fresh.

On a ship in Hong Kong after sniffing heroin, large profiles of statesmen of eternity appeared. They were benign and sizeless. Strength and beauty dripped from them. The silhouettes of darkness and color gazed at me from their warmth and made a soundless blessing. They smiled quietly with foreign but humane wisdom. I had believed that death by the atomic bomb was at hand and I was seeking some answer in mystic beauty. I was seeking some immortal evasion of death. The smile of the profiles was a strange answer—and I needed it.

Another time with eyes closed. I saw torsos and bodies twisting in air and turning out from me over my brows. Words of great meaning were spelled out before my eyes and rosy lambs moved their legs in darkness. It happened that it was a message of moment and I responded to it in life.

A fear of life that is the beginning of insanity is man's damnation of his internal energies by the part of him that is inert and unfeeling. Sexuality and spirit struggles are at the base of fear. Society will not be confronted with natural desires and hiding them causes a violation and a horror.

The unreleasable energies become more terrible. Men find less and less time to rest, and awareness of complexities grows. Heroin might bring moments of rest to the insane or about-to-become insane.

Heroin is only of importance when men are aided by it or when they suffer from addiction to it. Anything that creates an awareness of the depth and breadth of reality constructs an urge for reality. A man bound up in fear and sickness believes reality is tiny and closes in upon him. Drugs make a brief time when what is "narrow and constrictive" can be seen afresh. With luck a new view can be brought back to life and untie the binding.

Censorships are instigations of a bigoted and violent few who distrust mankind. Once cruel legislations are begun they grow blindly and lend power to those behind them. Making discovery of a cure a devotion, rather than persecution of addicts, would end all threat of narcotics.

The answer to drugs is cure for addiction—but addiction is damned and kept a mystery by any who can use it as a mystery. Narcotics authorities do not desire cures. The intellectually perverse do not desire cures.

A true warning system regarding addiction could be established till there is a cure—but it would be useless until the truths of narcotics are admitted.

Glimpses of reality should be open to all men. Gropings for power made by wringing the bodies and spirits of the uninformed should be exposed. A crack of light must be made. There should be no lie. There is no need for torture. I should not have recourse to heroin if it were legal or illegal, but there must be no blurs or confusions . . .

There should be no mystiques of language, drugs, or sex, or . . . !

III. COCAINE

Cocaine is an *ace of sunlight* that can be snuffed through the nostrils into the brain. For days it lightens the black interiors of the body and lends an ivory cast of sleekness and luminosity to the senses.

I had come from Walden Pond to New York City. In my hand was a new book of mine pressing an oak leaf from a branch above Thoreau's hearth. In the dim apartment a friend poured water out of a bronze vial onto my head. The water was from the Ganges. The cold oily rivulets trickled in streams through my hair, and over my eyes, and down my neck. I was joyful, it was three o'clock in the morning, hot July, in New York City. Perhaps the river water and Thoreau *alone* could have made me divinely high. The cocaine was powdered. (It comes in crystals and must be pulverized.) The mound of powder lay on a round hand mirror so none of it would be lost—even the tiniest grain shows on a mirror. It is so pure a white that it reflects tiny prisms of color. The little circular heap was flattened and divided into triangles. The Ganges still trickled over my scalp as we sniffed the cocaine through short pieces of drinking straw. Each one carefully sniffs a slice of the powder. It is medicinal and acrid. The mucous membrane immediately numbs where it touches—tongue, lip, nose burn for an instant and lose sensation. It takes five minutes to act. The darkness in skull and gut lights up. The cocaine dissolves and slips in moisture to the back of the throat. It burns, then numbs, then cools and leaves a harsh sweet taste. As the high comes, there is a flurry of excitement and speaking and laughter; eyes are bright and clear. It is erotically stimulating. There is friendliness and creativity.

For a week I passed through many states of emotion and intellect. All, all was reality. In the dark of morning by the East River I saw new nature made anew—as in any redwood forest of the West. The city becomes nature. The streets of the Lower East Side are pastoral and simple fields of summer haze. Minstrel children and shepherds moved among concrete and cars. Grimy barges and ancient factories leaned into eternity. If it shall be our nature to live this way we must know that Nature is here in a strange garment. Old nature and new blend together into virtue of meaning that we only begin to see. As we realize and feel the depth of it we shall rebel. But see the clarity of its passage! We need not live this way without eyes for it!

Color is enormously vivid. Simple things become elfin still-lifes. A small green plant is the living forest of its leaves, and trunks, and microscopic blossoms. The scent of the moist earth beneath it is a world of scents. The clarity of sounds is scary. There are reverberations and timbres with all sounds. Pallid pinks, blues and blue grays, the faded paper scraps and heaps of twisted and random rubbish are stark and cold or warm. They work themselves into a vast shifting work of art; men move in it creating it and leave to continue. The wind works it. The seasons toil upon it. The work of art manifests itself in islands that are not related. Space and Time are different. But it is all part of one melodious totality. Disjointed and sharp but always warm or cool—

it is alien, but humanly alien, close to human understanding, just a slight step beyond it. A green bar of soap with rusty granules is a monumental landscape—there are tiny blues and scarlets in the rust. It is lighted with the light of a tiny universe as the plants are, and as the sounds are. A vibrancy hovers over crimsons. There is intense excitement. Objects and acts still you to feelings. We are characters in a great drama, a romance where the tension of personality is an athletic absolute. A room is a large lighted chamber, truthful in its meanings. A glance to a white ceiling is a book of wonders. All things are perfect. You look for warm colors and tiny objects—they reward you. Everything has luminosity and intent.

Freud was an early experimenter with cocaine. After his initial rapture with it he denounced it. It is reputed to be addictive psychologically if not physically. The first time I took it I felt an addictive draw; after that I felt none. It is too hard to find to become addictive. The high is not supposed to last long but I found it continued for a day or two always. The high is easy to lose—though you can concentrate on it and pick it up again. With a needle the high probably goes out quicker. Anyone thinking the high is the initial burst of pleasurable energy would find it to be of short length. It brings excitement and spaciousness.

IV. THE MUSHROOM

The mushroom high isn't like any other. All of the hallucinogens—peyote or mescaline, LSD, and psilocybin (the Mexican mushroom)—lift you to an Olympian universe. Everything is timeless, huge, and bright and you're free to walk in it and do what you want to do. Each of the highs is a different continent in the Olympian universe.

Peyote takes you to lands of religiosity and physical matter—you study the physics of light and shade, and matter and space, and color and blackness, and hot and cold. LSD takes you to another place where you encounter deep psychological mysteries and revelations and mysticism. The mushroom is different. In some ways it is more beautiful than peyote. It opens you up so that you feel internally deep inside, and all around you, the utterly human and humane.

People are the main thing with the mushroom. A friend who was high cried: "My God, I am a temple !" Then he began talking about

Dutch painting and telling me Dutch women have little stoves of warmth inside them like the paintings do. At moments during the high you believe that everything is prearranged for you to see. The strangest, most grotesque, and most glorious people on earth are selected and paraded in front of you. It's one of the most elevated comic dramas ever seen. All is both comic *funny* and "comedy" in the sense that Dante wrote *The Divine Comedy*. You laugh and weep staring at the faces and bodies and weird costumes and godliness and beastliness of mankind.

A Charlie Parker lp is playing south-of-the-border pieces . . . I remember a woman I saw passing when I'd taken the mushroom. We were sitting in an outdoor restaurant in North Beach sipping at big crystal glasses of cold wine. We had just had an amazing conversation. My friend told me about a mushroom session he had with people I knew in a faraway city. As he told the story I was there with them. I experienced the beings of each person—one of them during the high had changed into a giant Santa Claus and another had become an Indian chief worrying at the problems of the world. The man telling me had mentally travelled into the future through wars and blackness, and, then new light, and finally to the last crusty day when the earth was a cold cinder. (I was heartsick to hear that there would be more wars.) While he told me the story and about his time-trip I watched him right in front of my eyes turn into a French-Canadian trapper, then a politician, and at last into a great visionary whose eyes were unexplored planets rolling in the sockets of his skull while a lock of Byronic hair drooped onto his brow. I think he glimpsed into the future again as he told me about it. I wanted him to tell me more . . .

But back to the woman. As we left the cave-like void of the restaurant we stopped stone still at the sight of her. Her hips were swinging to some soundless and immortal Parker-like melody that only she could hear. She shook her shoulders and breasts. She shimmied and shook. Her walk was a moving flow of basic sexuality. Seeing her I understood the whole thing—what she was doing and why she did it that way. I knew the biological rhythms, the social causes, the karma, the predispositions, and the final outcome of the strange sex dance that she called walking. It was too much. It was great, *great* in the sense the word can be used to describe immortal works of art, nature, or children and women. Her walking was a work of personal art in moving sculpture of flesh—just as Mozart is a motion in sound waves. It was her piece and she was living it, and she still is somewhere. I was knocked out by HER. She stood out perfectly and solely. Everyone came through to me that way. They showed what they were physically and spiritually—it is all one thing.

Half of the restaurant is under a marquee in the fresh air. The frontmost tables are in the sunlight and flood out over the sidewalk. The other half is a shadowy cave of bricabrac, plaster, and painted concrete. Small ornamental fig trees grow in front. As we sipped the wine (you don't drink much—only for the pleasure of the cold wine) I studied a tree moving in the wind like an animal-creature created out of emerald and bark. The tree was a symbol of perfect love and a bridge between the organic and inert world.

I was so deep in euphoria that my eyes pressed tightly closed with pleasure—wind-pleasure, sun-pleasure, air-pleasure, human-pleasure. It was so intense that I could not turn to look at the people behind me in the dark pit indoors. Now and then I would sneak a quick look from the corner of my eye. What I saw would break me up in gales of laughter or bring me to tears, or both. I saw PEOPLE'S FACES as they can only be seen with the mushroom, and more than that I saw their hands, and bodies, and their clothing!

It was the first day of the world's creation and ten trillion billion years old, bright, shadowless, and fresh and gleaming: an Oriental city as huggable as a teddy bear is to a child. A dazzling shiplike convertible pulled up to the fig tree. It backed up with infinite grace and deliberation and stopped exactly and perfectly illegally in front of the fireplug. Three strange animals stepped out. The seediest, most grotesque and most beautiful I had ever seen.

A skinny weirdly erotic hustler with long black roots to her hair (I could see every fraction of her physical and mental being), face covered with big sores beneath a layer of make-up, looking like she was going to fall off the thighs of her too-thin legs, wearing a fur stole in the heat of afternoon, smiling proudly and girlishly like a goddess she stepped out. *She radiated real shining light beams of joy and happiness to be alive.* She scattered auras of pride in joining herself to the company of the restaurant. She stepped a little to one side to miss the fireplug. IT WAS MONUMENTAL AUDACITY worthy of Homer's singing.

"The best is none too good," whispered my friend referring to the fireplug scene. I had to bite my thumb to keep from roaring with love. Next, out stepped her companion creatures—two male beasts or gods. People are no longer like our conception of them. They are like godly beasts. Every line, wrinkle, freckle, reflection of color, hidden motivation, and apparent desire stand out in technicolor, on their bodies and faces. Both were wearing sublimely ill-fitting and tailored suits shimmering with freshness and creases. They stopped and stared at all who watched them from the coffee shop. Arabian oils dripped from their hairlines onto olive brows. The youngest one smiled his smile of pride, pleasure and joy in life—he also sidestepped the fireplug. As he smiled his lips rolled farther and farther back till scarlet red gums showed over crooked and gleaming white teeth. He stood hands in pockets and radiant—he stared and stared, smiling and smiling—a natural lumbering creature proud to be a male beast. He grinned for another hundred years; we gaped at the drama. The older man also stopped to smile, then he hurried the hustler and friend into the depths to their awaiting table. They were more than stately—they were exquisite, and all eyes were watching them. Homer plucked the lyre for them.

I tried not to watch people. I could only look in small doses or I would exhaust myself with laughing and crying and my attempt to hide it from the waiter.

My friend sat across from me looking down the sidewalk—he prepared me for people coming up the street. He'd say, "Here comes another," or "You won't believe this. . . ." All humanity passed us by covered with sores and bandages, and tee-shirts, and furs, and psychoses, and raptures—not one of them looked like anything I had ever seen. Every shadow or detail of face, emotion, highlight of lip or hair, or arm-hair stood out in unique radiance.

All of our notions of the human body's shape are wrong. We think it is a head joined on a torso and sprouting arms and legs and genitals or breast, but we're wrong. It is more unified than that. It's all one total unity of protoplasm and our ideas of its appearance are too much a matter of habit. The human body and the clothing it chooses are weird and godly—it is often sickening, distorted and crippled. Strangely, it is not any the less beautiful if you can see the whole of it—and the reasons for the grotesquery.

The high lasts six hours and you don't eat. We ordered a sandwich. It looked like it was going to eat us. An escaped tongue of pink pastrami attempted to lap at the plate from slab lips of rye bread. The potato salad came from a dinosaur's dream—it was a miniature yellow mountain covered with green coral of chopped parsley. Nobody could eat it.

I wanted to see the great show of Chinese art at the Museum while everything was still radiant and timeless. (When we did go later in the afternoon the show was no different than it had been when I saw it days earlier. The landscapes of the Sung dynasty are perfect, immortal and untouchable in their beauty. They are from a marvel world of their own. I heard a long scroll of shark-fin hills as if it were a whistled song. Everyone seeing the show in the gleaming rooms was as high as I was. *They had been turned on by the paintings!* We were at home! I became interested in the tiny figures and houses in the paintings, and in a mysterious wide-eyed Eurasian woman who was looking at them. I decided to stop stock still in the middle of the show and begin a cosmic and inspired meditation. Everyone will come and sit at my feet, I thought—then I will have to protect them from being carried away to a mental institution. I laughed—I had caught myself in a cosmic illusion of grandeur.)

As we stared at the sandwich an old man strutted in. His hair was dyed black with shoe polish and he was mustachioed. He stopped at each table. In mute silence he winked at each customer then smiled and traced 1920s dance gesture in the air with his forefinger and danced robot-like to the next table. His enormous face was contorted with the desire to frighten us, and the simultaneous desire to amuse and assure. He was under almost superhuman strain—it was eerie. We left them.

On the street I stood in the sun, my eyes closed tight with pleasure at the warmth of the sun's rays. I was touched by the new clear beauty of billboards become luminous with hidden meanings and colors freshly arisen to the surface. The whole city was cuddlesome and near enough to touch and caress. I saw the most glorious face I've ever seen on a man—an old newspaper vendor sitting on a little ledge in the doorway of a bar. The dark marble behind him reflected green light. He was a strange pre-Greek deity sitting in a grotto. His forehead was dark brown and his big nose was pink-red and fleshy, the rest of his face was luminous flesh color. He looked at me through steel-rimmed glasses and then out on the whole world with primordial compassion.

In the car we drove up and down the hills, heading in the direction of the museum, and talked about Ireland and the Irish earth spirits. We careened up and down hills at thousands of miles an hour in utter timelessness and sunlight. (*Actually were we motionless and everything taking eternities?*) To amuse myself and to keep from being scared in moments of strain I'd make growling sounds to myself and repeat a little verse by Robert Burns that I'd found in the park. Then I'd say it over again and growl the R's like a lion. At moments the high can be a strain. We talked about what everyone is in the great scheme — one was a faustian man, another was surely an alchemist, another was a visionary . . .

We parked. I'd never been in the church before—it is quietly lovely and partly designed by the old California architect Maybeck. Two doors open from the stone hallway, one into an English garden and the other into a worship room. We went into the room. There is a fireplace at one end and a lectern and stone baptismal font at the other. Large natural tree trunks serve as ceiling beams—it is dim and gray and cool. (A friend saw a photo of it and described it as "haunted." He meant haunted by beauty.) I walked up and fingered the Bible and stood behind the lectern.

"Did I ever tell you I wrote a play in Beast Language?" I asked my friend.

He said, "No."

Then I began to speak in the language of beasts—roaring and growling in that language and I proceeded into a sermon and ended it with a song. Here's a poem I wrote to describe it:

At the altar of the Swedenborgian Church
with tiny white flowers behind me,
delicate in their glass vase—in half darkness.
By stained glass windows
of dream hills and landscapes—I raised back my head
AND SANG

into the Olympian world, growling with the worshipping
and directing voice of Man-Beasts!
GROOOHOOOOR GROOOOOOOR SHARAKTAR
GRAHR GROOOOOOR GREEEER
SHROOOOOOOLOWVEEEEEEEEEE.
The white flecks of my spittle
floated like clumps of alyssum in the dimness
of the here, now, eternal, beauteous peace and reality.

Throwing back my head with arms upraised.
Smiling. The blotched ceiling
of redwood became mother of pearl.
And I bowed my head, and I bowed my head,
and my arms dropped.

NOTE

1. *Lophophora williamsii* is a small spineless cactus. It is divided radially by a number of ridges. Small gray hair tufts (probably atrophied spines) prickle in circular bands on the dark green flesh. Sometimes peyote grows in a clump, several plants converging on one root or a group of joined roots. I've seen seven plants in one cluster.

Peyote grows around Laredo and southwards into Northern Mexico. Seen from above the plant is circular, a rounded mound peeping an inch or more from the earth. The harvesters clip off the plant at ground level with a sharp spade—the root will grow a top again.

The green buttons are laid in the sun to dry. They shrink and become wrinkled and brown. They peel and become desiccated and irregular in shape, but usually they remain somewhat circular and flat. Finally they look like dried mushrooms or pressed and battered buttons of dark leather.

Sometimes the buttons and roots are eaten green or made into a tea. Five or more dried buttons must be taken—the level of toxicity is extremely low and any number may be eaten.

Allen for Real: Allen Ginsberg

MICHAEL MCCLURE: I met Allen Ginsberg at a party for W.H. Auden given by the San Francisco Poetry Center in 1955. Everybody else there were academics or older people, and Allen and I found ourselves leaning against a wall and began speaking to each other. We felt simpatico at that moment, and it grew. I'd see Allen sometimes after that, and he told me about his friend Jack Kerouac, from whom he was receiving letters at the time. He had either the manuscript or parts of the manuscript of Kerouac's great religious poem *Mexico City Blues*, and I liked it very much.

At the time that I was seeing Allen in those days he had a show of his poems on the wall with paintings by Robert LaVigne, the Beat painter. That was at The Place, a North Beach artists' bar. LaVigne had done a series of flower paintings. Beautiful things in gouache paint—bright, vivid portrayals of real flowers in a detailed and up close and imaginary garden of consciousness. Ginsberg wrote a number of poems that were shown with the paintings. In those early poems, Allen said that he was not writing the voice, but writing the actual sound of the mind. They were long, dense poems. They're somewhat like Williams's descriptions of the poems in *Empty Mirror*. Long lines, and similar in that way, but each line being intensely different, and each one penetrating into a personal but almost universal level of consciousness, at the same time being a commentary on the outer world as well as the inner world of consciousness. That was the poetry of Allen's that I knew before *Howl*. So for me *Howl* is like the obverse, the other side of the coin. In one sense you would see Allen as the quiet, burning, intensely intellectual bohemian poet, pre-*Howl*. And then with *Howl* the coin turns over and you have flames of a Ginsbergian/Blakean vision coming out. It's a long poem that describes the wreckage

Conducted by Jerry Aronson in 1992, this interview is previously unpublished.

of his friends' lives, a poem in which what had been the traditional landscape of poetry in another century—Nature—is turned into a different landscape—the urban—which is seen with such intense vision that it becomes the new poem of Nature, as well as a master poem of social comment. I first heard *Howl* at a reading with Allen.

JERRY ARONSON: You read also, didn't you?

McCLURE: Yes, in October 1955. Kenneth Rexroth was master of ceremonies and Allen, Gary Snyder, Philip Lamantia, Philip Whalen, and I read our poetry. Jack Kerouac was there.

ARONSON: You said that was the night you first heard *Howl*.

McCLURE: Yes, it was the first reading of the poem. All of us were interested in bringing poetry to life with voice, in a heroic and visionary tradition that we associated with Mayakovsky or with Blake. So, on first hearing *Howl* that night, I found it deeply moving, and it laid a line that we all chose to commit ourselves to. *Howl* has founded a couple of generations of broader and more liberal, deeper and more profound, and more socially engaged poetry and art.

I'm afraid that many people today that were not alive in the fifties have a vague idea of what the fifties were like. This was the period of the Cold War—you can imagine Bob Dylan as a twelve-year-old boy watching the McCarthy hearings on television. One of the first things that I saw in San Francisco was a House Un-American Activities Committee riot, where liberal and radical San Franciscans were protesting against a meeting of the House Un-American Activities Committee that was taking place in the city. So at twenty-one or twenty-two I saw mounted police go in to break up a crowd that was peacefully objecting to the meeting of a most undemocratic association of congressmen and their henchmen. We were living in what Eisenhower himself called the military-industrial complex. A Military Industrial Corporative State, a state of corporations, feeding the military industrial complex. People on the streets, if they had any substance, were white men wearing grey suits, and they had crew cuts. People lived in tract houses, and they drove cars that we think of as looking quaint—big

Buicks with the ring on the front, with the little torpedo going through it, which is symbolic. The beginning of missile consciousness, and we were beginning to build our nuclear weapons arsenal out of control. Young men were looked on as cannon fodder to be sent to the Korean War, and to kill Asians to stop an absurd domino hypothesis of politics. It was a time of intense psychic pain because of the alienation, the polarization into two groups that was taking place—those who wished to maintain their feelings against the growing one-dimensionality and the majority who adulated the whole thing because they saw it presented to them on television, the American Dream. As young poets we were poor, not privileged in any way. We came from whatever class we came from but had renounced whatever we had inherited to be the artists that we knew we could be. So when Ginsberg drew the line with *Howl*, we had to decide whether our toe was on the line too. It was great to make that decision while Kerouac was there at the reading shouting, "Go! Go! Go!"

ARONSON: What was the audience at the reading like?

MCCLURE: Electric. The kind of audience that San Francisco is able to produce. There were elderly women in fur coats who were radical social leaders of the time, and there were college professors there, young anarchist carpenter idealists, artists, poets, painters associated with the gallery. So it was a broad spectrum, intensely radical, and intensely hoping for a change to take place. We all saw this not just as a change in poetry but as a change in consciousness. It was exciting.

ARONSON: When Allen read *Howl* that night, what went on between him and the audience?

MCCLURE: We were all intense young men, and Allen was intense in his special way—on the verge of shaking with inner concentration. At the same time Allen has always had an enormous gift for relating what he does to an audience. I think those two things came together for Allen at that moment, so there was a brightness to that—seeing the poet Allen and the audience come together. Of course, San Francisco had already had readings through the Poetry Center—Rexroth, Auden,

Dylan Thomas. But everyone knew there was something special about the Six Gallery reading.

ARONSON: So the Beats were born at that reading. I've heard so many stories, so many definitions from so many different sources.

McCLURE: Some critics feel that the Beat Generation began with that reading we gave in October, 1955. There are others who believe that the Beat Generation began in New York, that it was the coming together of Kerouac, Burroughs, and their immediate associates in the earlier 1950s. I see no contradiction between the two perspectives. The Beats first came together in the earlier 1950s in New York, but the Six Gallery reading transformed the movement, offering consciousness as nature. I see the Beat Generation as the literary wing of the environmental movement, but an environmental movement that is not different from consciousness, and an environmental movement that is not different from the urban aspect of our lives either. For example, Philip Whalen is a nature poet, as well as a Zen abbot. Gary Snyder is deeply involved in the study of environment and nature. Ginsberg is involved in consciousness, and consciousness is very much a part of our nature. The spread of consciousness through the universe is in fact manifested as nature, is manifested as flesh, or tree, or bird, or stars.

ARONSON: Where are we in 1992 in terms of the deepening of consciousness in this country?

McCLURE: I'm doing what I've always done. Gary Snyder is doing what he's always done. Allen Ginsberg, Philip Whalen, Philip Lamantia, Diane di Prima, Amiri Baraka are too. In the sixties there were people that we thought of as young, as seekers, who deepened consciousness on a community level. They broadened it, made it more community oriented, more social. In a sense, the young people in the mid-1960s came to their start from what we did, and what they saw in jazz, what they heard in Black music, what they heard in rock 'n' roll. They were the ones who resisted the Vietnam War.

I'd like to point something out though. The first resistance to the Vietnam War was primarily by elderly women, and then it was followed by the young people. First you saw old women standing out there, then younger women with their kids in baby-carts. And we built up demonstrations to the point where there'd be thirty, forty, fifty, one-hundred thousand people resisting the war. But that's also conscious-ness, that's also nature. Now we hear Noam Chomsky and Daniel Ellsberg saying without what the resistance did the war would not have ended as it did, not that it ended easily. It was a horrible and brutal, longlasting massacre.

If you look around and ask what happened to the 1950s and 1960s, you don't see grey flannel suits. You often see a man with an individual hair style, he's wearing an earring, he's wearing casual clothes, he doesn't believe in war, he doesn't believe in killing Arabs for American property, he doesn't believe in killing Asians. This is not the 1950s. A profound change has happened, Anybody so ignorant, or so ahis-torical as to ask where did the 1950s and 1960s go, needs some history other than the pre-prepared corporate history handed out by television.

ARONSON: What are you doing now?

MCCLURE: Ray Manzarek plays the piano while I recite my poetry at colleges and music clubs, at the Jack Kerouac Festival, or on television or radio. What we do is committed, environmentally and politically. We go to places like long-haired, rock 'n' roll, working-class blues clubs in Milwaukee and do our poetry there. I remember the first time we appeared there—I didn't know if we were going to get attacked for what we were saying, whether with music or not. While reading I looked at the house and they were dancing, and I said, "Hey, you can't dance to this!" Then I thought, why not? To work with a powerful, gifted fellow artist like Ray Manzarek allows the art we do to become a new experience. Manzarek was interested in Beat poetry as far back as the early sixties.

In part this comes out of what was happening in 1955 because one of our points—aside from the political and the intellectual—was an intense need to bring the voice back to poetry. The academy, with its tinkly-page poetry and know-nothing poets, and the brutal-minded jingoist crew cuts of the time, had essentially done away with poetry through lack of attention, lack of love, and active dislike. We decided to bring poetry back to people, and they came to hear us, to hear the voice. They came to hear the poetry alive in the air. Our instincts were that poetry was like an organism, or that poetry was an extension of our organism, as well as our consciousness.

ARONSON: Allen worked with Phillip Glass, you work with Ray Manzarek. Do you think that adding music does something that poetry by itself doesn't do . . . ? I'm thinking back to Thelonius Monk in the 1950s.

MCCLURE: Ray is as deep and profound as Monk. Ray is a deeply moving and soul-stirring artist. Ray and Monk are great, luminous pianists.

I wasn't doing poetry and jazz in the 1950s. I watched it, and I was interested in jazz, but it was not something I was participating in myself. I did not have a partner I wanted to work with. I didn't want to work with musicians that I barely knew, and just sort of have them engagingly and good-naturedly back me up. That's not what I do with Ray. When we work together it's like two beings coming together to create a third living organism—a symbiosis. Ray brings the art of his music, I bring the art of my poetry, and together it's something completely different. That's McClure/Manzarek, which is what we call ourselves. In solo poetry readings I read some of the poems I do with Ray, but it's not the same thing. I like both modes, but I actually prefer to be with Ray because when people hear poetry and music together, it speaks inside, way inside. If you look in a recent issue of *Science*, you'll see that the vocal center on one side of the brain interacts with the words that are being said, while the pitch center on the other side interacts with the music being played, so you have a much more complex experience than just the words. It's a reverberation. This complex experience has usually been part of poetry, from Greek poetry on, from poetry at the time of Confucius, 600 B.C. in China, through the Troubador poets, to what the best lyrics today are doing.

What the Beats did was take the poetry that was on the page, that had gotten separated from the music, and they said we're going to put the music back in this by bringing it to life with our voice. We are going to deliver it, and our voice will be the music.

There was great communal support for the arts among young people in 1965; they were experimenting with many forms of consciousness and anti-corporate, anti-progaganda activities, and they traded their consciousnesses with their musician poets of the day. Then the corporations bought those people out. Now people are saying, hey, wait—there used to be some thought to this, some profundity to this. When Ray and I are playing, or when Allen is working with musicians, and people who are trained to use both sides of the brain in listening to art hear us, they're able join into whatever we do. The same person who might not understand one of my poems if I read it from a stage hears Ray and me do it and says, "That's visionary, man. I get it." There's plenty of room for both modes, because the voice is poetry too. And poetry is beautiful on the page if you know how it sounds. But I'd rather somebody hears me first, before reading my poetry on the page. If someone sees my poetry on the page without hearing me, it's hard for them to understand. You have to be an initiate of contemporary poetry. With Ray, with music, there's no problem. They understand.

ARONSON: Sometimes Ginsberg's power of delivery is astounding.

MCCLURE: When I say the Beats are about nature and about consciousness, remember that nature is our body, consciousness is everything around us. The power that Allen has in delivering his poems, those long lines, that massive alchemical energy that he puts into it, and all the charm, and all the charisma he puts in there too, that's body expression. By body expression I don't mean how you move your body, I mean what's coming out of the whole body. If you move your hand, every muscle in your body is reacting. That's the way he treats his poetry. The figure of speech goes, "Say what you mean." That's wrong. Mean what you say! Allen means what he says. So when you hear somebody say, "Say what you mean," say "No, no. I want to mean what I say." That's the way it works with the body. There's a physical difference there.

ARONSON: Did you ever hear Ginsberg read "Kaddish"?

MCCLURE: Yes. As a matter of fact, recently Allen wanted me to read it for him. Allen was scheduled to read "Kaddish" at the Modern Language Association Convention here in San Francisco but he had heart failure. My friend Amy and I were on a trip to East Africa to look at animals and meet tribal peoples and Allen's message was on my machine when we returned, too late to do it. I've heard Allen read "Kaddish" several times.

Some people think of the Beats as outlaws, but we are also scholars. Gary Snyder is scholar. Philip Whalen is a scholar. Allen is a scholar. When I first heard *Howl*, I thought of Shelley's first long poem, "Queen Mab." At the age of eighteen, Shelley wrote his long, philosophical, visionary, moral, idealistic, flaming, incredible poem of the imagination called "Queen Mab." And he also wrote twenty pages of notes to go along with it, just in case anybody missed the point. The notes are as good as the poem. When I first heard *Howl*, I thought of it being like "Queen Mab."

My other thought was that *Howl* was like Antonin Artaud's great poem, "To Have Done With the Judgement of God." Artaud was the French poet who died in a madhouse in 1948. He was truly a great gnostic, anti-body poet. Although we were all body poets, we looked to Artaud as our immediate ancestor. I saw him as an older brother, though my feelings and beliefs were the opposite of his, and he spoke to me profoundly. He wrote "To Have Done With the Judgement of God" as a radio program, with the help of Roger Blin and a woman friend of his, for broadcast over French radio. It was so insane, and so right. If you look at it today, it's exactly about the Cold War, exactly about the state of Europe and America in those days. But French radio was not ready for such a vocal poem, and after having been commissioned it was banned from the radio. Even a committee of French intellectuals—from Sartre to Camus—could not get that piece (which is about the length of *Howl*) on French radio. It wasn't until 1968 during the rebellion in Paris that Jean-Jacques Lebel, a young poet, went with others into the basements of the radio center, got the Artaud tapes out, made copies, and sent them back to us in the States.

When I think of "Kaddish," I see the application of *Howl*'s burst of energy, that broke the dam, into an obsessive subject. Much great art is obsessive, whether it's by Cézanne or Ginsberg. In "Kaddish" you have Ginsberg's obsession with the mother's death, the obsession with things that happened to one as a child, the obsession with the outrage wrecked upon your community and your friends. "Kaddish" is Allen's obsession with his mother's body. I see it as the powerful obsession that we have as infants, the obsession that never leaves us. If we are to believe Freud, it becomes part of the unconscious. It never ages, never changes, never weakens. Allen's mother was taken away from him, and that obsession finally liberated itself in "Kaddish." And it helps those of us who have also lost our mothers.

ARONSON: You introduced Ginsberg and Jim Morrison?

McCLURE: Yes, one night in Los Angeles, and they spent part of an evening together. My feeling about Jim's poetry—not the lyrics to the Doors songs, which I also admire, but the poetry on the page—my feeling is that there's no better poet in his generation. Jim and I gave several poetry readings together because he wanted to learn from me how to read to an audience without music. Jim had a terrible problem reading to an audience. I've seen Jim stand up and sing to thousands of people until four in the morning. But that was another thing.

ARONSON: Who were his influences?

McCLURE: I've never liked the word influence. I realize that "influence" has become a popular word, but I think it's more appropriate to say *source*. I look at people as my sources. A source for me is Howling Wolf, a source for me is William Blake, a source for me is Shelley, a source for me is Whitehead. Allen Ginsberg, Gary Snyder—my friends are sources for me. Artists' works I love are sources for me. And I think Jim's sources were the Beats, as well as the Elizabethan poets, with their very beautiful sense of lyric poetry. Of course many of those Elizabethan poems that Jim was reading had been accompanied by music or were so close to the tradition that they might as well have had music with them.

What Jim and I talked about most in poetry was nineteenth-century English poetry: Blake, Shelley, Keats, Coleridge, and maybe even Wordsworth. But we just took it for granted that we both knew the Beats and we knew the contemporaries.

ARONSON: I remember a story about you and Allen talking about Blake—that Allen considers Blake a prophet and you consider Blake a liberator.

MCCLURE: One of the things that Allen and I had in common was that we were both deeply moved by Blake. Allen and I had had visions of Blake in our childhood, and we had two different Blakes. Allen has a Blake who is a Blake of prophesy, a Blake who speaks out against the dark Satanic Mills. My Blake is a Blake of body and of vision. Blake was such a powerful, such a great being that it's possible for every one of us to have an entirely different Blake. But Allen told me about his early visions of Blake and I told him about my dreams of Blake. I had dreamed that I was William Blake, and recited some poems of him that I had written. I recited poems for Allen that I had written in my understanding of Blake's style: "My mother said to me tonight / That I am dead ten years / And bending o'er my crib she bled / A multitude of tears."

ARONSON: What about Bob Dylan—was he a source?

MCCLURE: I met Bob Dylan, Joan Baez, and some Hell's Angels in, I think, 1964, at a Dylan concert. Afterwards, I hung out with Dylan and Allen for quite a while.

Freewheelin Frank of the Hell's Angels used to stay at my place while we were working on *Freewheelin Frank, Secretary to the Angels, as Told to Michael McClure.* I was a speed typist at that time, and I would type what Frank was saying. Afterwards, Frank would stay for dinner, and I'd take out the autoharp and we'd sing together. Frank loved "Mr. Tambourine Man," so he got himself a tambourine, and then he got a harmonica. My composer friend George Montana, who is a genius with any musical instrument, would bring over his autoharp, or an Indian instrument, or an African instrument, and we would make up songs. We would sit around in a circle on the floor and entertain ourselves making up songs. We played a few performances and called ourselves Freewheelin, McClure, Montana. We wanted to go amplified electric but we couldn't remember to get all the equipment there. Sometimes Frank would forget his harmonica.

ARONSON: Do you think the Beats had an effect on Dylan?

MCCLURE: Lately, I looked again at a pirated copy of *Tarantula*, a novel Dylan wrote. Looks like an amphetamine novel, but it's fascinating, in real Kerouacian spontaneous prose. It shows Dylan's immersion in the Beat scene. Plus the fact that there is great simpatico between Dylan and Ginsberg; and when I met Dylan there was an equal simpatico. It's the same scene. There isn't even much difference in age; maybe Dylan's ten years younger than me.

ARONSON: He's fifty-one.

MCCLURE: Yeah, fewer than ten years. I think that when people look back and talk about the music of the period being such a power on their lives they don't understand the community that the music grew from. Those people on the stage were our friends. Jerry Garcia was a friend, Paul Kantner, Grace Slick. Janis Joplin was Freewheelin Frank's girlfriend for a while. These are all people we knew on Haight Street. You all knew each other—the people who make the furniture, the people who design the posters, the people who make the music, the poets. These are all artists in a community. And there wasn't that cold distance of the stage that takes place now, that stage thing: "Oh, my god, we're worshipping the Gods! Look at that! Wow! Look at those lighting effects, all this massive stuff that's going on! Look at them up there."

I'm speaking about what goes on at the Oakland Coliseum when you go to a concert, even to something like an Amnesty International Benefit Concert, which is modest and even old-fashioned. There's a huge distance between the performers and the audience, though Peter Gabriel broke it beautifully. He walked to the edge of the stage, fell over backwards, the audience caught him in their extended hands, passed him around, and then put him back on the stage. That was wonderful because it gave some idea of what it was like in the sixties, or some idea of what the expression of our poetry was like in the mid-fifties, when the audience was as much a part of it as we were. The audience was yelling, "Go, go, go!," or, "Wow, man, tell it!" That's missing now, so Ray Manzarek and I put that back in our performances. If it's a heckler, we'll laugh with him. If it's somebody who wants to tell us something, we'll stop. If it makes sense, we'll listen. If somebody wants to ask something, we'll answer it. Our performances have that feeling; it's real. We're not a corporation. We're not selling tennis shoes and tee-shirts. We're putting our souls into it, and we're building our souls by putting them into it.

These Decades Are Echoes: Robert Creeley

In the early mid-fifties in San Francisco Robert Duncan and Jonathan Williams were recommending Creeley and Olson to me. I read Creeley's *Gold Diggers* and I liked those metaphysical stories.

Beautiful Creeley books bound with silk tassels and with drawings by René Laubies were beginning to appear. "My mind to me a mangle is . . ." is a line in one of them—it stuck in my mind—the enigmas of those short poems hinted that something gorgeous was happening. When poems like "The Whip" began to make themselves known I knew Bob was not just good, was not merely exciting, but was a master.

In March 1956 my wife and I and James and Beverly Harmon and sculptor Ronny Bladen and others were living in a rented mansion converted into a commune—we'd just edited the magazine *ARK II Moby I* incorporating poets from Rexroth to Zukofsky and Levertov. We had our West Coast scene but Creeley's anticipated visit added a dimension. Bob slipped into the kitchen grinning, solid, nervous, asked for a drink and when we didn't have one he drank off the gin and garlic that we used for fish sauce. We knew that not only was Bob a "literary man" but he was one of us and we were the same breed.

Bob is a touchstone for me—a measure of what poetry is. Creeley is a genius of the sensorium as Kerouac was and he is a master of the ear as is Miles Davis. He is a carver in space like Van Gogh.

Creeley's poems are sometimes like Van Gogh's paintings of work shoes—so real you can shake them in the air—and other poems are as mystical as the shifting point where the waves lap against the black slate beaches of my childhood.

Originally published in *Sagetrieb* 1:3, 1982.

Sometimes I ransack a new (or old) book of Bob's. "Is there a way I can use these couplet ideas? How about triplets? Look, how he uses this quatrain! What handsomeness I find in these syncopated intuitive syllabics. And there! That *volta*! It's as good as the pause in any Elizabethan sonnet."

———————

I go to look for a poem of Bob's and I can't find it but I realize as I search that he has carved the tiny black figures on a distant beach in my mental field as an etcher carves with his tool upon the metal. For days I saw the figures, far away and dark, and they added a dimension to my thoughts.

———————

Look how Bob creates his body in his book *Pieces*. What is the politics of shaping an extension of the body that will outlive the meat body and yet be an inextricable—or an inseparable—part of it? When Bob consciously discovered his body and told us about it he tore off his clothes and rolled drunkenly down a hill at two in the morning in the darkness of a deserted campus in San Diego. We were seeing the physiological counterpart of his meatly poems *Pieces*. That's bio-scholarship! What is the biology of *Pieces*? Chunks, gobbets—but all in the same animal soup. Bob is an American Inventor—he invents excitement with the antisystem of his long poem. Bob is an Existentialist—he assumes the full responsibility for being what he writes and for writing what he is. He is post-existentialist—he is free to move back and forth from the situations of the human world to the REAL BEING of the interior sense world.

I think I read Creeley like nobody else does. I see Bob as a jazz musician, as a physiologist tracing out where the past lies in the muscles, and as a new expressionist on the cutting edge of his own consciousness. I find that very often I am not reading for subject matter—I am reading the man there.

But probably everybody thinks they read Creeley like nobody else does. Possibly that's one of the greatnesses of his poetry.

Bob is as much a part of my life as the bed I sleep on—or as the sky I see out of my window—or Mount Tamalpais there in the distance—or Point Bonita where it slips out into the Pacific Ocean like the head of Disney's Pluto the Pup. Like those things, and the billowy, anise-scented fennel plants on the corner in the lot, Bob is a part of my life every day. If it were not for Bob and his poetry I'd be somebody else.

When I was first finding his verse I used to try—to find that feeling—to write poems like Bob's. But his poems were inimitable. If the poems I wrote were good they were mine and not like Creeley's. I made some fair poems trying to write like Creeley. Someday I could get them out of notebooks where they are stuck away with other attempts to imitate—and with quotes from George MacDonald, and scribblings on thoughts of Seurat, and *The Cloud of Unknowing*, and word lists from Shelley poems.

There are few poems from those days that I like as much as "The Whip":

I spent a night turning in bed,
my love was a feather, a flat

sleeping thing. She was
very white . . .

It begins that way—but it is not excerptable. "The Whip" has the compound possibilities of being an emotional aggregate that could be made by no one else—it is utterly unique like Creeley himself. The poem is open—almost innocent—yet sinister. It is sinuous as one of those long black whips that tenses and coils on itself. It is manly—virile—male. It is trapped and plighted. It is fiercely active as only a child or live being can be. It has a quality of being honest beyond honest—there is something foreign and challenging in it. The poem is out of control—but it is out of control within its own High Art bio-cybernetic system.

In recent poems Creeley is a time-buster. In "First Rain" he sees

"Along the grey iced sidewalk" the unveiling, like shimmerings in the
body memory, the

> piles of dogshit, papers

> bits of old clothing, are
> the human pledges . . .

The wind blurs his glasses and clothes as he passes the "pledges" on
the sidewalk. It is Creeley, it is Buffalo, is it Past unveiled in Present,
in poem stuff.

Every once in a while I have to write a poem for Bob and here's a
recent one:

FOR CREELEY

LIKE WATER LILY BUDS
RISING THROUGH BLACK WATER

all things

we
know

we
find

in self,
that matches

clown mask
patterns

in
the world

and then
we see

we're faces
smiling at

the
sun.

Just as day is done
we exhale our perfumes

into the night
we've won.

Pastures New: Gary Snyder

Since the early fifties when Charles Olson published his "Against Wisdom As Such" in *Black Mountain Review* there's been very little wisdom literature written by those of us in the new thrust. But Gary has always written practical visionary poems that can be touchstones and stepping-stones for us. We can always go back to Gary's thought for a base and say, look, we can do this or that good thing, and we should know all the names of our flowers and birds and mountains. But one poem of Gary's, more than all the others, has stood out in my mind for the last few years. I've had the broadside of it on my wall and read it many times and return to it each time with even more and greater pleasure. Then one day I began to realize that Gary's poem "High Quality Information" is wisdom literature—as much as is the *Tao Te Ching* or *The Cloud of Unknowing*. What I've done here is something like a gloss and something like a savoring of this poem.

HIGH QUALITY INFORMATION

A life spent seeking it
Like a worm in the earth,
Like a hawk. Catching threads
Sketching bones
Guessing where the road goes.
Lao-tzu says
To forget what you knew is best.
That's what I want:
To get these sights down,
Clear, right to the place
Where they fade
Back into the mind of my times.
The same old circuitry

Originally published in *Gary Snyder: Dimensions of a Myth*, ed. Jon Halper (San Francisco: Sierra Club Books, 1991).

But some paths color-coded
Empty
And we're free to go.

A *life spent seeking it* (I'll say! I've been watching Gary seeking that high-quality information for almost thirty-five years, seeing the lines deepen on the face and the gaze grow deeper, too, looking down past the surface of things. And the smile has grown more gentle.

Like a worm in the earth, (—turning and lithely swimming through the damp gritty particles and the tasty sheddings and off-shimmers of near countless preceding lives.

Like a hawk. (I remember how one day near Kitkitdizze we looked down from the gorge and saw an eagle fly slowly below us. We could almost see the cloudy mottle on the primaries.

Catching threads (Woolgathering. As old Zen wise men went woolgathering with a wine jug, watching a spider drop down on its thread in the moonlight.

Sketching bones (Goethe sketched bones too. There must be a hundred or a million bones beneath our feet at every step through the meadow in the forest.

Guessing where the road goes. (While recalling that we come from nowhere and it's nowhere where we go—with our children clapping their hands in the last clack of our heels.

Lao-tzu says (He says the whole thing is an Uncarved Block. Sometimes it's a block of pollywogs, or of deer in the yard.

To forget what you knew is best. (—to make it not painful, to join the forgetting at the end of the road. Going to sleep by the fireplace, with muscles forgetting a day of chopping and carrying and typing.

That's what I want: (Gary, you speak for so many of us, for what you see is what we'd like to see too. I trust what you want.

To get these sights down, (Gary, we'll get out of the greedy drunkenness. It's an age of addiction to population and petroleum, as you point out. But we see the high things because we are mammals.

Clear, right to the place

Where they fade (This poem is so beautiful that, though I've read it many times, I love to feel it fade and shift its meaning into a dimming moire pattern. Then after a few more lines I go back and read and come at it again, and try to guess how to imagine *śūnyatā*.

Back into the mind of my times. (Our thoughts fade as we drive and as we write our poems, as our bodies rest on the plastic plush that was created, in part, by the wars of our times and partly by gentler acts that had no intention to pollute.

The same old circuitry (All these years of the circuitry—and it is less than a sand grain in the earth that the worm moves through as he/she creates information affecting a future that spreads along the road to forgetting.

But some paths color-coded (We were sitting in H.T. Odum's front room in Gainesville and he pointed out the color coding of the cardinals in the trees. But is there a color coding of an ecotone of the land where the road goes?

Empty (No nothing. No more. Not even *nada*.

And we're free to go. (Thank you, Gary. As John Milton said, "Tomorrow to fresh Woods and Pastures new."

Sixty-six Things about the California Assemblage Movement

1. "Assemblage" in California in its early stages represented a view of how consciousness works. It was a new viewpoint, a new eye, turned on the American cities just as they began to become old. It was keen to the mysterious and almost alchemical meanings of the space between objects and of the emptiness in storefront windows that perhaps contained an old shoe, a tin can standing on a box, and three toothbrushes tied together with a piece of brown twine.

In this sense it was Romantic: esthetic considerations had been heightened to considerations of perception.

2. Only after matters of sensory perception had preeminence was the assemblage movement involved in esthetics.

3. Each mainline assemblage artist has his or her own esthetics.

4. The art was made of ordinary materials but the intent of examining sensory perceptions always verges on the mystical. Perceptions made an even greater thrill with dusty or worn materials. The ordinary became strange, romantic, almost scientific.

5. Decay was involved in perception but not decay of mud and bacteria. Instead, this was the decay of aging, of wear, even sometimes of entropy.

Originally presented as a lecture at UCLA's exhibition, "The Art of Assemblage in California," these "notes" first appeared in *Artweek* 10 (March 1992).

6. Part of the assemblage creed was to reverse entropy—much as living beings reverse entropy and create negentropy. The pieces became thrilling because the unspoken agenda was dynamic: to create objects that had bypassed entropy and become beautiful and alive, even in the aging "urb."

7. With perception as the basic agreement of the field, each artist became an evolved temperament on the background of the field.

8. Bruce Conner was the Leonardo of the assemblagists. He was the renaissance man, equally capable in his energetic subtlety of drawing, his uncanny skill with assembled film, his craft as a sculptor in wax. (Even his skill as a musician and still photographer.)

9. Bruce Conner's youthful skills as an oil painter are not yet acknowledged.

10. Conner's collage *Ratbastard Number One* is a turning point in assemblage. The "ratbastards" are objects of vivid beauty and sexuality and fetishism. They separate the thrust of Conner's intent from Merz, from Dada, and from Cubism, which are European, and though intellectually vivid, fall short in emotional range.

11. The ratbastard is as American as Pollock's "Jungian" work and his drip work. It is the next step.

12. Conner uses the collage to torment, with beauty and sexuality, the consciousness of the onlooker. They are the esthetic tease, so beautiful you want them. The perceptions of space are intense and go beyond perceptions of space and color into texture—into popular consciousness of Ray Charles, big-titted magazines, broken mirrors, and lovely spider goddesses with skulls between their legs.

13. Bruce Conner's work is the work of a little boy who still loves what is bright in sexuality and texture before invention is stifled.

14. In 1957 artist Wallace Berman became my peyote father by giving me five buttons of peyote.

15. Probably no one has pointed out the significance of psychedelic and psychotropic substances on the artists of the assemblage movement. It is of intimate significance in the work of George Herms, Wallace Berman, Dennis Hopper, and Bruce Conner.

16. Wallace Berman sent assemblage artist George Herms to meet me while I was high on the five peyote buttons. I saw that George was the God of Foxes with dirt under the nails of his paws, fresh from his den. (As I put it in my *Peyote Poem.*) A few weeks later, I introduced Bruce Conner and George Herms. They had never seen each others' work.

17. Not long after that, Wallace Berman published *Peyote Poem* with his own cover photo of a peyote button, as an issue of his assemblage magazine *Semina*.

18. George Herms is the most religious of the assemblagists. He believes that art and energy are holy.

19. Herms's work is the most delicately and intentionally negentropic—that is, it goes against entropy—and it is the most involved with creating pristine—even if dusty and cobwebbed—new aggregates of life for the old materials of wood and photo and rubber bands and rusty bike wheels.

20. Each piece of Herms's is a challenge to decay. For a moment, or a month, or a week, or ten years, or a thousand years (but always temporary) the assembled objects defy crumbling and become art. The religious intent is clear if one realizes that this work which defies mortality is eminently and especially mortal.

21. Conner fights the mortality of pieces, hoping to keep them alive. Herms may repair his assemblages but he is sure they will pass on.

22. Herms is interested in the poetic purity of what he is doing—that it shows for a moment, or for a few years, the depth of his love. He has purified things in bringing them together, and they shine even if dusty. Conner is obsessed with the sensory or intellective perceptions that he can bind upon the assemblage awareness of space. He wants to show you blue-black feathers and rhinestones.

23. Herms wants to give you a poem written in faded brown ink on an old photograph stapled to a chairseat lying in a broken aquarium tank.

24. Conner dazzles you so that your mind tells you that you are looking at a poem.

25. Herms is going for the deep strata of profound feeling of silence, or silent music and purity of feelings with perhaps a wry and wistful twist of humor.

26. Sometimes Conner's work is clown-like and sometimes Conner is a social realist in the media of castaway junk or brown-black wax.

27. Oftentimes, seeing Herms's works, one thinks that they are by someone who is near-saintly in his care for the objects that are put together.

28. Bruce Conner lived in the communal group with Timothy Leary in Newton Center, 1963.

29. George Herms was arrested and did time in the late fifties for possession of marijuana.

30. There is a complex relationship between poetry and assemblage.

31. Herms began as a poet and became a visual and tactile artist.

32. Editor Wallace Berman published his own poems in an issue of *Semina* under the *nom de plume* Pantale Xantos. One poem was a list of

drugs followed by the word *mother*. It went something like: Heroin mother, Peyote mother, Opium mother . . . and so forth.

33. Among writers most often mentioned by Berman were Cocteau and Hermann Hesse. Hesse appealed because of his bead game mysticism which bears some resemblance in its apparatus and stochasty to assemblage.

34. Conner saw a distinct relationship between the Ratbastard Protective Association, which he formed, and the Pre-Raphaelite Brotherhood. Membership in the RBPA included Conner, Herms, Jay DeFeo, Joan Brown, Manuel Neri, Wallace Berman, and other artists and poets.

35. Conner set out to illustrate Dante's *Divine Comedy*. The important result of this project were his images of Geryon—the monster Fraud. I appropriated Geryon from Conner and Dante for the title of my first book, *Hymns to Saint Geryon*.

36. In the late fifties, Conner ran the Ezra Pound for President campaign—publishing "Ez for Prez" literature for the election, and he had some correspondence with Pound, who was then incarcerated in Saint Elizabeth's Hospital in Washington, D.C.

37. Conner was an appreciative reader of Michael McClure, Allen Ginsberg, Gregory Corso. Conner created a film portrait of Michael McClure (subsequently lost) and a sculpted portrait bust of Allen Ginsberg in assemblage style. His assemblage sculpture *Bomb* had its source in part in Corso's *Bomb*.

38. Conner was a friend of writer Richard Brautigan. Conner was an admirer of the poetry of Philip Lamantia. One can see a relationship between the styles of the poet and the artist regarding tactile and visual and sensory intensity.

39. It could have not been lost on Conner that Pound's *Cantos* are a collage or assemblage of Pound's mind and history as well as of History itself.

40. The Ubu Gallery was the gallery of art that preceded the Six Gallery in the same location in San Francisco. The Ubu gallery had been supported intellectually and artistically by poet Robert Duncan and his companion, the painter and collagist Jess.

41. When the Ubu Gallery gave way to the Six Gallery, it became cooperative and its members included Wally Hedrick and Jay DeFeo and poet Jack Spicer.

42. In 1955, Wally Hedrick asked Michael McClure to put together a poetry reading for the Six Gallery.

43. Poets Kenneth Rexroth and Robert Duncan did much to furnish the intellectual fundament of the California Bay Area for the tiny but intensely engaged artistic community. Both men were self-taught scholars—both were anarchists. Kenneth Rexroth spoke of the artistic proximity of San Francisco to Asia and the Pacific Rim, and he asserted the importance of Paris and London over New York. Both poets were strong in ego and self-measured in their success as literary artists—both were anti-academic. Both were anti-materialistic. Both were believers in domesticity and supporters of nature. Both were intensely involved in the arts and especially the plastic arts.

44. Any major show of California assemblage should contain works by Robert LaVigne from the mid and late fifties. Some of these pieces were parts of sets created for the Actors Workshop in San Francisco. Robert LaVigne was the nearest thing to an official Beat artist. However, in the broadest sense, Wallace Berman, George Herms, Jay DeFeo, Joan Brown, and Manuel Neri were all Beats, or were for a time. An assemblage show should also contain collages by Russ Tamblyn (one of the stars of *West Side Story* and seen more recently in *Twin Peaks*). Russ Tamblyn gave up acting for many years, after discovering Wallace Berman and the new art. A major show should also contain collages by Dean Stockwell, who turned his attention to collage and 16mm films after becoming friends with Berman.

45. In the late sixties, actor/director and assemblagist Dennis Hopper was able to recite large passages of the gnostic Gospel of Thomas by rote memory.

46. To my knowledge, no one has ever collected and published poetry by George Herms, though Herms has published books of poems by Michael McClure and Diane di Prima, among others.

47. George Herms has printed small assemblage books and eccentric books with herculean zeal—these books and prints that he made with the printing press deserve to be seen on their own in a special show.

48. Poet David Meltzer is a close friend of George Herms and was good friends with Wallace and Shirley Berman. More than one poet learned his or her sense of style in personal life from the Bermans and from the Jess and Robert Duncan ménage.

49. Herms has used books extensively in his assemblage work. He also has made collage books as single works of art—for instance, he might take an old album for 78 rpm records and glue and staple it with other images and write upon it.

50. Jess is one of the most literate of modern artists. He has written nonsense poetry on a par with Lewis Carroll or Edward Lear, and he has done translations of the German nonsense poetry of Christian Morgenstern.

51. Jess has done many abstract poems as visual works of art. In the early fifties, he took words from periodicals and books and pasted them up in patterns that made haunting and evocative poems as well as esthetic objects. (This literary strand is perhaps even more stunning in the texts of his "Tricky Cad" pieces, which are collaged *Dick Tracy* strips.)

52. Jess has collaborated on books and broadsides with poet Robert

Duncan and many other poets, and has illustrated a children's story by Michael McClure.

53. On receiving a copy of McClure's book of poems *September Blackberries*, Jay DeFeo sent the author a collage titled *September Blackberries*.

54. One gets the idea that after the Abstract Expressionists, who were mainly anti-intellectual and macho (with such noteworthy exceptions as Art Reinhardt, Barrett Newman, and Clyfford Still), the mainline assemblage artists were brightly literate.

55. One gets the impression that the drug of choice among Abstract Expressionists was alcohol, and it was either pot or psychedelics among those assemblagists who used drugs.

56. One can almost imagine the assemblagists as the bad, brilliant children of the Abstract Expressionists.

57. The earliest art work of Jay DeFeo's that I saw was in North Beach, in the Grant Avenue bar The Place, where the Beat poets went to drink and socialize in 1954.

58. DeFeo's work was a sudden esthetic illumination: pieces of posterboard with daubed single splotches of grey and white tempera and maybe a few stringy lines or part of a brush stroke or sweep of dirty red. But none of it was careless—it was perfect. And it was on perfectly worn and slightly uncared-for backgrounds.

59. When I looked at her early pieces, I had a sudden feeling that, regarding visual art, I was happy to be in San Francisco and not Paris. That was 1954.

60. DeFeo rode Abstract Expressionism in a direction that it had never been before—it was the placement of her incredible shabby daubs or exquisitely worn splotches and loose sprawling offbeat bars that was the message. She was dealing with paint as the assemblagists would deal with worn materials. She was part of a vision, of a new way of

seeing. She was beat, she was elegant, she was worn, and she was glimmery. DeFeo is the visionary of the assemblagists.

61. Jay DeFeo was as calligraphic and as minimalistic as Robert Motherwell was, in a later decade, in his brush paintings. Robert Motherwell was a pure painter looking to Paris or perhaps Tokyo. DeFeo was a gambler and an alchemist. She was translating her vision into painting and gambling her spirit on the *coup* of her dusky materials.

62. I have seen three great crosses. One is by Cimabue or another post-Byzantine master, and is in the Accademia in Florence. The second is an assemblage by George Herms. Long-haired at the time, Herms carried the cross on his back up Downey Street in San Francisco, followed by a group of children. The Herms cross is composed of scrap wood and shelving and a tree branch. The crossbar supports a small "museum" of assemblage that ranges from a photo of a man with elephantiasis of the scrotum to a statue of Robbie the Robot to a plastic box containing human teeth. The third memorable cross was entered by Jay DeFeo into a San Francisco Art Annual of the mid-fifties. It was of butcher paper stretched over a lumber frame, and around twelve feet high. It was outrageous in scale and beauty—it had an enormous delicacy. The cross's sole decoration was a splash or splot of tempera. At the Museum, the piece was scribbled upon by vandals. The added obscenities made the piece seem more profound and consequently more beautiful.

63. At one point in the late fifties, I found that DeFeo had destroyed, by cutting in half, nearly all of her tempera on posterboard works. The destroyed stack of work was eighteen inches to two feet high.

I wish she had not done it, and I have thought about her act for thirty years.

64. My guess is that DeFeo destroyed the work so that she might go beyond it. It may have taken twenty years for her to go beyond that work. In its spiritual substance, it was the most advanced work that I had seen until that time.

65. Bruce Conner is working with sensory and intellective fire—and then spirit—in that order.

66. Jay DeFeo is working with spirit, contemplation, and gesture. She proves that the minute gesture in a perfect daub is as fine as a great slooping drip in Pollock's work or a color field by Rothko.

Wallace Berman and *Semina*

EDUARDO LIPSCHUTZ-VILLA: What effect did the assemblage magazine *Semina* have in the creative community?

MICHAEL MCCLURE: First, I want to talk about *Semina* as an act in itself. *Semina*s are a form of love structure that Wallace Berman made, drawing friends together. Friends are drawn together into the assemblage of the magazine, but then the magazine is also sent to acquaintances who are drawn into the circle of friends, so it expands and becomes a larger event. Friends become respondents, that is, to Berman, and some of them become correspondents to the magazine and in that way they are included in the magazine. *Semina* has some aspects of the religion of art and friends. There's an initiation to *Semina*, i.e., if Berman chose you. One is chosen. One cannot purchase or command having a *Semina* but it comes to one. The magazine is out of the line of commodity and merchandising and purchase. There's nothing to consume. And so it's completely different, and precious. In fact, the way one loses *Semina*s is that one lends them to a friend and they keep them because they also find them to be a wonder.

Like George Herms's work, *Semina* is made of the materials of mortality, such as poster papers, cardboard, twine, slick industrial papers. The senses are being appealed to and the magazine *is* an esthetic in itself. The unpurchasable bundle of beautiful art has a color range even more specific than Cubism, when you stop to look at it: the textured range of papers and twines. Also, the actual act of the hand-folding and gluing is there, the artist putting the pieces in the pockets—it's there, still present to the eye, like the smell of the glue in a new *Semina*. *Semina* contrasts the glossiness of hand-produced photographs

Conducted by Eduardo Lipschutz-Villa in October 1992, this interview first appeared in *Support the Revolution* (Institute of Contemporary Art, 1992).

with the almost Japanese-ness of the background of industrial materials that are used. There is also the luridness of nudity and sexuality contrasted with the various spiritualities of Hesse, or Cocteau, or Artaud, or of David Meltzer, or of John Wieners, or of Allen Ginsberg.

Another thing about *Semina* is that it's un-American. In the fifties, when the magazine first began, it was against what we called "The American Way." *Semina* was a long way from the American Way. The American Way was the Korean War, the starched shirts and ties, the military preparedness to battle against the Iron Curtain or the Bamboo Curtain.

Semina is also about rules. There are so many rules in the putting together of a *Semina* and it is so precise a game of art that new freedom is created for the imagination, as in information theory: the more rules there are, the more specific something must be—then more powerful channels are created for freedom. *Semina* poises like the work of George Herms or Bruce Conner on the crack of crisis, on the lip of entropy— it's about to fall apart. Like love, a *Semina* has to be tended and displayed to exist.

I want to give you an example of what I mean by being poised on the lip of entropy. When Wallace bought a TV set on time from Sears-Roebuck when he first moved to San Francisco, he collaged it. He put drawings and photographs all over it, and it became unrepossessable. It had become poised on the lip of entropy. Another time when Wallace bought a motorcycle, a new motorcycle (and he bought it on time, also), he took olive-drab spray paint and sprayed it. It was then on the lip of entropy. It was no longer useful to the American Way. It was unrepossessable. It had become Wallace, in the same way that the *Semina*s were Wallace, and poised out of the consumer loop. Pushed to the edge, *Semina* became unsellable. What Wallace made was his, and he kept it, and he also gave it to his friends.

I see *Semina* on the cusp exactly between love and generosity and selfish appetite: Wallace's appetite for art, and for friendship, and for spirituality. This is where the most meaningful art exists, and where the most meaningful art comes from, that crack of crisis. A poet said a poem is like an ice cube on the stove, floating on itself. *Semina* melts into itself; it's the ultimately precious object; it's valueless. It gives a gift to the imagination through its net of laws and rules. It gives a glamour of appreciation through the physical textures of twine, board, and papers, and it has the smell of photo chemicals and Wallace's potsmoke on it. To the eye, it is a fastidious range of both handmade and glossy (speaking of the photographs) to cheesily machine-made and already about-to-crumble-papers.

One of the things I remember in regard to *Semina* is that when I advised Jim Morrison to publish his poems for the first time, he was concerned that people would not appreciate his poems, that they would only look at them because he was a rock star. I suggested self-publishing to him as being what I had done, and what Shelley had done, and then giving, as Berman had done, the poems to friends to see their reactions. Apparently I'd shown Wallace's *Semina* to Jim because the first secret editions of his poetry, *The Lords* and *The New Creatures*, are brought out in such a way that they look like Wallace might have done them. So Jim also had been influenced by the *Semina* aesthetic. It hit a wide range of poets in surprising ways.

Regarding *Semina*, it was always old by the time you got it because you were interested in it and waiting for it. Since this was a love structure, an assemblage of meaningful materials, that you waited for— an esthetic, a spiritual occasion, an act of soul-building—it was also a slow-moving process. It would take Wallace six months or a year to get an issue of *Semina* out. You'd say, "Well, what are you doing now, Wallace?" and you'd get involved in the process. He wouldn't ever quite tell you what he was doing. So by the time it came out it was old, you'd waited for it for a long time, and then it was in your hands and it was brand-new. But there it was on that edge—it was about to fall apart again. Papers would fall apart, a photograph by Walter Hopps could peel off the page it was glued on; it was poised in a special place where nothing else existed. Even if friends were doing "mail art" or things like that, that was an entirely different thing. *Semina* is not a secular magazine; it's a magazine of the spirit. In the same way that we misunderstand today what the Dadaists were doing, or the early Russians—we misunderstood what Kandinsky was doing, or what Malevich was doing—we don't realize that the roots of those things are in deep, old spiritual beliefs from Hwa Yen Buddhism to Swedenborg to Meister Eckhart. Wallace's work had those old deep roots of spirituality, whereas mail art was secular and immediate. It had to do with the person's spiritual growth, but did not have the roots that Wallace intuitively tapped into with the production of *Semina*.

Like cool jazz or bop, *Semina* didn't ask for any approval. It didn't expect any approval, except from the circle of friends it went to. One couldn't subscribe or purchase it, so it didn't cater to anyone. The only catering it did was to the love of one's friends and their love for you, and the love for art that was part of the instinctive process. It was an outlaw publication. Being outlaw, it reveled in the contradictions of love and pain, and of drugs and of deep thought. We knew these were not contradictions but they were seen as contradictions by mainstream culture. This was something we hadn't really seen before, even in our own Beat milieu. It matched what we poets were doing and it matched what the painters were feeling.

Semina was unwholesome. In the age where the eight-cylinder car and military uniform represented wholesomeness, *Semina* was the ultimately unwholesome object, and we gloried in it. It was a magazine, or an assemblage, that would fling together Jean Cocteau and Orson Welles and David Meltzer and Charles Bukowski with no thought of the inherent contradictions of doing so. Part of the game rules was to do away with rules, with the rules of separation and distinction that were taken for granted. How could you print Bukowski side by side with Artaud and Hesse, or with Cameron? *Semina* is a poseur with the slyness and charm of a swami, but one who does, in fact, quietly and secretly know deep things. *Semina* is like the smoke and mirrors used by the Wizard of Oz in the movie, but behind the smoke and mirrors are views of the reality of the structure of nothingness. That's basically an Eastern, un-American view, regarding seeing through, and moving through, the veil of Maya. *Semina* says, "Everything is as flimsy as this magazine is. Here's a dose of reality for you. It's not like the four-door sedan, it's like this. Everything is all some kind of religious experience. You can look at it all as being love, or God."

Another thing about *Semina* is that it doesn't have any credentials. *Semina* has no credentials, no authority, no badge from the 4-H or the American Insurance Institute. *Semina*'s a real outlaw act, as complex as outlaws in the Old West, as sexy and cool and hip and pop—and at the same time religious. Furthermore, it's sabotage. It's a decor for soul-building. And those of us who were interested in building our souls used it not only as our decor but as a pointer to new directions for us, and as an outlet that we might follow with the portholes it created for our imagination.

LIPSCHUTZ-VILLA: I'm looking at this cover of *Semina* 7, and I see in the corner "Art is Love is God."

MCCLURE: Well, "Art is Love is God" may be in that same issue where Wallace prints a part of Juan de la Cruz, St. John of the Cross. You can hear the echo of Gertrude Stein, at the same time feeling the feet of St. John of the Cross on the moist soil of Spain.

LIPSCHUTZ-VILLA: I read somewhere that William Burroughs called Berman a poet-maker.

MCCLURE: I think that's a wonderful thing for William to say. I would call Wallace a spirit-maker, a soul-maker—because I don't see *Semina* as a poetry magazine. I see *Semina* as an assemblage, and the visual art in it is as interesting as the poetry. The act of creating it is an act that coincides with the poetry. I tend to look at the production of it. In other words, in the era of the slickest production values, here's probably the least slick magazine or the least slick assemblage that anybody had ever seen.

LIPSCHUTZ-VILLA: I'd like you to go through *Semina* 1 and just talk about what comes to you.

MCCLURE: All right. I'll pretend I'm twenty-three years old and seeing *Semina* for the first time. Here's *Semina* 1! Hmm—strange-looking woman on the cover, with eyes of such mixed emotion that I think of the paintings of Francesco Clemente. This cover is very beautiful—and it's got a WB under it. What is WB, and what is *Semina*? The face is like a hieroglyph, it's so vivid. I'm not sure of the emotions, or what that face means. I have a lot of ancillary thoughts about it, but . . . And here it all is, this publication in this envelope used by insurance companies or brokers of some unknown substance, or maybe left over from a ship chandler's office. I open it up, I say, "My god, here's a poem by David Meltzer!" I know David Meltzer—we're both renegade Beat poets in San Francisco. I like that! Then I find a poem by E.I. Alexander. I say, "Oh, I've heard of Bob Alexander. He's a legendary figure in Los Angeles. I'll have to read that one later." In the meantime, here's a wild-looking photo. It seems to be a triple exposure, no, a quadruple exposure. It's by Walter Hopps, *that's* why Walter gave me this! So I could see his photo, and see this magazine. That's great! Now I see what Walter's doing. And then here's another strange and beautiful piece by Walter also which could be part of a liquid projection. I heard about liquid projection shows and there's a man named Lee Romero doing them in Venice, California. Maybe this is a photograph that Chico took of a liquid projection—Whoa! And here's a slinky drawing by a woman with a snake's tongue meeting a Mr. Back Door Man, who looks like he escaped from Pavel Tchelichev. I like that, that's interesting. Here's a poem by Cocteau! It's hard in whatever year this is—1956 or 1957—to find anything by Cocteau. Cocteau's seldom printed in English. I've got to look at that in a minute. Then here's something that just says "Marianne Grogan." I don't know who that is. Oh, and then here's an assemblage sculpture! I know about that. My friend Bruce Conner does that. This is called "Homer," and the photo is by Charles Britten. He's one of the Venice or Los Angeles artists. And then here, wait, there's one more thing in here—"To a Toccata by Bach"? It's a poem by Herman Hesse. I didn't even know Herman Hesse wrote poems!

LIPSCHUTZ-VILLA: Thank you, Michael. That was great! A surge of remembrance.

Out of the Sixties:
Dennis Hopper

Dennis Hopper's photographs are the photos of angels, not just Hell's Angels and Grateful Dead Angels and Human Be-In Angels and Michael Angels and Andy Angels and Hockney Angels but also Angels of Dripping Heart Graffiti. Dennis Hopper is in for the big gamble, showing not just flat angels but ones who receive their depth, their roundness by the resonance of the expressions of their faces and postures of their bodies and muscles.

These people are able to be angels in front of Dennis—to lift the arm, to look down, to stare out with the look of creativity—and it mirrors both the creativity and the intensity of the author of these shots.

Whitehead says, "We think in generalities but we live in detail." But this is neither generality nor detail.

A woman with a crest of pheasant feathers, birdlike, stands almost on tiptoe, face in profile, gazing into the eyes of a stolid soulful man who might or might not be a lover—no matter who they are: this is an enigma of angels and it is both chic and eternal. Her hands will always be that way, one upon another, relaxed upon his shoulder, both possessing and liberating in the same compound gesture relating to their interpenetrating stare. His arm and hand will always hang stolidly and his feet will always be gracefully in that posture; and they may both move gracefully away. They are bound but free, and their specialness creates another dimension of spirituality. This is Hopper's dimension and there is no quarter or compromise in it, whether in *The Last Movie*—which may be a great disastrous wreck of Hollywood

Originally published in Dennis Hopper, *Out of the Sixties* (Pasadena: Twelve Trees Press, 1986).

finances or may, eventually, be to film what Joyce's *Ulysses* was to the novel—Who are we to say? We are to watch as we watch anyone we honor, admire, emblemize, idolize, stand in awe of, clasp hands with, feel bound to by brotherhood or sisterhood, whether from Kansas—as Dennis was—or Kenya.

Flip the page. Oh, look there, there's Allen Ginsberg Angel at the Human Be-In in 1967: but Allen, who wishes to be a saint and a spiritual beauty and with great grace poses for so many photographers with his intensity, is not as he is in other photos—where he may be powerful, soulful, burning bright; here there's an almost puppyish, kittenish sweetness that only Dennis's film can reflect—for it's not so much capturing or fixing but reflecting what Hopper sees that's taking place.

We're all high all of the time, even when we have quit all drugs and drinks. It is the natural high, the marguerita of the mind and muscle, looking back into our everpresent lucidity, creating our own dimension that is the ultimate high. We're always playing with the dolls and lariats of our consciousness and leaps and acts and stances. The *ding an sich* is flexible as a rawhide rope when we're stepping through the twirling.

Goethe discovered the principle of phyllotaxis: the relationship of leaves, one to another, on a plant, on a tree, on a wall; and an artist finds playful faces among the leaves.

Everyone gets to be the conquering Alexander or the pirate of themselves—that's the sixties: to become one's own beauty, to have the nerve to live it out, and to have an artist to be that thing for and to be encouraged by—that's the fifties, too, and the nineties, and the year 1200 or 609. Art moves through time in its own way.

How we stare right though it all with our dark brown eyes or silvery blue eyes or hazel eyes—right into Dennis. Into Hopper. He's there, and our backgrounds can be madcap self-made montage; or the foregrounds may be dissolving into hypnogogia. What a profound stare Peter has—and how open. In a portrait of myself taken in a studio in Marysville, Kansas when I was a year and a half old, I looked out with the same boyish interest, vividness, clarity, intellectivity, and hunger for experience. My little wool sweater had snakelike patterns woven in it. I was wearing short pants and my bare knees protruded as I sat alertly and yet *almost* self-contained on the chair.

My God, is that Morrison? No, it isn't him. But I dreamed last night of Jim. He hadn't died, and was going to an old building in dream-Seattle where there'd been a riot. Inside, where I was trying on shoes, Jim came up. He hadn't died. He was living in hiding and he hoped to become a dancer. It hurt, because I cared for him so much. I could hurt looking at how much Hopper cares, in these pictures.

There's Dean, with the flashlight, being playful while his lips are put on. What a thing to photograph. What an odd moment that would be lost otherwise—without this picture—and here it is.

There's Paul Newman in the net shadow!

I guess this is Hollywood. Not the raw gutty underside or the glitter of tinsel, but the invisible Hollywood known only to those who inhabit it or have inhabited it. There's a sweetness and a lack of fear of sentimentality; there's something about it that's like the Canadian or Mexican temperament. The Hollywood here is not afraid of friendship, love, or sentiment—and it's not nostalgic, either. Nostalgia is a product. These urban sophisticates keep their feelings a secret, and they let them out for their friends. It may be summer and they return from editing the film, as Dennis did, then we got high and turned on the electric waterfall—and it was *real* water falling. I remember it. And the motorcycle roar and the awful tragedies are there for the decor! Oddly, there's no glossiness in this world. Did you notice that! These are kids from the country, whether it's old Anaheim or Tarzana or Lake of the Ozarks, and they've grown up and kept the seasons alive in them; and they've been polished by the seasons: winter writing of frost on the window glass and the spring rains and the hot tar streets of summer. These people carry it all along with them, and they let a little out for Dennis and he lets them. He understands it. There's a profound consciousness here and it is willing to do what we call *resonate* with another consciousness. Let's say he lets another consciousness, which is a face, be beautiful right in its face, and its arm, and its shoulder.

Sure you can stop our motorcycles, but there's a world behind my glasses—and behind my head—and another beyond that—and another past there and they can all move forward and be one thing. Be one photograph, be one resonance, be an image. An image? What's an image? A poem is not comprised of images but of real perceptions, it's really happening in real life there on the page; it's as immortal as it ever was or ever will be, as these pictures are—except for Dennis there is a determining intense, push toward simplicity that is filtered through one of the most brooding, active, innocent, and furious minds.

Each one of these pictures is *sui generis* and defines itself as the sole example of its type, and yet each one proposes that there is a world of such photos, fields of faces and muscles and actions, and each turning of the page proves there is a larger field that is composed of each special type. It is clear that one is dealing not with photos which are representations made on film and reproduced, but with a very high level of art made by an artist who is casual and is willing to take chances— for what's existence but chance?—as with a Mozart or a wolf howling and scribbling his *griffonage* upon the ear's night.

Dennis and I were at the Monterey Pop Festival and the whole event was tossed up in the air—it never came down. It floats there as a spiritual occasion. I wrote to Janis Joplin in a poem after she died,

> . . . Big Brother danced like mad geniuses,
> electronic Rimbauds
> and Amerindians. Then,
> like everyone else, you became mad
> with
> arrogance.
> What do we have but that?

And thank god for the belief in our arrogance, that these photos hang in time and space as spiritual occasions, mortal or immortal is immaterial—everything as permanent as the North Pole or the Big Dipper or the Assemblage Movement. And it all keeps hanging there for us after Dennis has shaped it and let the grace leak out and show forth.

One time long ago Dennis and I were walking just after dawn through rain in Muir Redwood Forest with scent of mulch and decaying leaves and bright rainsparkle in the air. Dennis and I were high and he was reciting the Gospel of Thomas. Then he put his hand out on a fallen redwood and he showed me how he'd left a burned print of his hand on the bark—and it looked to me like maybe he had—but these prints of the eye and soul are even more indisputable. They're there!

Laugh on, James Brown, the open joyful soul in your face gives soul and broad Heart to those around. Keats said the Heart is the hornbook from which he might learn of the world. If there's Heart and soul in these photos then they're also a hornbook, an old-fashioned or new-fashioned primer to learn of the humanity of the human world around. We can be fenced off in the graves of our lives or we can hide in our veils too. Dennis doesn't ask us to lose our privacy. There is not a thing in any photo here that is intrusive. It appears that everyone is willing to give, to let go, or to be their special selves for Hopper.

Everything has life—a bare photo has a pepper tree or an oak in the middle distance through the window.

The politics are very real—the politics of generosity—of the Freedom March and of the screwy loveliness, absurdity, hope and pain of it. This is not a naive politics. The innocent eye was always intense and never naive.

There is a distinction in freedom and that is what Hopper's politics stand for. It is the politics of Giordano Bruno—of open eye and imagination, searching through space, acting in huge gatherings of ramshackle monuments and ghettos. There's nothing very sullen here; this is the politics of doing, feeling, being, marching, striding.

There can be a sweetness even, especially in those who can threaten. When the threat becomes sweet it becomes deep. Hopper sees deep by seeing the surfaces so luminously. Not that the photos are luminous. The subjects have become luminous for Dennis.

There is no exclusion of wit for it is part of a total charm and Dennis can be wholly charming. When wit is the primary focus it is exuberant wit. To quote Blake: Exuberance is Beauty.

A man stands full length in striped trousers, his shadow beneath him, almost like a surf board—above him there's a sign, bare feet on a skateboard; above that is the naivete of a *Challenge* milk billboard.

The visual wit of this piece could stand a long scholastic dissertation, but how dry. How much better to see it—no more, just see it. It needs no more. It is inherently playful, broad, subtle, and utterly without slyness or caprice. It is art.

It seems impossible for these personages to threaten us because their souls show though and we see that Dennis, like Shakespeare, at boy-level believes in a democracy of souls—no, not an equality, for that would be foolish, but a *democracy* of souls. Lear, the Fool, Ophelia, the Gravedigger, Macbeth—no one is threatening in such superior politics. We might find love or friendship or warmth or admiration for all of them. If they glower it ceases to be a glower. A transformation.

How does a young man turn out mature art? Ask Arthur Rimbaud. Ask Dennis Hopper.

Brian Jones and David Crosby get to be themselves here. It's all right to pose as themselves, to be as soulful—as full of soul as they are. These are not public photos—these are shots for the Heart's gallery. Who ever imagined that Hopper would get them printed anyway? There's no need to pose for that other thing that holds the money inside of it and bubbles over with pearls and gold. These are the naked looks that are freed of the need for lucre and show the interest in power and madness and modest subtlety. This is what, in fact, may be the daily news and that which is ever pop and the state in which each being is huge, or tiny as mice kissing, or a superstar.

What does one say of the enigma of collages of billboards with faces torn, scattered, graffitied, mustachioed, signed by "Hecto"—or utterly anonymous as a representation of the power of an almost benign dictator out of Orwell, or breast flashes of a lovely lady? I'd say that such things are common and the trick in representing them is to let them be no less normal than they are and still allow them to demonstrate their own scale. If they are monumental, allow them to be big as Behemoth. Hopper seems to know somehow in his secret wisdom that that which matters is beyond scale and is proportionless—is without proportion. We react to it as if it is very large, but in a universe invaded by measurement and logic we're informed it is in fact tiny or insignificant. Art, whether it is pottery or photography or poetry, liberates us for a moment of timeless clarity of the obligation of scale. Imagine using graffiti, montage of billboard, Third World scrawl, to show that. Someone else photoing the same thing has an utterly different effect.

We're all on the bandstand, we're all using the cameras, making the movie, we're all in the film, we're all cowboys and cowgirls lying together on floors, sitting on couches, we've all paused for just a minute to look at this artist with camera. We think we like him. He's easy to respond to. There's some charm here and we respond with our charm. The experience is intense but there's nothing drippy or creepy. We're comfortable in this dimension. This is an intimate experience, but it's open. There are no hooks or claws or commandments. It's not chic— it's real. The face behind Roy Lichtenstein, contrasting with Lichtenstein's own, allows us to know at a deep, gut level that he is a kind of a human elf—a man-creature with great and lightsome strengths and the capacity to create flowers of strokes and deliberate magical splashes while he sits, as casual as a human, on the old wooden floorboards. Look, he's even wearing a watch and has wrinkles in his sweater and under his eyes.—Or we can even be big, serious babies if we want and play games, or be seriously, earnestly cute—maybe nobody else has shown me just that.

Bruce Conner hangs like a saint over all of us and he fills his art boxes, his icons, with beauty, blonde and brunette and leggy. For just a moment, Dennis shows Bruce doing just that. It's all a pose for eternity where everything is being the reflection of itself turned inside out and opened up like a rose and profound as a play by Beckett, though less fearful of playfulness.

Climb on your old tractor in your dark glasses and go for a ride through Mex Town. We're as hip as the Chicanos or the slashing strokes so carefully, exquisitely planned and then written out by Franz Kline. We don't have to talk about our selves—we're right there in front of, or inside of, our possessions, with furs and necklaces and our looks and our breasts and our shades. It doesn't matter how much we know or don't know about photography; we know what this is about. We may, as the song says, cover our eyes as the animals die, but these animals are mucho alive, and most of them obviously have the depth and grace of a Terry Southern planning assaults on the culture from the Chateau Marmont. Wallace Berman was, for everyone who knew him, in search of the Grail, the Kabalah, clearly a mystic. BUT for no one but Dennis did he show that above, and below, it all he is and was a knight. Though you're gone, Wallace, now we all know you better, your aleph and your pistoned steed like your art and your speech are in our dreams.

There are no portraits here. These are not portraits. Portraits are like plots in films. We don't need them all the time. We need release from portraits as much as we need portraits.

Rauschenberg is inside of everything, everything is inside of him, George Herms sends his babes out in the world, Claes stands there as clearly as Claes—a deep one. It's all in the air like a ball tossed from the hand.

That's the Net of Indra on Paul Newman's face and shoulders. The goddess Indra had an infinitely large net, and at each knot of the net was a mirror, and each mirror reflected every other mirror in the net. Each reflection of each mirror showed all the other mirrors reflecting every other mirror, and in each of those reflections was the reflection of the reflection of every other mirror. One story says that materiality is built up that way out of nothingness, merely reflecting nothingess in illusion. Another good story doesn't have the net metaphor quite so clearly, although it says there is a manner of a net; it states that quarks comprise large particles, which make atoms, atoms comprise molecules, and so forth. But we all know just as Paul Newman's arm and cheek show that those are both just metaphors for our lack of knowing, and what is real are those faces and bodies we have that look inside and outward upon one another.

Towards Perception:
An Interview with
Francesco Clemente

MICHAEL MCCLURE: Francesco, I was remembering a poem by William Blake:

> The Good are attracted by Men's perceptions,
> And think not for themselves;
> Till Experience teaches them to catch
> And cage the Fairies & Elves.

The poem seems pertinent when I look at your work, and I wonder what your reaction is to "The Good are attracted by Men's perceptions, / And think not for themselves"?

FRANCESCO CLEMENTE: Well, what's beautiful about that is the idea that there is this movement toward perception. Meister Eckhart wrote a moving and reassuring line: "Matter's deepest desire is for form." Here again, there is the movement toward perception that makes you free. It's reassuring to believe that, I suppose.

MCCLURE: Yes, I wonder if it has something to do with your idea of trusting the concept of "fragmentation." Does trusting fragmentation allow perceptions to happen in another way?

CLEMENTE: Fragmentation has to do with interpretation. Perception is always there; fragmentation only happens when you begin to interpret

Conducted in 1992, this interview was originally published in *Testa Coda* (New York: Rizzoli Books, 1992).

what you see. Fragmentation means there are gaps in between the fragments and in those gaps something happens. I believe in those spaces "in between." The main question is how to make room.

McCLURE: And then you trap the fairies and elves. Does the work then become a kind of experience that's a form or shape of the perception itself?

CLEMENTE: The fairies and elves also are always there, and it's always a matter of removing the weight of what we think more real; to see it all with the same weight and form for a thing to have a voice.

McCLURE: An art historian I spoke with said that in the past there have been portraits of psychological states that are very moving—by Ensor, Gauguin, Van Gogh, Munch. One of the engaging things for him about your work is that there has never been anyone who portrayed the psychological states you portray, psychological in the broadest sense of the word. It's almost as if new hieroglyphs come together out of perceptions or emotional or psychic states and though we've never seen them represented by anyone else, we recognize them.

CLEMENTE: Do you think that's true, or do you think that's true only for the Western tradition?

McCLURE: At moments it's as if you tear something out of those states, something familial, almost as familial as the household paintings of Bonnard, except that it's unlike anything we've ever seen before. I'm thinking of a pastel you did: a representation of two figures almost melting into each other. One figure is leaning against the other, and to their left is the top of another figure. I believe the head and shoulders of that third figure is wrapped like a mummy, and sitting on the mummy's head is a small graceful figure, and the interior of that figure is spotted with a series of eyes. We look at the pastel and say we've never seen that condition before; we can't paraphrase it, but we understand it. We look at the figure with the eyes on the mummy's head and we understand it on some profound level, but we don't have words for it.

CLEMENTE: I don't know how it happens. I believe my activity is almost ritualistic. I organize places, I trace a border around myself, and then I start a series of movements or actions that I believe are correct within that border. As in a ritual, I preserve the memory of something that I've seen or that has happened, that has lost meaning somehow, but is there. Just as in a ritual it happens that you have movements and actions that nobody knows the meaning of anymore, but they know that's the correct way to perform them. Somehow, in a mysterious way, these actions preserve the memory of this previous moment when something meaningful happened—before it was forgotten.

MCCLURE: You have many qualities of a religious painter.

CLEMENTE: The etymological meaning of "religion" is to bring together, to connect. In that way, I am a religious painter; in my impulse toward connecting, a gathering of meaning or elements.

MCCLURE: It's not a specific religion.

CLEMENTE: Obviously, it's not a specific religion, not a formal religion in any way. I suppose religion is rooted in functions in our mind, and, as far as my work relates to those functions, it may be religious.

MCCLURE: But not a religion that we follow formally.

CLEMENTE: It's not a formal religion, and it's not even, in any way, a systematic set. I imagine that every solution that I arrive at leaves room for other possible solutions. None of my images is dogmatic in any way. They are all images that are there. You recognize and accept their reality and their necessity. But somehow they leave room for other possibilities. The lines, too. I think there is a vulnerability to the lines that makes you always believe, "Oh, yes, that's correct." It could have been different, also.

MCCLURE: You mean the lines of the drawing?

CLEMENTE: Yes, the lines themselves.

McCLURE: Vulnerability is an issue. In an age when people are so heavily body-armored in the sense of Reich, which is psyche-armored at the same time, you have the nerve to be vulnerable, not to be pounding your chest, and to be presenting us with things we recognize as beauty, and I find this very moving.

CLEMENTE: I believe in softness. It's an extremely important quality to achieve. Softness, and I want things to appear where they belong, in time, worn by time already at the very moment they're made. I try to make them look worn already. Regarding immortality, I always think of the line I heard from Krishnamurti one afternoon in Madras long ago. He said, "I'm eternal, not immortal." It's an obvious statement, but somehow I never thought about it in such a clear way. Things can be eternal, but it doesn't mean they're immortal. It's a distinction that I have never heard stated in such a blunt way.

McCLURE: You mentioned Meister Eckhart, who unveils himself as a true atheist, somebody truly without a god. To paraphrase him, he said that belief in God prohibits the ability to experience God. You could say that believing that one is immortal and has this particular shape and continues as this specific shape prevents one from being whatever one is.

CLEMENTE: There is a lineage of these iconoclast contemplatives who leave everything open, just as before.

McCLURE: But with these iconoclasts an entire horizon of their personality comes through. Many people respond with joy. I think some other people respond with a certain amount of fear in that they recognize familiar states that are happening at all times but they feel unsure when they recognize the experience.

CLEMENTE: I think all these functions of ourselves are all there and they all happen at the same time; fear and whatever are needs. There are many ways to face that or not to face that.

MCCLURE: In the book of black-and-white pastels that was done with an accompanying text by René Ricard, there is a recognition of the intermingling of sexual joy and sexual grief. Everybody thinks that they experience sex, and it's a dull thing in their consciousness because they believe they understand it. It's happening to them, but it's s-e-x, sex; so they don't recognize the complexity of psychic elements woven through it. It's almost as if you, in the figures you're using, allowed the edges of the states that are combining to show some unravelling and that is part of the work.

CLEMENTE: I have no sympathy for the idea that death is like the period at the end of a sentence—the end of one's life and that is what gives meaning to one's life, because it is the end. I think death is to be brought into every single day of the week, into every action, into everything that you see. It has to be there, woven in with everything you do.

MCCLURE: Death has to be there . . . ?

CLEMENTE: Yes. If one is able to keep alive this memory of the presence of death, then one realizes that things are either much more simple, or as complex as you want. You realize that a lot of these movements that seem antagonistic are actually the same movements. Then again, to quote this village sage in India. He was another contemporary sage like Krishnamurti. He was a cigarette seller, a man in his eighties, and his disciple was a Polish man in his nineties. In one conversation the disciple said, "Oh teacher, in all you say the detachment is so great and promising, yet the desire to live is so strong." And the teacher answered, "But the desire to die is even stronger." To see that these two movements are really the same allows you to accept a lot of confusing experiences.

MCCLURE: Blake said: "The Tygers of Wrath are wiser than the Horses of instruction." And it occurred to me that Blake is separating out the two elements in a way of showing us that they're one. Tigers of wrath are the horses of instruction. He unpeels it far enough so we can say these are the elements of something.

CLEMENTE: Maybe we're talking about the basic alchemical strategy of *solve* and *coagula*: to discriminate and then to be able to separate the elements of experience and then to experience them fully in one moment.

McCLURE: To make the philosopher's mercury and the philosopher's sulfur, then the gold.

CLEMENTE: I have always thought of my work as a form of breath: it breathes everything out, then everything in again. I guess the moment you are able to discriminate—which means to separate interpretations—between grief and joy or fear and hope . . . these are just names of feelings that we have and are really like a modulation of one breath, of one voice. The sound is one, it just modulates in different ways. And the only art that one can learn is how to adapt to this merciless modulation that keeps happening no matter what we do. Like the Hindus say, the only thing that never changes is change. And the only art you can learn is to adapt to change. And the only intelligence that matters is the intelligence of being able not to cling to the previous state and to accept a new state. Just to be able to be there for every new challenge.

McCLURE: That's wonderful. Charles Olson said, "What does not change is the will to change." He was paraphrasing Herakleitos.

CLEMENTE: The most beautiful way that has been said was by Herakleitos in two words. I can't remember the Greek, but in Italian it reads: *Mutando riposa*. "Changing, it rests." To be able to rest in change is all that you need to know.

McCLURE: Herakleitos also said, "Movement can only be perceived by that which is in motion." And I thought that the strategy of fragmentation is a way of experiencing movement. When one makes a tank of oneself, there is no motion except that one hauls around the piece of armor. One of the things that I wanted to bring up while we are talking is a sonnet of Shelley's. It was written in 1818, and he clearly had been reading Eastern thought. The poem begins with a reference to the veil of Maya:

> Lift not the painted veil, which those who live
> Call Life: . . .

That must be the veil of Maya. Then it continues:

> . . . though unreal shapes be pictured there,
> And it but mimic all we would believe
> With colors idly spread,—behind, lurk Fear
> And Hope, twin Destinies; who ever weave
> Their shadows, o'er the chasm, sightless and
> drear. . . .

Did you notice Shelley's reference to hope and fear? I've always heard that hope and fear are the partners of the religious experience.

CLEMENTE: I thought the religious experience is an experience of helplessness.

MCCLURE: Or grief and joy.

CLEMENTE: I'm surprised you say that. I would think that's the map of our worldly experience: hope, fear, grief, joy. Those are the four directions, the four points on our horizon.

MCCLURE: And we're aswim in it. It's our religious universe. In New York, I see something exciting going on in painting. It looks as though painting has eased free from the structure that it has been gradually building around itself, the kind of consciousness of itself that has become much like a wall. I see new extremes. Your work being at one extreme. I think all art should be extreme, I think if it's not extreme, it's not high art. It's as though painting has opened up.

CLEMENTE: I'm happy you've noticed the vulnerability, because I think in terms of a communal effort, that's where my contribution has been most useful, to introduce this element of vulnerability and timidity and lightness and softness. To make it acceptable as compared to this kind of male universe that was there before. I see it elsewhere now. I see other painters that before would always have a stronger, more somber format now accepting the possibility that they can work even more openly, vulnerably—that I consider a Mediterranean approach.

MCCLURE: On the one hand you enjoy reading Freud's case histories and on the other hand you don't believe in the unconscious. I have sympathy with that because the unconscious itself, as presented to us by the psychological philosophers Freud and Jung, has become an icon. As artists we experience what is identified as the unconscious all the time, we just refuse to name the lineaments drawn around it. It's as if the unconscious has been made with stained-glass pictures when it seems to us to be really quite flowing.

CLEMENTE: Planets and stars and galaxies and the Earth are changing all the time and destroying themselves and giving rise to new systems. If so, why should the unconscious be a fixed system? Why shouldn't there also be some organisms and structures that destroy themselves and new structures that come into place?

MCCLURE: We are like the people before Copernicus when we talk about the unconscious.

CLEMENTE: I just don't think the universe is waiting for our awareness of it to happen. It just goes on whether we understand it scientifically or not, thank God.

MCCLURE: Lots of times you laugh when you look at your work.

CLEMENTE: I do consider laughter to be the most intelligent response. I am always pleased to see someone laughing while looking at my work. Laughter is the poor man's elegant reaction to defeat. When there's nothing else left in terms of language, when you don't have any vocabulary for what's going on and you can't get out of it in any way, the only thing that is left is to laugh. I imagine there is some objective tie between poetical solutions and humor, in the sense that they both deal with the double-bind situation: a situation where you create a bind, a place for yourself where you have no way out.

MCCLURE: Are you ever troubled getting the image of a complex of experiences and having it pour away from you as you work, or are you most of the time able to contain it within the frame?

CLEMENTE: No. There are many sides to these functions of our mind. One is a healing side, which is the image. There is a moment when our perception fixes itself on a point. That is the moment when the image arises, and the image has a healing power on our mind.

MCCLURE: Is it there that you make a connection with Joseph Beuys? When you were a younger man and you discovered Beuys, I imagine that you found in him a shamanistic and healing function?

CLEMENTE: Yes, the connection has to do with this ritualistic activity, which I think is how he did his work. The connection with Beuys has also to do with the place where he put himself—mediating between the healing power of forms and a new strategy of ideas. My position is more traditional than his. I'm turning my gaze away from ideas. Ideas divide people into good people and bad people. I have no interest in that, as I have no interest in formal religions, because all religions create an "us against you" situation. I don't think our world needs that anymore. I want to turn my gaze toward the world of forms—that is a healing world, because forms bring us together, as opposed to ideas, which divide us.

MCCLURE: If Beuys was taking the role of a healer, then you are looking at a more Eastern tradition?

CLEMENTE: In terms of Eastern traditions of knowledge, to choose the way of the shaman is still a form of limitation, in a way, because you still want to heal. In Eastern traditions it is believed that there must be some people who don't even want to heal anymore, they just want to sit there and wait. And I somehow accept that, without claiming that I'm anywhere near that totally compassionate view of the world. But I do have faith in this possibility for living.

MCCLURE: I know that in the pantheon of artists that you are engaged with Twombly is important, yet there is a wide distance between Beuys and Twombly. You've said intriguing things about Twombly before, but I didn't understand them at the time.

CLEMENTE: I know that what we have said so far has had nothing to do with painting. With all my programmed indifference to painting, I still know I have to compromise and set myself within a lineage of painters to give a reality to where I stand. In that sense, Twombly has been a connection, a bridge to the lineage of the New York School, which is the moment in our time when there has been this push towards painting. Although Twombly comes out of this milieu, somehow he has nothing to do with it. To me the most important thing about Twombly is his line—talking about vulnerability and fragility and nondogmatic strategy. Twombly and Beuys draw a line that has gotten thinner and thinner and more vulnerable and more tentative, which is both true and not true. On one side, Twombly is a neoclassical painter with a very strong line, but with a sensibility for a weaker line, which has made it possible for me to get a line as arbitrary as mine. Mine is an extremely arbitrary line, an extremely unorthodox line.

MCCLURE: You say that, but I watched you work with pastels the other day and I was astonished by your absolute sureness in the manner you were following a line.

CLEMENTE: The sureness that you saw I think has to do with some-thing else, which is the quality of the line that has to be there for any painting to be correct, which is a fullness of the line in the same way you have a full line when you throw a clay vase. If you throw a clay vase and your line is not full in all places, the vase will collapse and break. When you make a drawing you're doing exactly the same thing. The line has to be always full as a chest that is inflated. If you don't do that then it's going to be weak. Not tentative as I meant for Twombly, which is a way to look at the world or a sensibility but structurally weak, weakness that's going to break under the eyes of the viewer. It's no good.

MCCLURE: I can see that both Twombly and Beuys are willing to be tentative. They can be absolutely correct but still willing to be tentative.

CLEMENTE: They both also have had a fascination for the Mediterranean, for the European, for the feminine possibility of the Western world, the same way I have. They have been looking in different directions. My interest in India is really based on the fact that we are the Hindus; that is, the Hindus are Americans who instead of going to California went to India. They are the same people. They just chose the mother instead of choosing the father and chose to turn their back on the sun instead of following the sun as the Americans did. We are desperately following the father. The Indians are following the moon. But somehow Twombly and Beuys gave me more confidence in my native lineage of Mediterranean painters.

MCCLURE: You are one of the painters making it possible to move from medium to medium and from outward appearance of style to another style with a freedom that is a relief to many people who love art. I look back on boyhood heroes and see that they were fixed on heroism rather than on vulnerability. When I look at Pollock and see him, finally in 1951, go ahead and drip those figurative heads that he poured in black and white, I say, "Oh, how wonderful." It is a high point that he was able to move on from his style and take a chance and be vulnerable again.

Here's a poem by Emily Dickinson:

Split the Lark—and you'll find the Music—
Bulb after Bulb, in silver rolled—
Scantily dealt to the Summer Morning
Saved for your Ear when Lutes be old.

Loose the Flood—you shall find it patent—
Gush after Gush, reserved for you—
Scarlet Experiment! Sceptic Thomas!
Now, do you doubt that your Bird was true?

And we're all splitting that lark, and it seems to me you're constantly splitting the lark. In the same way that Shelley's poem is an admonition, "Lift not the painted veil," she is telling us, "Split the Lark— and you'll find the Music. . . ." It is under there. Are you splitting the lark? Do you feel you have an endless number of larks to split? Is this trail of creativity that you're making one that is already there, or does it grow and create new possibilities?

CLEMENTE: As you remember, Blake called Satan the unprolific, again guiding us toward the idea that Satan is what is rigid and what stops through ignorance, stops knowledge from proliferating and multiplying itself into a million new possibilities. I believe in contemplation. I really believe that all you need do is remove the obstacles that prevent you from being an instrument of the proliferating force in the world. That's all there is; there is nothing "yours" to contribute. Again, it's a very traditional position.

MCCLURE: Would you resent it if somebody said you are maturing, that as an artist you have matured enormously in ten years?

CLEMENTE: It's possible. I think it would be childish to refuse that idea. There is maturity in art just as there is in animals. If you talk about maturity in terms of the acquiring of skills, the acquiring of abilities and authority in what you do, yes I know that happens, but it does not make things easier at all. It actually can make things even more difficult because, again, what you do as a poet and what I do as a painter is really to work this distance between an experience and the material fact that is a poem or a painting. And being able to cover that distance with more ease doesn't mean that the poem or the painting is going to be better. If you cover the distance with more comfort, a lot of accidents that could have been of interest may be lost.

MCCLURE: From looking at the body of work I sense enormous growth.

CLEMENTE: It's possible. But then maturity goes along with a diminishing awareness or control that you have on how things develop. Maturity is proportionate to your giving up what you think you are and what you think you want to do. I believe you if you say you see that, but in my eyes what you call maturity is a form of disappearing, me disappearing from my own eyes.

MCCLURE: My early essays were about the problem of having the head take control of consciousness rather than letting consciousness speak from the entire body.

CLEMENTE: Which is why I couldn't find an answer to an earlier question of what would I do if there were no obstacles. Fifteen years ago I knew exactly what I wanted to do, but now I have absolutely no idea.

Francesco Clemente:
Field Notes of the Imagination

Francesco Clemente is putting black edges around a nude in pastel. The figure is an extremely beautiful female torso with open labia and generous breasts. Francesco had said the figure was unfinished, and now he's in the small back room of his enormous studio working at it on a flat low table. "The secret, Michael, of pastels, is that you must sit down to do them," he has just explained. Francesco has deep furrows in his face today and several days of beardy growth. It's hard for me to believe that he is continuing work on this pastel; it seems so fine that it should be left alone. The hand with the black pastel begins to thickly outline the shape of the hips and waist of the figure. What was striking before stands with more force than it did, and it now begins to shine. Beneath the nude, in a yellow field shaped like the brow below a widow's peak hairline, are the vowels A E I O U—the poet Rimbaud's vowels. Each one is given a color in the system of the visionary: A is for black, E is for white, I is for red, O is for blue, and U is for green.

I'm an aficionado of painters and sculptors. I like to see them or, should I say, feel them create; I also like to be in a room with a poet friend when he or she is creating. It is a special field of consciousness. Francesco has just finished the pastel, now it is startling; in this last outlining he's created what is altogether a new piece—I feel like whistling at it. On the wall behind Francesco is a photo by Allen Ginsberg of de Kooning and Francesco together in the de Kooning studio. We talk about his visit to see the painter with Ginsberg: "de Kooning, when we walked in, was just sitting in this big studio, and

Originally appeared in Francesco Clemente, *Testa Coda* (New York: Rizzoli Books, 1992).

he was laughing." We both laugh with pleasure at the thought. In the photo, de Kooning is grinning and there's an upright thrust to him—one can see that he is shooting for the stars. In the photo, Francesco is rumpled and looking out with a vivid light in his eyes: stylish, shabby, intense, and kind all at once. This might be a still from a production of *Waiting for Godot*, with Didi and Gogo being played by genius hobos from a distant, but similar, planet.

Francesco has taken the pastel into the studio and there's the giddy smell of fixative in the air. There's the rustle of a big sheet of glassine paper that covers the pastels finished and unfinished, to protect them from the feet of the gray Maltese cat. Far away, in the distant end of the studio, the perky mynah bird whistles and makes that deep-throated, croak-talking sound they sometimes make. Clemente walks in with another pastel that looks complete but now I'm convinced that he'll improve this one too.

This sequence of pastels is radically different from those I've seen before. The earlier ones remain in my mind with a visionary lucidity. For instance: there's the large face with furtive eyes looking to the right and slightly up, as one does in the act of memory, but in this case the memory is crossed with fright. There is the huge, voluptuous mango-like pink scarlet pair of lips, but, in a way, the most important part of the hieroglyph of this gray silvery visage is the blotched gold ocher band shape that crosses from one side of the work to the other. It is in the position of the nose, and it is a horizon of dark, almost randomly placed nostrils—twenty of them. They are outlined in black pastel.

The pre-Socratic philosopher Herakleitos believed that if all the objects of the universe were turned to smoke, the nostrils could distinguish among them. But what is this being in this "combine" of emotions perceiving? One must remember in Clemente's work that one is not seeking to answer the works as they stand there or to find some question that they themselves answer. The works this artist makes are literally statements, the statements of an artist, and they exist in most cases as both statements of themselves and as pauses in the flow of a "circuit" that has opened to him and that he is pursuing in a stream of works. But these circuits or streams or currents—varying as they do from watercolor to fresco—may be complete in themselves and at the same time may make complex cross-references to one another in their unorthodox mythologies and secret or blatant symbologies.

One could wake in the middle of the night thinking about that ocher band of nostrils in that haunting pastel face. In Clemente's iconography, or to be more truthful, in my view of Clemente's iconography, nostrils are also eyes. Nostrils, like ears and mouths, are apertures of sensory and sensual experience—that which one makes permanent within himself, or herself, from what passes in the flow of the world about. The nostril shapes in Clemente's world of art are also egg shapes, and the egg, being a beginning, an origin, is a powerful mental emblem. In looking at other circuits of this artist's work, it is clear that eggs are often filled with skulls. That's understandable—the mortal beginning holds many mortalities and deaths.

We know these tiny skulls contain eggs. The nostril, or egg, is also an elliptical white or luminous shape: a shape of light, and it is certainly consciousness. One imagines that it is consciousness in itself as well as consciousness of sexuality and the painful joy of that manifestation. However, at this point one also remembers in referring to these Clemente circuits, or fields of reference, that these ellipses of light are not only eggs-of-beginning but also shit or excrement. This is not the shit of an adult to be disposed of and condemned; it is the shit of a young child or baby before an opinion has been formed about it and while it is still an object of wonder—still seen, felt, smelled, at that time when both birth and evacuation are processes linked in the perceptual imagination of the very structure of the universe that has the artist-babe as its center source.

In the series of strong paintings that are hanging on the heavily overpainted walls of Clemente's studio is *Foot*. The dark, elongated, prone face stretches from one side of the canvas to the other. The face is sleeping, though the viewer doubts that the consciousness within the face is at all asleep. There is a momentary state of grace involved in this expression. It is surrendered to the almost impossibly light, soft foot that is firmly standing on the brow above the slitted, closed, and sleeping eye. One realizes, without any thought on the subject, that the horizon of the sleeping, gray-black face is the same horizon as the band of nostrils in the earlier pastel just described. In *Heart*, another new painting upon the wall, it becomes clear that this horizon of noses and features of the face is also a mouth. This brown figure with a heart for a face and a phallus and testicles for a sternum holds its hands over the position of the second chakra (or the diaphragm), and the hands make an horizon-like aperture that is incontestably a mouth, and in that mouth is a large luminous pair of eyes.

It is easy to have a fantasy about the nature of Clemente as one watches. He is a painter one watches because he is ceaselessly changing, and yet the changes, the new loops that he pursues, are friendly, in one's perception of them, with the loops that one already knows in the work. Because of this tendency to watch Clemente—as one, over a life, might watch the changes of a forest—there is a participation in his work. One can easily participate as an observer, and then the work that one watches and the "things" of it become naive and dense and intellectual. The contradictions that apparently exist in these qualities disappear—naive and intellectual become complementary; we have let ourselves out of our thought structures by being aficionados of an art. The physical aspects of color and iconography may both have a mental side. But meantime we have experienced mouths of eyes and nostrils and skulls and also the spaces between gently touching foot soles, which become vulva-shaped portholes to the night sky that is often forgotten in the city smog.

Again, there's a slight rustle of paper over the muffled noise coming up from Great Jones Street. Francesco comes back into the little room carrying another large pastel. Finishing this group of pastels calls for an intensely particular state of creativity and an unvarying accuracy of execution. The outlines of figures are widened in black and areas of color come into being under the sure strokes of the pastel. In this pastel most of the field is filled by a man who seems almost bloated in his own bulk; his head is round against the small horizon at the top of the work. He has grasped his body at the center of his torso, and he has pulled back the flesh and opened a large aperture, window, porthole, cave of himself, and inside is another world, and what shows of it is a nubile kneeling nude woman: her torso, breasts, and knees. There is the physical energy of a man tearing himself back, perhaps to his own surprise, to reveal the kneeling, voluptuous, and gracile nude. In works like this one, Clemente shows the vigor of a sudden perception, executed and managed so that it carries forth the lucidity of the original moment of conception.

Hanging with the collection of new works on canvas is a painting titled *Heart*. It is a decapitated brown torso with smoke pouring from it into the wind. The shoulders of the headless torso are humped upwards with the energy or power of a physical gesture, and the gesture, the act, is seen in the man's hands splitting back the chest as if it were a zippered jacket broken open at the waist and still clasped together near the top where the hands are tugging it apart. There is not a kneeling nude inside, but a skyscape of a pattern of parapet-like white clouds against a delightful clear blue. This skyscape is as peaceful and calm and emblematic as representations of ritual symbols in Tibetan tantric scroll paintings. It is a mandala of the sky, but like almost all of Clemente's work, even when it is focused on a center of symmetry, it is skewed, perhaps as a nondeliberate acknowledgment of the movement of all things, moving even when they are apparently in a stasis.

Near that painting in the collection on the wall is a square canvas in muted blends of yellows, browns, pinks. This painting, *Head*, is not two hands tearing back a torso but four hands in a gesture of containing. In these loving and arranging and gently grooming hands are the faces of two lovers. These faces are laid prone and horizontal, as is the face with the graceful foot treading upon it in *Foot*. Both lovers are awake, and in the wide opening of the two visible eyes, one eye of each lover, is an emotional and psychic state that is seldom seen represented and yet felt often. We have no name for this mutual state in which two must commingle to create or imagine it. One can read in this image such rarely acknowledged bedmates as fulfillment, calm, the edge of fear, and a drift of consciousness into a state that allows for the little-noticed meaningfulness of peripheral visions. This is not daydream or reverie being represented, but an alert, calm equipoise— a small but hugely important moment of grace. Like many moments of grace, there is a dry velvety texture to the moment of danger that accompanies it.

Near this studio exhibition of canvases, against another wall, stands a large four-poster bed in the Memphis style by the designer Ettore Sottsass. To the right of the bed, lying on the floor, spread as a rug, is an old kilim with a pattern of diamond-checkered stripes. Near the bed on the kilim is a little tower of books. At the foot of the stack is *Gita*, which is a Sanskrit-English commentary on the *Bhagavad Gita:* each word is presented in Sanskrit, then the romanized form of the word in Western letters, then an English translation of the word. These are followed by a flowing translation in English. On top of the dog-eared *Gita* is a new Italian book on architectural ornament. A paperback of the Bantam *Bhagavad Gita* rests on that. Next is another book in Italian, on the anthropology of ancient cities. *A Quick Graph*, a collection of essays and notes by Robert Creeley, weighs down the stack, and lying on it, open and hanging over the edge of the pile, is a paper edition of the sermons and fragments of the fourteenth-century German mystic Meister Eckhart.

In the large workspace and studio where the Memphis bed stands and the canvases are hung, it is easy to imagine and feel a complex state of well-being, orderliness, calm, and energized continuity. The old patched and repatched plaster ceiling looks in one place, wholly by accident, like a graffiti fresco and in another place like a ceiling mural from the heyday of Abstract Expressionism. In the large studio one becomes alert to the painterliness of things: a purple and yellow spot of encaustic upon the green denim cover of a sofa pillow might be a gouache painting by a dryly elegant existentialist.

A burst of truck roar and honking rises from the street below. On a varnished wooden table in the middle of the large room is a stack of watercolors. The watercolors are folded like a book and wrapped in a big piece of ecru-colored rice paper that crackles when opened. The rag paper of the watercolors is grayer than eggshell; it is clearly hand-made and dappled or dimpled in pattern. Done on a recent trip to Southern India, they are unlike any watercolors Clemente has shown before. Usually Clemente's watercolors are seen to be swift glidings of rich and nearly pure colors, often with much white as the background. This suite, this circuit, has steeped quickly into the paper, spreading gentle and alert and thoughtful as it portrays a set of processes of vision and imagination in the wet movement of the watercolors into the soft solid paper. This paper is a co-substance with the watercolor that has joined it to become a mutual act. There is a new sheet showing large eyes with fern tendril chakra swirls. (In Tantrism the goddess is called up through the body to the brow through seven lotuses called chakras.) Then there is the bottom of that face. Then there are eyes with more burstings of tendrils and sprouts from the head chakra in some virtualization of a higher moment of consciousness, but it is all seen through passing screens of arms, legs, mouths, scarlet nipples, an anus, and the suite closes with a dark brown hand in midair holding an even darker foot that tiptoes down onto the hand as lightly as the foot on the sleeping gray face in the painting *Foot*. Around the edge of the painting the watercolors have formed themselves with a seepage of color into a wavery border of a tint that varies from red brown into magenta and back to brown.

"Yes," says Francesco, "I am never really involved with the way the work finally looks. That's all there in itself. After the work is done, I'm in exactly the same position as you are as a viewer, and I recognize that this thing was necessary but have no idea where it comes from, or what it is, in any sense." He speaks softly and nearly mumbles but is quite clear. His fingertips go across the tip of his chin for a moment. On the wall of the large studio, a theme, one of multiple overlapping possible themes, pops into the foreground for a moment in the way a line flickers in op art or as neon flashes for a moment on the street down below: many of the paintings on the wall stand out as images of crucifixion. *Foot* has the shape of a cross, and if it were inverted the image would be more clear. In that case the crescent moon and stars held between the gentle soles of the feet would be the head of the crucified person or god, and the chest of the crucified would be the lips of the female sexual organ and labia. This wholly iconographic image of the universe brought in its concentration to the open secret of sexuality for a moment has the subtext or "overtext" of a cross with flesh upon it. Why not?

"It does not help that we are all trained to be on a restricted diet in our ways of experiencing the world, living and selecting what's good for us and not good for us. I think that makes things seem unique, when they are not that unique. There is an endless tradition, a stream of things that have been done. I think we have seen it all along, but to have seen it doesn't mean you see it now. You have to do it all over again." There is a thoughtful pause.

It is clearly a dead man in *Head*. A pointed red blade comes out of each of the orifices of the head. The angle of the head and shoulders of this "crucifixion" clearly says this one—this being—is dead. But there's no possible visual autopsy, for the viewer could not say for sure whether these blades, as pointed as the black-handled Scottish daggers, are driven into the head from the outside or whether they have burst through the head's windows and doors from the inside.

"I think we forget everything and have to find it out all over again. I don't believe knowledge is an accumulation of memories. Knowledge is how much experience you can have of what's there now, today. . . ." The crucifixion in *Oblation* is almost joyful in its grisliness, as a young child might be cheerful playing a role in some scatological scene that he or she has not yet been taught is a horror. The decapitated neck pushes into a bloody, smoky, grainy band of wood or sky. Blood that is, in fact, not only gore but the pollution of our petroleum-addicted and mechanized society floppily drizzles and cloudily pours downward from the swollen stumps of the upper arms. The vagina spews smoking gore (or is it the opening of the stump of a hermaphrodite's penis!) onto a besmirched or crusted table of stone that supports the remaining stumps of the legs. There is as much innocence in this image and as much visionary truth, or even serious humor, as there is in the thinking of pre-Socratic philosophers, who considered that men who did not believe war was necessary were fools. (For better or for worse, we could use more true fools.) So perhaps it is the ghost of the crucifixion that is one of the numerous forms that Clemente feels appearing to him, and the crucifixion lies in the cauldron with breasts and lips and stars and excreta and gentle touches of hand to foot or lips to nipple.

These canvases on the wall seem more *painted* than previous works; that is—they seem to exist before the artist paints them. This circuit of works is as independent of other circuits as are the earlier gold paintings, which were monumental blocks of eyed, sepia-colored rectangles painted on backgrounds of gold. All these circuits, strategies, and suites clearly derive from the same ceaselessly active and highly contemplative mind or consciousness. This mortal mind moves the pigments through open moments of energy when inner pictures can come right to some outer surface. A viewer believes that sometimes this happens with struggle and sometimes it must be a surprise. However, there must be an organicity or animalness to these occurrences of art. There must be inherent principles that are less than obvious because of Clemente's use of his concept of fragmentation. This principle is reminiscent of Keats's negative capability in that, in the moments of inspiration, the artist trusts in his art and he trusts in processes that lift it out of himself onto the bare surfaces of the paper or the cloth or the wall that are under his hands or in front of him.

The *Tao Te Ching*, the Book of the Way, composed in China in the fifth century B.C., says:

> Man, when he enters into life,
> is tender and weak
> and when he dies,
> then he is tough and strong.
>
> That is why the tough and strong are
> companions of death,
> the tender and the weak,
> companions of life.
> For this reason:
> if the weapons are strong, we will not be victorious.
>
> *As translated by Richard Wilhelm*
> *and Eugen Diedrichs*

The artist never loses the babe in himself or herself, never ceases playing. The strong man or woman kills off or boxes-in the child in the self and becomes a soldier or banker or fireman who proposes and follows a path through life. One castigates oneself for not following one's duty. One's capacity to act is directed by a plan. Clemente does not believe in having a plan. If anything, he is always checking with his work to see what the plan is, what his art will show him of it. Or pehaps to see if there is a plan at all in the world out there that is at once, to him, most ancient and simultaneously potently modern. This is one of the organismic aspects of Clemente's body of the work, which is, of course, inseparable from the course of his life. Though he is highly organized, Clemente does not plan to be something—to be something that he is not already. He is moving through his experiences and his perceptions of them. They are not melioristic, they are not leading somewhere. They are not going somewhere. There is no apparent goal. This is foreign or strange to some people. A cougar kitten does not plan to become a cougar and to practice the virtues of cougarness and go to cougar school to become a better cougar. The cougar takes what is there in the stream of the world passing by, or standing still, and moves in it, playing in it, exercising it, sniffing it, raking its claws over the rough bark of it, and staring dumbly and thoughtfully and thoughtlessly at the stars and moon of it, taking mice and rabbits and deer as the mother teaches it and as they come into vision. Thus is Francesco Clemente.

Jack Kerouac wrote each novel and each book of blues poems as if it were a separate circuit. Each novel is in a unique style that is not clearly related to the style in any other novel. *Subterraneans* was written in a dense and sparking dark frantic style reminiscent of Dostoevsky on amphetamines and sweet wine. *On the Road* is a lucid *bildungsroman* foundation novel, of a young artist forming his self with his friends and their travels. *Big Sur* is an internalized brooding introspection of regret in another style. All the works of Kerouac put together (or imagined) in order form a large coherent pattern of an artist thinker. Kerouac's business was not to explain but to do. There are ellipses, and times of quiet, then there is the huge looping and toss of a flesh coil and a surge forward—or what looks like a sudden break-through. This is as wholly organic as life, which does not only grow steadily, it moves also in streams and circuits and looping coils and deaths and mutations and surges of energy.

It is not surprising that Clemente is a reader of the Beat poets. The Beats are the most organismic movement in modern poetry. They also understand, as Clemente does, that consciousness is as physical, or non-physical, as everything else and indeed it pervades everything. It is no wonder that Clemente works with poets so compatibly in his many collaborations of poetry and painting.

It is notable that Francesco Clemente's early watercolors of psychological portraits and self-portraits are absolutely achieved and accomplished and especially finely executed. These works stand out in one's memory as among the surest contemporary watercolors. The SHEER PLAY, the refusal to be bound by the skills of earlier work, reminds one also of Kerouac. After writing his great novels, Kerouac dared to let it all go in *Mexico City Blues* and laid out his genius in choruses of overheard mumblings and wordplays that fall together into a work of the highest religious art. It was sheer play. It is the field notes of the imagination.

In Francesco Clemente's work there is an almost blatant confession that can be both truth and fantasy. On the other hand, there is shyness. With daring representations of sexual intimacy and decapitations there is concurrently a shifting and draping of veils of iconography. On one side it seems perfectly clear and on the other smokily elusive; sometimes both happen at once. Clemente's reply is, "I think the clarity of expression of accomplishment . . . the *execution* . . . has to be clear." There is a faraway look in Francesco's eyes, but he speaks precisely with occasional pauses: "The memories and experiences and feelings legitimize the fact that I set to work, those are obscure matters that can only be described obscurely, and I think have to remain so. It would be a lie to show as clear-cut something whose importance is really there by the fact that the borderlines are not clear, they are fuzzy, continuously flowing into something else." Just as this might become cyclic reasoning, Francesco continues, "First of all, every one of the experiences in states that I'm concerned with doesn't have a name in our vocabulary. Secondly, it is their nature to overflow into other states as soon as you are there to fix them, to describe them." There is a pause with no sound from the street. "If you want to get attached to them, they just elude you."

Inherent in all of us, in our human nervous systems, is the ratio of bodily experience and sensory perception as it is perceived and measured by the cerebral cortex. In *Gray's Anatomy*, there is a figure of the motor homunculus. This plate shows a cross-section of the brain and the outer cortical areas that figure in the use and experience of the body. Around the hemisphere of the brain is curled a man with his body corresponding to the active areas of the cortex. It is blatant and almost titillating in its raw truthfulness. There is an enormous head and staring eyes and large nose. The open mouth of the homunculus is huge. Behind the individual, and the artist, is the exemplary individual. Since Clemente is not in the process of creating an ever-growing and ever-perfecting "autobiography," because he immediately values all the selves that make up himself, he is vulnerable. He is bare and he is alive in the storms and summer days of sight, sound, taste, touch, and smell and an old and steady but constantly shape-changing universe.

His pastel portraits of sleeping children are as personal and unique in themselves as any of the larger circuits he works at. One of these portraits depicts a little girl, perhaps a year old, eyes closed, fast asleep. Her facial expression is a mixture of otherworldliness and the strained balance between tension and bliss that a child has as it struggles sometimes to hang onto sleep. The face, as portrayed, does not sentimentalize babyhood, though it seems to adore babyhood. The face shows those lines, which are sometimes seen fleetingly, of the adult that the child will become. The child is lying on her stomach, and her right, gray-stockinged leg is tossed up at one of those odd angles that limber children manage. A brown hand has taken the ankle of the raised leg and clasps it gently as would a loving parent or a kind doctor. The child is in an irregular pool of silky yellow light. The yellow in this application is sensuous in its enjoyment of the medium. This sensuousness is not so much an enjoyment of what may be done with the medium as it is literally an enjoyment of the medium for its oleaginous and gritty self. There's no great effort at smoothing or sleek marbleizing in this work. The mauve background of this portrait is as straightforward and unmanipulated in its clarity of tint as a color field by Mark Rothko.

Returning to the paintings on the wall, *Foot* has a background color of the same simple clarity, a medium-colored blue purple. It could be the color of a suit or a cape in a comic book or it could be the color that corresponds to the scent of a sweet perfume. The figures of the painting are two bare feet, natural feet with widespread toes that may have never known any shoes except sandals. There is a sense of innocence about these feet, seen as they are from a view looking at the soles. One thinks for a moment of the verbal pun of soles and souls. Through a spread and open gash in the sole of each foot pours a stream of excreta making ever-higher mountain-shaped mounds. As one continues to look it becomes possible that several toes on each foot have had one joint amputated. As with the portrait of the sleeping child, this is not a traditional representation, not an unusual symbology; it is a wholly personal experience, a recorded and created event coming from recogizable horizons and verticalities. There is the sense that this is new, but all quite well understood and understandable in the world of imagination that steams and sleeps and laughs and strides and purrs and gently taps and incessantly hammers all in the same moment.

Noguchi Notes

While putting the final touches on the steel *Pierced Table*, Noguchi added a curved, finlike piece resembling a feather in an Indian headband, and said with a smile, "I am a native American." Isamu Noguchi is *twice* a Native American. First he was born in California, and second his maternal grandmother was part Indian.

These sculptures pull together aerospace and the world when it was still young. Landscape shapes of cactus, rock, cloud, and mountain can be seen. Some forms are in chrysalis, as a moth when pupating; others are in a metamorphosis that could be either rock or butterfly. Among these sculptures are unexpected and newly invented contours bringing to mind the powerful, repetitive elegance of Thelonius Monk playing *Round About Midnight* or *Ruby My Dear*. As in the best jazz, spontaneity is an outstanding quality, but the spontaneity of these works is close to the swiftness of calligraphy and ceramic. As in calligraphy, the sculptures have been freely, broadly, and almost instantly drawn. They are the works of the inspired instant. Like ceramics, the sculptures have been made quickly and have been through fire.

In the galvanizing process the sculptures passed through boiling zinc and returned with newly made surfaces of nature. The surfaces resemble those of rocks in a stream. Each skin, epidermis, outer layer, is unique in pattern and texture.

> Wave   pock   blur
> mottle   blotch
> ripple
> thickness
> flow pattern

Originally appeared in *Isamu Noguchi at Gemini* (Los Angeles: Gemini, 1983).

diffusion of mat shimmer

silver   gray   blue   stone color

The sheet steel has been cut with a plasma torch—an ultra high temperature flame. The plasma torch is employed for cutting airplane parts, heavy equipment, and hard metals. The cutter is a large, sleekly moving machine with an electric eye at one end that follows Noguchi's line. At the other end of the machine, the plasma torch cuts a template from a sheet of steel. As in welding, the silvery blue flame of the burning is so bright that it cannot be looked at directly. (Through a black-glassed welding mask the torch beam is seen as a narrow bright rod of light of a coppery green-yellow.)

In conversation Noguchi says, "Industrial process has its own secret nature—its own entropy, its own cycle of birth and dissolution. . . . We try hard to subject the industrial process to man's supervision." But, he says, that industrial process could be freed of strictly human and civilizational preconceptions.

One piece had been marked on with a grease pencil before galvanizing— the galvanizing then made the quickly, deliberately written technical letters (silvered above the surface) a permanent part of the sculpture. Noguchi enjoys the unexpected marking—the unexpected appearance of the writing laid upon the unpredicted patterns of zinc. Noguchi says, "Preconception is the death of art." He does not open art to chance but lets down the strictures of preconception so that new occurrences may appear on fields that he has cleared.

Ramon Margalef says that information is that which influences the future. Noguchi speaks with pleasure of the recognition of myriad accidents in the world. Accident is a result of clear and evident causes. It is fine to be appreciator and instigator of accident. It makes a brighter world.

Commenting on a consensual style (that which is commonly and normally agreed upon as style), Noguchi stated: "That's when a style loses its keen edge of originality. That's why I'm always off on my own investigations. In a way, I'm an eternal novice."

Some investigations are of great scale. There is ceaselessness in Noguchi's movement from material to material and in shift from attack to attack. A profound artist changes our lives and freely gives the myriadness of his aspirations and consciousness. Consciousness can have a real physicality—sculpture is real physicality—thought is real physicality.

ETERNAL NOVICE
is a master of style
beyond style.
The mountain
of shapes
is the stone
to be carved
for
the perfect
lyric.
Real hands
reach across
memories.
Fur. Boulders. Scales
to weigh
the grams
of Experience.

As a child, Noguchi's mother read him William Blake. Probably she read him *The Marriage of Heaven and Hell*. One of Hell's proverbs is, "The Cistern contains; the Fountain overflows." Noguchi is a fountain pouring forth sculptures. These pieces are his physical thoughts. They are rivulets, waves, ripples, spray, bubbles, splashings from the flow of work. They are not referential because they speak in the thought of sculpture but they do create real pieces called sparrow, persimmons, cloud mountains, and wind catchers.

Art since Cubism shifts quickly from stance to stance to perceive matter and explore spirit-biography (as with the Abstract Expressionists). Noguchi utilizes what precedes him and goes within to a music-like, interior, self-creating, fountainlike thought—these pieces are the real splashes and solid metal bubbles that emerge.

Noguchi's garden park in Costa Mesa is his gift to California. In it the textures and patterns of the stones under foot (as well as the trees, cacti, grasses, silhouettes on the walls, and reflections on glass) are reminiscent of the work in galvanized steel. The stones underfoot were carefully and deliberately chosen. Building the garden was an act of play, but active, spontaneous, and quick play. As a fountain is said to play, these pieces are part of an act of play. Play is beyond seriousness or comedy—it is either and both.

> "It is my desire to view nature through nature's eyes, and to ignore man as an object of special veneration. There must be unthought-of heights of beauty to which sculpture may be raised by this reversal of attitude."

The landscape scrolls of mountains and rivers painted in the Sung Dynasty of China have an ambition in common with this desire. The sleek, jagged scrolls by Mi Yu-jen and the abstracted dreaminess of Mi Fu step into the dimension they create to view nature through nature's eyes. In those paintings man and his bridges and huts are no special objects of veneration.

Some of Noguchi's sculptures resemble the upward looming, intensely-geologic mountains painted by Emperor Hui-tsung. The memorable karstian, water-carved, wind-eroded peaks of China are the universe experiencing itself in an open-ended, growing self-intelligence. In Sung scrolls there is sometimes a farmer-philosopher standing by his tea house, head down, in contemplation. It would be possible to stand that way beside *Cloud Mountain* or *Atomic Haystack*. Another thrust of Noguchi's is his consciousness of the interdependence (at this time especially) of nature and man. He would like to do a monument to the holocaust—but he thinks of the holocaust as all present and past human destructions including the apparently terminal war on nature as we know it.

Speaking of the sea palm, a small palmtree-shaped plant which will grow only upon rocks that are heavily crashed by tidal surge, Noguchi says, "Adversity is necessary." How appropriate to create with the adversity of industrial metals. A crisis is observed by the artist as he creates. The adversity of substance is acknowledged.

The steel of the hawk-beaked *Giacometti's Shadow* stands in its grace of self. It is a stele that could be imagined on a Southwestern desert or in a Hawaiian or Chinook rainforest, but it also has the implied shadow of a memory and a mysterious linkage with the world of art as well as nature.

Garcia Lorca's poems give the gift of the writer's sensorium, his special vision of how things are, the sound of horses in the night or the odor of jasmines on beige sand. Noguchi's works give one the artists's sense of angle, surface, texture, solidity, space, and surprise at the perception of solidity and emptiness.

Noguchi says, "One should be free of style." His sculptures refer to all his work and to all of his experiences. He is an artist of reason. The work embraces its own apparent contradictions, and refuses to be narrowed. It is appetitive of new sensation, exploration, and ideas. Human figures, when they appear in Noguchi's work in stone or metal, are not of one culture or lineage. They vary from the eighteenth-century mystic Zen master Hakuin (who wrote, "The universe loses its body at midnight") to the Greek tragedian Euripides (playwright of Dionysos in the intense and bloody *Bacchae*).

The black granite *Night Wind* (1970) and other horizontal pieces such as *This Place* appear in Noguchi's oeuvre in various materials—and they seem to be the sculpture of the earth experiencing itself. They refer to each other. In turn, they all refer to the artists' playgrounds, and the designs of the playgrounds reflect Noguchi's gardens. *Cactus Wind* points to those pieces but with a new extension of materials into galvanized metal. In this manifestation, the horizontal sculpture is a little above the earth, perhaps afloat with the energy of the constructive materials—the plasma torch and heli-arc welding.

Pieces reflect and counter-reflect one another as they are created. Noguchi's core pieces and machine drilled sections of the late sixties and seventies are the predecessors of the use of metallurgy. ("All previous works are mistakes," says Noguchi.) The stainless steel, burnished aluminum, and welded pieces are predecessors and reflections on this idea. Earlier works that appear to be mounted and hanging stones cast in bronze are the brothers and sisters (if once removed) of similar new works. Noguchi's investigations of many decades blossom and become manifest. Noguchi's work is exactly like nature. It is nature, in fact. Look into Noguchi's work at any point—the world of it is growing, extending. It is solid and moving in time. Like nature and reason the work does not stand still—it evolves and devolves, always becoming more complex as the body, the field, becomes more complex.

Nile Insect Eyes:
Talking on Jim Morrison

FRANK LISCIANDRO: Could you talk about the first time you met Jim Morrison?

MICHAEL MCCLURE: It was sometime in 1968. I believe Michael Hamilburg was going with Pam Courson's sister, and Jim wanted to meet me and had heard that Hamilburg was my agent. Hamilburg got hold of me while I was in New York rehearsing *The Beard* and arranged for Jim and me to meet in a bar in the Village. I was wearing a pair of dark blue leather pants, and I think Jim was wearing leather pants with a tee-shirt. It was one of those things where we walked into the bar, I took one look at Jim and he took one look at me and we decided we didn't like each other. You know how young men are. We sat and glared at one another, sort of cold-fished each other out of existence. I don't remember how it happened, but one of us bought the other one a drink and we started talking. Hamilburg remembers getting stomach cramps watching us stare at each other.

LISCIANDRO: What kind of impression did he make on you, other than young men staring each other down?

MCCLURE: Well, I liked Jim. I'm not talking about that initial cold stare at each other. That moved over pretty quickly into warm response to one another. I liked his intelligence. I liked his style. I liked the way his mind moved and I liked the way he moved. He was a pretty

Conducted by Frank Lisciandrio in May-June 1990, excerpts from this interview appeared in Lisciandro's *Morrison, A Feast of Friends* (New York: Warner Books, Inc., 1991).

well-integrated human being, both physically adept and mentally adept, the whole individual working in one direction. You could sense the poet there.

You've got to remember that at this point I was not interested in rock 'n' roll. I had already been through it. So Jim being with The Doors meant just about nothing to me. I mean, it certainly wouldn't have been in his favor. It was through the artistry of Ray Manzarek and Jim that I became interested in the music again.

LISCIANDRO: What was his literary background?

MCCLURE: What Jim had was not specific knowledge of, or readings in, a lot of poets but a large, stable, working, vivid, imaginative, and lively picture of what post-World War II poetry is. To some extent— and he may have owed this in part to our conversations—he also had a picture of what nineteenth-century poetry was. Jim did not like to talk about anybody's poetry in particular, not I think out of vanity or modesty but simply out of an accurate feeling that he wasn't an authority and that he was still in the process of learning as he created. But he had a sense of it.

LISCIANDRO: How do you think he learned the mechanics of his craft?

MCCLURE: He taught it to himself. I think almost all poets teach themselves the craft. I would also think that somewhere along the line he had good explication of meter and form, but in the early sixties such things were still not uncommon in high school. You would have some wise, old instructor who would tell you what the sonnet was, and would explain iambic pentameter to you, how the ballad meter worked. It was clear Jim knew that. But the poetry itself—if you go to *The New Creatures*—is well-paced poetry with an understanding of what contemporary poetry is. A person is a poet, a person is a painter. Doesn't it amaze you that some people can pick up a paintbrush and begin? The person just takes up the brush and the figure he's painted looks like his Aunt, and he's got Aunt Fanny sitting in front of him, and he's doing a portrait. It's remarkable. You see Kerouac sit down at a typewriter and start turning out novels. Some people are novelists. Some people are poets. Some people are painters. It's only to be expected that those people are capable of teaching themselves their craft. And Jim was a poet. I taught myself enormous amounts of craft—all the forms, the meters, the styles—when I was about seventeen, and I would think that Jim taught himself sometime in his late teens or early twenties.

LISCIANDRO: What might have prompted him to start writing poems?

MCCLURE: What prompted him to start writing poems would be that he was responding to poems that he saw or heard, poems that spoke to him. Say he saw a poem by e.e. cummings that he liked a lot. That's what started me, in a sense. Actually, I had started writing rhymes and reciting them to people very early, comic rhymes which were complex word plays. I must have been eleven or twelve, and I would make those up and recite them to people for my entertainment. When I was about fourteen, I found some poems by e.e. cummings that I responded to. I thought they were wonderful and lively, and I could see the structure of the imagination. And I said, "Wow, this is really interesting. What power there is in the language, and what an entertaining facility there is in the language, and what a possibility to explore structure." I heard biologist E.O. Wilson say on the radio yesterday that important science consists of play that is disguised as work. You see the possibilities of the play of imagination within an art form, and then the art form begins to speak to you. You wish to perform such feats yourself. You're listening to the blues, and you decide you're going to sing the blues. You say, "Oh my god! Muddy Waters is sensational! Listening to the complexity of that form, how might I do something like this?" I think the beginning of poetry writing probably is—unless there are some unusual circumstances—a response to poetry. One finds oneself; a baby eagle starts to fly by practicing standing on the edge of its nest beating its wings.

LISCIANDRO: But that's a little bit different. That's genetic imprint. Do you think that poets have genetic imprint?

MCCLURE: To an extent some people are more verbal than others, some are more visual, others more imaginative, others are more playful. It's a complex thing that makes a poet, but the propensity has to be there. Part of that propensity has to be hard-wired.

LISCIANDRO: There is a certain facility or a certain openness towards that particular way of doing things?

MCCLURE: Yeah, and I have no doubt that both Jim and I were people with that given propensity, ready to go with it, and probably not liable to do anything else very successfully.

LISCIANDRO: He couldn't be an architect necessarily.

MCCLURE: No. It's not a lack of intelligence but a lack of the right medicine bundle, as the Native Americans might say. I was fortunate because not only was I writing poetry but found that I had a facility for novels, which I did not necessarily expect because I wasn't interested in writing prose. I had a gift for theater also and could write plays, so I began to make a flush. I could begin to be myself as I began to write plays, and Jim was crazy about them. He was more guarded about my poetry because I think my poetry was having an influence on him. If you look at the poem "Brian Jones" you'll see that Jim had the same kind of problem with me that I might have had with Robert Duncan. One doesn't want to be overwhelmed.

Jim had a lyric gift, not in the sense of song lyric but poetry, which we usually think of as page-oriented. And then he also discovered he could sing and he could write songs. He did the smart thing—he kept them separate and the more separate he kept them the better off he was. Still, as Diane di Prima says, it is all one life anyway. It's all coming out of the same imagination.

LISCIANDRO: To go back for a moment, who among poets prior to the 1950's do you think he read and admired?

MCCLURE: Jim avoided specifics like that. Everybody knew Jim was quite interested in Nietzsche. Oddly enough, as I look at it I see the possibility that he paid a lot of attention to Kenneth Patchen. He had some things in common with Patchen that I thought only I had in common with Patchen, and you have to remember how Patchen is being ignored. Kenneth Patchen was always the most secret thing locked in the heart of just a few admirers of his work. His was a kind of romantic creation of other, haunted worlds. Jim had that quality. I would imagine Pound and Patchen are two of the people you might not ordinarily think of in terms of Jim, but I think he may have looked to Pound for the feel of the Classical world and to Patchen for grace of statement. For that world where people are wandering, or killers are wandering through that world. I'm speaking about the early, intensely romantic agonized poetry of Patchen.

LISCIANDRO: What about Hart Crane as an influence?

MCCLURE: I'm an admirer of Hart Crane's poetry. I find it beautiful, but I think it is so contrived—so hard-edgedly contrived—that it's difficult for me to imagine a young man doing anything more than reading it. There's a kind of perfection to Jim's poetry that's in Crane's poetry, where you feel it's set just perfectly the way Crane's often is.

LISCIANDRO: What about the "lost manuscripts," Morrison's work which was supposedly in his portmanteau? You had the portmanteau in your possession for a time.

MCCLURE: Yeah. Jim's wife Pam called me when she got back from Paris after Jim's death. She was living in Sausalito with some strange associates in a house where people were just sort of melting in and out of back doors. She was extremely distraught about Jim and telling me about their last days, and she gave me his portmanteau, which was a leather doctor's bag that opened on top and had a handle. I had it for about six weeks. At the time I was writing a novel, being sued by a man who is now a congressman from southern California, and dealing with the Hell's Angels. I didn't think I could handle another thing. Clearly, she wanted me to edit it, and if Pam hadn't been there I would have kept it and edited it myself in the future. I gave it back to her and said that it was my clear understanding from things that had happened in London and after London that Jim considered her to be his editor, and I thought it would be a good thing for her to edit it. I told her to put it in a safe, some kind of bank vault before it disappeared.

The portmanteau itself was one of the most impressive examples I've seen of how a poet works. Taking the material as it stood my guess is that it would have made a manuscript of between 100 to 130 pages. Mostly shorter poems, very few over a couple pages long. And in almost every instance there were multiple versions held together by a paper clip. You'd open up the portmanteau and there were perhaps sixty or seventy little files in there. I've never seen anything more orderly.

LISCIANDRO: Were the manuscripts typed or handwritten?

McCLURE: They were mostly typed. Perhaps the only other people who saw it were Freewheelin Frank and my wife of the time and poet David Gitin and perhaps Maria Gitin. By that time Jim was a legend; I didn't want somebody to take it and drive away with it, so I wasn't showing it casually. It was a miracle of order and it astonished me because that's the way I work. As a poet, you've got to be that orderly. The world is not exactly waiting for your poems. You've got to protect them, keep them together. Nobody else can or will do it for you.

Regarding the manuscript, it would have been a matter of carefully going through and picking out the right version of the surviving versions and, I think, eliminating some of the poems that were not resolved. In a sense, none of them were resolved, but in another sense two-thirds of them were resolved enough to publish. This was a re- markable thing about Jim. For a couple years I had been Jim's best friend—and he had no other literary friend—and he had not told me about the portmanteau. I laughed about this. I thought that he's as secretive as I am. He's as secretive as any writer.

LISCIANDRO: And each file had drafts of poems?

McCLURE: Sometimes three or four, sometimes seven or eight, and two-thirds of them were realized. These should have been his third book because these were intellectually mature poems. You go to his first book, *The Lords*, and what is that? His UCLA film school . . .

LISCIANDRO: His notes on vision that he was keeping for a long time.

McCLURE: Yeah, maybe even a thesis he had "deconstructed," which is a good way for a poet to work. Perhaps he alchemically collaged his UCLA film school thesis into an incredible document. I looked at it the other day and I'm still interested, maybe more interested at an acute intellectual level than a few years ago. Then there's *The New Creatures*, which is a book of imagistic poetry with hints of seventeenth century, hints of Elizabethan drama, tastes of classical mythology. It's a kind of romantic personal viewpoint in a nineteenth-century Shelleyan/Keatsian sense. "Snakeskin jacket / Indian eyes / Brilliant hair. . . ."

Very nineteenth-century, very personal. Yet the poetry itself is almost mainstream twentieth-century imagist poetry. It's good poetry, real fine poetry, as good as anybody in his generation was writing. But until that material in the portmanteau is found it might be better not to publish more because the stuff in the portmanteau is the next step after *The Lords* and *The New Creatures*. I don't recognize anything in *Wilderness* as being from the portmanteau.

LISCIANDRO: What do you think the basis of his material was? Was it autobiographical? Philosophical? Visionary?

McCLURE: Jim shows an excellent capacity for dealing with information, both inventive information and real information. The poem that begins "Snakeskin jacket / Indian eyes" is as good an autobiographical poem, as good a short autobiographical poem, as I know. Ginsberg's also written personal autobiographical poems, but considering the condensation of Jim's poem, a poem of, like, six imagistic lines . . . One thinks of a sonnet of Shelley's, or a flake, an obsidian chip flaked out of a sonnet of Shelley's, but one also thinks of the best rock songs at the same time. Think of how simple-minded and yet beautiful some of those Mick Jagger songs from the same period were: "When I see a red door, I want to paint it black." There's another imagistic "poem." But I don't think Jagger ever wanted to be a poet, and this is why he was never acclaimed as a poet. I don't think he ever wanted to be anything but the blues singer he is. In *The New Creatures* you have some autobiographical material, and when it shows up it's real nice, like the poem about Ensenada. But at what point does something stop being autobiographical?

> Ensenada
> the dead seal
> the dog crucifix.
> Ghosts of the dead car sun.
> Stop the car.
> Rain. Night.
> Feel.

Is that autobiographical? Is it an imagistic poem or autobiography? The two are very nicely conjoined in it.

And then when you come to transcendental visions, maybe they were not transcendental but its opposite. The transcendentalists spoke of the oversoul. I used to like to say my work was coming out of the undersoul, that I felt I was a mammal. But with Jim it's not that. His poems are almost narratives rather than being transcendental visions. Some of them could be Roman poems, except for their very Englishness—goddess hunters, bows and arrows, people with green hair walking by the side of the sea. It's a little bit like science fiction. A little bit like some Roman poet writing in Latin had been reading nineteenth-century poetry. I know these are not standard takes on Jim's work, but I'm giving you a friend's view.

LISCIANDRO: Morrison said real poetry doesn't say anything, just ticks off possibilities, opens all doors. You can walk through any one that suits you. What do you think he might have meant by that? Or was it just a glib answer to an interview question?

MCCLURE: It's an exaggerated answer to make a point. He's saying that the function of poetry is to liberate the imagination and create possibilities, and it is the liberation or the use—simply the use—of the imagination that creates possibilities, new worlds. Imagine the

Vietnam War could be stopped and it stops. It was the imagining on the part of a few people that then became the imaginings of hundreds of thousands of other people.

LISCIANDRO: You see the poems as content rich . . .

MCCLURE: Yes, the poems are content rich is a good way to say it. Also, there is an intent of content, and I don't see any of his work that doesn't have a content. Even where there are sketchy poems and I think they are something that he wouldn't have published. On the other hand, sketches are sketches and they have their own kind of content. The content in a sketch by Rembrandt is entirely different from the content in a painting by Rembrandt. Levels of detail. Color.

LISCIANDRO: Returning to the autobiographical sense, "Ode to L.A." seems self-reflective.

MCCLURE: That poem is one that shows why Jim liked to talk to me about my plays more than about my poetry. I think my poetry is getting to Jim's style there, not in any sense that he's derivative but the way he's handling the subject—where he and the subject melt together. It is about Brian Jones, and it is about Hamlet, and it is about Los Angeles. It was a way that Jim and I thought alike.

LISCIANDRO: And it is about Jim too in some sense, isn't it? He is the poet, the rock star, the "porky satyr's leer"?

MCCLURE: One would say Jones had become Jim's metaphor for himself. Wallace Berman was seeing Brian Jones in the same way, but Wallace had taken photographs of Jones and had gotten to be good friends with Jones shortly before his death. Ray Manzarek and I performed that poem once, the only time we've ever done it. When we used to do poems of Jim's we'd tell the audience about his books. We try to turn them on to Jim's poetry, my poetry. I find the "Ode" to be one of Jim's deepest poems. We're talking about poems by a man who died at twenty-seven.

LISCIANDRO: You once wrote that Jim was sensitive that his poetry might only be read because he was a rock star.

MCCLURE: He was afraid that the poetry would be adulated because he was a rock star and that it wouldn't be taken seriously by the people that he wanted to take it seriously because it was being adulated because he was a rock star. And it was for that reason that I suggested that he do a private publication of those poems when I first saw them in London. When I saw them I was moved. A wonderful first book. I did not see *The Lords*. I saw *The New Creatures*.

He left the manuscript on the table so I'd see it in the morning, it was obvious. And I said, "Jim, this is real fine. You should publish it," but he was concerned. And I said, "Well, because of that concern, why not do what so many people have done, and I did with my book *Ghost Tantras*? Publish a private edition." "What would I do with it?" he asked. And I said, "Give it to people, and see what responses you get, and then decide what you want to do about commercial publication." So he published *The Lords* and *The New Creatures*, in the style of Wallace Berman's handmade books. They were the model. He'd seen work of Wallace's around my place, and he went for the same handmade look. When the books were finished, he gave me a stock of them and asked me to give them to literary people so that he would be able to get feedback. I gave them to people from Allen Ginsberg to rare book dealers to spread them out as much as I could. But he was right—he did not get the reaction that he should have gotten. Everyone was cautious because he was a rock star.

————————

LISCIANDRO: While we were filming the experimental movie HWY, Jim called you on the phone and told you that he killed somebody in the desert.

MCCLURE: When Jim said something like that it's not something that I would totally believe, though it's not something that would be totally impossible.

LISCIANDRO: Why do you think he chose to call you?

McCLURE: Maybe he wanted to connect outside the film world and the rock 'n' roll world. In other words, he's up to his chin in the rock world, and he's certainly up to his chin in the film world, and maybe while he's filming he just wants to make contact with another world of art. Jim admired my play *The Blossom*. It's about Billy the Kid and those murders in the Lincoln County Range War. I think maybe if he had killed somebody he would have wanted to talk to me. I was nine or ten years older. I think I told him, "Take it easy. Figure out where you are. Keep your equipose." I think he was really in a state, that the call wasn't a prank. But he wasn't a violent person.

LISCIANDRO: You never saw him raise his hand to anyone?

McCLURE: Well, I saw him break a bottle over Babe Hill's head. This was at a poetry conference in San Diego. Robert Creeley was there. Ed Dorn was there. It was the middle of the night. Everybody was extremely intoxicated. We were sitting out on the greensward. Creeley had his clothes off and was rolling down the hill, drunkenly yelling that he was his body. It was wonderful. Richard Brautigan was sitting under a tree brooding about noble Brautigan thoughts. Jim, Babe, and I were sitting there sort of cross-legged under another tree. I don't remember what anybody was saying, but Jim reached over with a bottle and broke it over Babe's head. I said, "Jim, that was a rotten thing to do," and he said "Oh yeah?" and he picked up another bottle and broke it over his own head. So, I can't say I never saw Jim do a violent thing, but he did it back to himself—immediate self-retribution. It was touching and crazy.

LISCIANDRO: Did you ever see him get angry with anybody? Shout or scream? We all had heard him shout "nigger."

McCLURE: Yeah, I have. Jim and I went to a performance of *Paradise Now* by The Living Theater in San Francisco at the Civic Auditorium. And we walked in and the troup had already started—they were at that point where they'd stripped down to their jockstraps. Remember Rufus, the black actor? It was Rufus who let us in the door, or was standing by the door when we came in. Jim took one look at Rufus and he yelled "nigger!" at the top of his lungs. He really yelled nigger—loud, drawn out, with violence. And I thought, the best thing for me to do now is to yell nigger too, so I yelled nigger at Rufus, which I think made it a little better because I knew Rufus well. And then we kind of got into the thing of yelling nigger. It was quite an experience. A mob of people in San Francisco Civic, *Paradise Now* going on. Jim yelled, "Rufus is a nigger!" I yelled, "Rufus is a nigger!" Jim yelled, "Nigger!" I yelled, "Judith Malina's a nigger!" Jim yelled, "Nigger!" I yelled, "Julian Beck is a nigger!" Jim really went off the deep end, so I thought the best thing for him was to join him.

Well, eventually they pushed us on stage. Jim was yelling "nigger, nigger, nigger" over and over, and I kept yelling "so and so's a nigger." We got to the point where we were doing those theater games that I'd been doing earlier with The Living Theater where you'd stand and drop over backwards and somebody would catch you before you hit the floor. It went on for quite a while.

Jim had on one of his jackets made out of Morrocan goatskin, or something like that, and I believe that he thought he was in a performance with The Doors. We were raging drunk, and I remember seeing him at one point thinking that he was singing in a concert. He took off his jacket and he flung it out into the audience like he'd do at a Doors concert, only it was to people who didn't know who he was. It was probably a two-thousand-dollar jacket and some hand flew up and grabbed it and it was gone. But nobody there knew he was Jim.

The next day I was sick and hung over and cleansed and fearful and trembling, a deep experience. Frightening and cleansing, but it had started out violently. Jim had gone into the area where one's yelling was connected with violence and it had to be carried out and exorcised.

LISCIANDRO: When did you and Morrison start working on the screenplay to your novel, *The Adept*?

MCCLURE: Early summer of 1969. But some other events preceded it. Jim asked me to come over to London to talk to Elliott Kastner, the film producer, about a month or six weeks before *The Beard* opened in London. That was late 1968. I flew to London, Jim met me at the airport.

LISCIANDRO: Was that the occasion when you wrote a poem about Shelley on the plane and when you showed it to Jim he wrote a spontaneous poem back?

MCCLURE: Yeah, that's exactly it. We spent several days conversing about poetry, going around London. The idea was to talk to Kastner about a film version of *The Beard* starring Jim, but after some serious talk we decided that there was no way in 1968 that the play could be done without censoring it for the film media so that it could be shown. So we decided against talking to Kastner about the project.

In the meantime, Jim had read my new manuscript, my novel *The Adept*. He was crazy about it. He loved *The Beard* and wanted to play Billy the Kid, but when he read *The Adept* he was sold and wanted to do that instead.

Jim had a beard and both of us had hair down to the middle of our backs and were pretty hung over, and god knows what Kastner thought, although he was a pretty hip guy.

When he saw us in his elegant English office Kastner asked about *The Beard*. Jim said that we'd changed our minds, that we didn't want to do *The Beard* but, instead, a new project based on *The Adept*. Then Jim explained the novel in detail and elegance to Kastner. That says something about memory—he told the story with a great sense of drama, great detail and full recall of what happens in it. That's a complex job because the novel is basically about the sensorium, basically about sensory experience, and it's a mystical novel, an adventure novel about an anarchist, sixties idealist coke dealer, who is also a motorcycle rider. Sort of a sociopathic idealist back in the days in the sixties when there were such people. The characters are based on people I knew. People believed in drugs, sold only certain drugs, more harmless types of drugs. Coke was then thought to be a diversion, a rarity, not a social plague. People were making fortunes and using their money to do things like back plays. I had a play at the Straight Theater in San

Francisco angeled by someone much like this person in *The Adept*. Jim
pitched the entire novel to Kastner and Kastner was interested, but I
think possibly because of Jim's condition he passed on it. His physical
appearance, much as I hate to say so.

LISCIANDRO: So Kastner didn't see him in the starring role.

MCCLURE: Maybe not. I did not have any trouble seeing it because I
imagined at that point that Jim was able to get himself back in shape.
And certainly his intellectual abilities were sharp. I was pleased to be
working with Jim. I was just beginning to know Jim, so it was a
demonstration of his power—how he was able to recall the novel in
its totality and explain it to Kastner, changing it into a film as he told
it.

When Kastner passed on it, I went back to San Francisco and then
returned to London a few weeks later to see the opening of *The Beard*,
which played in the Royal Court Theatre, the same theater in which
George Bernard Shaw had so many of his plays start. The theater Censor
had just been abolished in England, so *The Beard* was the first play
that threatened the Establishment to go to the theaters without a
Censor. There was a question of whether *The Beard* would bring the
Censor back or not.

On opening night everybody was there, from the Beatles to Vanessa
Redgrave. Sir Ralph Richardson was there. I remember talking with
him before the play with Rip Torn, who was directing *The Beard*. We
had the same cast as in New York.

In the meantime, Jim had made contact in L.A. He was intent on
doing the *The Adept* as a film, and we were determined that we would
write the script and that Jim would star in it. Bill Belasco wanted to
produce it, so Jim and I made arrangements to start writing a film
script together. I went to L.A. and got a room at the Alta Cienaga
Motel, where Jim was always staying. Belasco rented an office for us
on the top of the Scam Building on Sunset Strip. It's that big glass-
fronted building right in the middle of the Strip, down a couple blocks
from the Whiskey-a-Go-Go. It's about a twelve-story building, and
we had a corner office there on the eleventh or twelfth floor. A couple
of rooms. Jim and I made a deal with ourselves—no drinking during

the day, until six o'clock. This was critical for both of us. We came in with copies of the novel by ten o'clock every morning. Jim was never late. I said, "Jim, I'm going to tell you the same thing that I told Freewheelin Frank—if you're late we'll just have to stop this." Jim took it seriously.

Since Jim had been at UCLA film school he said that we should do an outline before we did the script, but I didn't think we had to. He was right; we should have done the treatment. We started working directly from the novel, just adapting the novel. We got a fair distance into it, and then at some point we were not doing what we wanted to do. Jim and I had seen so many things together in Los Angeles and in London, that we wanted to put in the script. Jim would say, "You remember that violinist we saw in Grosvenor Square, man? The kid with the rag hat? I want him in the film right here, playing down below in the street while the protagonist comes to the window and looks out." I'd say, okay man. Then I'd remember something else, and we started adding everything we ever wanted to see into the script. It became voluminous. We were getting ideas rapidly. Jim would shoot some of the dialogue and a twist of the plot to me, or we'd go back to the book. We realized that what we were doing was that we were sitting there rapping it back and forth to each other, so at that point we hired a secretary and began dictating it. We did this all day for three or four weeks.

I went home to see my wife and daughter on weekends. Jim and I were playboys, and did what we did. And we worked hard during the day, but so energetically that we ended up with a script that was about the size of *Moby Dick*. It was a couple hundred pages typed up and we realized that we had not shown it to Belasco. A proper script is seventy-five to ninety pages.

Then in the middle of the night Jim cut it down to a ninety-page script, but he missed the point of the novel. We gave it to Belasco, but I didn't like what it ended up being because originally we had created a redwood tree, we had created a huge script, and in cutting it we should have said, "Ah, let's go back and do a treatment and see if we can use any of this new stuff or scratch it off to practice." I think despite Jim's mental acuteness while we were working, he had a depression setting in regarding his physical self. I think it was beginning to dawn on Jim that he wasn't going to get himself back in shape. I don't like saying that, but that's the subtext of what went on by the time we got the script done. I think he was feeling some despair about himself. But despair for Jim was like hangovers—he didn't acknowledge it.

So what happened was that in a fit of creativity Jim took a redwood tree and cut it down to a ninety-page toothpick. And it didn't cut well because there was some real good stuff in the script. What we cut the script to was not worthy of what we'd done. I thought we should have begun over again following Jim's initial insight regarding a treatment.

That is essentially what happened with *The Adept*. It would have been real fine with Jim in it. People saw *The Adept* as an experience, a fast-moving adventure about drugs. It turned out, oddly enough, that while I was writing the novel Dennis Hopper was making *Easy Rider*. There's a similarity between the two works, but then Dennis and I have some similarities. Both of us come out of the same milieu, even the same place—Kansas. Dennis and my wife and daughter and I were living together with Leo Garen the previous summer at a huge mansion made out of cast-concrete in the Hollywood Hills. We called it Chateau Zsa Zsa because its mythology was that it it had been built for Zsa Zsa Gabor by her Mafiosa cement contractor lover. It had an indoor swimming pool, and up above it on the hill there was a cliff, and on the cliff there were cast-concrete Tahitian cabanas, with little streams that could be turned on and off to trickle through them. There was a tunnel through the hill at the back of the house which came out on the other side of the mountain in the Hollywood Hills. Leo had been granted the right to live in the place if he kept the grounds up, the banana trees and vines.

Everybody was coming by to visit. Jim used to visit all the time that summer, actor Tom Baker, Antonioni, Nico. I think *The Beard* had closed. We were having a great time, and we lived there a good part of the summer. Bob and Toby Rafelson lived across the street.

LISCIANDRO: Whatever happened to the film project?

MCCLURE: Actually, I couldn't see going on to write another script because of Jim's condition. So the producer paid it off and that's the last I saw of it. *The Adept* has been optioned by other producers since then, but the thing is that now, because it's pro-drug as a visionary experience—it's like an historical document. At the time of its writing it was speaking out about the anarchist, visionary strata of consciousness of the 1960s. It was not really about drugs—it was about consciousness, it was about the politics of individualism, equality and rebellion.

I would not care to write a script again unless I wrote with a skilled scriptwriter. It is a craft that I began to admire as a craft at that point. Two of the most highly-crafted word genres are the film script and the haiku. I don't mean in the sense of people who write poems in English called haikus, but the real haikus by Basho or Buson that follow the constructs in the Japanese language and follow the tenets of Zen philosophy. The Japanese haiku is as crafted and honed as a film script is. Except that a film script is a commercial work of art. A haiku is a window to a deep world.

LISCIANDRO: As I understand it, Jim was trying to find out the allure of cocaine, its properties, through the experience of using a lot of it.

McCLURE: Not while we were working on *The Adept*, but either before or after Jim was doing massive amounts of coke. I don't mean he was doing it like a cokehead, but Jim would score some grams and share it and then he'd snort the rest of it in a few minutes or a few hours. It was a large amount of coke for the days before everyone was pushing it into their heads and noses. But this was typical. I just took it as Jim's hedonistic gluttony. Jim was a glutton for experience, a glutton for pleasure, though I mean that in a good sense. One of the things I admired about Jim was the intensity with which he sought out pleasures for the experience—not because he was a creep hung up on pleasure but because it was an experience. I think that's why he was doing the coke, and he'd do some huge amount of it and then seem to forget about it.

LISCIANDRO: Do you think he was trying to filter this experience through himself to make an expression of it or just to experience it?

MCCLURE: I think it was basic research for a poet: pleasure, pain, consciousness, love, hate, rage, joy, alcohol, sobriety. This is the basic field of possibilities that we have to play before we get a little older and we have more going on so that we can actually play with consciousness itself. We have to play with our sensory perceptions until we have enough experience in life that we can begin to play madrigals and arpeggios, with consciousness and its relationship to perception. And remember, at this time Jim was twenty-five years old. He knew a lot, but a twenty-five-year-old person isn't supposed to be out there quite yet.

LISCIANDRO: Jim seemed very interested in Rimbaud.

MCCLURE: Well, we talked about Rimbaud while we were working on *The Adept*, of course, because the protagonist in the novel has much in common with Rimbaud. But Jim and I were fascinated with Rimbaud's idea of the arranged derangement of the senses. When you arrange to derange the ratio of your senses—whether you do it with alcohol or lack of sleep or starvation, or whether you do it with drugs—you not only add to the body of knowledge, but you jar the body of knowledge so that you are looking out in a different way. And once you look out in a different way, you widen your sensory field. It's as if you made the porthole looking out into the world a trifle larger, and this is what a meaning seeking young poet must do. Not a young poet writing poems about running over frogs with his lawnmower, but a young poet writing about acts of adventure, and consciousness, and perception.

LISCIANDRO: What is the place of the poet in our society?

MCCLURE: The same as any other artist—to maintain the thoroughfares, to maintain the pathways of the imagination in a society that would close down the pathways of the imagination. We all find other social functions, also. We'll be environmentally inclined, or biologically inclined, or socially committed. But what we do as artists is to maintain free pathways for the imagination.

Secondarily, we are like athletes. We maintain the connections between our sensoriums of sight, sound, touch, taste, and smell, and all other modes of perception we have. All the seventeen or twenty-seven modes of physical perception that we have. I'm not talking about anything metaphysical here. We maintain those in language connections with our consciousness so that we are really speaking about something. In other words, we are constantly subverting, we are constantly undermining, we are constantly eroding and sabotaging social discourse, which is about nothing. Social discourse is about things that have been taken for granted, habit patterns, the death of the imagination. Discourse is about structures that no longer have any relationship to reality. Instead, we maintain a direct contact between what we perceive with our affective perceptions and our language, and that's important. A sculptor does it with volume, a painter with color and form, a musician with those aspects of consciousness that go through the ears. All the arts have the same function—to maintain a state of crisis.

LISCIANDRO: And given that sense, was Jim fulfilling the role of artist?

MCCLURE: Yes, absolutely. And so does Jack Kerouac, and so does Lawrence Ferlinghetti and so does Anne Waldman, and so does Amiri Baraka, and so does Diane di Prima, and so does Denise Levertov.

LISCIANDRO: In another piece you said something about how Jim enjoyed picking up a microphone and singing in a bar with a house band.

MCCLURE: I remember Jim sitting down at my dinner table with my wife and daughter and singing "House of the Rising Sun" or some Presley hit just because he was a natural singer and loved to do it. Or walking down the street through Chinatown. Just walking down the street Jim would start singing some blues right out of nowhere, probably jogged by seeing some fruit in a stand or fish lying on the cracked ice.

I was struck with that because somebody who is a guitarist never comes to your house and plays the guitar. Even if you have a guitar sitting right there they never pick it up. They only play guitars if they are on stage or when they are in recording studios or rehearsing. That doesn't seem like a full life of an artist to me. But Jim sang spontaneously, and I enjoyed that.

LISCIANDRO: I had several experiences walking into bars with him in New Orleans and he'd do that.

MCCLURE: I've seen him do that because he wanted to draw attention to the fact that he was Jim Morrison. But I'm talking about when he was wearing an engineer's hat and had a beard and a pot belly, and he was walking down the street through Chinatown and he did it because he loved to sing. Not a Doors' song. Nobody's going to know it is Jim Morrison. They're just going to think it's some crazy guy who's got a great voice, right?

There was the time I was at the Cow Palace when the Doors played and they had a big video projection of Jim while he sang. There's Jim down there very small, and a huge video screen of him up above, and he started singing and the Doors went through their whole repertoire. Then they kept playing blues and Jim went on singing, and finally it ended with a few hundred people left in the Cow Palace lying on their backs looking up at the ceiling. That's being an artist. And it wasn't just Jim. It was Ray Manzarek, and Robbie, and John Densmore. Working together they are special as a symbiosis is special. A symbiosis is like the lichen. In the beginning there is an algae and another organism, but when they join together there is a streaming, growing plant. Join them together into a lichen and they'll grow and cover an entire tree and blow in the wind, like Spanish Moss. California's Spanish moss is a lichen. It has the capacity to grow and stream in the air and be beautiful pale green, and reproduce and cover whole forests, giving a romantic edge to everything. That's what The Doors were like. Ray Manzarek is a musician and artist with prescient powers; Jim had the words and the voice to go with it.

A Conversation with John Lion

MICHAEL McCLURE: I decided the theater wasn't for me. After the fourteen busts in L.A. I said enough of the theater. Then after *The Beard*'s success in London, I was feeling so good about the theater that I wrote a little play called *The Cherub*. Soon after that I saw John Lion's Magic Theatre production of *Ubu Roi* . . . It was one of the best things I'd seen. Lion asked if I had a new play, and I said Yeah, and he took *The Cherub*. I was so turned on in the process of watching the rehearsals that I wrote ten more short plays in the genre of "Gargoyle Cartoons."

JOHN LION: The thing that distinguishes the Magic Theatre from so many others around it is how it's set up, financially, and how it runs. It originally came out of the extreme dissatisfaction with the Drama department at U.C. Berkeley, although this probably wouldn't be very good material for the *Daily Cal*.

THOMAS MAREMAA: On the contrary, it's the best material for the *Daily Cal*.

LION: I realize theater departments everywhere are preparing people for "Show Biz" and not preparing them for the theater . . . not preparing them to think for themselves.

MAREMAA: What turned you on to Alfred Jarry?

LION: Jarry is a fantastic character. I happened to get hold of *Ubu*, and it seemed to be a reflection of so many things in my experience, particularly in the public school system . . . the way power is given

This conversation originally appeared in *Every Other Week*, *The Daily Californian* (October 7, 1969).

out to people who are the biggest and the dumbest. Anyway, I came out here from Chicago, and when I did a play I took it to the Steppenwolf cabaret . . . it was Ionesco's *The Lesson* . . . and founded the Magic Theatre. A friend of mine at school, a professor, Kerry Prescott, got a commission to do something at the University Arts Festival, and so I picked out the Dada play *The Gas Heart*. We got that down, and caused a riot and ruined their theater for them. Then we brought theater to the Mandrake Bar, and then one thing led to another. The way to start a theater is to get one show up and then follow it with another.

We gradually evolved a cooperative form . . . as general director I don't get paid any more than any one else in the theater. This is the way to create a kind of spirit around a show which you need to keep it tight. We're looking towards being able to support our people and to provide an alternative to boulevard theater.

What I liked so much about what Michael was doing was that it was full of joy . . . It had a new vision to it. And it had something which, by virtue of what it was doing, happened to be in collusion with what was going on in the student protest on the streets. So of course I jumped at the chance to do *The Cherub*. It took a while to accustom the theater to doing it, because people weren't used to that genre yet. We finally put it on the second day of the Siege of Berkeley.

MCCLURE: We had helicopters going over and state troopers with bayonets outside on opening night. It was when Reagan tear-gassed the campus. It was like the ecology of keeping a sense of pleasure and a sense of being alive in a situation like that . . . and people did turn on to it.

LION: It was also one of the only safe places to go.

SAM SILVER: Have the cops been hassling you more now that you ride a chopper?

MCCLURE: No, they seem to go easier on motorcycles. I had a sports car and that's when I really had trouble. I had long hair and a sports car, and they couldn't resist that.

SAMMY EGAN: Well, there's a real affinity. You and a motorcycle cop are riding the same thing . . . just wearing different uniforms.

SILVER: My Hell's Angel friends tell me that a lot of police are remarkably frustrated. They tend to stop Angels just to talk to them. It bespeaks of a common illness among a lot of law enforcement officials.

———

MAREMAA: What do you anticipate for the coming performances of the new plays?

LION: There's no telling. We're anticipating everything. We have no idea what the people coming in are going to think. You're so busy thinking about getting your production out that you really can't think beyond the necessity of getting it on stage.

MAREMAA: What about the mise-en-scene?

LION: There's going to be fog in the lobby, large weather balloons and dancing girls. There will be a bed with an elderly couple having breakfast. What we're hoping is to turn the lobby into a kind of moving sculpture. There'll be simultaneous poems, in the style of the Dadaists, read over tapes . . . and they'll probably involve Tweety Bird and Hot Stuff.

The collective name for the thing is *The Charbroiled Chinchilla*—a kind of post-Hollywood ritual frying of Marilyn Monroe. Everytime I think of charbroiled chinchilla, I think of coats and openings . . . sitting there simmering like meat. The three plays in the evening are *Spider Rabbit*, *The Pansy*, and *The Meatball*.

EGAN: Was that inspired by cartoonist R. Crumb's "Meatball"?

LION: I kept saying so, but Michael didn't have Crumb in mind.

MCCLURE: No. I took some unusual pills called "meatballs."

LION: Actually, there are two meatballs. One is by Joel Beck and the other is by R. Crumb. The first is where they all gather around the

pile of dogshit in the street, and they start tripping on it. It turns
into the entire Polish Army. Crumb's is "Once the meatball hits things
are never the same." That's what we hope will happen.

MAREMAA: Is there any attempt to involve the audience in these plays?

LION: Involvement is an elusive term. It's misused a lot. So many
theaters now are going out and doing everything from giving the
audience a bath to taking the audience to bed with them. You can't
really think of involvement in this sense anymore. Involvement is
something that happens to you when you read a good book.

What we're trying to do is to create a pin-point universe on stage—
a focus, which will destroy normal conceptions of time. We experimented with the characters coming off stage, but this doesn't work.
When they leave their universe, they're in another universe. As Michael
says, this is a kind of reverse return to Ibsenism, and there is a kind
of fourth third-eye wall.

McCLURE: I prefer to think of it as meat enacting itself on a shelf in
space with lights. I like to see it that way. I liked what the Living
Theatre did in *Antigone*. They writhed down the aisles, and I was
actually involved. But they were relating themselves to me and took
me out of being a witness. All they were doing was extending the
stage, and I dug their being out in the audience.

McCLURE: It's as if you invent a vision and you rise up with it, and
as you rise up with it, you burn each other out. But in the process of
burning that vision out, you discover that all the people that want to
keep things mysterious are really wrong. One of the things that you
tell them as a poet is that they're shucking and jiving. Because when
you keep something mysterious, what you're ignoring is the fact that
behind each mystery, there is another mystery, and that they become
more fascinating and more intriguing.

So you sit down and write something which may be ridiculous and
undignified, but maybe more visionary than you dreamed possible. I

wrote two hundred and fifty rhymed stanzas about my childhood non-stop. They sound like a cross between the worst of Lord Byron and the best of Terry Tunes.

LION: What André Breton used to say to the Surrealists was when you find yourself dry, sit down and write . . . write anything.

MCCLURE: And what happens when you do that—create something that you know no one will ever look at, or will ever judge, or will ever form an opinion about, or will ever know the existence of—part of you comes in and says, "Oh, boy, I've been waiting for that for a long time." And with that part of your mind comes the possibility of the angelic and the divine; you make a space for an intelligence to secretly occur.

In one Gargoyle Cartoon, I started with an image: three girl fairies dancing, while Mama, Papa, and Baby Panda Bear watch, and a giant frog hops across the stage. And that image just extends itself. Of course, you've seen the same thing happen at the Greyhound bus depot. And Aristophanes used a chorus of frogs hopping around the stage.

MCCLURE: Someone said to me that *The Beard*'s an avant-garde drama; I said *The Beard* was done in the eleventh century A.D. in India. It's at least that old.

LION: When we rehearse there is this concept, which kind of spreads itself out over the people: that we're approaching something as an event—to turn other people on. Particularly when we're dealing with Michael's plays.

MCCLURE: Particularly when I'm there, because I laugh my head off.

LION: We're looking for some kind of fluid, some kind of emotional transmission to the audience. I believe this is real—and when there is something real on stage, this is something an audience cannot resist.

MCCLURE: The fine thing about *The Cherub* was that it remained an organism with integrity. Almost at all times, it was an improvisation within the play as an organism. If you think of the play as being a cell, with an infra-structure, and an ultra-structure, and cytoplasm, and nucleus, and golgi apparatus, and mitochondria, and the DNA, and it all functioning together.

EGAN: How do you react to the arbitrariness in any creative process? If you sit down to write something, and you decide, for no reason at all, that you'll wait ten seconds, the probability is that you won't write the same thing when you start again. Do you really believe that everything follows a biological order?

MCCLURE: I don't think I like the word "arbitrary." All life on this earth is part of a protoplasm that's in the process of making a surge. It's all the same material, and it will all surge within possible patterns, and all these possible patterns will inter-act beautifully.

EGAN: Is there such a thing as artistic failure within this "surge"?

MCCLURE: I guess so, because I print only a small part of what I write.

LION: It is amazing that any plays ever get put on and are successful. There are so many different places for failure. You have to find the right people—people who have a natural affinity for the central image. Professional show biz throws people together. You come in, you have your lines memorized, you do the play, and you split. The new theater is more tribal in structure. The life style becomes intricately connected with the product itself.

MCCLURE: One of the reasons the Elizabethan theater was amazing was that in a rigid English social structure, it was one of the only fields one could go into, regardless of one's social class, and make a relative fortune. In that sense, rock 'n' roll is more comparable—socially, if not artistically—to the Elizabethan theater.

LION: Michael's claim that *The Beard* is really ancient is appropriate here. Certainly rock is getting to the beginnings—to the original Greek satyr dance, where they just stood there and listened to their own heartbeats. And out of that they created their vision.

MCCLURE: There's a thing you can do with the Magic Theatre that's out of sight: you're making meat sculptures—real meat sculptures of bodies. You can't make meat sculptures with a T.V. set, no matter how hard you try. You can make electronic dots move around, but you can't make flesh do anything. And the impact of fifty people seeing such a play might be more generative in the long run than fifty million people seeing electronic dots move around.

LION: You can always tell where people are at when they come to the Magic Theatre. I have people come up to me and say, "I liked the production very much, but the faces weren't big enough." You aren't going to do with theater what you do with film. That's why theater is beginning to claim back all the things that have been stolen from it, say since 1900, by the technology. You can make a film of the theater, but you can't do a theater version of the film. In that sense, film will always have it over theater in terms of reaching an audience. It's a piece of celluloid that will never go away. And it'll always be the same. Theater is a constantly changing thing. The theater has something which film will never have, and that is immediacy. There's only one ritual in film, and that's the ritual of putting the thing together. Theatre is a constant ritual. Films in the sixites, via Kenneth Anger, Stan Brakhage, and all those people, are attempting to recreate the same kind of ritual that the theater will always have. *Scorpio Rising* is nothing but ritual.

MCCLURE: In *Scorpio*, Kenneth is taking a vibration, and he's doing the *whole* vibration. I mean, it's all there. It exists, as a sculpture, it's on celluloid; but he has the whole vibration.

MCCLURE: You were talking a minute ago about going to a theater piece more than once. Here's a review from a Vancouver paper, by a man who went to see *The Beard* twice before he reviewed it. In fact, *Time* magazine went to see the New York production of *The Beard* twice. They sent the first reviewer; he came back and wrote a rave review of it. They said we're not publishing that, then he said that's the third time you haven't published one of my reviews and he quit. Then they sent their second reviewer out.

—————————

LION: You posed the question earlier, Sam, "When do you fail?" I think there's a kind of internal unconscious sense which keeps you, at your best moments, in touch with your vision. At your worst moments you're completely out of touch, and you're deceiving yourself. There's nothing else to go on at the internal level. When we were talking about the concept of shamanism, the almost trance-like state, which is part and parcel of what's been going on in art, for forty years, from the Dadaists on. Of course some of the attempts were successful and some were unsuccessful. We took a Dada play which Saroyan wrote as an automatic writing exercise and transposed it for a setting with the images we found in 1968. We got something which was intrinsically Saroyan's and intrinsically ours. As it was originally performed, it was shouted as a kind of protest.

—————————

SILVER: How effective is the Magic Theatre as a vehicle for your writing?

MCCLURE: Their production of *The Cherub* inspired me to write ten plays.

—————————

MAREMAA: What are you doing with ecology? I understand there's a poetry reading on ecology next week in Berkeley.

MCCLURE: This is the third or fourth reading for ecology. In recent years a few people have been trying to spread the word as much as possible to start the momentum—the urgent radicalization that's necessary. I'm tremendously relieved that the issue has become popular so swiftly, because people are aware.

SILVER: I don't think you'll solve the problem of ecology, until you start getting a humane society.

MCCLURE: We'll have to have a cherubic civilization. We'll have to have a change that's so far beyond politics, that it will have to be biological. We're not citizens now, we're consumers. That's not good! And Spengler was right: this civilization is Faustian in the negative sense. It is destructive, and it does not have to do with the protoplasmic surge toward whatever we're surging. It's not even evil; it's bad.

Poet Playwright
Director Magic

MICHAEL MCCLURE: In the late fifties I began considering the poetic tradition in drama. There was the input of Artaud, Genet, Georg Büchner, Sartre, Camus, and Beckett.

STEWART BRAND: You were reading all of them at the same time?

MCCLURE: Yes, and I discovered Artaud's dramatic vision in 1958. I had already developed a projective verse to use for theater.

BRAND: Projective verse means what, exactly?

MCCLURE: Charles Olson says it is the witnessed object, or event, passing through the sensorium of the poet and then being projected onto the page or air in the breath line of the poem. It's almost a one-for-one transmutation of the energy involved. In that way, it's related to Blake's energy defined as "eternal delight."

In *The Theatre and Its Double* Artaud is calling not for masterpieces, but new texts. He says something like "down with masterpieces, but let us have new texts by poets." I was tremendously impressed with that, and I went back and reread the Elizabethan playwrights, reread Tourneur and Ford, and then reread Shelley and his play *The Cenci*, and was involved at about the same time with the plays of Büchner. The result was that my first play, which was *The Blossom*, a play about Billy the Kid and the Lincoln County Range War. It was written in 1958. Earlier, I'd written a farce called *The Raptors*, which is a shaman farce;

This conversation took place in June, 1976 and was originally published in *Theatre* I:1 (Summer, 1977).

the characters being Wolf, Planarian, and the Oracle of Newark (who was a giant vulture), and a Rose, and a Boulder.

BRAND: I'm curious about John's own genesis.

JOHN LION: Well, I was struck by Artaud in '62, the first year that I was at the University of Chicago. Someone had laid a copy of *The Theatre and Its Double* on me, also some early Genet, and I was mesmerized by *The Maids*. It seemed to unlock a lot of suspicions I had about the way things really worked. It turned out to be the first play I directed—I was eighteen at the time.

MCCLURE: Nobody was doing Genet then.

LION: It had just been translated, I think. I started working on it. *The Maids* led me to Genet's *Death Watch*, *Death Watch* led me circuitously to *Ubu The King*, which I've staged three times—twice in Chicago and once here. *Ubu* also unlocked a whole other aspect of the way things worked for me. At that point, it was mostly intellectivity because I was trying hard to be a student and an intellectual. It seemed to be the thing to do. But as time went on, I began to realize that a playwright is doing more than writing. As I had to direct, I wanted to find out about these things. Finally someone told me I used "playwright" and spelled it w-r-i-t-e as a sophomore. Someone said, "Plays are not written, they are wrought," and that seemed to be another key for me. So, I started to feel, every time I picked up a play, that it was more like a symphonic score than a piece of literature, although some have attained the status of literature. And, I'm not sure that's really good for them, because it makes them sort of a "divertissement" as opposed to a living thing in theater.

BRAND: How did you guys encounter each other?

MCCLURE: It was through the play *Ubu*. We had a mutual friend who was a writer for the *Berkeley Barb*. He told me I must come over and see the *Ubu Roi* that was being done by the Magic Theatre in Berkeley. I had just gotten interested in theater again at that time. *The Beard* was done again in London, and it was reviewed favorably, and it was compared to Eliot's plays and to Yeats's plays and not to pornography. Then I wrote two new short plays that I liked. Our mutual friend asked me to come over and look at John's work at the Magic Theatre. John's *Ubu*, and I had seen several *Ubu*'s, was by far and away the most incredible.

BRAND: A masterpiece of invention! There are things that there was no equivalent for in the text. Like *Ubu* holding a corkscrew and holding a doll, screwing the corkscrew into the doll's ass. And one of the characters being a living table and a living footstool. Another thing was a way of going from solidity, being in one place on the stage, to everybody sort of moving at once, as if a ripple had gone across the stage. It was a different kind of action than I'd seen on the stage. Non-rational action, more interesting action. Action that had to do with the movement of the play and not the way people moved in everyday life, and it was probably more like people actually do move in everyday life, rather than the realistic presentations that are done on stage.

LION: One of the things I did was have Ubu begin the play by pulling a live worm out of his mouth, so that, before he spoke a word, we understood "where he was at," as they say. It was a totally manic production. It was madness. It scared me. After I had finished directing it, I ran away from it. I could not believe that I did it. I could attend only a few times.

MCCLURE: It was, as Richard Ogar said, the way Jarry intended the play to be, but in a way he hadn't foreseen.

BRAND: So you were impressed. What happened then?

MCCLURE: John asked me for a play. I showed him *¡The Feast!*, which was a play I'd written in beast-language many years before at about the time he was directing *The Maids* in Chicago.

LION: Right.

MCCLURE: That play, by the way, is sourced in Blake and Genet; that is, Blake and Genet were in my mind as I wrote. The other play I gave John was one that I'd written just after *The Beard*'s success in London when I decided I was going to go on writing plays. *The Beard* finally was a complete "success." It was a "masterpiece." Now people wanted me to write plays like it, and I could not, did not want to, and had no interest in that. I decided I would write a few little plays that would burn everything down. I wanted to reduce things to the original cinders of creation. One of these plays was called *The Cherub*. That's the one that John picked to do. It was the first *Gargoyle Cartoon*.

LION: *The Cherub* opened during the Siege of Berkeley, the People's Park protest, and it was an extraordinary sort of "wraparound" experience, or environmental experience, I guess, because outside the theater the air was filled with bullets, mobs of people running around completely insane . . .

MCCLURE: Tear gas was drifting down the street on opening night and there were troopers with presented bayonets outside the door of the theater.

LION: And inside, the theater was essentially this fairy playground, which was sort of quiet and . . .

MCCLURE: Musical?

LION: Musical. And . . .

MCCLURE: Cherubs that stuck their heads through the ceiling and had long hair and beards and green faces, naked girls and panda bears, and talking beds.

BRAND: Say a little more about that medium, because it seems to me to be one you're sticking with for plays now. Fairyland. Where did that come from? Why are you staying with it?

MCCLURE: Well, we're looking at it after the fact and calling it Fairy-land. Okay, most plays start with a playwright rather than a poet. They start with a playwright thinking about a plot, or thinking about scraps of dialogue, or verbal occurrences that are stimulating. In the case of the poet, in the case of Lorca, and probably in the case of Yeats, the play comes from an entirely different area. But there's a difference between a play being written in poetry, and a play that is a poem. Robert Lowell can write a play in verse, but it's not a poem, it's a play in verse. When they succeed, my plays are poems and they do not come from the idea of a plot or ideas of dialogue or rhetoric; they come from an image. At first there's the conception of the image, then the image expands itself or unrolls, or grows, or takes on color and dimension on the stage. Each image is a universe or a dimension of its own and its own being. It has to have that dimension around it that it may grow into. For instance, if I conceive of a Spider Rabbit, (a being who's half spider and half rabbit), with a briefcase full of hand grenades and copies of scholarships to the Mystic Order of Rosicrucians, then one has to postulate that there's a dimension that he can exist in. And then that dimension comes into existence. If I wake up in the morning and imagine that there are two giant garter snakes named Bjorn and Sam, and one speaks with a Swedish accent and one with a Japanese accent, and that they have platonic dialogues about the nature of the edibility of objects, why, then, the image demands, if it's going to be enacted, a universe that they can expand into. They have a diverse universe or dimension, but it's not really Fairyland—although it may be what Fairyland really is, because Fairyland may really be other dimensions and universes.

BRAND: It strikes me that this theater domain of yours is like Stein-beck country is to Steinbeck, in some sense. This is McClure country—naked girls with fairy wings.

MCCLURE: And, if a costumer turns up who makes beautiful panda costumes, there are going to be pandas.

LION: Right. Don't like what you see around you?

BRAND: Build it again.

LION: Build it again. It's interesting that in directing these *Gargoyle Cartoons* and dealing with some of the scripts which have come out of them, my *a priori* dispositions toward directing, once I had discovered that plays are wrought, not written, was essentially to start with an image and to tend to hang a text in several places on it.

MCCLURE: Genet starts with an image—that is something that John and I both found in Genet.

LION: I was thinking of what one sees from a directorial point of view when one starts to direct a play. For instance, a sort of Artaudian *"gestus."* You know, Brecht is the inventor of the *"gestus,"* which is one thing which puts a handle on a scene for him. It's something, according to him, that the audience can automatically identify, and which is the handle to the suitcase. For example, one of the classic ones is in *Mother Courage* where she stands there with money and she's got to raise more in order to keep her son from being hung. The scene starts with the money in her hand, and it ends with the money in her hand. While she's haggling over how much graft she's going to pay, her son is hung. She is there at the end of the scene with the money, which has never gone away, and there's no comment made on it. The audience has to sit there and look at the money. The money is there; the son is not.

MCCLURE: That's also an image of symbolic theater.

LION: That's an image, you see, that's a *"gestus."* In *Ubu*, it's pulling the worm out of the mouth—immediately, the *"gestus"* of *Ubu*. It prepares you for everything that is to follow.

BRAND: I got that in *Gorf* when the angel band all pick up their slide whistles together and blow, and, I guess, hit a C note together or something, but instead out of the loudspeakers comes the New York Symphony Orchestra. I've never been suspended so fast and so thoroughly.

LION: That is supposed to let you know that anything can happen.

BRAND: It works. It short-circuits the intellect at that point. Whose idea was that?

LION: That was mine. That was just there, you know, it just came out. But at any rate, to get to the center, when I start to think about how a play is going to look on the stage, I start with a vision, a center, an image, and it continues on from there. What I imagine when I'm directing a play is that the dialogue and the course of the characters has got to get me from image to image, and it continues on from there. What I imagine when I'm directing a play is that the dialogue and the course of the characters must get me from image to image, and I begin to work. If I work and no image comes up, then I stop until it's there, or I can find it, or we play with it, or I encourage play so that we can find it. Of course, as we've gone on working, Michael and I, this has been a tremendous aid, because he tends to work the same way when he writes. In *Gorf*, for instance, when you're done with Gorf and his relationship with the Blind Dyke, you come up with the Shitfer, or . . .

McCLURE: One *coup de theatre* follows another.

LION: Right. Or the landscape of bones, for instance. How can we show that the Blind Dyke is trapped without having her stumble all over the stage in a tragic way that fits most modern melodrama? Well, bind her. Bind her in a landscape of bones; we need a landscape of bones. There's the question of finding the objective correlative for the images.

McCLURE: *Gorf* is Ubuesque, so there are more correlatives in *Gorf* than there are in the other plays. In the other plays, we got down to literally making the event that was called for. Naked girls with fairy wings really *were* naked girls with fairy wings, giant garter snakes really *were* giant garter snakes. The giant balls of fur with plaid berets really were giant balls of fur with plaid berets in *The Meatball*, another Gargoyle cartoon, thanks to a great costumer.

MCCLURE: John and I work so closely together that I do little commenting. It's the same way with Regina Cate, the costume designer. When she hands in the costume sketches I say, "Okay." Her creativity should not be stunted. Also, the inspiration of the set designer should not be held back. Everybody should be allowed to go full-blast. But in one case, in one play, a fire was represented by hands, and I said, "John, I think the hands poking through the floor don't work. We've got so many things sticking through the wall in the accompanying play that I think the hands being a fire are too much." John went ahead, and it's one of the things that people like most in the play. That image of the hands goes back to an earlier case where fire came through the floor, a play called *The Pussy* . . .

LION: Where the war was treated as a light show—which is a tremendous image.

BRAND: That's how we felt about Vietnam, wasn't it?

LION: Sure. You know, standing on the side of a battleship with a cocktail, watching the fireworks at night, which was a much-related story about the officers in the Navy. They'd meet and play shuffleboard and watch the bombardment. It was leisurely entertainment. I guess these guys were just imitating their superiors. You were saying?

MCCLURE: I was making some loops . . . the hands coming through the floor and the earlier use of fire coming through the stage in *The Pussy*.

LION: We got an outsize Ronson lighter for that one, which had a flame this big.

MCCLURE: The idea was that napalm was landing all around. A fire would flare up out of the mud earth. One of the soldiers would reach over and swat it, putting the fire out. It was as if napalm were flapping or falling all over. The soldiers continued hallucinating and shooting Asians with their big rifles and cursing when they missed. Then three naked blue women with fairy wings arrived with beer. Then they all drank beer and had an orgy and a growling monster appeared.

LION: From a directorial point of view, the play interested me as a sort of concrete example of the expansion of hallucinations. I decided that what the play was about was these fellows who had indoctrinated themselves to the dada reality of war. The idea of taking amphetamines and generally getting fucked-up becomes so real to them that the energy from the drug state actually transferred to the audience as the play progressed. By the time the women appeared we understand that the energy of the soldiers' hallucinations had created the women's presences. It didn't matter whether the women were there or not.

MCCLURE: My concept was that the women were real, and that the universe was hallucinating the event. The universe was the hallucinator.

LION: My prejudice is anthropomorphic; it has to be when you're dealing with an audience. You have to start from the "I," the ego, at least some form of the self. You have to trust that that is going to make the connection to the audience. So, I'm a little more conservative when I have to get a practical idea out.

MCCLURE: Some people were disturbed about the play in New York. Rip Torn directed *The Pussy* there. I said, "Who is booing the play" and "Why are they booing it?" "Because it's not anti-war," Rip said. I said, "Well . . . what do they want if this is not against war?"

LION: No war, that's what they wanted. They wanted no war. No war, no theater.

BRAND: How's that again? No war, no theater?

LION: They wanted no war; they didn't want theater. They came to see no war. They came to see the war as idea rather than as isness.

BRAND: Was there an audience for all this raving you guys were doing when you began working together?

LION: Oh yeah, it was quite a fullsome sort of audience.

MCCLURE: We seemed to be cutting through all the lines. We weren't getting the formal theater audience. We were getting people who had intellectual curiosity and alertness and a sense of humor, from all strata and types.

LION: I think those who were attending the theater were performance-goers, or almost literally, sensation-seekers.

MCCLURE: Yes, in the best sense. I meet more people that I didn't know who were going to our plays in '72 or '73. They are the most alert, warmest type of person. I had that realization lately.

LION: Moving right along . . . The thing that attracted me about doing theater in the West is that there was no theater audience here. When I got here I realized there was a Kulture-Konscious audience that was mainly in for the old social "shot in the arm" when they went to see the opera or see some "classical theater," or whatever; and the scene around the attendance of these things appeared as if they'd just go and mill around and the going was the event. The play was the excuse for the event. So I immediately reacted against this, because I had been used to chamber theater in the East. If we were going to find an audience, we were going to have to go and find the audience that existed in the cracks. I believe that we did that to a large degree. I remember that there was a tremendous mix that came to the theater: elderly people, kids, all sorts—odd characters, a kid came to the play the other night with Mickey Mouse gloves on.

MCCLURE: I don't believe the audience has been stolen from theater. The audience has been driven away by the plays since Ibsen's day. Walter Kerr blames it on George Bernard Shaw, who advised, "Do as Ibsen does." Then Shaw was the only one who didn't do as Ibsen did.

LION: Yes, but there are many more people blaming it on Walter Kerr.

MCCLURE: The musical *Minnie Mouse and the Tap-Dancing Buddha* is the next play we did after *Gorf* because once the Taoist universe of *Gorf* was established, then Shakespeare could pop out beside the tap-dancing Buddha and Minnie Mouse; it's a swirl; it's completely malleable.

BRAND: The thing that gets me about the recent play *The Grabbing of the Fairy* is the stuff coming through the walls of the rose petal room: hands coming through the walls and pulling rabbits out of hats, brushing themselves, opening drawers, etc. Where did that come from?

MCCLURE: Childhood fantasies. Where Cocteau got it for *Beauty and the Beast*. It is a prevalent childhood fantasy with many persons.

LION: I'll say that from a directorial point of view, it's understood that the play was to have taken place inside a rose, and I did not necessarily interpret it to mean the center of the rose, but maybe inside a petal, inside of anything, inside a biological membrane. I thought of the arms and everything coming through as cilia.

MCCLURE: Absolutely. Extrusions and intrusions into a cellular being is the idea. The movements of the dancers, of the four women with tails, are cytoplasmic flow. The intrusions and the extrusions are cilia and flagella penetrating the cell. There's nothing one-to-one there. You can't say something's a mitochondria, something's a golgi body—but it's a biological universe.

BRAND: From the audience's standpoint, it is just fantastic theater because it's multimedia in a way that multimedia never really accomplished, which is that there's more going on than you can track. You just cannot stay ahead of the action because it's coming at you in more directions than you have eyes. And, as a result, the overwhelm, which still has contact, is rather marvelous. The feeling I got from everybody I talked with was that they wanted a great deal more because it felt so good. I think a lot of it was that although the audience really outnumbered the actors it was as if the stage could outnumber any number of audience by virtue of the way it was presented.

LION: I agree with that—the biological surge of the stage as an image in and of itself with its own complexities which appears to be endless. It's interesting, I think, that Michael is writing two kinds of plays. I prefer the plays with so much plot that they are plotless, such as *Gorf*. I think that the way the other plays, such as *The Pink Helmet*, function is that they are like serial music, like a Steve Reich piece or a Terry Riley piece.

MCCLURE: *The Pink Helmet* is a radical play. Male nudity is clearly still radical. It's bothering to many people. You have a universe posited in which there are naked soldiers with fairy wings and slingshot-shaped weapons. They're the last three males left in the war. One begins to realize, hearing them, that they are telling, through their actions, about a complex universe. It is a world in which there are sacred rites, sacred dances, in which there is an enemy that shouts, "Blam. Blam. Blam." It's only through sparse dialogue that one is told about the spirit and topology of that dimension. The viewer is allowed to realize that dimension is endless. It can go as far as the imagination lets it go. How many people were there in the army? How did they get there? They are just points of all that universe out there. The audience is confronted with an endless package of its own imagination.

BRAND: *The Pink Helmet* seems, for me at least, to have worked better in the reading than the viewing. The Mothers-in-Law of the Milky Way are fantastic in the reading of it, but maybe not connected enough with "shimmery chrome hooks" in the theater play to go together. For me *The Pink Helmet* made it on details, rather than the wholeness of it, but it seems like an essential work to have as part of a sequence. Dan, a Zen priest, was raving at me from the top of the stairs in Baker-Roshi's the other day, saying, "You know, that was only a goddamn first act. I think McClure owes us at least two more acts of *Pink Helment* and *The Grabbing of the Fairy*." There seems to be an endless sequence of such fairy stories. A fairy story book is always a very big book. By the time you get back to some of the early stories, you're enough older to have forgotten them.

LION: Right, or if they're the same, you aren't. And so they're totally new.

On Julian Beck

URI HERTZ: When did you first become aware of the work the Becks were doing with the Living Theatre?

MICHAEL McCLURE: In the later 1950s. Of course, I saw the Living Theatre's production of Jack Gelber's post-Pirandellian play *The Connection* on a trip to New York a couple of years earlier. My first contact with Julian Beck was in 1958. I sent my my first play to Julian and Judith Malina. Unfortunately it was lost, but it was done soon thereafter by the Poet's Theatre with Diane di Prima and Alan Marlowe producing it. The Living Theatre was rising like a phoenix out of a lot of important avant-garde theater troupes. It was the energy and beauty of Julian and Judith which made it that way.

HERTZ: When did the Living Theatre make their first appearance in the San Francisco Bay Area?

McCLURE: I remember the Living first came here around the mid-sixties and they started doing theater exercises. My wife of the time and I participated in them—games where five or six people would stand and throw the living body of another person high into the air from the stage, ten, fifteen, or twenty feet into the auditorium below where they'd be caught by other actors. It was a kind of bonding exercise that I remember most strongly. *Antigone* was done in the San Francisco Civic Auditorium. I remember a great deal of wonder. It was as if all the things we'd been hearing about the Living were all true. There was the huge cast of the play lying on their backs with arms up in the air, so it looked like the tiny legs in the water-vascular

Conducted by Uri Hertz, this interview first appeared in *Third Rail* No. 7, 1985/1986.

system of a starfish covering the stage, waving in the air as if the stage were a starfish on its back. The body of Antigone's brother was passed along over their hands. It was an extraordinary thing to see. At the same time, other members of the cast crawled down the aisles of the theater and over the laps of the spectators so that while the action was taking place onstage, the concept of the stage was being taken into the audience.

HERTZ: What about the Living Theatre's other productions?

MCCLURE: I remember that Julian and Judith came back next with *Paradise Now*. That had less of a reception here. It was a great sort of liberating drama of free form and shape and protest. They had done it in Europe and it had shocked people there. But at that point Berkeley, California was terminally hip. It was probably the most hip place in the world. The Living performed *Paradise Now* in Berkeley. In one part they take off their clothes and say, "I'm not allowed to be naked," and they take out joints of marijuana and say, "I'm not allowed to smoke marijuana." But in Berkeley, a lot of the audience took off their clothes and chain-danced up and down the aisles and smoked dope.

HERTZ: They were ready for it.

MCCLURE: They had already been there, in a sense. Julian's reaction to that—and I remember a lot of us were impressed by it—was to stay in the Bay Area and say, "I'm going to stay here and learn." That's one of the marks of a real man.

HERTZ: How long did the Living Theatre stay?

MCCLURE: Some months, as I remember.

HERTZ: Did they participate in the activities of the poets and theater people?

MCCLURE: Yes. They made themselves available. They had a place where they exercised and did their work. Both Julian and Judith were social persons, so they were around the community and the members of the troupe were also. Anybody had access to come in and do theater games with them or see what the troupe was doing or come in and talk to Julian. At the time, there were many of us who wanted to run away and join the Living, as when I was a kid people wanted to run away and join the circus. There was that sense of freedom.

HERTZ: What was their impact on you as a playwright?

McCLURE: They've always been a source and example for me personally. Their freedom from prejudice and their desire to be free of governmental strictures has always struck me. And in my theater and writing, they've been an example in their sense of freedom of image and the flowingness of it . . . And also in their use of stage, which is remarkable. It's not enough to write plays. One has to think about the stage as a physical part of the organism a play is. They gave some wonderful examples of that in *Paradise Now, Frankenstein*, and pieces like that.

HERTZ: What further contact did you have with the Becks after the time they spent in the Bay area?

McCLURE: As a matter of fact, I saw *Antigone* in Paris two years ago. It's much as Julian did it back then. In Paris they had been appointed to be the theater in residence for Paris, as I understand it. They had access to a theater which I think was a huge rebuilt stable or horse-grooming area in a park and they were doing *Antigone* there. There was still the grace that there was in the sixties performances of *Antigone* and, at moments, it was heightened to a translucence, as if they had become eagle-angels of the anarchist spirit, and they glowed. It was really quite remarkable. I wish that someone in the U.S. had done what the French Ministry of Culture did, so Julian and Judith and the Living could have been theater in residence for San Franciso or New York or Los Angeles.

HERTZ: When did you last see Julian?

McCLURE: At a reading we gave in Paris in June of 1984 with Judith and some French poets. Afterwards, after an evening at La Coupole, Julian gave me the manuscript to the book of poems that he read that night as a gift in response to a poem of mine which ran down the page one word at a time like a Japanese poem, so it sort of hung in space, which goes like this:

HOW
SWEET
TO
BE
A
ROSE
BY
CANDLE
LIGHT
or
a
worm
by
full
moon.
See the hop-
ping flight
a cricket makes.
Nature loves
the absence of
mistakes.

Julian is one of the great non-mistakes of nature.

Writing *The Beard*

LEE BARTLETT: How did you get interested in writing plays?

MICHAEL MCCLURE: It started early because once Theodore Roethke told me that he recalled a letter I'd sent him asking if he was writing plays. I'd gotten that idea somewhere and I was fascinated with Roethke's poetry when I was in high school. In the mid-fifties I was beginning to keep journals and in those journals I was writing dialogues that were spoken between the alchemist and his wife or the biochemist and his muse. These dialogues became aspirations for plays.

BARTLETT: What about early reading?

MCCLURE: As a teenager I was reading Yeats—not just the poetry but I was most interested in his theater pieces. Around the same time I was reading Federico Garcia Lorca and became fascinated with Lorca's theater, particularly the more unusual plays like *The Love of Don Perlimplin for Belisa in the Garden* and his surreal pieces like *After Five Years Pass*. There was that kind of background for my growing interest in drama.

BARTLETT: What about the Elizabethans?

MCCLURE: I had always been moved by the verbal and dramatic electricity of John Webster and the Elizabethans, not to mention Shakespeare, and I was fascinated by the outrageousness of the Greek comedy of Aristophanes. And then I discovered the works of Frank Wedekind—*Spring's Awakening* and the *Lulu* plays—which were part of the atmos-

Conducted by Lee Bartlett in 1991, this interview is previously unpublished.

phere of the beginning of sexual liberation and enlightened politics at the time.

BARTLETT: How did the San Francisco Actors' Workshop come to first produce *The Beard?*

McCLURE: *The Beard* was first produced because Harold Pinter was in San Francisco and I heard from someone that Pinter didn't know anyone in town. I called his hotel and said that I was a poet, and he asked me to come on down to the hotel and have a drink with him, that he was going back to London the following day. During our conversation I mentioned that I was writing plays, and later Pinter got hold of the Actor's Workshop and suggested that they look at my work. I had given the Actor's Workshop a play in beast language called ¡*The Feast!*, which must have looked quite strange. I'd also given them a play called *The Blossom*, which was about the Lincoln County Range War enacted by Billy the Kid and the other actual personae—Alexander and Susan McSween and John Tunstall—the active participants in that battle in the New Mexican range war. *The Blossom* was a play in which the characters were already dead but did not know it. They knew each other—like psyches of people who had been killed in battle swirling around one another trying to align themselves. I knew that this was more outre than Beckett and Genet but I couldn't understand why they wouldn't consider the plays. I was pleased when Pinter made the suggestion that they read them, and sure enough they got hold of me and asked me for a play—so by this time—it was 1964–65—*The Beard* had been written, so I sent them a copy and never heard another word until one day Mark Estrin got a hold of me. He'd been given the okay for a directorial project, and he'd found *The Beard* and said that he'd like to do it.

BARTLETT: The poster you created for *The Beard* is very striking.

McCLURE: As you know, *The Beard* is a play between Billy the Kid and Jean Harlow as they confront each other in a blue velvet eternity. I was flying to Los Angeles to visit a friend there and earlier I'd been talking with Norman Mailer and had become interested in boxing. I had a copy of *Ring Magazine* with me and while I was on the plane a boxing poster flashed into my mind—on the boxing poster were pictures of Billy the Kid and Jean Harlow. In boxing posters of that time you had photographs of the two contenders, one on each side of the poster, and in the middle the text would say Muhammad Ali versus Joe Frazier. But on this poster I saw Billy the Kid and Jean Harlow, and the poster was printed in beast language. It was like a vision—almost comic, like a lightbulb over my head.

I finished in Los Angeles and returned to San Francisco, taking a cab back from the airport to my home. As the cab passed the Uganda Liquor Store at the corner of Haight Street and Masonic I saw one of those boxing posters in the window, so I asked the cab driver to wait and I got out and looked at the poster to see the printer's name in the corner. I got up the next morning and began laying out a poster in beast language, with Billy the Kid and Jean Harlow on it. Then I phoned Telegraph Press and said, "I want to know if you'd do a poem poster for me." I got a tough, working-class voice on the other end of the line, a middle-aged man saying, "Polo poster? Sure kid, we can do polo posters. Bring it on down and we'll do it." I laid the poster out. From the two available pictures of the Kid I chose the head shot, then I went through photographs of Harlow and found a photograph that I liked.

BARTLETT: What about the text?

MCCLURE: As if it were as clear as a vision, I knew what the poster words would say. They began: "LOVE LION, LIONESS, GAHHR THY ROOH, GRAHEEER." I wrote it all out and then I went downtown to the Telegraph Press, which was a huge basement printery, and it turned out that they did nothing but boxing posters except for one instance—they did a Rolling Stones concert poster. It looked like the right place. Ed Jelinsky was there chewing on a cigar; he had talked to me on the phone so I spread out the poster for him. He said, "Yeah, okay—these words will be blue, these will be red." It was all in huge, circus typeface. "The picture will have to be this size, and down here the text must go right there," and he explained the principles behind the boxing poster, some of which I've used in my writing to this day. So I told him to go ahead and print it but he said no—he didn't like the picture of Jean Harlow. He said, "You young guys think you know what Jean Harlow looked like but that picture doesn't look like Jean Harlow at all. Look, she's got wrinkles under her chin in this one." So I went to the library and did some research and I found another photo of Harlow that I liked a whole lot. I took it down to the press and gave it to Jelinsky's assistant. A couple days later I received a call saying Jelinsky wants you to come down here, he wants to talk to you about the poster. When I arrived Jelinsky got out the proofsheet, which was printed on flimsy paper, and we started reading it. He looked at me and said, "LOVE LION comma LIONESS—is that right?" I said Yeah, and then said, "GAHHR." We went through the spelling of the beast language in detail. We got all the way down to near the end, and he looked directly at me and asked, "What is this shit anyway?" I told him it was a poem and he said that he had a friend who worked for the WPA who was a poet and he had a book of his, so he'd print the poster.

BARTLETT: How many did you run?

MCCLURE: I think about 150. I took one back to the liquor store where I'd seen the fight poster in the window and I asked to put one up there. The proprietor looked at it and said he couldn't do it because he always got complimentary tickets for putting posters in his window. I went back down to Telegraph Press and told Jelinsky that we had to run some tickets. So he got out a boxing ticket for me to see and I wrote up another boxing ticket in beast language. He printed it and I went back to the liquor store. The proprietor looked at me, and I put two comps on the counter. The poster was up in the window for a long time. I used to park across the street to watch people walking past and then stopping to look at it. Some people would walk right on by and shake their heads. Some would come back and read it. Some would get someone else to come look at it too.

BARTLETT: Where else did you hang them?

MCCLURE: I took posters and put them up in places where boxing posters were put up. I put them up on walls, fences, and took one and stapled it on Kenneth Anger's door, and took one over to Kenneth Rexroth's apartment and leaned it against his door, and I gave them to friends. I folded one of them in half and stapled some comp tickets to it and mailed it to Wallace Berman. I took one home and put it on the wall of the room where I worked. The desk was in front of a window which looked out on the Pacific Ocean—I was living on top of a hill, a peak above the Haight Ashbury.

So I sat at my typewriter and looked out at the western sky and the ocean, with the poster behind my head. In a day or two I could feel that Billy the Kid and Jean Harlow had entered my consciousness. It was as if the poster, from the wall behind my chair, had focused them into my head, and they began acting out a play. It was strange. It began: "Before you can pry any secrets from me you must first find the real me. Which one will you pursue?" That's Harlow speaking. Then the Kid replies, "What makes you think I want to pry any secrets from you?" She says, "Because I'm so beautiful. Before you can pry any secrets from me you must first find the real me. Which one will you pursue?" And they go through it again. They were doing it in my head, so I typed it out.

The first time they came to act it out, I wrote out a few pages. I felt a little like Jelinsky: "What is this? What's going on here?" William Blake said, "The authors are in Eternity." Yeah, okay, I guess they're in Eternity. I didn't know if any more was going to happen or not and then sometime the next day, when I sat down at the typewriter, Harlow and the Kid came back and picked up just where they were before. Soon I was involved in whether they'd come back again, and the next day they came back and there was another number of pages. There were no changes—I just typed out what they said and it took about a week. I have been told that *Waiting for Godot* was written much like that, that Beckett wrote out *Godot* with no changes in a tablet—one of those "Big Chief" notebooks. When I tried to make corrections in the text or make it more coherent, or edit it in any way, *The Beard* became incoherent and lost its fineness. Then I had to go back and restore the original. That's how the play came about. Looking at it, I thought, this is a kind of nature poem, or a ritual of Shakti and Shiva.

BARTLETT: How did it come to be published?

MCCLURE: Robert Hawley at Oyez Press said he would print a limited edition, so we had it typed as a play script and had them bound and stapled. We gave the play scripts to friends.

BARTLETT: And then The Actors' Workshop picked it up?

MCCLURE: Yes. Director Mark Estrin called me, having found the play in the bottom drawer of the nethermost abysmal basement under The Actors' Workshop, at the back of the bottom-most drawer. It had not only been filed, it had been put in eternity, and the fact that Mark Estrin found it and saved it from eternity was great luck. Now The Actors' Workshop was going to allow two performances of the play at midnight on the Encore Stage with a tiny budget for it. It happened that they had a pair of really fine actors there who wanted to be in it and Mark cast them for it.

BARTLETT: Who?

MCCLURE: Richard Bright was one. You see him often nowadays as a talented character actor—he's in the "Godfather" films. The actress was a woman named Billie Dixon, who is no longer acting as far as I know but she had a career afterwards and was asked to join a distinguished British company. They were novice actors and Mark cast them for the play, Robert LaVigne did the set, which was a beautiful small set of blue velvet and pinpricks of light. We had gone into rehearsal on the play when I received a phone call from the artistic director of The Actors' Workshop who said that he was cancelling our two performances. I said he couldn't do that—I had announcements printed up and mailed and had arranged for people to be ushers and be in costumes too, and it was to be a major artistic event in my life and also in the San Francisco art scene that I was in.

BARTLETT: What was the problem?

MCCLURE: He insisted that *The Beard* threatened the acceptable image of The Actors' Workshop, which was in the middle of fundraising. We argued about it back and forth. He finally said that there could be a single performance of the play if I would cancel the reviewers whom I had invited. I didn't know anything about reviews anyway, so I said I'd do that as long as we had the play—one performance. I did in fact cancel the reviewers and we had the play and then it was all over. A few days later there was a major laudatory review of it in the *Chronicle*.

BARTLETT: Who wrote it?

MCCLURE: Michael Grieg, who was a staff writer for the *Chronicle*, and an old-time radical. It didn't occur to me to cancel Michael's invitation because he was not a reviewer, and I was only dimly aware that he wrote for the *Chronicle* because I knew him for other reasons— as a poet. So in all innocence, I had not cancelled Michael. The artistic director of the theater phoned and—talking about obscenities—yelled and screamed obscenities for a long time about my ruining his theater. Of course, this wasn't true since San Francisco loved a scandal anyway. It caused no great trouble. It was a work of art and it was a mistake to keep it off the stage.

BARTLETT: Wasn't the next production at the Fillmore?

MCCLURE: Yes. Billie Dixon, Richie Bright, and I wanted to do it again, and Bill Graham said we could do it at the Fillmore Auditorium. Tony Martin set up an enormous and beautiful light show with every- thing from movies of horses running through liquid projections to other projections of movies of little girls skipping rope and clouds passing by. We took the set and put it up on the Fillmore bandstand, and decided that Billie and Richie would use hand-held microphones so that the play would go over the amplification system. It was like classic Greek theater where one looked down from the amphitheater onto the orchestra where the play took place, and behind the stage the ocean was visible in the distance. So, although we were looking upward at the play, it was as if the universe or the ocean of images was behind it. It was an ocean or universe of moving colors and lights and pictures, and we were hearing huge voices coming over the amplification. It was spectacular. It felt like Aristophanes or Sophocles. And it was a spectacle because we were using the equipment of rock 'n' roll with the talents and gifts of the theater. But at the end of that performance Bill Graham told Richie Bright that he had to cancel our second show because he'd heard from the police that they were going to arrest us at our next performance, and that would cause him to lose his license. In those days rock 'n' roll was new and the last thing we wanted to do was to lose our only rock 'n' roll hall and the scene around it.

BARTLETT: Was it just the performance that evening, or did a band play?

McCLURE: I asked Bill Graham last year who the rock group was and he said it was the Sons of Champlin.

BARTLETT: And was it the usual Fillmore rock crowd?

McCLURE: There wasn't a usual Fillmore crowd, or if there was it was not a bunch of rock 'n' roll heads. The Fillmore crowd in 1965 was the art scene. What I mean to say is that there wasn't a rock 'n' roll scene and a separate art scene. There was an art world of young people and rock 'n' roll was part of it. There were painters, dancers, a lot of poets. Then there were friends there that night who would be thought of as literary—the chances were that they were going to the Fillmore as often as I was.

BARTLETT: The next performance?

McCLURE: That was thanks to Richie Bright, who is as tough as The Kid in his own way. The Committee, an improvisational comedy theater, was black on Monday nights so Richie made an arrangement for the Committee on a Monday night, a few weeks later. At the end of the performance there was a loud clattering, the clattering of a movie camera—back in those days a 16mm camera made lot of noise. A cop had been sitting in the audience, literally in a trenchcoat, with a 16mm camera under it, and he jumped up to film the last part of the play. In a few minutes police dragged Billie and Richie down to the police station and booked them.

Even with this arrest, Billie and Richie believed in the play as art and wanted to go on. By this time we were getting deeply upset about censorship. The Vietnam War was going on and we were in the middle of the war atmosphere. We were thinking, why are we being censored over an artwork about eros and the divine when there is a bombing of fishing villagers with napalm in Southeast Asia? It was a moving situation. We think, "We're artists. We're being censored. We don't see anything wrong with this play. We're not making anybody go to this play. We've been censored by the Actors' Workshop. We've been censored by the police who've threatened Bill Graham. And now we've taken it to the Committee on a Monday night, which certainly ought to be safe ground." We decided to continue the performances and we formed a production company which we called Rare Angel Productions. We knew we'd be arrested if we did it again in San Francisco so we decided to take the play to Berkeley—Berkeley is liberal. Richie went to Berkeley and rented the Flora Schwimley Little Theatre, but he didn't realize that it was the Board of Education's theater. Almost immediately we had letters from the Chief of Police and the District Attorney of Berkeley telling us that we could not use the Flora Schwimley Theatre for our obscene play.

BARTLETT: This was before the production took place.

MCCLURE: Yes, and they told us that we would be arrested on sight. We all had a conference and Billie, Richie, and I decided that we'd go on. We knew police would have movie cameras and tape recorders so that they could take evidence and arrest us. I invited the intellectuals in the Bay Area who were lively enough to want to attend—everyone from Alan Watts to Mark Schorer and Lawrence Ferlinghetti, as well as religious leaders. They were all given seats in the front row. The auditorium was packed with policemen and their cameras and tape recorders. I also had friends with tape recorders to tape-record the police. I went on stage before the play to read the letter forbidding us to use the theater, and the audience cheered and laughed.

I remember that one of the police tape recorders was lowered from the ceiling. It came down lower and lower until it was right over Mark Schorer's head—Schorer was the Blake critic at the University of California at Berkeley—to record anything he might say. We got away with no arrest that night, but then they arrested Billie and Richie with warrants the next day, and so we had two busts against us. The ACLU had offered to defend us so we stopped performances at that point. And we saw the whole trial through with the ACLU, and then to thank them after we won we did a benefit performance for the ACLU at California Hall.

BARTLETT: Was the trial held in San Francisco?

MCCLURE: Yes, but that was only the beginning of arrests, lawsuits, and trials. Berkeley dropped the charges after we won in San Francisco, but later the heavier censorship problems began.

BARTLETT: Who testified at the San Francisco trial?

MCCLURE: Expert witnesses from my side and police witnesses from theirs. The whole thing went on for weeks but the actual trial only ran for a few days. It took a long time to move up the dockets. When we won the trial we formalized Rare Angel Productions, found a producer, and rented the Encore Theater. We had an art show in the lobby by George Herms, and another show of works by Kathie Bunnell, and we began performing the play. After a while we moved it to Fisherman's Wharf, and it ran for a fair number of weeks, though we lost Mark as director somewhere along the way. Consequently, the play became progressively looser and was not holding together. Some plays have to be redirected occasionally.

BARTLETT: Didn't *Evergreen Review* publish the play?

MCCLURE: Yes, Grove Press's *Evergreen Review*. Barney Rossett the publisher asked if he could have *The Beard* for the first production in

The Evergreen Theater that he was opening in New York. Rossett had been defeating U.S. censorship laws by publishing Burroughs, D.H. Lawrence, and Henry Miller. I said we'd have to have the play redirected because of its condition. Rossett asked me what I thought of Rip Torn and I said that I liked his acting but didn't know anything about his directing. Rip came out to San Francisco and looked at the play as it was, and we spent some time together. We decided he was the right director and then we all went back to New York and began work. The Evergreen Theater was being built around us as we worked. We had the inside of the theater lined with stretch cloth and contacted USCO, the big East Coast multi-media light show people, so that the whole interior of the theater preceding the play would be like a light show— the walls, the ceiling, and everything else would have lights and projection going on all at once. I suggested some Blake songs I'd set to music before the play, during the light show. I wanted a Hell's Angel, an angel, and a cowboy to come in with amplified autoharps and sing the Blake songs as an induction. I searched for somebody who knew how to play the autoharp, to be a teacher to the actors who played the roles of motorcyclist, angel, and cowboy. I went walking across the park in Greenwich Village and I found a guy in fringe leathers and asked him if he knew how to play the autoharp. He said yes, and I asked him if he wanted a job teaching some actors. He smiled and turned me down. A few steps later the man I was with told me that I had been talking to Tim Buckley. Then we went up to Folk City and found someone who could teach autoharp and went on from there.

I thought of another thing that would be good in the lobby. I wanted to have cages of doves and cages of ferrets stacked near each other to get an adrenalin rush moving through the lobby, so then we needed animal handlers for that. We had a light show going on, we had animal handlers, we had a costumer who has since become one of the famous ones on Broadway, Ann Roth. USCO was constantly wanting to work the light show and at first Rip could barely get time to rehearse with Billie and Richie. We had gone from an art performance, to the Fillmore, to commercial theater with our own company, and now we were legitimate off-Broadway. In a period of a year I'd gone from not being a playwright at all through a street-education to being an off-Broadway playwright, as well as initiating the opening of Grove's new theater in New York, dealing with animal handlers, directors, PR people, and Grove Press.

At the same time, Rip and I were acting in a film that Norman Mailer was shooting, playing outlaw motorcyclists in "Beyond the Law." I was going to a lot of New York theater to see what was going on—*Hair* and *The Beard* opened in the same year. When it came time for the awards, the Obies, *The Beard* received an Obie for Best Director for Rip and Best Actress for Billie Dixon.

Later we took the play to London, and Rip directed Billie and Richie again, with a British light show. This was at the Royal Court Theatre, where George Bernard Shaw started. It was all burgundy velvet and pleasantly old and solid inside. We were nearly the first play put on after the abolition of the British theater Censor, so everybody was there on opening night, from Vanessa Redgrave and Ralph Richardson to the Beatles, wanting to see what would happen—to see if *The Beard* might cause the re-establishment of the Censor. Apparently the reviewers felt themselves liberated and it was the most glowing single bunch of reviews I've seen in my life. I woke up the next morning in an Art Deco hotel and, over that day and the next, eleven great reviews came in from British papers and magazines. Then we took the play to Paris where Billie and Richie did it in English a couple of times.

BARTLETT: Wasn't Dennis Hopper somehow involved in the Los Angeles production?

MCCLURE: Yes, after the New York production and before the London production, a producer had asked to do *The Beard* in Los Angeles. It was to star an old friend, Dennis Hopper, and starlet Alexandra Hay. In rehearsal Dennis was intense and vivid. Meanwhile, he and the producer had many fallings out and many disagreements. Almost regularly I'd fly down to Los Angeles and put Dennis and the producer back together, get them speaking to one another. Then three days later Dennis's pal Peter Fonda would call me up to say, "Dennis and the producer aren't speaking again. You've got to come down here." That went on for weeks.

In the meantime, Fullerton State College in Orange County had done an unauthorized student production of *The Beard* without my knowledge. The conservatives in Orange County went wild. They went pretty nearly crazy and the newspapers in Orange County—there must be a dozen of them—were running banner headlines about the filthy play being produced at the College. In reaction to that, the *Los Angeles Times* published an editorial against *The Beard* while we were rehearsing the play. But that was not enough. They waited another week or so and ran another editorial against *The Beard* before the opening night. I wasn't able to reconcile Hopper and the producer, and Richie Bright was free by that time, so Richie arrived to play The Kid, which was a break. On opening night there were klieg lights outside the theater, searchlights beaming through the sky and all over Hollywood. All the birds and beasts and glitterati, actors and actresses and producers of Hollywood were there to see what would happen. That night the police made the first arrest of fourteen arrests. They arrested fourteen performances in a row—at the end of each they took away Richie and Alexandra Hay and booked them. But in the meantime, a wealthy financier, who had been radicalized by the play, put up bail for us. Each night he put up a huge bail sum or the play would have been stopped. The arrests were a media circus for weeks, with regular front page photos of Richie and Alexandra. Someone tried to burn down the theater by setting a fire on the roof, so we had to move to another theater in Hollywood.

The State of California reprinted the play in a document as part of the evidence against us, and a state law against obscene plays—a law that specifically named *The Beard*—was rejected in the Criminal Committee by only one vote. Charlton Heston denounced the play. Nancy Reagan, wife of then-Governor Ronald Reagan, spoke against the play. I was sued for a huge amount by Robert Dornan, who was then a talk-show host and is now an ultra-conservative congressman from Southern California. He's the one who claimed that Bill Clinton made trips to Moscow to get his orders from the K.G.B. My lawyer claimed that I was being shadowed when I was in Los Angeles. Rip and I were on television to explain that the play was an award-winning work of dramatic art. The law that was being used to arrest the actors was a law that gave the right to Los Angeles police—distinguished for their brutality and beatings of poor whites and non-whites, as well as other neanderthal fearsomeness—to deny production to theater pieces. The only other use of the law that I know about was regarding a production of Aristophanes' anti-war play *Lysistrata*. Our position was always that of Alan Watts, who pointed out that "obscene" means that which is done offstage—which in Greek theater was violence, violence was done offstage. We said the obscenity was in the violence of the United States' bombings and napalmings and massacres of Asians in Vietnam, Laos, and Cambodia. We believed that a play that claimed that the universe and eternity is divine—as *The Beard* does—is intolerable to murderers and those brainwashed or self-deluded into napalming innocent Asians. Eventually we won. The lawsuit against me was dropped and the play has been done in French and German translations. It's performed in colleges and workshops and theaters all over the U.S.

I went on to a relationship with the Magic Theater in San Francisco which did eleven productions of my plays. Sam Shepard and I were playwrights-in-residence at the Magic Theater. In 1979, another of my plays, *Josephine the Mouse Singer*, received New York's Obie for Best Play. There were other busts of *The Beard*, also. One was in Vancouver, B.C., where it won the case with help of the CCLU. I also understand the play had censorship problems in Boston and in Israel.

At an early point in my theater life, before *The Beard*, a production of my play *The Blossom* was forcibly cancelled at the end of a long rehearsal at the University of Wisconsin. The actors would have been expelled from school if they'd gone ahead. My second poetry book— a long poem titled *Dark Brown*—was nearly impossible to publish in 1959, though it was called one of the great American poems by Jack Kerouac, who tried to get a publisher for it. It was a visionary and sexual poem, and when it was finally published it had to be sold under-the-counter to those interested in my poetry.

People have said that *The Beard* cases were to the theater what *Howl* was to poetry and *Naked Lunch* was to the novel. When I was a young man I saw Lenny Bruce letting himself be destroyed by censorship, and that was a thought in the back of my mind—not to be destroyed, and not to be censored.

The Lion Roars

WILLIAM PERKINS: Let's talk about your new book, *Rebel Lions*. I hear echoes of Wordsworth and Keats in these poems. Were you influenced by the Romantic poets in writing these poems?

MICHAEL MCCLURE: I've always been deeply moved by Keats and Shelley, especially Shelley. In my previous book of poems, the quote on the title page is from Shelley:

> Rise like lions after slumber,
> In unvanquishable number,
> Shake the chains to earth like dew
> Which in sleep had fall'n on you.

That's where the title of my new book, *Rebel Lions*, comes from. Shelley and Blake are the nineteenth-century poets that I read the most.

PERKINS: Judging by the poems in *Rebel Lions*, it appears to me that you had just fallen in love again after a long respite. Care to comment?

MCCLURE: I wasn't expecting that! Yes, I am in love again, deeply, and that's clear in my poems. In fact, the major poem in *Rebel Lions*, called "Stanzas from Maui," recounts the exact moment wherein one who believes that he is dying of one love, finds the birth of another love. The poem is like a word sculpture of the occasion. It's a long poem that some people might think was some kind of spontaneous chant. Whereas, in fact, it is a meditational, highly constructed work, as someone would work on a string quartet, a carefully wrought piece.

Conducted by William Perkins, this interview originally appeared in *Howl*, 1992.

PERKINS: I noted many metaphysical references in "Stanzas From Maui"—god, goddess, python papa, Bodhisattva. What's your metaphysical reference?

McCLURE: Well, I'm a spiritual seeker. I'm on a grail quest, as most artists are, and any spiritual seeking includes the writings of the great mystics and religious thinkers that I'm familiar with, from Lao Tzu and the *Tao Te Ching* to Confucius to *The Cloud of Unknowing* (the great fifteenth-century English book of knowing through not knowing) to Hwa Yen, which was introduced to me by Gary Snyder. Hwa Yen is an eighth-century Chinese Buddhism from the time of the first uniting of Taoism and Buddhism. It's the sister sect of Zen, but it's about physics. It's about the non-physics of nothingness; whereas Zen is about the practice of meditation. But it's essentially the same thing.

PERKINS: I'm quoting now from your poem, "High Heels," a selection from your new book *Rebel Lions*. The lines read, "What does it mean if we melt together in a pool of rippling silver? I've got a soul I'm building. I'm soul making." What do you mean by soul building and soul making?

McCLURE: Well, I take the term from Keats. You started this out by asking a question about Keats, and I said Shelley was more of a source for me. Now that you bring that up, I recall Keats's letters have been as powerful a source for me as Shelley's poetry. Keats, in one of his letters, brings up the idea of soul building, "soul-making" he calls it. He believes that life is soul-making. What Keats means is that all of us are born with a propensity for a soul. We are always introjecting parts of the world that we move through that are meaningful to us, and we create an inner life. That inner life that we create balances and joins, in part, with our unconscious life, or with the forgotten life of our childhood, or the life of our father, and that makes a complex and richer interior. With that interior we are able to recognize greater complexity and self-organization in the exterior world. And we take it back within ourselves, and that becomes part of us again. So, finally, there is a kind of nimbus or halo around ourselves—and I don't mean that in any religious sense—there is a kind of metaphorical glow around ourselves, which is the creation of our own field of being. So that we become more autonomous and more able to direct ourselves, more appreciative, constructive, and permeable to nature, both interior and exterior. So that finally we realize we are our soul.

PERKINS: Some of the poems in *Rebel Lions* allude to the earth movement, the ecology movement, and the goddess movement. Do you have anything other than a poetic involvement with these issues? Or, in other words, what are you doing to save the planet?

MCCLURE: I have been involved with the environmental movement since about 1957. As many people did in the Bay Area, I attended the United Nations meeting on Human Environment in 1972 in Stockholm.

PERKINS: What about these days? That was about twenty years ago.

MCCLURE: Well, it is a major preoccupation of mine. I do not separate the environmental movement from my own studies in nature. What Ray Manzarek (keyboardist for The Doors) and I are doing in performance now is, to a great extent, political and environmental. A lot of the poems at our performances are about the planet. We do one long environmental poem called "Antechamber" and we close with a powerful political-nature poem called "Stanzas In Turmoil." So I consider myself both a political and environmental activist—at the level of the city, the music club, the college—as a public messenger.

PERKINS: Actually, when I saw you and Ray Manzarek at "The Great American Music Hall," I was pleased to see that many of your comments, between the poems, concerned the environment.

MCCLURE: That is deliberate. Much of the conversation at the show is political. I try, generally, to talk about Noam Chomsky; and I usually bring up Allen Ginsberg to make young people, who are into music, aware of the American dissident position. And Ray gives them real wisdom and advice from his perspective. Political and environmental activism is a major part of my work. But it springs from my interest in nature. I have always considered myself to be a biologist as well as a poet.

PERKINS: You seem to be having a lot of success with Ray Manzarek. How much longer do you think you'll be working with Ray? And/or when are you going to go solo again?

MCCLURE: I give solo readings, and I enjoy giving solo readings. I enjoy working with Ray more at this point. Ray and I have been working together since March 1987, and we have no plans to stop. We are both artists, so we work without a plan. We never made a plan to start. We never made a plan to stop. We keep doing it because we believe in what we're doing, in taking it to people and reaching them.

PERKINS: What is it you see or connect with in music that compels you to perform your poetry with music? Is it music's commercial appeal? So that your poetry will get heard?

MCCLURE: About five or six years ago, another poet named Michael C. Ford, who is a mutual friend of Ray's and mine, gave a reading with me at a small night club in Santa Monica called "McCabes." Ray came over to play piano with Ford. I thought it was wonderful. Ray heard my new poems, and he liked the new poems a lot. By the end of the evening, Ray and I believed we should work together. Within six weeks, by some strange act of nature and the goddesses and gods, we were asked to perform at a college, and that was our beginning. At that performance we got a standing ovation, and we've been doing it ever since. The first couple of years working together was spent building a repertoire. This was never a commercial endeavor.

PERKINS: I'm trying to get you to compare today's resurgent poetry scene with the scene back then.

MCCLURE: You're asking me about the poetry scene on the street today, but the poetry scene that I see today is when I go to colleges and music clubs. After performances, young poets come and speak to me; they give me their books; they ask me what they might be doing, if I have any suggestion what direction to go. So my contact with the scene is coming from clubs and colleges where we're performing, as well as the college where I teach.

PERKINS: Back in the sixties you were very involved in the street scene. You would appear at the concerts and recite a poem; you would show up at various events and demonstrations. Do you have any connection to the street now?

MCCLURE: Well, I'm not sure. I consider our performances to be an intense kind of activism in places that are almost subversive in their unexpectedness. For example, we will perform at a rock 'n' roll club in Milwaukee where the audience is young, blue-collar longhairs and their girlfriends, drinking hard. And we're doing music and performing environmental poetry and talking about Noam Chomsky. The first time we did that four or five years ago, I didn't know whether we were going to get attacked or what would happen. In fact, half-way through the performance, I saw that they were dancing. So they're hearing us. We're very involved. People are hearing us at levels that have a positive impact. We're reaching an unexpected and lively audience of all types and styles.

PERKINS: One last question. Do you think, like many of us poets would like to think today, that another poetry renaissance is now taking place?

MCCLURE: Renaissance means *rebirth*, and being reborn never ceases.

Cinnamon Turquoise Leather

MICHAEL MCCLURE: I'm going to give you a set of rules for making a deck of fifty cards containing one hundred words. This is a complex set of rules. Feel free to ask questions. They may remind me of something I'm leaving out.

This is to make a *personal universe deck*. It is going to be your personal universe exemplified in one hundred words. James Joyce was supposed to have had an English vocabulary of one hundred thousand words. Joyce also spoke a dozen languages. If he had five or ten thousand words in each of those languages, you can imagine the scale of Joyce's vocabulary. A normal active vocabulary may vary from five thousand to twenty thousand words. To pick only one hundred words from your vocabulary to exemplify your personal universe is a challenging process.

To follow this set of rules you will pick words that exemplify your past, your present, and, if you can imagine it, your future: some of these hundred words will reach into your future and exemplify it also. These hundred words will represent your *personal universe* in the past, present, and future.

The next rule is that the one hundred words must sound good together. It's even better if they sound beautiful together. But, at least, they must sound good together in *any random combination*. As I understand it, someone found from Edgar Allen Poe or Baudelaire, that he thought that the most beautiful word in English was "cellar door." The recognition of what sounds good, or beautiful, to you is in your own ears. For instance, anybody would agree that Chaucer sounds good. Just say the *Canterbury Tales* aloud:

Originally given as a talk at Naropa Institute in July, 1976, this appeared in *Talking Poetics From Naropa Institute*, ed. Anne Waldman and Marilyn Webb (Boulder: Shambala, 1978).

Whan that Aprille with his shoures sote
The droghte of Marche hath perced to the rote,
And bathed every veyne in swich licour
Of which vertu engendred is the flour;
Whan Zephirus eek with his swete breeth
Inspired hath in every holt and heeth
The tendre croppes, and the yonge sonne
Hath in the Ram his halfe cours y-ronne,
And smale fowles maken melodye,
That slepen al the night with open yë. . .

There's no disputing the fact that those words sound good in those combinations. Or, if we recite Blake:

How sweet I roam'd from field to field,
    And tasted all the summer's pride,
'Till I the prince of love beheld,
    Who in the sunny beams did glide!

He shew'd me lilies for my hair,
    And blushing roses for my brow;
He led me through his gardens fair,
    Where all his golden pleasures grow.

We know that sounds good. Or to take something that's not in English, listen to this in Spanish:

Nadie comprendia el perfume
de la oscura magnolia de tu vientre.

That's the "Gacela of Unforeseen Love" from *The Divan at Tamarit* by Lorca.

What if you randomly say: "Shit, Venezuela, Hamburger"? Sounds terrible? What if you said "Shit, Musk, Velvet"? Or "Shit, Musk"? Or "Velvet, Musk, Shit"? If you say "Shit, Venezuela, Hamburger" it doesn't sound good.

QUESTION: Shit doesn't sound good to me.

MCCLURE: Well, you're going to make up your own list of one hundred words.

Here's the next rule. You must show your good side as well as your bad side. The hundred words can't all come from your angelfood self. You want some of the dark meat in there too. Some of your negative aspect. Don't use a hundred words to tell the world that you're an angel. Remember the demonic, sinister side of yourself also.

Okay. It's going to be a personal universe, one hundred words from your past, present and future. The words should sound good, or beautiful together, in any random combination. A word that sounds bad to your ear by itself may sound beautiful in combination with ninety-nine other words that enable the word to express its beautiful aspects. For instance, when Allen Ginsberg says "Hamburger, Shit, Venezuela," he'll add ninety-seven other words to fill those words out. Then when they combine you'll hear their many facets, and the fricatives and the vowels interacting, and the beauteous parts of the breath that are in their interdependence. That's exactly what *Howl* does, as a matter of fact.

QUESTION: Does the repetition of one word over and over make sound more beautiful?

MCCLURE: It might or might not. It depends on the circumstances. When you're drawing up a list of a hundred words, if a word comes up obsessively two or three times and you don't notice, if it sneaks in, you may use that word more than once in your hundred words. Possibly its multiple occurrence represents an unconscious, impulsive desire to join the list more than once. You can pay attention to that.

QUESTION: What about words that are synonyms or opposites for each other?

MCCLURE: If you've got a hundred words to express your past, present, and future, your good side and your bad side, how many synonyms do you want to use?

QUESTION: Can you make up words?

MCCLURE: Absolutely, make up one or two for feelings you don't have words for.

QUESTION: Do you want any particular grammatical distribution?

MCCLURE: The words should be bare of endings. If you want to say star, don't say *starry*. If you want to say *stare*, don't say *stared*. If you want to say *tooth*, don't say *toothy*. If you want to say *spark*, don't say *sparkly*. Don't use endings such as "ings," "ies." Don't use plurals. Reduce words to their most concrete, original, basic grammatical structure. Reduce words to their grammatic concrete base. In this hundred words, all except a few should be absolutely concrete.

QUESTION: What do you mean by concrete?

MCCLURE: That's a question I'll put off for five minutes. The one hundred words are going to tend to be nouns. But don't look at them as nouns. View them as basic concrete language. Let's not use grammatical terms to describe a word, because that limits the possibility of the word in this imaginative and experimental context. Mostly they will be basic nouns but that is beside the point. Some words will work in other ways. You'll discover that they have adjectival and verbal connotations when you free them. So, no endings. No plurals. We want to use real words. The words are to be concrete.

Eighty of these concrete words will be divided evenly among Sight, Sound, Taste, Touch, Smell. That's sixteen apiece. So, there will be sixteen words of sight, sixteen words of sound, sixteen words of taste, sixteen words of touch, and sixteen of smell.

Here's what would happen if you didn't follow this set of directions. About seventy-five percent of concrete, conscious, verbal information is visual. If you don't follow the rule that divides the words equally among sight, sound, taste, touch, and smell, you'll have seventy or eighty *sight* words in the hundred. That's the *natural, conscious* distribution. The function of dividing the words into five equal units is to achieve the arranged derangement of the senses, of which Rimbaud spoke. By evenly dividing our personal one hundred words' consciousness over the five senses, we break up our normal *set* or ratio. Then, other processes begin to take hold and we imagine in new or other fashions. There are other areas than the conscious ones. You'll see them as you begin this experimental exercise.

So, there will be sixteen sight words, sixteen sound words, sixteen taste words, sixteen touch words, and sixteen smell words. That's eighty of the hundred words.

Next, there will be ten words of movement. They're words describing movement—like *handspring, swim, talk, run, surf, skate*. Notice, no endings. It's not *skating, surfing, swimming, handspringing*, but *surf, swim*, etc. . . .

For this exercise, avoid terms like noun or verb. You'll find out that words aren't verbs or nouns anymore. There's no sense in thinking of them as verbs or nouns when you're making your list. You'll find out right away that they are something else also.

That leaves ten words.

Remember, these words are from the past, present, and future. They represent your good side and your bad side.

We'll turn to the concept of "concrete," which is puzzling some people. But before that, let's look at how one is going to delve for a hundred words from past, present, and future. You will have to be in a special state—a rapport with yourself. The best way to get to this state is to temporarily send away your roommate, your lover, your dog, your cat, the television set—and definitely, absolutely—the record player. You must sit someplace in semidarkness, quite still without persons coming in and out of the room. You must be really alone, able to find a companionability with your past, your present, your future.

You must be able to feel the aura of your past, your present, and future around yourself, and feel the weaving of your good and bad and sweet and bitter nature through the aura that you're allowing to exist. The best way I know of to do this is to go to a semidark room without even a cat there. The cat is not part of your interior personal universe. Nothing should be there except a candle—a little candlelight. If you do this list by candlelight it helps consciousness to expand at the peripheral edges. Just a candle in darkness, or maybe a dim desk lamp, and a pencil and a piece of paper. Let your verbal universe exist around you and then become conscious of it. There will be your whole vocabulary world, and you'll be able to move right through it to make the right choices quite easily.

QUESTION: You write down words as they come to you?

McCLURE: That's the intuitive way of doing it. An individual sits down and simply writes out his hundred words. You wouldn't believe how many people absorb the rules and write down sixteen sight, sixteen sound, sixteen taste, sixteen touch, sixteen smell, etc., and have their hundred words immediately. On the other hand, it's common for people to write sixty words immediately and then lengthily sort around for the last forty. I've also seen people write two or three hundred words and then cull the list to a hundred.

Okay, the last ten words. One or two will be parts of the body. Parts of the body that are significant to your personal universe. That puts the chips right on the table!

QUESTION: Does this have to be *your* body?

McCLURE: No, it doesn't have to be your body. It could be somebody else's. Your mother's, your lover's.

Also, in this last ten words will be names of heroines or heroes. And also, places in the universe. Plus invented words. And times of the night or day. Also, symbolic signs like astrological signs. Don't forget totemic animals. And birds and plants. You must also save one word for the *abstraction* that has the most significance to you. Could your abstraction be Patriotism? Thriftiness? Prayer? Industry?

That is the rule for ten final words. Use them for parts of the body, names of heroes and heroines, places in the universe, invented words, times of the night and day, symbolic signs, totemic animals, birds and plants, and one abstraction.

What is the most significant abstraction in your life? You shouldn't brood on it; you should possibly take the first answer that comes into your head.

Last thoughts on the deck are: avoid hyphenated words if you can. Use them when you need to. Remember, the one hundred words have to sound good, or beautiful, together in any random combination.

I'm going to pretend that I'm all by myself in a dark room with a candle. I've just put the cat out, turned the record player off, and I'm remembering the list of rules given at this lecture. I've got a pen and a piece of paper. My personal way to do it is by free association. I'll remember past, present, future, good and bad sides, sight, sound, taste, touch, smell, and that the words must sound good in any combination. Well, I've always liked roses. ROSES! Oh, It's supposed to be singular! Okay, ROSE! Let's see, is that a sight? A smell? A taste? It could be, in the case of the rose. This is one of the trickiest words you run into. Is it a verb? It *rose* up in front of me. It's either sight or smell. How many smell a *rose*? In my case it's *sight*. I saw it. Sometimes I smell it, but this time I see it. So, a *sight* word. Now I'm going to free associate. THUNDER! A childhood word, Kansas, thunderstorms, THUNDER! Then SWIM comes right out. Now I *know* what THUNDER is, that's sound. See, it's really up to you, isn't it? TURQUOISE. Strangely, TURQUOISE is a touch for me. TURQUOISE is a tactile sensation. I like to touch turquoises. LEATHER, there's another word. SWIM. There's another.

QUESTION: When you free-associate, do you keep all the other words in mind at the same time to see how they sound together?

MCCLURE: That's an important point. When you get some words down, you have to keep checking them to see if they're going well together.

Let me free associate a couple of smell words. By the way, smell is really tough to get words for. Sixteen good smell words? Remember spices when you're doing it. Often spices out of your childhood, or out of your future, have a particular strength. CINNAMON . . . MUSK . . . or a perfume.

I'll check randomly for their sound quality . . . TURQUOISE THUNDER MUSK ROSE . . . ROSE THUNDER LEATHER TURQUOISE . . . CINNAMON TURQUOISE MUSK SWIM LEATHER . . . THUNDER ROSE TURQUOISE MUSK. I like them all. Now let's say for a fantasy that I'm a hamburger addict. For the last twenty-seven years the only thing I've eaten is hamburgers. I have a couple for breakfast, and since that's kind of heavy I have one for lunch, and then I get hungry around dinnertime and have three hamburgers for dinner. Once in awhile at midnight I go to MacDonald's and have a hamburger. That's the only thing I eat. It doesn't seem fair to me to pick out a hundred words that are significant to my past, present, and future, and leave out hamburger. The candle is flickering and twitching and I'm looking at it and saying, "HAMBURGER, HAMBURGER, HAMBURGER." I don't want to say hamburger. I just had a horrible thought that hamburger isn't going to sound right with TURQUOISE and MUSK. My conscience is hot on my heels. HAMBURGER! I exclaim! ROSE HAMBURGER THUNDER. HAMBURGER has got to go with all of them! LEATHER HAMBURGER MUSK ROSE . . . CINNAMON HAMBURGER. . . That sounds good! But LEATHER CINNAMON HAMBURGER? No! This puts me in a dilemma! I want the list to be honest. How about GROUND BEEF LEATHER? Try this: ROSE GROUND BEEF?

I determine that hamburger doesn't work on my list. But it remains an enigma because it's too significant to leave out. The fellow in the back of the room suggests MEAT. So, MEAT is a constituent of a hamburger. What are the other constituents? MEAT is a category and I'd rather be more specific. So BEEF might be better. BREAD? BUN? ONION? MUSTARD? Could it be KETCHUP, MUSTARD, GREASE, PICKLE? If HAMBURGER doesn't work, I'm going to have to go after the essential quality. I've tried BURGER, it doesn't work either. I'm going to break HAMBURGER down into its constituents. I'm a purist at heart. I love them for the BEEF and the BREAD—or the MEAT and the BREAD. I like the sound of MEAT. I'm going to get rid of HAMBURGER. I found the word. It's MEAT. Maybe it's BREAD too.

MEAT. I wonder what category that goes into? That's a taste word. BREAD? Is that a *touch* or a *taste*?

Now let's go on. I love birds. BIRD! But I don't want categories. I'm going to have to say what kind of bird. A toucan, a sparrow, a falcon, a parrot, a hawk. I was thinking of a FALCON. I think that's going to sound good with the other words. I'm going to test this again. FALCON TURQUOISE LEATHER ROSE. . . I know a lot about falcons. It sounds good, too.